The Amish Heiress

Patrick E. Craig

The Amish Heiress

Copyright © 2015 by Patrick E. Craig

First Edition eBook: 2015
First Edition Paperback: 2015
ISBN (ePub): 978-0-9965334-1-6
ISBN (Paperback): 978-0-9965334-0-9

Published by P&J Publishing
Caldwell, Idaho
In cooperation with NCC Publishing (www.nccpublishing.com)

Cover by Garborg Design Works, Savage, Minnesota
Cover Photos © Chris Garborg, Bigstock / Voy
Author Photo by William Craig, Craig Prographica

This is a work of fiction. While set in a real town in Pennsylvania, the names, characters, and incidents are the product of the author's imagination or are used fictitiously. Any resemblance to actual persons, living or dead, is entirely coincidental.

20150720

Dedication

This book is dedicated to my mother, Cora Jean Hilbert Craig, for her untiring support of my creative endeavors and her delight in all things lovely.

Acknowledgements

To my wife, Judy, for her tireless efforts in proofing and editing *The Amish Heiress*.

To Lindsay A. Franklin for her great substantive editing and advice with this book.

To Ray Ellis and Michael and Debbie Sloane at NCC Publishing for their terrific help in getting this book ready for publication.

The Amish Heiress

Contents

A Note from Patrick E. Craig

When I first started writing Amish fiction, I had a short story in mind about a master quilter from Apple Creek, Ohio who found God, a little lost child, and a new life in the heart of a snowstorm. When I showed the story to my agent, he encouraged me to turn it into a full-length series of three books. Now, three years later, the last of those books, *Jenny's Choice*, has been released and I am still telling the story of the Hershbergers and the Springers. The setting has moved from Apple Creek to Paradise, Pennsylvania, but the characters and the stories are part of an ongoing thread that has captured my heart and kept me busy since 2010.

When I was writing the Apple Creek Dreams series, I was going to tell the stories of Jerusha Springer, her adopted daughter, Jenny, and then Jenny's daughter, Rachel. But I fell in love with the character of Jenny, and then there were two books about Jenny where I had only planned on one.

Now I finally get to tell Rachel's story. It's a different kind of story, but then I'm not exactly known in Amish circles as someone who writes a typical Amish novel. I think that's because I read too many Zane Grey books when I was a kid. His books had adventure, mystery, and danger, and for those of you expecting a typical light-hearted romance dressed in Amish clothing, you will certainly find far more than that in this story, so be prepared. But Grey was also one of the best romance writers that ever put pen to paper, and in the end, good Amish fiction has to have romance and plenty of it.

So sit back and enjoy *The Amish Heiress*, and remember, in the end, stories should be about love: love between people and ultimately, they should be about the love our God had for us when He sent His own son to solve the dilemma of the ages and bring peace and joy to our hearts. And that is the greatest story ever told.

Part One

The Key

Rachel, my darling girl, how can I tell of the joy you give me. In the dark days when we thought we had lost your papa, I was adrift in my grief but you were my ray of sunlight, and precious memories were bound into your very being. In all those years when Jonathan was gone, you were my rock, the one person I could turn to that always had an uplifting word or a loving gesture. I know your heart ached as mine did, but somehow you held yourself above the pain and were always there for me. And for such a long time, you were the one who believed your papa would come home someday.

That is why it surprised me when it was so hard for you when your papa did come home. You were fourteen, you were becoming a woman, and Jonathan had missed such a big part of your life. You and your papa were at odds for a long time. I think that you had finally reconciled yourself to Jonathan being dead—you had moved on. And then when he came home, you had to learn that relationship all over again. We were so close, the two of us and then there was another person in the house, a man who in many ways was a stranger to us both, especially on his "bad" days. I think you felt like he came between us. So when the opportunity came for you to go, you were ready, too ready…

Rachel – From The Journals of Jenny Hershberger

Chapter One

Trouble in Paradise

"I won't do it!"

"You will do what I say!"

"I'm eighteen, Papa, and my own person. You can't make me do anything anymore!"

"Rachel, Jonathan, please stop shouting at each other."

The cacophony of voices pushed out the open front door of the house like a symphony orchestra with every instrument out of tune. A girl stood in the doorway pointing her finger back at someone inside. She spoke again and this time her voice was low and icy.

"Mama, I hate him. Ever since he came back, my life has been...hell!"

The word crashed down like an avalanche of rocks and then there was silence.

"*Dochter*, you don't mean that. Please, apologize to your papa."

"I won't apologize to someone that's...that's *verrückt!*"

"Rachel!"

"So, I'm crazy, am I? Well, we'll see. Go on. You want to leave, just go. Get out of my house."

"Your house? Your house? I've lived here longer than you. You come back into our lives and think you can just take over and order me around. Papa, I don't even know you. I'll go, I'll go, and maybe I won't come back!"

With that, Rachel swung around and stomped out onto the porch, slamming the screen door in the face of the man who was following her out. She ran down the steps and out onto the lane and was gone before her papa could catch her.

Jonathan Hershberger opened the door and stood, watching his daughter run through the field next to the house. His wife, Jenny, came out behind him and watched their daughter go. Jenny's face was pale and her eyes were red.

Jonathan put his hand to his head. "My head hurts, Jenny. Help me inside."

Jenny dabbed her eyes with a handkerchief. "You know you are not supposed to get angry. The doctor warned you that you could have a stroke."

"I know, Jenny, but I can't seem to help myself. I don't want to be angry with Rachel, but there is something in her that just pushes me over the edge."

Jenny put her arm on Jonathan's shoulder and led him back inside. "In her, Jonathan, or in you?"

It was a cold and wet March day in Paradise. Spring had not yet arrived with her palette of vivid hues, and the predominant color was brown—brown stubble, brown earth, dead grass in the front yard. The small swale beyond the pasture fence was filled with runoff from the winter snowmelt, and a few solitary white ducks floated on the surface of the temporary pond, casting their reflections on the leaden surface that drearily mirrored the gray clouds gathered above the Hershberger farm.

Rachel Hershberger trudged down the path that led away from the house. Her feet sank inches into the soft mud, and the edges of her dress bore the stains of her ill-advised trail breaking.

Her face was red, and a single tear had coursed its way down her cheek. She spoke out loud to no one in particular, and her outburst roused the ducks from their peaceful repose to flutter a few feet across the pond and then settle back again. "Why did he have to come back? Everything was fine without him."

Now the tears began to flow freely down her face. She wiped them away, but others that seemed eager to mar the loveliness of her face quickly replaced them. Her dark auburn hair was held tightly in a bun beneath her *kappe*, and the wool jacket she wore over her plain dress kept the March chill from her skin. But it did nothing to ease the chill in her heart.

The squishing of her boots in the mud mixed with an occasional sob and the rippling sound of the little creek that ran through the cottonwoods, off to her right, played a strangely discordant concerto that jarred against the serenity all around her. Finally, she came to the gate out onto the main road. As she walked disconsolately down the asphalt, Rachel was absorbed in her sorrow and did not pay attention to the soft clop of the horse's hooves behind her until the small buggy pulled up next to her.

"A bit chilly for a walk in the mud, isn't it, Rachel?"

Rachel looked up into the kindly face of Daniel King, her friend from the neighboring farm. He sat on the buggy seat with a quizzical look on his face.

"Go away, Daniel. I don't need your indefatigable good nature right now."

"Indefatigable! *Ja*, now there's a fifty-dollar word. Come on, Rachel, I'm your friend, and you look like you could use one right now. Hop in and I'll take you wherever you're going and keep you tidy at the same time."

Rachel stopped and looked up at Daniel. His handsome, beardless face smiled at her from under the black hat, and he sat straight and tall on the seat. Rachel's shoulders dropped and she gave a sigh of resignation. She really wanted to be by herself, but her hike through the mud had worn her out. She climbed up on the seat next to Daniel.

"You and your papa fighting again?"

"Yes, if it's any of your business!"

"Look, Rachel, don't go there. You have spoken with me many times about Jonathan, so it's not like I'm prying into your secrets. What was it this time?"

Rachel slumped down in the seat. "I signed up for another class at the Junior College—a class in animal husbandry. I...I want to be a veterinarian, but my papa told me to drop the class."

"Why, because Amish girls are supposed to stay home after eighth grade and learn to be obedient little servants to the men?"

Rachel looked at Daniel in surprise. "Something like that."

She looked again. Daniel wasn't smiling. He was staring straight ahead, and his face was set in a stern mask.

Rachel suddenly realized that she might have an ally in this handsome young man. He was usually so...so traditional. "Why, Daniel, you surprise me. I wouldn't expect anything like that out of you."

Daniel shook the reins over the back of the horse and relaxed. The smile returned to his face, and he looked over at Rachel. "There's a lot you don't know about me. I'd be more than willing to share it with you if...if you'd let me court you."

Rachel turned away abruptly and stared out at the brown fields of Paradise, Pennsylvania. "Don't, Daniel. We've talked about this before. You're my friend, but that's all I feel for you. Besides, I don't want to get married. I have...other plans."

Daniel didn't let the barbed remark ruffle his calm demeanor. "So what are you going to do, Rachel? Run away to the big city and become an animal doctor? Wouldn't you find more work around here?"

Rachel turned back to Daniel, and now there was excitement in her voice.

"Don't you see? It's not the 1800s anymore, even for the Amish. It's 1990. There's so much out there, so much more to life than a little farm in Paradise, Pennsylvania. There's music and art and museums—the whole country and even the whole world to see. I want to float down the Nile and see the pyramids. I want to go to the Louvre and stay there for weeks. I want to torment the guards at Buckingham Palace and see if I can make them smile. Daniel, don't you ever want to go, to see, to do?"

Daniel looked down at the reins in his strong hands. "All I want is to stay here and work with my papa, and then when it's my time, take over the farm and raise the finest saddlebred horses in Pennsylvania."

Rachel gave an exasperated sigh. "And that's why we could never be together. I want to be part of a much bigger world, and in order to do that I...I..."

"Can't stay Amish?" asked Daniel softly.

Rachel looked at him without speaking. The answer lay heavy between them in a silence broken only by the soft clopping of the horse's hooves on the road.

When Rachel banged back through the door, Jenny was sitting on the sofa in the front room. Her face was soft and sad. She lifted her finger to her lips.

Rachel pulled off her coat and hung it on the hook by the door. "Where's Papa?"

"He's sleeping, Rachel. He got a bad headache when he got so angry. You know that it hurts him physically when you fight with him."

Rachel looked down. She felt bad, but she wasn't going to back down. "Mama, is he the only one who lives here? Why do we have to tiptoe around and make everything easy for him all the time?"

Jenny motioned for Rachel to come sit beside her. Rachel hesitated and then plopped down stiffly beside her mama. Jenny's arm circled Rachel's waist. She pushed through the stiffness and pulled her daughter up close. It took a minute, but Rachel finally relaxed and put her head on Jenny's shoulder. Soft sobs began to shake Rachel's body. Jenny reached over and stroked her daughter's forehead as Rachel began to calm down.

"I know it's difficult...to have Jonathan home. He still struggles with the disaster on the boat and the injuries he sustained. He watched his parents die and it hurt him so."

"I know, Mama, and I feel sorry for him, but he's so hard to live with."

Jenny turned Rachel's face toward her. "Rachel, your papa was a different man for eight years. He completely lost any memory of being Jonathan Hershberger, of being an Amish man, of you and me and our home here in Paradise."

"I know, Mama, but—"

Jenny put her fingers softly on Rachel's lips. "Let me finish. When your papa converted to the Amish faith before we were married, he came from a background that was very worldly. He was an atheist, or at least an agnostic. He had tried drugs and different religions. He thought he was going to be a famous musician, and if he hadn't met me, he probably would have been. When he lost his memory, he went back to what he intuitively knew—playing music. He became famous out there in the world and made a lot of money."

Rachel stirred. "I know the story, Mama, but it still doesn't explain why he's so strict with me."

Jenny sighed and put her hand to her face. An errant tear had attempted to run down her cheek and she brushed it away. Rachel saw the involuntary movement and her heart softened.

This really hurts my mama. She also wishes things were not this way.

Rachel's arms crept around her mama. "Oh, Mama, I'm sorry. I know all this makes you sad."

"Yes, *dochter*, I am sad. I am sad for the years we missed, you and I, with your papa. I am sorry for the pain that your papa went through, and I am sorry that you and he are not close like you once were. But I am also very grateful. I thank *du lieber Gott* every day that Jonathan came back to me…to us. I thank Him for the amazing miracle He performed when my heart was broken beyond hope. You must know that your papa and I were made for each other. We are two lives and one heart. It is a very special thing that *Gott* does for people. That is His plan for marriage, and someday I hope you will find the same joy. Jonathan and I had ten wonderful years together. It was especially joyful after you were born. When he disappeared and I thought he was dead…"

Jenny paused and dabbed her eyes. "Rachel, when your papa came home, he did not really know who he was. He still goes back to being Richard Sandbridge from time to time, and I think that is what confuses you. One minute he is a strict Amish man and the next he is a very easy-going musician. I know it's been hard. The only thing that has saved your papa is the *Ordnung*. He clings to them like a life preserver, because some days that is the only way he knows who he is. And he is so dependent on them that he forgets the *Ordnung* don't save us. And so he tries to live by them as best he can to stay grounded in our world. That's why he is so strict. My papa went through the same thing when he came back from World War II. He was so devastated by his experience in the Pacific that he swore he would come back to the church and keep the rules with all his heart. He believed that keeping the *Ordnung* would make him all right with *Gott*. It took a terrible tragedy to make him see differently."

Rachel took her mama's hand and put it to her cheek. She kissed it. "I'm sorry, Mama. I don't understand this sometimes, but I do love Papa. I'll try to do better."

"And I love you and will try also, *dochter*."

The women looked up to see Jonathan standing in the doorway. He held out his arms and Rachel rose and went to him. His strong arms enfolded her and she saw the love in his eyes. She held onto him and hid her face against his chest.

I hope so, Papa. I truly hope so.

Chapter Two

A Longing

Rachel was unhappy. Even though the sun was shining and the muddy fields around her were beginning to dry up, and the first faint breath of spring touched the air around her with a promise of the fragrance to come, for Rachel, it might as well have been snowing. In the trees along the road, bright yellow acacia blossoms were blooming, interspersed with the beautiful pink of the early plums, but Rachel didn't notice. The weather had changed for the better, but it hadn't changed the gloom in her heart. She pushed her scooter down Leacock Road, headed for the Old Philadelphia Turnpike. It was three miles from the farm, but she didn't care—she just wanted to get away, to get out, to be gone.

After the fight with her papa, things had been quiet for a week. It was like pounding down a wild, whitewater rapid and then, after the final set of huge rocks, sliding into a deep, calm stretch of the river. But soon Jonathan seemed to forget his promise and started riding her about little things again; the way she did her chores, the way she wore her clothes, her devotion to Bible study or lack thereof. Everything seemed to touch a sore spot in her *daed* and bring forth a caustic comment or a curt instruction. That is, when he was her papa. At other times, he seemed confused and disoriented, looking for the telephone that wasn't there or asking where his guitar was.

It had been four years since Jonathan returned to Paradise. He had been gone for eight years, and the day of his return, though miraculous and joyous, had been the first day of the most confusing and vexing time in Rachel's life. She knew it had been difficult for her mother too, because Rachel could see the sadness in Jenny's eyes as she watched her husband when he wasn't looking.

As Rachel pushed her scooter along, she tried to remember the days before the accident, when she and her papa had been so close. But the memories were hard to come by, like fragments of a wonderful dream that seems so real in the safety of slumber, but, upon awakening, can only be recalled in bits and pieces, finally to dissolve in the shadows of forgetfulness. And that was Rachel's remembrance of her papa—a dream that could not be recaptured, a golden time that had somehow been replaced with the reality of a confused and angry man who did not seem to care if Rachel loved him or not.

At last, Rachel came to the crossroads. She turned right and began to walk along the side of The Old Philadelphia Turnpike. She loved the houses along this road. They were grand and palatial—so different from the Amish houses—and Rachel wondered what life was like for the people who lived in them. She could only imagine what it might be like to be the daughter of one of these wealthy families. In her mind's eye she could see herself attending a private high school and then having to make the hard decision about which college to attend. She dreamed of all the things that rich girls would do—things like dating and proms, playing sports and owning a car, taking long vacations to romantic places.

I feel like a foreigner. Look at me, pushing this stupid scooter down the road in this silly outfit, wearing this dumb hat. Why can't I just be like everybody else?

Rachel wondered if it was a sin to think that way. After all, she was Amish, and Amish were supposed to be so religious and somehow more Christian than everyone else.

If they only knew what really goes on behind the four walls of a typical Amish home. We are just the same as everyone else. We fight, we treat each other badly, we can't figure out our relationship with Gott, or even if He's real...

Rachel stopped and looked up. She had never thought about the reality of *Gott* in this way and it made her nervous. She felt like He might send a lightning bolt down because she was thinking such awful thoughts, but the only clouds in the sky were high up and wispy. After an anxious moment, she walked on, trying to get her thoughts back to romanticizing the lives of the people who lived in the mansions along the Pike. But somehow her thinking about *Gott* got in the way of her dreaming. She was tense and ill at ease, and suddenly she felt like she might throw up. She wanted to take the scooter and fling it into the ditch. She wanted to pull off this silly *kappe* and let her long auburn hair flow free in the wind. She felt her heart racing so she stopped and took some deep breaths.

I have to do something. I have to get away from Papa...

"Rachel?"

The buggy had been driving on the grass along the side of the road, and she was so lost in thought she had not heard it approach. She jumped involuntarily and then turned. Daniel King sat on the seat with the reins in his hands.

Rachel felt a surge of anger toward Daniel. "Oh my goodness, Daniel, *sie erschraken mich!* Why are you always sneaking up on me? What are you doing here? Why are you following me?"

Daniel frowned and then he lifted his hand to silence her. "Rachel, I need your help. Your mama told me you would be coming this way. Contrary to what you think, I'm not spying on you."

Suddenly Rachel felt foolish. She blushed and lowered her eyes. "What's wrong?"

"One of my mares is foaling and the baby is positioned wrong. There's a good chance of dystocia."

"Have you called the vet?"

"Yes, but he's not available. He's away over on the far side of Lancaster, and my papa is in Hallam looking at some draft horses. I can't wait for them. The mare might die. That's why I'm asking you to come help me."

Rachel threw her scooter into the back of the buggy and climbed up on the seat beside Daniel. He turned the horse and started back toward Leacock and the King farm. Rachel sat on the seat with her head down and her cheeks burning.

After a while, Daniel spoke. "I'm your friend, Rachel. I only want the best for you. I came to find you because, next to the vet, you're the best person with sick animals that I know."

"Yes, and if my papa would let me go to college, I could be a vet."

Daniel chucked the horse again and replied, "You're eighteen years old. You can make some decisions for yourself."

"Yes, but the *Ordnung* forbid girls going to school past the eighth grade. What about that?"

"The policy toward extra schooling is not as harsh as you think. Often girls are allowed to continue if the elders see that there will be benefit to the Amish community. In your case, the benefit would be a good, non-*Englischer* vet to help the Amish farmers around Paradise. After all, Rachel, like you said, it is 1990. We don't live in the middle ages anymore."

"But you don't understand. I have a dream. I don't want to take some community college classes and become someone who works for a vet. I want to go to Cornell University's College of Veterinary Medicine."

"But that's far away, isn't it?"

"Ithaca, New York, to be exact."

Suddenly Rachel was excited and she reached in her pocket and pulled out a folded up piece of paper. "It's the very best college of veterinary medicine in the whole county. Listen to their mission statement."

Rachel began to read.

"To advance the health and well-being of animals and people through education, research, and public service."

Rachel grabbed Daniel's arm and began to rattle off the college blurb. "They have 211 faculty and 732 non-academic staff members for only 360 students. They have an incredible graduate studies program where you can work toward either a

Master of Science or Doctor of Philosophy degree. There are internships and residency programs. Oh, Daniel! Wouldn't it be wonderful?"

Daniel sat quietly and then smiled. "You must have that brochure memorized. Does Jonathan know about this? And how are you going to get in? You only have an eighth grade education."

Rachel slumped down in her seat. "I know, but I got straight As in school, and I did take some courses at the Junior College in Lancaster before Papa came home. I did really well in my studies there. And...I've already written a letter to the Dean of Admissions explaining my situation. Maybe they would let me in as a hardship case."

Daniel shook his head. "You have a lot to overcome. It might be very difficult."

Rachel felt a twisting inside her. She felt like she wanted to scream at Daniel, but she kept her thoughts to herself as she clutched the college flyer in her hand.

You just don't understand, Daniel. I don't want to be Amish, I don't want to be married, I just want this!

They sat in silence as they rolled into the lane leading to the King farm. Daniel drove straight back to the barn, and they climbed out and hurried in. The mare was lying down on her side in a stall, and her legs were sticking out straight and stiff. Rachel could see the muscles contracting as she pushed to get the foal out.

"Get a bale of grass hay and spread it all around the stall. And then get me a clean bed sheet. Quickly, Daniel!"

Daniel ran to get the sheet as Rachel knelt beside the mare.

She shouted after the retreating Daniel. "And bring a blanket, Ivermectin, and Banamine, if you have it. Oh, and a squirt bottle of iodine!"

Rachel turned back to the mare and gently caressed her face, rubbing around the ears.

"Come on, mama, we are here now. Don't worry, we will help you get this baby out."

The mare continued pushing. She was grunting softly and her tongue flicked in and out. Daniel arrived back with the supplies.

"Give me the sheet, Daniel!"

Rachel spread the sheet under the mare's hindquarters and examined the mare closely. "I see the birth sac and I can feel the foal's nose, but it looks like the shoulder is wedged inside. I'm going to reach in and grab a leg and shift the baby."

As she did that, the mare moved and suddenly the foal's nose and two front hooves emerged. Rachel tore away the sac and grabbed the front legs.

"Help me pull, Daniel, but only pull downward, just one tug."

Daniel took hold of the foal with Rachel and together they gave a quick tug downward. The head and shoulders popped out and Rachel moved back and smiled.

"Things will happen rather quickly now."

And then the foal was out and lying next to its mother. Rachel squeezed the liquid out of the tiny foal's nose with a gentle downward motion. The foal and the mother lay quietly, still connected by the umbilical cord. The foal shifted and the cord broke.

"Squirt the iodine right on the navel stump, Daniel. Now give me the Ivermectin and the Banamine."

Rachel estimated the mare's weight and gave her an oral dose from each bottle. As she worked, she explained to Daniel what she was doing.

"The Ivermectin is a wormer and keeps the mare from getting foal scours. The Banamine helps her with the contraction pains."

The little colt tried to stand up. It struggled for a minute and then suddenly stood up on shaky legs.

"It is a filly, Daniel, strong and beautiful. Put the blanket around her and keep her warm. It's a bit chilly in here."

Daniel looked at Rachel with admiration in his eyes. "You were wonderful."

Rachel smiled at the praise. "I'm surprised that you didn't know more about birthing. You love horses so much."

"I have watched many times, but my *daed* always has the vet do it and he helps. So this is the first time I have been able to really assist. You did a great job. My papa will be pleased and grateful."

Daniel paused. Then he put his arm around Rachel's shoulders. "You have a natural gift. If you want to go to college, then I support you in this."

Rachel stared at Daniel for a moment and then threw her arms around him. "Thank you, Daniel."

Daniel's arms wrapped around Rachel and they stood that way for a minute and then Rachel realized what was happening. She pulled away, her face burning hot. Daniel's hands fell awkwardly to his sides.

"But how will you do it, Rachel? Isn't it very expensive? And how will you convince your *daed*?"

"I do not know the answers to those questions, Daniel. But I know this. If I can get the money to go, I'm going whether Papa gives me permission or not."

Chapter Three

The Inheritance

Augusta St. Clair marched through the swinging glass door into the offices of Murray, Peterson and Lowell. Augusta was a formidable looking woman with perfectly coifed white hair wearing a low-key, but obviously expensive, charcoal business suit. The extremely handsome young man beside her was dressed in a modern, collegiate way. The look on his face let the world know that he did not want to be there. Behind them trotted an older woman in a frumpy suit and glasses, looking somewhat like a scared puppy. The startled secretary behind the massive reception desk raised her hand to stop the group.

The nervous woman behind Augusta tried to intervene. "Maybe we shouldn't go in Mrs. St. Clair. I think—"

"Shut your mouth, Eva," Augusta snapped. The young man looked at Eva's embarrassed face and shrugged as Augusta pushed her way past the protesting secretary and into the inner sanctum of the prestigious law firm. Several pieces of paper were clutched in her hand.

James Lowell looked up from his desk. When he recognized his visitor, his face paled and he started to protest. "Augusta, I can't see you right now. I'm in the middle—"

Augusta St. Clair cut him off with an imperious wave of her hand. "You will see me right now, James, if you know what's good for you and this firm."

James Lowell started to answer back and then looked over at the two men in the chairs facing him, smiling sheepishly. "Well, gentlemen, as you see, something very important has come up. We will have to discuss this matter at another time."

One of the men rose and looked at James with steely eyes. "You mean, you're asking us to leave, James? This is a five million dollar deal we're discussing. I would think—"

Before he could finish, Augusta cut in. "Good afternoon, Mr. Carrington. Perhaps you don't know who I am, but I know who you are and the company you represent. Let me be very clear. If I wanted to, I could buy your crummy little factory and shut it down today. So if you don't want that to happen, I would suggest you accept Mr. Lowell's request and come back another day. Goodbye."

Without another look, she turned to the man behind the desk as the chastened visitors slunk out the door. The young man who was with Augusta found a chair and started to light a cigarette. At a warning look from Augusta, he put the pack back in his pocket. Eva stood behind Augusta, shifting from one foot to the other as though waiting for a command.

Augusta shook the stack of papers in front of James Lowell's face and then flung them down on the attorney's desk. "Just what is this?"

Lowell swallowed hard, picked up the top document, and adjusted his glasses. "Oh, you got my letter," he said with a weak smile.

"Don't play games with me, Jimmy. I want to know what this means."

James Lowell pushed his glasses down on his nose as he glanced at the cover page. Then he put the sheaf of papers down and removed his glasses. "I thought I made myself very clear, Augusta. I have looked over all the documents and the family papers, and I have concluded that I must deny your request."

"You have concluded?" Augusta laughed. "You little pipsqueak! You don't deny anything I ask; you do what I say.

Now you get on that phone, call the trustees and tell them to sign the papers, or you will wish you had never been born."

A bead of sweat formed on Lowell's forehead.

He looked down and then back up at Augusta. "I can't. I tried but they won't have it. The inheritance directives are over four hundred years old and there is not a person on the whole board of trustees who will deviate from them—not one inch!"

"Oohh!"

Augusta's face began to turn red. Eva touched her shoulder.

Augusta turned sharply and spoke with a voice like knives. "What is it, Eva? Can't you see I'm talking here?"

The woman's face went pale. "Please, Mrs. St. Clair, you know what the doctor said. You're not to let yourself get worked up. Your heart..."

Augusta stared at the woman for a long moment while the muscle in her jaw worked furiously. Finally, she took three deep breaths and raised her hands. Her voice was evenly modulated and low.

"You're right, Eva. You're right. You know I told you never to interrupt me, but I don't want to have a heart attack right here in this man's office so I'll let it go this time. After all," she said as she turned slowly back to Lowell, "I wouldn't want to die before Jimmy, now would I?"

The young man blinked and tried to mollify things. "Threats probably won't help the situation, Grandmother."

"I'll tell you when to speak, Gerald."

Gerald started to respond, but closed his mouth and kept silent.

Augusta walked around and sat on the edge of James Lowell's desk. "Now, James, I wouldn't want anything bad to happen to you, so surely there must be another way..." Augusta paused meaningfully while Lowell mulled over the dark implications.

Then Augusta smiled and patted James Lowell on the hand. "Oh, I'm just playing with you, Jimmy," she said, but her eyes told a different story. "Now, I want you to tell me exactly what the board said."

Lowell wiped the sweat off his brow with a Kleenex from a box on his desk, adjusted his glasses again, and pushed a stack of papers toward Augusta. "It's all in here."

Augusta ignored the papers and kept looking at Lowell. "Just give me the Cliffs Notes version, Jimmy," she said sweetly, but there was ice in the air.

Lowell wrung his hands, looked over at Gerald, and then spoke. "You can keep your trust, you can keep the house and the estate, but no one inherits the bulk of the money unless they are a direct descendant of the oldest son and have the Key. That's the bottom line and I can't get around it."

"The Key? And what is the Key?"

James Lowell shrugged. "I don't know. You will have to ask the board of trustees, because I don't have the slightest idea. I would suggest you contact Michel Duvigney. He's the director of the board of trustees."

Augusta gave Lowell a steely look. She stood up and walked toward the door. Without glancing back, she spoke to Eva. "Eva, be a dear and get the pertinent information from Mr. Lowell and then set an appointment for me with Mr. Duvigney."

"Yes, Mrs. St. Clair."

Augusta opened the door and then stopped and looked back at James Lowell. "When I settle this, I will settle with you, Jimmy. Nobody stands in my way. It's a bad decision. Come, Gerald!"

With that, she picked up the sheaf of papers, turned and stomped out, her grandson and secretary trailing along behind like ducklings trying to keep up with their mother.

Three days later, Augusta sat in the dark office of Michel Duvigney. It was small and cramped with red cherry wood bookshelves lining the walls and a small fireplace with a gas flame burning behind glass doors. The desk was the largest piece of furniture in the room and it was covered with books and odd pieces of memorabilia. Pictures of Duvigney with well-known personages, including him shaking hands with three ex-presidents, hung on the wall. Dim afternoon light tried to force its way through the drawn venetian blinds, but the only real illumination in the room came from the small lamp on the desk.

Duvigney was old, but somehow the lines of age had not marked themselves too deeply on his features. His white hair and crow's feet around his eyes were the only giveaways. Augusta sat stiffly while Duvigney went over the paperwork in front of him. Finally, he lifted the whole pile in his hands, tapped the bottom twice on the desk to even the documents up, and set it aside.

Looking at Augusta he spoke in a quiet, sibilant voice. "I'm sorry, Ms. St. Clair, but there is no other decision that can be made. The directives for the succession of the St. Clair inheritance are quite explicit. First of all, only the direct descendants of an eldest son can inherit. It can be male or female as long as it can be proved that the eldest son was either father or grandfather to the heir."

Duvigney smiled but there was no warmth in it. "May I call you Augusta?"

Augusta nodded. Duvigney took a folder from a tray on his desk and opened it.

He scanned it for a moment and then closed it again. "I see from this file that you are the widow of Jerod St. Clair, the younger son of Maximillian St. Clair. Jerod was killed in World War II in a mission over France. You had one son with Jerod..."

Duvigney glanced down. "...Ah, yes, Francis, who is also deceased, as well as his wife."

"They died in a skiing accident in Switzerland," Augusta said with a frown. "An avalanche..."

"Yes, I have the details here. So, Augusta, even though you are the sole beneficiary of your late husband's will, which entitles you to the proceeds from his portion of the St. Clair trust, the house you are now living in, the property in Connecticut, and the townhouse in London, you persist in pressing your claim to the bulk of the estate which is in trust for the true heir, a claim that is without merit and will never be considered."

Augusta twisted in her chair. It was an overstuffed club chair covered in leather that somehow put Augusta's eyes on a plane lower than Duvigney's.

"Well, if I'm not able to inherit, what about my grandson, Gerald? Shouldn't he be considered?"

Duvigney's voice took on a tone that sounded like a snake hissing. "Augusta, you don't seem to be following me. The St. Clair family is over eight hundred years old and can trace their lineage back to the household knights of William the Conqueror. The precedents for preserving the lineage and the inheritance were established hundreds of years ago in Europe. I'm afraid that you, as a relative newcomer to the family, cannot seem to grasp the significance of the St. Clair traditions."

Augusta stiffened. "Excuse me, Michel, but my family has a very old and proud name. Why, my family is descended from the royal families of Russia. We have traditions as well."

Duvigney smiled again. "Augusta, you must think me simple. Your family is not descended from the Romanovs. Your grandfather was a Yugoslavian immigrant named Alexzander Bošnjaković who was a cheese maker on the lower east side. Your father was a used car salesman who changed his last name to Bosnan so his customers could pronounce it. Your real name is Francine Bosnan, and you were born to a lower middle class family in The Bronx. Compared to the St. Clairs, your family doesn't have traditions, it has habits."

Duvigney's face cracked for a moment at his attempt at humor. The effect was not pleasant.

He glanced down at the dossier in front of him. "Now, as to how you moved up so far in your life. It seems that you met Jerod at a USO dance in Manhattan in August of 1944 and began seeing him on a regular basis. You cleverly arranged to become pregnant before he was sent to England with his bomber squadron in February 1945. An honorable man, Jerod married you three weeks before he left and, *voilà*, suddenly you were the wealthy Augusta St. Clair, possessor of a proud name and a mysterious background, a background invented by you to make your way through the labyrinth of New York society. Which you did handily, I must say."

Duvigney glanced up and smiled a patronizing sort of smile that infuriated Augusta, but she held her tongue.

He glanced back down. "Sadly, Jerod was killed a week after he arrived in England on a bombing run over Germany. Your son, Francis, was born three months later in June 1945."

Michel picked up a pencil and tapped it a few times on his desk. Then he smiled. "You see, Augusta, we do our homework. Now let's go over this once more. Your husband's older brother, Robert, was the true heir to the St. Clair fortune. It has come to our attention that he was also married and had a child, but the wife and child disappeared."

Augusta stared at the old man. "How did you find out about Robert's wife and child?"

Duvigney showed the first signs of exasperation. "Ms. St. Clair! For years we believed that Robert died without an heir, and so Robert's trust was a closed account waiting until we could take action to declare a new heir. When you came forward to press your claims, the case was re-opened, and during that new investigation, certain facts came to light concerning Robert St. Clair. Our investigation turned up a copy of a marriage license listing Robert St. Clair and Rachel Borntraeger dated September 15, 1946. We also found a birth certificate for their daughter, Jennifer Constance St. Clair, dated January of 1947. We know that Robert St. Clair was killed in a car accident, but at this time, the whereabouts of the wife and daughter remains unknown. Our representatives are conducting a search for them. If we find her or the child and they can prove definitive relationship to Robert through DNA testing, or if the daughter has the Key, then they will be invested with the bulk of the trust estate which totals at this time…"

Duvigney reached over and rustled through some papers in a tray on the corner of his desk and pulled out a spreadsheet. "…around forty billion dollars in investments and properties."

Augusta clamped her jaw shut to keep from gasping. She gathered her emotions and then spoke again, trying to be pleasant. "May I ask you a question, Michel?"

"Yes, of course, Augusta."

"What is the Key?"

Duvigney's face took on a serious mien. "The Key is the St. Clair Key. It is, in fact, a birthmark that was found on the first St. Clair in 1123. It is a red, key-shaped mark that is located above the heart on the chest. This birthmark has been a factor in determining the heir for centuries. It sometimes skips generations but it has always followed the line. Your brother-in-law had this birthmark, but your husband did not. If we find an heir that carries the Key, there will be absolutely no question as to the validity of their claim. They will be immediately granted title to everything."

"Even if they are female?"

"The trust documents permit a woman inheriting if she has the Key. That only holds true to the second generation from the direct heir. If no heir is found, then fifty years after the heir's death, the board of trustees will follow the other lines of descent and name the closest St. Clair male the new heir. The long wait prevents internecine strife."

"Internecine strife?"

"Yes, strife of or relating to conflict within a group, a family, or an organization. In this case, family members killing each other for the money. It seems that in the fourteenth century, certain of the St. Clair brothers attempted to murder each other over the inheritance, so strict guidelines were set in place by their father."

"So you are saying that Robert's daughter could inherit, if she has the Key, or his granddaughter or grandson. But if they could not be found, then the fortune would go to the next St. Clair male which would be my grandson, Gerald?"

"Not exactly, Augusta. Robert died forty-four years ago. Gerald would become the next in line six years from now, but only his heirs could inherit. So he would have to have a child who reaches the age of twenty-one. Then the estate would be invested in that heir. And so the line would continue."

Duvigney glanced at his Rolex. "Now, I'm sorry, Augusta, but that is all the time I have. It has been very pleasant talking with you, but I'm afraid there is no further use in your pursuit of this claim. You need to learn to be content with the bounty that has been, might I say, generously provided to you by the St. Clair family. Now, if you will excuse me—"

A door behind Augusta opened and a large man in a butler's uniform stepped into the room. The signal was clear. The meeting was over.

As the limousine cruised up Park Avenue, Augusta sat in the back, fuming. "Why that pompous, overblown secretary! Who does he think he is?" she said to no one in particular. Augusta knew she had to make a plan. She picked up the car phone from the armrest next to her and dialed a number. After a few rings a man's voice answered.

"Gordon Randall Security."

"Randall, this is Augusta St. Clair. I need you to do some work for me."

"Certainly, Mrs. St. Clair. What do you need?"

"I need you to find a little girl; well, she would be grown up now. Her mother was married to Robert St. Clair. She was from Lancaster, Pennsylvania and she was Amish. Her name was Rachel Borntraeger. That's about all I have. I'll leave the rest up to you."

"Fine, Mrs. St. Clair. Any other instructions?"

"Yes, Randall. Some other people are looking for this girl also. It is imperative that you find her first, absolutely imperative. There can be no mistaking my meaning."

"Fine, Mrs. St. Clair. Consider it handled."

Chapter Four

Painful Days

The grey-green sea rolled in long, choppy swells beneath the boat. The waves were endless, moving toward him out of the mist and disappearing away toward the unseen horizon. It was dark, so dark, and the strange smell of the salt water was overpowering and somehow terrifying. A stiff breeze drove the icy spray off the tops of the waves into Jonathan's eyes. He raised his hand to wipe his face, but the mist and spray were continuous, blinding him. The chill of winter not yet dead…the gulls circling behind the boat…the plaintive cries whirling away on the wind. The sea, ominous and dead…

He stood in the gloom and the cold and the spray and the waves, the endless waves, rolling, rolling, rolling by, and where were they going? Suddenly, a great longing to see Jenny and Rachel swept over him like one of the swells rolling ceaselessly and vanishing away, beyond his sight. He was lost, gone, alone on the bridge of a ghost ship that cut through the waves like a sword. He looked through the window into the wheelhouse, but there was no one to pilot the boat. Where was the captain? Then he felt a hand touch him. He turned to see his dad standing there with him, but Dad was dead, dead as the grey-green waves. Or was he?

Craig

Jonathan felt his dad's hand squeeze his shoulder and then Dad smiled. "Thank you, son." And then Dad was gone, gone like a cool breeze that touches the face on a blistering day in the desert and then slips away leaving only regret behind.

But I'm not in the desert. I'm on this boat on the ocean and I'm alone and lost in the shadows and I'm freezing. Dad! Dad! Help me, please.

Then the boat lurched to the right as he heard the muffled explosion. The huge craft twisted like a snake, and the abrupt distortion of the boat's course threw Jonathan to the deck. As he lay there, stunned, he saw his mother come out of her stateroom and try to make her way forward.

Mom! But she's dead too! What's happening?

Then there was fire. Fire and smoke blowing through the middle of the boat. And then he was deep in the water, and above him he saw the churning waves. It was cold, so cold, and he couldn't breathe. And then he was swimming, swimming upward toward the light and the fire, the fire on the water. His head broke the surface and he gasped for air. Burning diesel fuel covered the waves. He was in the flames and he felt the fire burning his face, burning, melting, reaching for his eyes...

And then he saw his father again and his mother was with his father, not twenty feet away on the boat, and they were smiling. *"Dad, Mom!"*

Dad looked straight into Jonathan's eyes. He reached his hand toward Jonathan but he wasn't afraid. Jonathan couldn't hear him over the wind, but he saw his father's mouth forming words.

"Son, I believe!"

At that instant, the flames from the burning diesel fuel below deck ignited the propane tank in the galley, and the *Mistral* exploded with a roar. Jonathan struggled in the water. He was in the fire and the water, burning and drowning. He looked up as debris from the boat came flying toward him. He watched in terror as the grey-green waves rolled over the deck and Mistral sank. Within seconds, there was nothing left except some floating pieces of wreckage driving west before the howling wind.

Jenny! Jenny!

"JENNY!"

"Jonathan! Jonathan! Wake up!"

Jonathan groaned and rolled over. He opened his eyes and stared into the face of the lovely woman beside him in the bed. "What? Where am I? Who are you?"

"Jonathan, it's me, it's your Jenny. I'm here, beloved, right here. You were dreaming."

Jonathan clutched at the woman's arm. "I've got to find Jenny and Rachel. I'm lost and I can't find them. Can you help me?"

The woman placed her hand over Jonathan's eyes. Her skin was warm and alive, not dead like the horrible, killing sea. He heard her voice from a long way off.

"Close your eyes, Jonathan."

Jonathan closed his eyes beneath her hand.

"Now see your Jenny in your mind's eye. See her face, her red hair, the love for you in her eyes."

A face drifted into his mind. It was beautiful, framed by unruly golden-red curls... A white *kappe*, the eyes filled with love and compassion.

Jenny, it's you, my Jenny.

"Do you see her?"

"Yes, I see her. She's coming to find me. She's here to take me away from this darkness."

"Now open your eyes, Jonathan."

He opened his eyes. They were still covered by the woman's hand. Slowly, she lifted it away, pausing to lightly caress his face. He looked at her. The beautiful face with some age lines showing but still her face, the curls with a little touch of white among them, but still Jenny's curls...

It's Jenny, my Jenny.

"Jenny, Jenny..."

"Yes, beloved, it's me. I'm here with you. I'll always be here."

Peace flooded Jonathan's soul. He was home. Home with his wife and daughter, safe in his house in Paradise. He reached for Jenny and pulled her tight against him. He breathed the fragrance of her against his cheek. There was life here; life and safety and home. He felt relief wash over him, then joy. They lay quietly together.

"Was it the dream, Jonathan?"

"Yes, the dream. I was back on the boat. My dad was there, and my mother. I watched them die but they were smiling. They weren't afraid."

"Yes, dearest, they were not afraid because you gave them Christ, and they went to be with Him. That was your gift to them, Jonathan. That was why God took you to see them one last time."

"But it took me so long to get home, and now I get confused. Some days I wake up and I don't even know you. I think I'm late for work and I look for my guitar and...oh, Jenny! Will I ever get well?"

"You were gone for eight years, Jonathan. I don't know why God did that, but I know he worked everything for good while we were apart."

"But what about your folks? They died while I was gone. I never got to see them again. I loved your *daed* and your mama."

"I know, and you must know that they loved you also. My papa was so proud of you. He saw how *du leiber Gott* worked in your life, how much you loved me and cared for me, and how precious Rachel was to you. He never, ever regretted suggesting that you become Amish. You belonged to us. Never forget that."

Jonathan released his wife and swung his legs over the edge of the bed. He sat for a while slumped over, his head in his hands, quiet. Jenny reached out and softly began to rub his back.

Jonathan gave a deep sigh and straightened up. "I am sorry that Rachel and I are having so much trouble. I don't want to be hard with her. It's just that when she starts talking about going out in the world, I get frightened. I know what's out there, and I fear for her."

Jenny came and sat beside Jonathan on the edge of the bed. She slipped under his arm and laid her head on his chest. She was quiet for a few minutes. Then she spoke.

"When I was a little girl, I came to live with my mama and papa in Apple Creek. I did not know who I was or remember anything but a little bit about my real mama. But you know that because you helped me find out about my parents."

"Yes, but what—?"

Jenny put her fingers on his lips. "Don't you see, Jonathan? *Gott* sent me to Apple Creek to fill a terrible, empty place in my mama's heart."

"... After your sister, Jenna, died."

"Yes, and that was a wonderful thing. But if I never came there, I wouldn't have been walking across the street when you almost hit me. We never would have met, there would be no home in Paradise, there would be no Rachel."

"I understand that, Jenny. But that doesn't answer my questions about me, why I act this way, why I am so harsh when I want to be loving."

"My papa struggled with the same things for many years. During World War II, he rejected his faith, left the church, and joined the Marines. He ended up in a terrible place in the Pacific called Guadalcanal. He had to kill Japanese soldiers, often in hand-to-hand combat. It did something to his heart and his mind. My mama told me that when he came home he was different. He rejoined the church, but he didn't really know the Lord. He felt as though he had committed a terrible sin during the war, and he believed that if he just kept the rules of the church, somehow he would be allowed to go to heaven. It was because he was so strict that my sister, Jenna, died. It was a terrible thing, but *Gott griff nach seinem Herzen. Gott* was reaching for his heart."

Jonathan turned to look at Jenny's face. "Do you think the same thing has happened to me?"

Jenny paused. "In a way, yes. When you became a Christian, you understood that the church doesn't save us. Only Jesus can do that. But there were other parts of your life that you found difficult to surrender to God—your love for music, your gifts as a songwriter. You never sold your guitar, and sometimes I would hear you out in the barn playing softly so no one would hear you."

Jonathan grinned. "You heard me?"

"Yes, dearest. I never said anything because, truthfully, I love that part of you. I love your songs and your wonderful voice. It was your song that led me to you when I found you again in that nightclub. So I let you have your little secret."

Jenny smiled with the memory. Then she went on. "I think that may have been what the Lord was reaching for in your life—to surrender everything to Him so that if you did play music it would only be for His glory, or even to set it down altogether so that there would be no idols in your life that were above Him."

Jonathan's brow furrowed as he thought about what Jenny said. "So you think He might have let me live as Richard Sandbridge for all those years so I could see what my life would be like if my dreams came true?"

"Were you happy then?"

"No, Jenny. Even when I had hit songs and lots of money, I was never happy. There was always something missing—something that, if I could have found it, I would have traded everything for it."

"Like the pearl of great price that was found in the field?"

"Yes, Jenny, exactly. And when you came back to me at that nightclub, when all my dreams were coming true, I wanted nothing more than to put it all down and come home. This, this farm, this land, this is who I am. And you and Rachel are worth more to me than all the gold records in the world. But sometimes I get frightened."

"When you have the dream?"

"Yes, the dream. I'm lost and floating on the sea. I'm clinging to a piece of wood and the waves are crashing on me, and all I want to do is come home, to sit by the fire with my wife beside me and my little girl on my lap."

Jenny put her arms around Jonathan. "So maybe the *Ordnung* are like that piece of wood that you clung to all those days in the ocean. And perhaps that is why you are so strict—because the *Ordnung* are like a life preserver for you. They keep you centered in this life and hold the wicked world at bay."

"Yes, Jenny, you are probably right."

"So even if they are that way for you, maybe they are not that way for Rachel?"

Jonathan thought for a moment. "So I am forcing my fears on Rachel?"

"I cannot tell you that for sure, Jonathan, but from my own observation, it appears that way."

Jonathan stood up and went to the window. Outside, the air was bursting with the clean, strong smell of the fields—his fields. All around the house, stretching off into the distance, the first growth of the spring planting was beginning to show green against the brown earth. Jonathan saw a small bird sitting in a tree. It had black feathers on its topknot but brilliant yellow underneath. It trilled a short song and then flitted away.

That was an Oriole. I've never seen one on the farm before.

A spring breeze shook the pink flowers on the plum trees and the soft petals drifted down in a magical shower. The clouds above were showing golden and pink as the day began to grow around them.

"I think I understand what you are saying. I will try to remember, but sometimes it is so hard, Jenny. I will be working at something around the farm, and then I'll be staring at the tool in my hands, wondering how to use it. It's as though I'm standing outside my body, observing me and wondering what I am doing. Thoughts come to me and I can't unlock them, and I know that if I could just get back inside me, everything would be all right again."

"I know you struggle, Jonathan. The doctors have told me that you still suffer from the effects of your amnesia and your injuries. They could not tell me if you would ever be well, but I am trusting the Lord for that. I know that one day you will be healed, and until then, I will care for you and love you always, looking for that day with joy and hope."

Jonathan turned back to Jenny and pulled her up into his arms. The smell of her was like a beacon in a black night, the feel of her body pressed against him was like a breath of air to a drowning man.

"I am so grateful for you, my darling Jenny. I am also praying that I will be healed from this. I just hope I don't drive Rachel away before I am."

Chapter Five

The Search

Gordon Randall sat comfortably in the chair across the desk from Augusta St. Clair. He had a manila folder open on his lap and was looking at a few sheets of paper in front of him. A crooked smile broke the harsh contours of his hawk-like features.

"So what have you found out, Randall?" Augusta asked sweetly, though Randall doubted there was an ounce of sweetness in the woman's whole being.

"You've probably heard most of this before, Mrs. St. Clair, but I'm going to go through it, just to bring you up to speed."

Augusta leaned back and folded her hands in her lap, with the fingers intertwined. "Go ahead."

"As you know, Augusta, your brother-in-law, Robert, married a young girl on September 14, 1946. At that time, he was living in Lancaster, Pennsylvania, running his father's airplane factory. The girl's maiden name was Rachel Mary Borntraeger. It's on the marriage certificate I obtained from the county records. Rachel Borntraeger was born in Lancaster County, Pennsylvania, May 12, 1928. She wasn't born in a hospital. The records state that a midwife filed the birth certificate. I have the certificate here. She was eighteen years old when she married

Robert St. Clair. Robert was twenty-six. Robert and Rachel had one child, Jennifer Constance St. Clair, also born in Lancaster County, in January of 1947. Rachel Borntrager's parents were Abel and Eliza Borntraeger. They are both deceased. The interesting thing in all of this is that Rachel was Amish."

"Amish. Yes, I heard that from my mother-in-law. Robert alienated his father by marrying against his wishes and outside our faith. When Robert told Max that he had gotten the girl pregnant and he was going to marry her, Max, my father-in-law, told Robert to get the baby taken care of and dump the girl, but Robert refused. Max believed that Rachel Borntraeger had deliberately failed to take the necessary precautions in order to hook a wealthy young man into marriage. Max never forgave Robert, even though Robert asked many times to bring the woman and the child home to visit. Margaret, my mother-in-law, was heartbroken, of course. She loved children. She was such a sentimental old fool."

Augusta paused. "I met the girl, you know."

Randall was surprised. "When was that, Mrs. St. Clair?"

"In the spring of 1950. It was after Robert was killed in the car wreck. A few months later, a young woman showed up on the doorstep of the city house with a toddler in tow. She said her name was Rachel St. Clair and the youngster was Robert's child. She wanted to see Max or Margaret. Max had passed by then and Margaret was getting senile. I felt it was my duty to protect her from gold diggers and riff-raff, so I sent them away."

Randall made a note on one of the sheets of paper. "Uh-huh. And then what happened?"

"The woman persisted in contacting us. She came to the house a second time and I had the police escort her off the property and give her a warning as to what would happen if she continued disturbing us."

"Did she stop?"

"No, she was very tenacious. She called again and informed our butler that she had documentary proof that she and Robert were married and the baby was Robert's. I refused to see her or let her bother Margaret. I was only fulfilling my responsibility as a dutiful daughter-in-law."

Randall grinned, although the grin was hardly friendly. "Can I be blunt, Augusta?"

"Speak your mind, Randall."

"According to the research I had done on you privately, you were never a dutiful daughter-in-law. The truth is, you are not who you pretend to be. Contrary to your claims that you are descended from Russian royalty, you are a lower middle-class girl, the former Francine Bosnan, who married into a fortune, and you have been protecting your hard-won position ever since."

Augusta scowled. "Duvigney knew about me, too. You people have excellent sources. Somehow my life has become an open book."

Randall went on. "It's my guess you knew exactly who this girl was, and you were quite aware she represented a threat to your status in the family. I assume you took swift and determined action against Rachel Borntraeger St. Clair."

A look of mock dismay crossed Augusta's face. "Why, Randall! How can you accuse me of such a thing?"

Randall laughed. "You can stop blowing smoke in my ear, Augusta. Just tell me what you did to the girl so I can get on with this investigation."

Augusta shifted uncomfortably in her chair and tried glowering at Randall. He didn't bite. Finally, she spoke. "I sent the police to her hotel to find the alleged proof of her marriage to Robert."

"By police, do you mean the cops you own in the Manhattan NYPD?"

Augusta pulled herself erect and glared at Randall. "It is important for a family of our stature to have connections in the right places. We must cover all our bases, you know."

"Uh-huh. And what happened when you sent the boys round to steal the documents?"

"Well, I never..." Augusta snorted.

Randall laughed again. "Yes, you did. So what happened?"

"They found some evidence, photos of Robert and the girl, things of that nature—but no wedding or birth certificates. She must have hidden them somewhere."

Randall looked at his notes. "And what other punitive action did you take?"

"What makes you think I took further action?"

Randall sighed, put the notes back into the folder, and started to get up.

"Where are you going, Randall?"

"Look, I don't have time to play games with you. I know how you operate. Now just give me the facts or I'll have to go. I have other clients, you know."

A flash of anger crossed Augusta's face. "How dare you speak to me in that manner? You're playing a dangerous game with me, Randall. I can have you taken care of with a phone call."

Randall put his hands on the desk, palms down, and leaned forward. "Augusta, don't try threatening me. Maybe you've forgotten how this works. Sure you can have me beat up, or even killed. But if you attempt such a course of action, there are certain files that would be immediately sent to the police and the feds. You're in way too deep with me. And you should know that along with a record of our activities, there are certain incriminating materials I've gathered and retained in the course of my employment with you. I'm very sure you would not want those materials to be made public. So let's just play nice. What did you do to the girl?"

Augusta shifted stiffly in her chair and smiled at Randall again. She motioned for Randall to sit back down. "Point taken, Randall. All right. I had the woman put out of the hotel. My men watched her until she took up with a heroin dealer named Joseph Bender. She stayed with him for a few months. Then Bender and his brother were involved in a bank robbery. The brother was captured during the holdup but Joseph Bender escaped. Sammy Bender ended up in Sing Sing. Joseph Bender disappeared. When he left, I assume he took Rachel St. Clair and the baby with him, because they never returned to Bender's apartment. I was unable to track him down."

Augusta got up and went to the bay window and looked out for a moment. Then she turned and sat on the oversized sill. "My people talked to Bender's mother but she said she didn't know anything. In all the years since then, I have never heard from Rachel again. Since no heirs had come forward in forty years, I was sure that my claim to the estate would be undisputed. Now the board of trustees has informed me that only an heir in the line of an oldest son can inherit the principal trust, which represents billions of dollars. That's how the fortune came to Max, Robert's father, and it would have come to Robert if he had lived."

"Can it be inherited by a female?"

"Duvigney told me that it can be inherited by a woman but only if she has the Key, and she can be only two generations away from the elder son. If the older son leaves no heirs, the trust is held for fifty years and then a younger son or the son of another branch of the St. Clair family would be nominated as the principal heir."

"What is the Key?"

"It's a birthmark that has passed genetically down from the first St. Clair. It's a key-shaped red mark above the heart."

"So let me get this straight, Augusta. The daughter of Robert St. Clair or his granddaughter or grandson could inherit but only if they had this Key?"

"Yes. Duvigney informed me that it is the one irrefutable proof."

"And what about Gerald?"

"At this point, he could not inherit, being the second generation of a younger brother, my husband, Jerod. Robert died forty-four years ago. There are six years left and then another son or a grandson, in this case, Gerald, would come into the line, but there are conditions. Gerald would be the heir, but he would not receive the money. He would have to marry and have a son, and his son could only inherit when he reached maturity."

"Why the long gap in determining another heir?"

Augusta smiled. "They didn't want the boys killing each other for the money."

"So unless Robert's wife is still alive, the little girl that came to the house in New York with her is the heir, if she has the Key?"

"Yes, she or Robert's grandchildren, if there are any."

"Why don't you just find the wife and Robert's little girl and eliminate them so that Gerald could be in line for the inheritance?"

Augusta got up from the window bench and returned to her desk chair. "You don't seem to understand, Randall. Gerald would not come into the line for another six years. But only Gerald's son can inherit, and he can only inherit after he reaches twenty-one. Gerald doesn't have a son. I'm sixty-eight now. That's twenty-five years, if he had a son tomorrow, which he won't. I'll probably be moldering in the grave, or so old I wouldn't even know what money is, if and when Gerald or his heirs get any money. I can't wait for the fools on the board of trustees to dilly-dally around. I want that money, and I want it now!"

"So if I find Robert's wife or daughter, what are you going to do with her?"

Augusta scowled. "First of all, I don't think you will find Rachel St. Clair. She was very determined to prove that she was Robert's wife, but I have not heard a thing from her for forty years. I believe that she is dead. As for the little girl, she may be alive and if she is, I need you to find her."

"Why is it so important for you to have all that money, Augusta?"

Augusta's face narrowed and she pursed her lips. "I want it because I want it. The St. Clairs have always treated me as a second-class citizen, even though I married one of their precious sons. It will do my old heart good to take all their money and see them come begging to replenish their trusts and pay their bills."

Randall considered Augusta's words. "The only solution is to find the girl. If she is still alive, she should be about forty-three years old. But it won't be easy. You met her in 1950. That was forty years ago. A lot has happened since then."

"Randall, you are the only hope I have in this situation. We must find that girl. If we can, then we'll go from there."

"You say the man that Rachel St. Clair ended up with was Joseph Bender?"

"Yes."

"How did you know about the bank Robbery?"

"Well…"

"Augusta?"

"All right. I paid Bender a monthly stipend to keep the woman addicted to drugs. He reported to my contacts, without knowing that the St. Clair family was involved. He just knew that someone wanted the girl out of the way. Then he disappeared with Rachel St. Clair, and I never heard from him again."

"What about the brother?"

"Sammy Bender was sentenced to Sing Sing prison for shooting a bank guard and a teller in the holdup. My contacts have the information."

Randall put his notes back into the folder and slipped it into the leather briefcase next to his chair. He closed the latch and stood up. "I will need to speak to your contacts. You have my number, so have them call me today. In the meantime, I will go to Pennsylvania and see if I can find any Borntraegers that might know of Rachel or her daughter's whereabouts. And I will check with Bender's brother. I must tell you, Augusta, that this will not be easy."

"If you can solve this, Randall, I guarantee you'll be rewarded beyond your wildest dreams."

Randall smiled unpleasantly. "Augusta, you just said the magic words."

Randall turned and walked to the door. Augusta stared after him.

Randall stopped and looked back. "I hope I live to spend it, Augusta, for your sake."

Then the door closed behind him.

The private line on Michel Duvigney's desk rang once and then stopped. Duvigney pulled a notebook from his pocket, checked a number, and then dialed it. It rang twice, and then a cold voice answered.

"Randall speaking."

"You have some information for me?"

"Yes. I spent some time with Augusta today and will be following some leads she gave me. It will be hard but not impossible to find the girl. I'll be making a call on a source tomorrow. Hopefully, they'll give me some information that will set me on the right track."

"'Hopefully', is not a word in my lexicon, Randall. Either you can find the heir or not. There are a great many issues pressing the point here, Randall. They go far beyond the disgusting St. Clair woman's desire to get her hands on the estate. She is the lesser daughter of a Yugoslavian car mechanic, even though she pretends to be descended from wealthy stock. It would be a shameful thing if the old tart got her hands on the trust. And there are other issues."

"What other issues?"

"That is no concern of yours, Randall. Let's just say that if Augusta St. Clair gets into the middle of this mix, there will literally be hell to pay."

"I understand."

"On another note, does Augusta have any inkling of your, ah, divided loyalties?"

"At this point, no. But we'll have to play the game carefully, for my sake, if not for yours. You may have access to a lot more money than she does, but she is equally ruthless as you and your friends. If she thought you were doing an end-run around her schemes, she'd become a formidable foe. And I would find myself caught in the middle. A very delicate situation, as you can see."

"Just play it straight with us, Randall, and make sure that we get all the information before Augusta. If you do, you will be handsomely rewarded, I assure you."

"That's the second time I've been promised a big reward today. Things are looking up."

There was a click and the line went dead. Duvigney stared at the receiver in his hand.

Enjoy it while it lasts, Randall.

Chapter Six

Daniel's Heart

Daniel King stood on the high knoll behind his father's house. It was just before dawn on an early April morning. Far away to the east, a dark row of trees marked the horizon. Long, smooth clouds drifted through the slowly brightening sky. A golden glow began to grow around the tops of the trees, and as it did, the billows above were touched with a beautiful orange that faded into a dusky pink as it reached toward heaven. Above it all, the deep indigo of the dying night held time fixed in perfect suspension.

It was that mystical moment, just before the day begins, when all nature holds its breath, as though waiting for an unheard command from on high. Then the tiniest sliver of sun peeked over the eastern hills, and the world exhaled. A small breeze stirred and Daniel felt the soft brush of nature's breath against his face. A familiar peace flooded over him. His heart was filled with a deep sense of connection to the land, and especially to this place.

The light gathered itself into golden shafts that pierced the cobalt depths and the green fields of Paradise, materialized below him, reaching away to the east. One by one, Daniel began to pick out the Amish farms that surrounded Jonas King's property. Off to the right was the Beachey place with the finest milk cows in Lancaster County. Up the road, nestled in a thick stand of Chestnut trees were the Masts, and beyond them, the Nissleys and the Ottos. The three families were all related— carpenters and woodworkers that produced wonderful handcrafted furniture.

Down the hill to his left he could see the potato fields of the Glick farm, and beyond that, the Keim's first hay cutting was a bright patch of green that prophesied good feed for the King horses this year. Daniel could almost see the names on the mailboxes that lined Leacock Road: Umble, Troyer, Swartzendruber, Raber, Petershwim, Shetler, Stoltzfus, Yoder, and Zook. Each name held a story, not only for Daniel, but also for the Amish community that had lived and prospered here since 1720.

Daniel's eyes turned to the blue farmhouse a half-mile away. It was the old Borntraeger place, now the Hershberger farm. It, too, was part of the long continuum of Daniel's people in Pennsylvania, for Jenny Hershberger was a Borntraeger, and her story was a great illustration to Daniel of how *der kluge und liebende Gott* had kept his hand on the Plain people of Lancaster County and held them to their inheritance.

In a way, we are like the people of Israel, who have an inheritance forever in their land. Gott promised it to them and He always keeps His promise.

Daniel sighed and kicked at a large stone that was half-buried in the dirt. After a few nudges, the stone broke loose and rolled away down the hill. Daniel watched as it bounced into the small creek that meandered along the base of the knoll.

That stone is Rachel. She wants to go rolling away, and she will. She will fall into the river of the world and be swept away and leave this place. And she will never know the peace that is here, all around us.

A small, black buggy rolled along Leacock toward the Old Philadelphia Turnpike. Daniel could not make out the driver's face, but he didn't have to, for he knew that buggy well. A big, white gelding with a flowing mane pulled it.

It's Tuesday and Andy Peterswhim is on his way to the market for his mother.

As Daniel watched the buggy disappear around the tree-shadowed bend in the road, he took comfort in the symmetry of his life. The seasons came and went, the crops were planted and then harvested, the people were born, they lived, and they died. It was all part of a mysterious cycle that set his people apart, a cycle that only an uncluttered heart could see. It was timeless, stretching away into the past and moving forward into the future, like a great river that is always changing, filling its banks, ever-moving, catching the sun with a million different diamond-sparkle facets of its surface and yet somehow, to the casual observer, always the same, always there. For Daniel, that was the secret of the Plain Way. It was always there, appearing to be fixed, yet when each day started, it was always a new journey, without any missteps to mar the way. If a man was accountable for his actions, to himself and to others, and *spazieren gegangen im Licht des Gottes*, if he walked in the light of God, there was much grace for living and everything that happened seemed to work together for the good.

With a deep sigh, Daniel turned and started down the hill. The path through the small woods was as familiar to him as the walls of his room. He had been coming to the top of the knoll since he was a small child and it was, for him, a castle keep where he could take refuge from the pressures of the world and sort out his thoughts. Many times when they were small children, he and Rachel had come here to play. But then Rachel had moved away, and it seemed as though a great piece of Daniel's life went with her. And later, when she returned and began to blossom into womanhood, the dictates of the *Ordnung* had separated them even more, and Daniel had to content himself with watching Rachel grow lovelier each day from afar.

He stopped and picked up a broken-off branch that had fallen from the huge buckeye tree that stood a little below the crest of the ridge. There had been a storm a week ago and the ancient chestnut had shed many small branches and limbs, and yet it still stood, strong and defiant, unmoved from the place it had been growing for over one hundred years. To Daniel, it was a symbol of all that was permanent in his life. It was under that tree that he and Rachel had pledged to be friends forever when they were only six years old. He began to absentmindedly whisk the trail in front of him with the branch as he walked, and as he did, the old yearning rose inside. Rachel! Rachel!

Sie leben immer in meinem Herzen...always in my heart!

He struck the stick against a small bay tree as he walked past, and the branch broke in his hand. His heart sank as he tried to come to grips with his feelings for the girl. She was an enigma to him. Daughter of an *Außenseiter* father and a half-Amish mother, Rachel had not lived the normal life of an Amish girl. When Rachel was seven her father, Jonathan, disappeared at sea. Everyone thought he was dead, and Rachel and her mother, Jenny, went to Ohio to live. They were gone almost three years, and then suddenly one day, Rachel was back at the farm. But she was no longer the carefree child that had been Daniel's playmate. Word filtered back to Paradise about the tragic events that had taken the lives of Jenny's parents, and Daniel began to understand the deep sadness that wrapped Rachel like a winter coat.

Daniel tried to reestablish their friendship, but Rachel was standoffish and quiet. Once, Daniel asked her whether she still liked him. She would not answer him, but Daniel knew somehow that Rachel was afraid of getting close to anyone. And then when her father had literally come back from the dead, Rachel grew even more distant. Jonathan had been an amnesia victim for almost eight years and he still struggled with physical issues that made him unstable emotionally, and the volatility played havoc with his relationship with Rachel.

With nowhere else to place the blame for her circumstances, Rachel had come to blame being Amish as the root of all her sorrow and confusion. Now she looked elsewhere for her joy, and Daniel could see it in her eyes when he was with her. Even when things seemed normal between them, it was as though she was looking through him, past the everyday of life in Paradise, to a place that Daniel could hardly even comprehend. When she began talking about going away to school, his heart ached. And yet Daniel could see the gift in her, a gift of healing and caring, and he knew that it was something that *Gott* had placed within her. So Daniel's heart was torn—torn between wanting to be close to Rachel again and letting her go to fulfill her dream, if that would make her happy.

"Daniel! Daniel! Stop moping around and give me a hand here. *Wir vergeuden Tageslicht.* Time's a wasting!"

Daniel's reverie was broken as he came down the path and into the farmyard. His *daed* came out of the barn, leading the great black stallion that was the pride of the King farm. The smile in his eyes belied the gruff tone of his remark.

"Ja, Papa, ich komme."

Daniel stopped by the well pump. He hung his black hat on a nail on the barn wall and levered the red handle. A stream of icy spring water poured out, and he filled his hands with it and splashed his face. He brushed his hair back with both hands and put his hat back on. Then he quickly walked to his papa who handed him the halter rope. Black Dancer put his face down, and Daniel stroked the smooth skin around Dancer's nostrils, then scratched behind the silky ears. The horse pushed his nose against Daniel's overall pocket.

"Looking for something, Dancer?"

Daniel pulled the apple out of his pocket and the horse nickered and took it from him in one bite.

Jonas King smiled at his son. *"Ja,* with you he acts like a pig, not a horse."

"He's a good boy, Papa."

The two Kings admired the beautiful animal for another moment. Jonas put his hand on Daniel's shoulder. "You look troubled, my son. What is it? Rachel?"

"Yes, Papa. I am worried for her. She does not have peace in her heart. I see it in her eyes."

"Is it her trouble with Jonathan?"

"That's part of it, Papa, but there's more. Rachel is different. All these things that have happened to her have changed her. She does not see the world out there as we do. Instead, she sees it as a refuge, a place where she might escape from the hurt and the pain she has found in Paradise. Sometimes when I'm with her and she says something to me, it is from such a different point of view that it's almost as though she was never Amish.

She takes no joy in the simple things. She is always looking away, out there somewhere. It troubles me."

The two men walked toward the pasture together with the horse following them. Black Dancer pushed his nose against Daniel's back, cadging for another apple. The early-morning sun warmed the air and Daniel's papa sighed and pulled a handkerchief out of his pocket. He wiped his face and then spoke again.

"Daniel, perhaps you need to let this girl go her own way. You are Amish to the heart of you. I know how you love this land and the ways of our people. Rachel will never be happy here, I think, and if you were ever to marry her, she would bring you unhappiness, too. You should look for a good, plain Amish girl who will be content to make a home for you and give you children. Hettie Troyer has made it very clear that she would welcome courtship from you. And there are others—beautiful, simple girls who love our ways as much as you do. "

Daniel walked beside his father silently. There was wisdom in his *daed's* words but no joy. He remembered how good Rachel had been with their mare.

If only she could see that everything she really wants is right here in Paradise.

"If only I could make Rachel see, Papa. She has a gift and she would be of great benefit to our people if she would just stay here."

"*Ja, mein Sohn, Sie sind richtig...*you are right. Rachel would be an excellent veterinarian. But I am afraid she has many crossroads before her, choices she must make, before she can even see clearly enough to make the right decision about the rest of her life. I am thinking that, for you, it is best to forget her and go on with your own life."

Daniel's heart felt like a great hand was squeezing it, and he couldn't breathe. He stopped and looked at his father. "But isn't there a way, Papa? There must be a way!"

Daniel's papa stopped and looked at his son. "I think that you love this girl more than you have told me, Daniel."

Daniel looked back and then slowly nodded his head. His papa sighed.

"Then, the only thing you can do is to bathe this girl in prayer. If she is *das Mädchen, das Gott für Sie geplant hat*, then you must trust Him to work His will and way in her heart. Nonetheless, I am afraid there is much sorrow in all this for you, and it troubles me. But I will pray with you and for you...and for Rachel."

"*Danki*, Papa."

But at that moment, Daniel knew only two things. He knew that Rachel *was* the girl God had for him. And he couldn't see how prayer would change anything.

Chapter Seven

Closing In

Sammy Bender looked through the crack in his door. The man in the hallway was medium height and powerfully built, with a sharp, hawk-like face set off by a short crew cut and black turtleneck under a brown, houndstooth wool jacket. The tan slacks were sharply pressed, and the black brogans bore a high-luster shine, military in its perfection.

"Whaddaya want?"

The hawk-faced man glanced down at a small notebook in his hand, checked the number on the apartment door, and smiled. Somehow the smile made Sammy shiver.

"Sammy Bender?"

"Yeah."

"Formerly of Sing Sing Correctional Facility?"

"I done my time..."

"Brother of one..."—the man glanced down at the notebook—"Joseph Bender?"

Sammy didn't like the turn of the conversation. "Say, what are you, a cop? I'm clean, see. I visit my PO every month, and I don't cause no trouble."

Sammy started to close the door, but the man put his shoe in the opening, reached into his pocket, and pulled out a crisp, one-hundred dollar bill. He held it close to the crack.

"I have no interest in you, personally, Mr. Bender, or your brother. I only need some small pieces of information that you might be carrying in that drug-addled brain of yours. So if you let me in, perhaps I can help you in your determined desire to escape the cares of this dreadful world."

Sammy closed the door, released the chain latch, reached out, grabbed the money, and started to close the door. It was the wrong move, because the next thing he knew, he was up against the wall in the hallway with a small but deadly-looking revolver pressed painfully against his face and a steel grip on his arm.

"Not a good way to begin a relationship, Sammy."

Sammy Bender slumped his shoulders in defeat. The man kept his grip while he put the gun back in the shoulder holster where it had resided so invisibly, and then he pushed Sammy down the hall.

When they got into the front room, the man pointed to the ragged, cigarette-burned stuffed chair by the window. "Sit down, Sammy."

Sammy Bender sat. "Okay, I'm sitting. Are you going to shoot me?"

"Why would I want to do that? Then I wouldn't be able to find out what I need to know." He glanced around and smiled the same joyless smile. "Besides, it would make an awful mess in this otherwise elegant sitting room."

A ray of hope splintered the darkness in Sammy's brain. "So, what do you want, and how do you know about Joe?"

"How I know about Joe is my business, and that's not what I'm here for anyway. I need to know about the woman and the little girl."

"The woman? What woman?"

"The woman, Rachel St. Clair, and the little girl, her daughter, that lived with you for a while back in the fifties."

"Oh, Rachel…" Sammy paused, thinking back. "That's a long time ago, man. I ain't seen Rachel since I seen Joe. And Joe's dead."

"Dead?" The man reached for his notebook. "How did that happen?"

"I think he died in a car crash out in Ohio. The cop told me all about it."

"The cop?"

"Well, he was actually a sheriff from someplace by Akron—Woozer or Weiser, I don't know."

"Wooster?"

"Yeah, that's it. Wooster."

"And what exactly did he tell you about Joe?"

"When Joe and I robbed the bank, Joe drove the car. I got caught inside the bank and went to prison. Joe split. The sheriff who visited me told me Joe died in a wreck in Ohio. He had a little girl with him. The girl was Rachel's daughter, Jenny. The sheriff was looking for Rachel. That's all I know."

The hawk-faced man pulled the hundred-dollar bill out of his pocket and snapped it flat between his hands. He laid it on the coffee table in front of Sammy and then he pulled out two more and laid them beside the first in a perfectly even row. "I need more, Sammy."

Sammy looked at the money, and a hunger began to grow in his belly. "Okay, Rachel's dead, too."

"And how do you know that?"

"The sheriff went to my mom's house in Patterson. They got a tip from her that Rachel had overdosed in Stroudsburg. When they were at her place, there was an Amish guy and a hippie and a girl with the sheriff—a real human 'Incredible Journey' or sumpthin'."

Sammy cackled at his joke and spittle flew out of the hole where his front teeth used to be. He went on, looking at the money while he spoke. "The girl was Jenny."

That got the hawk-faced man's attention. "So, you're telling me that Jenny is still alive?"

"Yeah, she was at my mom's house."

The man reached down and pushed one of the bills over to Sammy. "More, Sammy."

"Jenny stayed in touch with my mom. She and the rest of them went to Stroudsburg and found out that Rachel was dead. She let my mom know."

The man reached down and pushed the second bill over. "And…"

It felt hot in the room. Sammy wiped his brow with the sleeve of his shirt. "Uh…"

"C'mon, Sammy, just a little more."

"Halverson! The sheriff's name was Halverson! And Jenny married the hippie. My mom told me she sent her a letter."

"And what was the hippie's name, Sammy?

Sammy's brow furrowed. "That was a long time ago, pal."

The hawk-face man reached for the third bill and put it back in his pocket.

"Wait. Uh…the guy's name was Johnny or John. That's the best I can do. When my mom told me, I wasn't really paying attention."

"Good boy, Sammy."

The bill appeared magically and made its journey to Sammy's side of the coffee table. Sammy picked up the money and felt the crispness of it between his fingers. "Brand-new Franklins. This will keep me up for a week. Thanks a lot."

Sammy heard the click of the door latch closing and looked up. The hawk-faced man was gone.

"So Rachel St. Clair is dead. What about the girl?"

Augusta listened intently while the voice on the other end of the line replied to her question. Then she spoke again. "All right, she was alive in 1965. That's twenty-five years ago, Randall. Have you made any progress in finding her?"

Again, the voice spoke while Augusta listened. "Uh-huh, all right, Randall. Where are you now? Wooster? Why Wooster?"

Another long pause and then Augusta smiled. "Good work, Randall. Let me know when you find out more."

Augusta hung up the phone and turned to her grandson, Gerald. He was sitting stiffly on a couch in an elegant sitting room at the St. Clair mansion. He tapped his fingers together nervously and then reached into his pocket and pulled out a pack of menthol cigarettes.

Augusta waved her hand. "Not in here, Gerald. If you want to smoke those filthy things, do it outside."

Gerald frowned and put the cigarettes back in his pocket. "So what did our spy have to say?"

"He's not a spy, Gerald. He's a former Special Forces and CIA. That makes him exactly suited to our needs. There is nothing Randall can't find out."

"Well?"

"All right, Gerald, calm down and I'll tell you where we stand. Rachel St. Clair, your great aunt, is dead. She overdosed on heroin in Stroudsburg, Pennsylvania, in 1950. The man she was with, Joe Bender, left her body behind in a motel room and drove west with Rachel's child, Jenny St. Clair. He crashed his car outside of Dalton, Ohio and was killed. The girl survived the wreck and was adopted by an Amish couple in Apple Creek, Ohio. She was still alive as of 1965."

"How in the world did Randall find all that out?"

"Gerald, you must never underestimate Randall. He is ruthless—without feeling. His intelligence-gathering capabilities are superb. He was able to gain, umm…access to police files in Stroudsburg. In them, he found that in 1965 one Bobby Halverson, who was the sheriff of Wayne County at that time, paid a visit to the department there. Jenny St. Clair, along with her adoptive father and another man, Jonathan Hershberger, accompanied him. They were able to give the police information that established Rachel St. Clair's identity. It was all in the file. Randall is in Wooster following up on Halverson. He'll be back to us soon."

"Well, I wish he would hurry up. I'm getting tired of this whole game. I don't see why they won't just give me the money. I'm a St. Clair, too!"

Augusta looked at her grandson. He was such a beautiful boy, but he was so impatient. She smiled anyway. "Now, Gerald, dear, don't get petulant. Things have changed and it's not going to be as easy to get our hands on the money as I thought. But I'm working on it. So just relax. Your grandmother will take care of everything."

Augusta stood up, walked over behind the couch and began to stroke Gerald's hair and forehead. "Haven't I always taken care of you, dearest? Why don't you relax. Grandmother will handle everything."

Gerald turned to look at Augusta and then shrugged his shoulders and accepted the caresses.

The black BMW drove slowly up to the small house in Wooster, Ohio. Yellow daffodils bloomed along a white picket fence, and yellow forsythias blossomed on large bushes under the windows. Birch trees in the front yard were putting forth their lime-green leaf buds. An older man stood by the front porch with a hose in his hand, absentmindedly watering some juniper bushes that grew on either side of the steps. The whole place was immaculate. The man in the yard was big and carried himself with a military bearing. He looked very tough, despite the years that had lined his face. Randall stopped the car and watched the man for a moment, assessing him. Then he climbed out of the car and walked up to the fence. The old man glanced up at Randall. "Mornin'. Can I help you with somethin'?"

Randall looked down at his notebook. "Ralph Halkovich?"

"Bull Halkovich. Nobody's called me Ralph since I broke my Aunt Daisy's window when I was ten."

"Okay, Bull. I'm looking for Bobby Halverson. The folks down at the Sheriff's Department said you knew how to reach him."

"Uh-huh."

Bull went back to watering the bushes.

"I said I'm looking for Bobby Halverson."

Bull sighed and glanced up again. "I heard you."

"Well, can you help me?"

Bull twisted the nozzle on the hose until the mist he was directing toward the junipers was cut off and then he laid the hose down. He walked over to the fence and looked down at Randall. "Mister, I don't go handing out Bobby's info to any Tom, Dick, or Harry that comes driving into Wooster in a fancy car with New York plates and smoked windows. Bobby's retired and he's getting old and he doesn't like people to come around much, so you'll have to give me a real good reason to spill my guts."

Randall smiled and took a guess. "Semper Fi, Bull."

"You a Marine?"

"Yes, First Division, Vietnam, then Special Forces. How about you?"

"Nope, but I fought side by side with them in the Pacific."

"Wasn't Halverson a Marine?"

"Yep, won the silver star on Guadalcanal. He was a real tough customer..."

Bull's eyes narrowed. "Say, you trying to squeeze something outta me? How did you find out so much about Bobby?"

"Take it easy, Bull. I'm just trying to be friendly here. In my line of business you have to do your homework."

Randall realized that it didn't seem wise to try and outfox the old guy, and he better tell Bull as much of the truth as he could. "Look, Bull, I represent a family that is looking for the heirs of one Robert St. Clair. We understand that Bobby knows quite a lot about the subject and we'd like to contact him."

Bull put his hand to his chin and rubbed it contemplatively. Then he shrugged. "I don't know about any Robert St. Clair and I ain't giving you no info on Bobby until I check with him. Gimme your card and I'll have him call you."

"I assure you that I'm on the up and up here, Bull..."

"Gimme the card!"

Randall reached in his chest pocket to retrieve a business card. He felt the handle of his pistol and debated using a different tactic, but Bull was ahead of him.

"If you're thinkin' about pulling that popgun you got in your pocket, I can tell you this. I may be old but I'm still in army shape, and I could come over this fence and break your puny neck before you got it out. And besides, I'm too big to kill with that little .38. So leave that idea in the filing cabinet."

Randall's hand moved past the gun and pulled out a card. He handed it to Bull. "My number's right there. I would appreciate any help. Have the sheriff call me."

"And who should I say you represent?"

"I represent Augusta St. Clair, Robert St. Clair's sister-in-law."

Bull looked down at the card. "Uh-huh."

Randall reached out a hand. "Well, nice to meet you, Bull."

Bull just stared at him with steely eyes, so Randall turned, went back to the car, climbed in, and pulled away. He drove to the end of the block and looked back. Bull was still staring after him. Randall watched as an old cat that had been hiding under the hydrangeas walked slowly out and began bunting against Bull's leg. Bull reached down and picked him up, turned, and headed toward the house.

Randall smiled. "And now Bull goes in and calls Halverson. Army guys are so predictable."

He glanced at his watch and then headed back toward Pennsylvania.

Chapter Eight

An Open Door

The Paradise Post Office was a small brick building right on the corner of Highway 30 and Leacock Road. Rachel parked her scooter by the phone booth, went around to the front and walked up the stairs to the big glass door. She peeked through the glass and saw Mrs. Shoemaker, the postmistress, behind the counter. Rachel went inside, but before she could say anything, Mrs. Shoemaker waved at her and smiled.

"Yoo hoo, Rachel! It's here!"

Rachel glanced around to see if anybody heard Mrs. Shoemaker and then went to the counter. "Please, Mrs. Shoemaker, I don't want everybody to know."

"Whoops, I forgot."

Mrs. Shoemaker looked around furtively, too, and then, with a secretive air, handed Rachel an official-looking envelope.

Rachel's heart leaped. She stared down at the envelope, her heart pounding. An elegant logo was printed in the upper left corner. There was a red double circle with a book in the center and the words "Cornell University—Founded 1865" printed inside the lines. Off to the right was a red rectangle with the words, "Cornell University College of Veterinary Medicine."

"Aren't you going to open it, dear?"

"I'm afraid to, Mrs. Shoemaker."

"Well, there's only two answers that could be in it, yes or no. So you might as well get it over with."

Rachel nodded in agreement and took a deep breath. She had been waiting for six weeks for an answer from the admissions department and now here it was. Her hand shook as she gently undid the seal on the letter and pulled out the folded paper inside.

My Dear Miss Hershberger,

We received your application for admittance to the School of Veterinary Medicine. As you may know, our standards are very high and only a small percentage of applicants gain entrance to the school. What makes your case interesting is that we have never had an Amish applicant before. Normally, a person in your position, that is, one who has technically only completed the eighth grade, would not be considered for entrance, but your obvious passion for the field of animal husbandry, as detailed in your charming letter, convinced our committee to pursue this matter further. After careful review of your middle school transcript, which, by the way, was exceptional, and the records you sent us from the community college where you took several courses in which you ranked at the top of your class, we are willing to pursue your application further, with a few conditions.

First, you will be required to take the Scholastic Assessment Test (SAT). You must demonstrate high aptitude on this test (in the top ten percent) in order to be eligible for consideration for entrance. You will also need to take the GED test to show us that your education has reached high school level or beyond. Once you have completed this testing, you will need to come to Ithaca for a personal interview. Our final decision will be based on your performance in all of these areas.

As Dean of Admissions to the college, I must say that your letter was very interesting, and we were all quite impressed. If your skills can be shown to be as high as your desire, then your application may have a positive outcome, after all. Please contact me personally if you have any questions and let me know as soon as possible if the conditions we have stipulated can be met by January. In the meantime, I want to wish you all the best in the pursuit of your dream.

Dr. Eloise Tillinghast
Dean of Admissions
Cornell School of Veterinary Medicine

Mrs. Shoemaker leaned over the counter. "Well? What?"

Rachel folded the letter and put it back into the envelope. Then she burst into tears. Mrs. Shoemaker came around the counter and took Rachel in her arms.

"Did they say no, Rachel?"

Rachel took a breath. "No, Ma'am. They…they said they will consider me if I can meet a few more requirements. If I do, they want me to come for an interview."

"So, that's good, right?"

"Yes and no, Mrs. Shoemaker. It's wonderful, but there's a big problem."

Mrs. Shoemaker looked at her, and Rachel saw the question in her eyes.

"I have to convince my folks to let me take the tests, and if I pass, to let me travel to Ithaca for the interview. That's not going to happen. I don't know why I had my hopes up. I wish Cornell would have just rejected me."

Mrs. Shoemaker pulled a Kleenex out of a box on top of the counter and handed it to Rachel. Rachel dabbed her eyes and blew her nose. The postmistress put her arm around Rachel once more. "Is it your father, Rachel?"

"Yes, Ma'am. It's just…well, it's just that he's so strict. We have fought over me just taking some classes at the community college, so this will put him right over the edge."

"What about your mom?"

"I think she supports me in this, but she loves my papa, too, and doesn't want to upset him. He's had some real physical and emotional problems since he came home and…oh, I shouldn't be telling you all this. It's really kind of personal."

Mrs. Shoemaker sighed. "It's okay, honey. You're a sweet girl, and from what I hear, you would make a fine vet. I won't say anything about your problem to anyone, but I will pray about it."

Rachel looked at the woman in surprise. "Are you a Christian, Mrs. Shoemaker?"

The postmistress chucked Rachel under the chin and smiled. "The Amish aren't the only ones around here that love God, sweetie."

Rachel blushed and looked down. "I…I'm sorry, I didn't mean it like that."

Mrs. Shoemaker gave Rachel a hug. "It's a big world, Rachel, and there are all kinds of people in it. Now, you should head on home. You have some things to work out, and I don't envy you. But, like I said, I'll be praying."

Rachel hugged Mrs. Shoemaker back and smiled through her tears. She walked to the door and then turned. "Thank you, Mrs. Shoemaker; you are very kind."

Rachel walked to the post office door. Then she turned. "If you wouldn't mind, Mrs. Shoemaker, I could use some…"

Mrs. Shoemaker waved her hand. "I know, honey. I've already been praying for you, too."

Rachel peeked around the doorframe into the front room. The weather had cooled, portending rain. A fire popped and crackled in the fireplace, and her *daed* was sitting in front of it, staring into the flames. Jenny sat in her rocking chair, sewing a torn pair of Jonathan's pants. From time to time, Jenny looked up at Jonathan and smiled, but he seemed lost in his thoughts. Rachel ducked back behind the doorframe and stood with her heart racing, the letter from Cornell clutched in her hand.

I've got to say something, but I'm so afraid. Oh, Gott, *why is everything so hard? Vielleicht sind Sie nicht ebenso freundlich, wie Mama sagt. Perhaps you are not as good as mama says.*

Rachel turned to go back down the hall to her room. The thought that maybe *Gott* wasn't as kind as her mama said confused her. Then she felt a soft hand on her shoulder. Her heart leaped into her throat, and she turned to see her mama.

"Rachel, what is it?"

Jenny had come quietly out into the hall and was standing beside her. Rachel stared at her, and then took a deep breath.

"I...I have something...I mean...I..."

"What is it, Rachel? Are you in some sort of trouble?"

"No, Mama, it's just that I..."

Rachel's hands were trembling. Jenny took hold of them and looked deep into Rachel's eyes. She nodded toward the back and together they went down the hall into Rachel's room and closed the door.

"What is it, Rachel?" Jenny asked softly.

Rachel looked at her mama and then handed her the letter from Cornell. Jenny looked at the address on the outside and then back up at Rachel. "What is this, *dochter?*"

"It's...it's... Oh, just read it, Mama."

Rachel sat down on the edge of her bed and put her face in her hands. Jenny opened the envelope, took out the letter, and read. When she finished, she looked down at Rachel and sighed. Rachel looked up at her mama's face, hoping for a reaction that she could read, but Jenny's face remained stoic. Then Jenny came and sat down on the edge of the bed next to her. She put her arm around Rachel's shoulders and drew her close.

"What, Mama?"

Jenny drew a breath and squeezed Rachel. She held her that way for a long time. Finally, she spoke. "This is a hard thing, Rachel. My heart is torn for you. On the one hand, I am so proud of you and what you have become. You are so smart, *Sie machen mich so stolz*, you make me so proud of you. You have your papa's mind and my determination. But I am afraid that you have chosen a path that can only bring sorrow and strife to our family. Your papa, he…"

"He will say no, that's what I know," Rachel said.

"Perhaps if you let me speak to him first. You two are not good with words and you make each other so angry."

Jenny sighed and then continued. "It was not always so. Sometimes, I think it would have been better…"

But the thought remained unspoken. Jenny folded the letter and put it back in the envelope. "Also, there is more to this than just taking the tests and going to the interview, Rachel, even if we can get your papa's permission. There is your faith and your commitment to the Plain Way. It would not be easy to convince the elders that this is a good thing. They believe that higher education can promote ideas that are counter to Christian values, and rightly so. But they also believe that education is useful when it can be shown that it is for the good of the Amish community. The elders could decide that a good Amish vet would be of great value to all of us. So this is a matter that could be decided either way."

Jenny stood up and handed Rachel the letter. "Keep this and let me pray the matter through. I will see what *du leiber Gott* has to say. If I do not have a check in my spirit, I will speak to your papa. But I cannot promise anything. Will you abide by Jonathan's wishes in this matter if he says no?"

Rachel's insides twisted. "If Papa will think it through and give it a sincere consideration, and if he can give me a good reason why I should not do this, I will obey him. If he just says no without any consideration, then I do not know what I will do."

Jenny sighed and reached down to stroke Rachel's face. "That is an honest answer, Rachel. *Wollen wir dem Herrn in dieser Sache vertrauen.* We don't want to trust ourselves so let's trust *Gott.*"

Jenny turned and left the room. Rachel remained sitting on the edge of her bed, staring down at the letter. Her head whirled with the possibilities it represented. If she could get accepted into Cornell, it would mean that her dream of being a vet would be on its way to fulfillment. She knew she could handle the classes—that wasn't the problem. Handling her father was the greatest obstacle. Rachel's heart sank.

He will never, ever give his permission!

Rachel stood up and began to get ready for bed. After she took down her long, auburn hair, she went into the bathroom and washed her face and brushed her teeth. She came back to her room, got into her nightshirt, and slipped under the covers. But for Rachel, sleep did not come easily. Her mama's question kept running through her mind...

Will you abide by your father's wishes in this matter if he says no?
Will you abide by your father's wishes in this matter if he says no?

Rachel tossed and turned trying to get comfortable. She twisted from one side to the other, but her mind kept racing. She knew what Jonathan's answer would be, even though her mama had promised to intervene.

It's no use. No matter what Mama says, Papa will never give in. He is too stubborn and besides, he is verrückt! *He's crazy! I wish he had never come back.*

A profound sense of guilt swept over Rachel as she thought about her father. She lay in the darkness and tried to remember the good days when she and Jonathan had been so close. Finally, her eyes closed and she drifted off.

But Rachel did not find peace, even in sleep. Strange images and thoughts began to play in her mind. Her papa, floating in the ocean, clinging to a piece of wreckage; her grandparents, Reuben and Jerusha Springer, lying dead in the front room of the little house in Apple Creek, Ohio; Jonathan returning home after so many years, not dressed as an Amish man but an *Englischer.*

Images of death and loss and deep feelings of fear and sorrow swept back and forth through her mind like the restless sea bringing flotsam and jetsam to the shore, only to drag it away again to be lost forever. Rachel groaned in her sleep. Her mouth opened, but she couldn't speak. Finally, with a great effort of will, she broke free from the grip of the dream and jerked awake. She lay in her bed and felt the sweat on her arms and back.

Then she knew the answer.

There was no life for her in Paradise. If she wanted to fulfill her dreams. she would have to leave, to go far away and never look back. The tears began to fall, and then the quiet sobs shook her shoulders. The truth that she could not—would not—entertain, pressed to the front of her consciousness.

No, I mustn't think that, I must not...

And then the words forced themselves from her lips, and she spoke quietly into the darkness.

"I cannot stay Amish."

Chapter Nine

Phone Calls

Michel Duvigney tapped his fingers nervously on the top of his mahogany desk. Then he got up and went to the antique carved oak Louis XIV Lion Head wine bar against the back wall and got out the bottle of Le Voyage de Delamain Cognac. He held the bottle up to the light and admired the beautiful color of the amber liquid inside. Then he reached for a small, hand-warming crystal glass and poured himself a drink. He set the bottle down and then picked it back up and added some more cognac to the glass.

Then he sighed. The cognac cost $8,000 a bottle and after today, he probably would not be able to afford to buy it anymore.

The phone rang, a quiet clicking sound instead of a bell, and Duvigney returned to the desk, warming the cognac in his hands as he walked. He swirled the drink in the glass, put his nose down to savor the wonderful aroma, and then took a sip. The phone kept ringing. Finally, he put down the glass and picked up the receiver. "Well?"

The indistinct voice on the other end spoke a few words.

"All of it?"

Again, some words.

Duvigney put the phone back in its cradle. He sat at the desk and then put his face in his hands. Ten minutes passed and then Michel Duvigney raised his head and sighed. He picked up the glass and finished the cognac. Then he punched the discreet intercom button on the silver inlaid panel at the side of his desktop.

"Yes, Mr. Duvigney?"

"Get me Randall."

Randall sat at a table looking out on the East River in Manhattan. The Brooklyn Bridge soared over his head and boats plied the calm waters. A garbage scow chugged by, followed by squadrons of seagulls. From his table he had a sweeping view of the New York skyline and off in the distance, the Statue of Liberty. This was Randall's favorite restaurant and he came often. A waiter approached the table. "There's a call for you, Mr. Randall. We'll transfer it to the phone booth for you."

Randall didn't like being disturbed, but very few of his clients would call him at this place, so he knew it was important.

"Fine, Peter. Tell the chef to hold off on the steak until I get back."

Randall pushed back from the table and walked to the private phone booth in the hallway. He went in, slid the dark, mahogany wood door shut behind him, and picked up the phone.

"Randall speaking."

"Mr. Randall, Mr. M would like to speak to you."

"Fine, put him on."

Randall smiled. Mr. M thought he had hidden his identity, but Randall knew that his name was Michel Duvigney and that he was in the highest rank of the elite financiers of New York City

Really, these people must think I'm a muscle-bound cretin.

M came on the line. The man's sibilant voice always reminded Randall of a king cobra. He'd seen plenty of those in Vietnam and he didn't like the sound. When you heard a king cobra hiss, you knew something bad was about to happen.

"Randall?"

"This is Randall."

"Good. I need to speak to you right away. Privately, not on the phone."

"Name the place, M."

"You're in Brooklyn. How fast can you get downtown?"

"Forty-five minutes with traffic."

"Great. Meet me at 145 Avenue of the Americas. Park your car down the block. It's a storefront. Just walk in and tell the guard you're here to see me. He'll show you where to go.

"Fine, I'll see you in forty-five minutes."

Randall left the booth and headed toward the door. The waiter approached him.

"Are you leaving, Mr. Randall?"

"Yes, Peter. Something has come up."

Randall pulled one of the ubiquitous one hundred dollar bills from his pocket and handed it to the young man. "Sorry for the inconvenience, Peter. This should soothe the chef."

"Thank you, sir. Will we be seeing you soon?"

Peter picked up a phone by the front desk and spoke into it.

"Mr. Randall's car, please."

Randall smiled and patted Peter on the shoulder. "If my business doesn't take too long, I may come back and try for the steak again. Not a better one in the city."

Randall walked out to the curb. In a few minutes, his BMW pulled up, and a kid in a white jacket got out and handed him the keys. Randall tipped him twenty dollars and got in the car, leaving the young man with a huge smile on his face. Then he drove onto the bridge approach and headed for Manhattan.

It was midafternoon in Paradise, Pennsylvania. The old man sat on his porch and gazed off into the distance. He wasn't really looking at the green fields and the rolling hills, though. His thoughts wandered back to another time and place, in a steaming jungle with the screams of men dying all around him. He was lying flat on his back in a ditch and his hip felt like molten-hot steel stakes had been driven through it. A tall Marine with black hair stood over him, covered in blood, clutching a broken rifle in his hands. Japanese soldiers pressed up the trench, and the man was singlehandedly beating them back. The man screamed like a banshee. Wounded and dying men lay all around, and the black-haired man was the only one standing. The Japanese were blocked by the narrowness of the trench and could only come at the Marine a few at a time.

"Reuben…"

The old man spoke the name softly and it slipped away on the breeze.

His thoughts fast-forwarded to another day. He was in a hospital waiting room and the same man was being attacked again—this time by a lovely woman in Amish clothing. She was striking the tall man's chest over and over and calling him a fool. The tall man just stood there with horrible suffering, distorting his handsome face.

A tear came to the old man's eyes and he groaned softly. This time the golden retriever at his feet stirred, whined, and looked up. The old man glanced down at the dog. The retriever whined again and stood up, wagging his tail. He put his muzzle under the old man's hand and pushed his head against him.

"It's okay, pal. I'm all right."

The old man stroked the dog's head and scratched the long ears. The dog responded by pushing his head harder against the man's hand. The old man reached over to the little table next to his chair. A pack of camels and some matches lay there. He took one, lit it, and took a deep drag. He looked down at the dog.

"Funny how those memories come back, isn't it boy?"

The dog whined and wagged his tail, then lay back down on the rug at the old man's feet. The man took another deep and satisfying drag.

"You know, they say these things'll kill you, but they can't prove it by me. Must be good genes or somethin'."

The dog's tail thumped once on the porch as if to answer in the affirmative. The old man went back to his reverie. Another picture came into his mind. He was plowing through deep snow in a covered tractor, and a tall man was seated next to him. Outside the cab, the wind howled with a fiendish roar. Up ahead through the blinding sheets of white snow, the two men could see a small cabin. It looked abandoned. Then they were inside and the lovely woman was there again, but this time she had a little girl and the tall man was wrapping her in a blanket. Another fast-forward and the old man was standing in a nightclub with his arms around two people who were weeping and clinging to each other.

He spoke to the dog. "It's been a long, strange journey, Rufus."

Another thump of the tail as the dog stretched out in the warm sun. The old man smiled and looked around. This time instead of memories, he saw the beautiful fields stretching out below his house and the trees over by the small stream. The sweet melody of a songbird lifted on the air. Down the hill from his porch stood a blue farmhouse surrounded by a white picket fence. As the old man watched, a man came out the front door. He was tall with longish, black hair under a straw hat. He wore a blue shirt tucked into denim pants and a medium-length beard obscured his face.

"No mustache, though," said the old man.

The dog looked up again. The man in the hat looked up the hill, saw the old man, and waved. The words floated up to him on the breeze. "Hey, Bobby, how goes it today?"

The old man smiled and waved back. "I'm alive and well and still takin' nourishment, Jonathan."

"Good to hear, Bobby, good to hear."

Then two women came out on the front porch of the blue house. One was tall, with auburn hair and a lovely, but unsmiling face. The older woman was shorter and had golden red hair, now touched with white. A few unruly curls spilled out from underneath the white prayer *kappe*. She had her arm around the younger woman. They both looked up and waved.

Rachel and Jenny—my beautiful girls. Rachel sure doesn't look happy. It's been hard since Jonathan has been home—real hard.

Then a discordant sound broke the stillness. It was Bobby's phone ringing from the kitchen wall. It was persistent. Bobby got up slowly and went into the house. The screen door banged shut behind him as he made his way to the kitchen. Bobby picked up the phone.

"Halverson here."

"Sheriff?"

The deep gravely voice was very familiar.

"Bull, is that you?"

"Yeah, Bobby, it's me."

"Well, well. I haven't heard from you in a long time. How are you doing? What's up in Wooster that would engender a call to Paradise?"

"Well, I am sorry to bother you, but something happened that I found a bit odd, and I felt like I needed to touch bases."

"What's up, Bull?"

"A guy came by my house today. Very clean-cut, military style, nice clothes. Said he was a former Marine and Special Forces guy and he looked it. He drove a BMW with New York plates and smoked-glass windows. He was looking for you."

"Why was he looking for me?"

"Well, actually he was looking for Jenny. At least that's what I deduced. He was looking for the heirs of Robert St. Clair, and he said you knew about that. I didn't tell him anything, especially when he told me who he was working for."

"And who was he working for, Bull?"

"Augusta St. Clair."

There was a moment's silence as Bobby pondered this bit of information.

"Wasn't Robert St. Clair Jenny's father? And didn't you tell me that this St. Clair woman had a big part in Jenny's mom ending up strung out and dead?"

Bobby gave a low whistle. "Augusta St. Clair. That is very interesting. I wonder how she got my name. And you're right,

Bull. Robert St. Clair was Jenny's father and the son of one of the richest families on the planet. Augusta St. Clair is not someone that Jenny feels particularly good about."

Bobby paused and then he spoke back into the phone. "So, did this guy leave a card?"

"Yeah, I got it right here. Got a pencil?"

Bobby dug through the pile of stuff on the little stand under the wall phone. He found a pencil stub and a scrap of paper. "Okay, go ahead."

"Gordon L. Randall. 2200 Park Avenue, New York. 718-533-5443."

Bobby held the phone between his chin and his shoulder and scribbled down the information. "Okay, Bull, got it."

There was a pause, and then Bull spoke. "What do you think this is about, Bobby?"

"I'm not sure, Bull, but I don't think it's a good thing. From what we found out about Augusta St. Clair when we were looking for Jenny's folks, she didn't sound like a very benevolent person. I'll need to talk to Jenny about this. So, how are you doing, Bull?"

"Oh, I'm good, Bobby. I don't like retirement much, but I got my place in Wooster, and I got Timothy, my cat. I eat three squares a day and get my social security and my pension check every month. I get by. What about you?"

"I like it here in Pennsylvania. I got Jenny and Rachel and Jonathan, when he's having a good day."

"A good day?"

"Yeah, Bull. Jonathan's had a hard time since we found him. He's got a lot of physical problems and emotional ones, too. He's been home five years but he and Rachel don't get along, which is sad, because I know they love each other. But Jonathan's real erratic and Rachel is a very organized girl. So it's like east is east and west is west and never the twain shall meet most days."

"Ever think you'll get back to Wooster and Apple Creek, Bobby?"

"Yeah, I'd like to come see the old place, although it doesn't draw me as much as when my folks were alive. I would like to see you and some of the guys."

"Well, let me know when you're coming. We'll kill the fatted calf."

"Okay, Bull. I'll stay in touch."

Bobby hung up the phone. He looked at the piece of paper and shook his head. Then he went back outside and looked down the hill. Jenny was working in the vegetable garden and Jonathan and Rachel were nowhere to be seen. The dog got up and stood beside Bobby. Bobby reached down and stroked the dog's head and then sighed.

"Augusta St. Clair, Rufus. Now what in the world would she want with Jenny?"

He shook his head. Something was up. Bobby could smell it and it didn't smell good.

Chapter Ten

The Trail

Bobby Halverson studied the note in his hand as he walked along the path leading from his house to the Hershbergers'.

Augusta St. Clair. Now there's a name out of the past.

He put the scrap of paper in his pocket as he walked around the side of the blue house to the garden. Jenny was kneeling down, digging up a bed. She had a basket with some tools and paper bags in it. She reached up and wiped the sweat off her brow with the back of her hand as she dug. She looked up and saw Bobby standing there. She smiled at him but kept after her digging. "Morning, Bobby. What brings you down the hill?"

Bobby laughed. "I'm not so old I can't get up and walk a few hundred feet, Jenny."

"Give me a minute while I finish this, then we'll go inside and I'll pour you a cup of coffee. Get your motor turned over."

She smiled up at him. He stood watching as she finished working the soil. At forty-three, Jenny Hershberger was almost as lovely as she had been when she was a girl back in Apple Creek, Ohio. Time had been kind to her. The red-gold hair still shone in the sun, and except for a few wrinkles around the eyes, the perfect face was nearly unlined. The only change that Bobby noticed beside the few strands of white in her hair was the deep sadness he sometimes saw behind Jenny's violet eyes. But given the events of the last few years and the circumstances surrounding the death of her parents, that was understandable. Finally, she turned over the last few clumps of soil. She got up, wiped her hands on her apron, and beckoned him to follow her.

"Where are the rest of the Hershbergers today?"

Jenny pointed out at the potato field behind the barn. Way out on the back of the property, he could see Jonathan at work with a team of horses and a cultivator.

"Jonathan is weeding the potato rows and Rachel...Rachel left. I think she's at Daniel King's place. She said something about a new foal that needed looking after."

"Are Rachel and Jonathan doing better these days?"

Jenny looked at Bobby as if measuring him and then sighed. "Does that question have anything to do with why you dropped by?"

Bobby smiled. *Not much gets past Jenny.* "Kind of...but mostly just asking."

Jenny held the screen door open and they went into the kitchen. She stopped at the cupboard and fetched down two mugs. Bobby pulled up a chair at the kitchen table while Jenny poured the coffee and added just the right amount of cream. Then she sat across from Bobby and pushed the mug toward him. Bobby put his hands around it, feeling the warmth in his aching fingers. Then he looked up at Jenny. "I got a call from Bull yesterday."

"Bull Halkovich?"

"Yep, Bull Halkovich."

"And...?"

Bobby loved that about Jenny—no shillyshally, always cut to the chase. "Someone came to his house asking questions about your mother."

"About Jerusha?"

"No, Jenny. They were looking for Rachel St. Clair or her daughter."

Jenny's eyes opened in surprise. "Who even knows about Mama Rachel?"

"Augusta St. Clair."

Shock passed over Jenny's face. She looked down at the table for a minute and then up at Bobby. The shock had turned to puzzlement. "Why in the world would Augusta St. Clair be looking for me? From what Mama Rachel wrote about her in her journal, I know that Augusta St. Clair is not a nice person. She was the main reason for my biological mother's death. She threw her out on the streets of New York and left her homeless there. And now she's looking for me? This can't be good."

Bobby nodded in agreement. "You're right about that. And after hearing Bull's description of the messenger, I don't have a good feeling either."

"Why, Bobby?"

"Well, the man who came to Bull's place sounds like a professional. A marine, Special Forces, probably owns his own private investigation company or maybe provides security for the St. Clairs. In other words, he's a man to be reckoned with. He gave Bull just enough information. When he left there, he knew Bull would call me."

Jenny took a sip of her coffee. "Why can't we just ignore it? He doesn't know where you live."

"That's what I'm saying, Jenny. If he's the pro I think he is, he'll find me. The St. Clairs have plenty of money, so sooner or later, one of us will be getting a knock on the door."

"What should I do?"

"Let me handle it, Jenny. I'll call the guy and see what he wants. If Augusta knows about me, it's probably because she found Sammy Bender and 'interviewed' him. So she's probably been out to Patterson to see Magdalena Bender. If she follows the same trail we did, eventually she will find out about your grandfather and this farm. It won't take them long to dig around and find out that Rachel Borntraeger St. Clair's daughter is now Jenny Hershberger and that you're living back here."

"Why do you think she's looking for us?"

Bobby looked in his cup. The cream had made swirling patterns, dark brown like Guadalcanal mud...

"Bobby?"

"Oh, sorry. It probably has to do with money. Probably something that your grandfather Robert had access to but she doesn't. That's just my guess, but people like Augusta St. Clair operate that way. I've seen it before. Unless something has happened to stir up the hornet's nest, I'm sure she would never look for you."

"So, what does that mean for us?"

"It means that you need to let me do the talking and don't volunteer anything. Don't speak to their agent unless I'm in the room. And whatever you do, don't sign anything. She's after something, most likely money, and remembering what she did to your mama, she'll probably do a lot to get it."

Gordon Randall pulled his black BMW into a parking garage down the street from the address Duvigney had given him. He drove clear to the top level and parked the car overlooking the street below. He checked the rooftops across the street. It was a habit that had been trained into him during his Special Forces' days, but today he was particularly keyed to his surroundings.

Michel Duvigney or "Mr. M," as he preferred to be called, had never called him for a face-to-face meeting, and Randall didn't feel good about it. All of Randall's clients were either very wealthy or very crooked, most of them both. He had developed his clientele with the utmost care. He only took on those with impeccable financial references. Duvigney was one of those, as was Augusta St. Clair. Of the two, Duvigney was the one he could not read. Augusta St. Clair was an obvious gold-digging female who had clawed her way into a very wealthy family. Her agenda was patently obvious—get money and power at any cost. Duvigney, on the other hand, was like mist in a graveyard. Randall couldn't put his finger on what was bothering him, so he just raised his antennae and stayed alert.

Randall went down the stairwell to the ground floor and exited the garage. The address was not on the main street, but up where Avenue of Americas started before it merged with Sixth

Avenue. There was a little park on the right and a smattering of foot traffic.

He saw the address. The sign above the double glass door read "Trans-European Trading Company." He pushed through the doors and walked in. There was a foyer with a large reception counter. A couple of worn couches were pushed against the wall, and there was a table with magazines on it. The titles were in Cyrillic script. Behind the counter lounged a seedy-looking character with a mustache and a green fedora. He looked up as he stubbed out a cigarette.

"Vat you vant?"

Randall noted that the man's accent was either Russian or Yugoslavian. "I'm here to see Mr. M."

The man stared at Randall and then got up and walked toward a hallway to the right of the foyer, motioning Randall to follow him. They walked down to a green metal door. The door was very new and very strong. Randall noticed the red flash of a tiny camera that was mounted above the door and had an unobstructed view of anyone who entered the hallway. His guide pressed a keypad by the door. There was a click and the door swung open.

"Mr. M is vaiting for you in da room at ze end of za hall."

He waited until Randall stepped through the door and then closed it. Randall turned and noticed that there was no handle on his side. He continued down the hall until he came to a wall. He stood there wondering what was next, and then the wall opened to reveal an elevator. Randall stepped in and the doors closed behind him. He felt motion but there were no floor markers or buttons, so he wasn't sure just how far he traveled. The car stopped, the door opened, and he stepped into another short hallway with a door at the end. He walked up to the door and knocked. A quiet buzzer sounded and there was another click as the lock moved. There was a handle on this door, and he pulled it open and stepped into a small room.

A thin, old man with white hair and sharp features sat behind a desk. The room was on the upper floors of the building and the window commanded a view of most of uptown

Manhattan. The old man motioned to a chair across the desk from where he was sitting. Randall sat.

"So, Gordon, we meet at last."

Randall recognized the sibilant voice, and even face-to-face, it still put his teeth on edge. He also knew the protocol. "Mr... ah...M, I presume?"

Duvigney smiled. "Yes."

Randall leaned forward. "Why the secrecy and why the rush...?"

Duvigney fidgeted for a moment and Randall sensed that the old man was under a great deal of pressure.

"Gordon, some things have occurred that have accelerated events concerning the St. Clair woman and her pursuit of the inheritance. I can't tell you more than that except to say that I felt it was very important that we meet face-to-face so that I could impress you with the absolute necessity of finding the heir to the St. Clair fortune."

"Well, Mr. M, I think I understand the importance you place on this matter, but I can also tell you that you will have to raise the stakes. Suddenly the money you're offering doesn't seem like it's quite enough."

The old man looked at Randall and then began to sputter. He stood up and shook his finger at Randall. "Why you..."

"Sit down, Michel!"

Randall's voice was cold and quiet, but Michel Duvigney sat down like he had been shoved.

"That is your name, isn't it?"

Duvigney looked like a fish on land as his mouth gaped open and then shut. Randall took the black notebook out of his pocket.

"Michael Duvigney, President of the Board of Trustees of Rosslyn Foundation, the group that manages the fortunes of the American branch of the St. Clair family."

Randall flipped over a couple of pages.

"The St. Clair family's lineage can be traced back to the Normandy area of France and earlier to the Scandinavian Viking days when they were known as the Sinclairs. The family's history is closely intertwined with the crowns of France, England, and

Scotland, and ancestors have been involved in many of the pivotal events in western civilization. Throughout the history of the last one thousand years, there are places and events where Sinclairs or St. Clairs have left an indelible mark in the history books. For that same one thousand years the Duvigneys have always played a role in this family as counselors, administrators and, might I add, assassins."

Randall closed the pad and put it back in his breast pocket. Duvigney sat back in his chair, looking like someone had struck him. Randall smiled. "Really, Michel, you don't think I would take on the mysterious 'Mr. M' without thoroughly checking you out. Now, let's get down to business. There's something amiss in the St. Clair kingdom or we wouldn't be meeting face-to-face, am I right?"

"How did you find out about me?"

"Your money bought you the best in the business. I am not a man who likes surprises, and I am the very best at what I do. When I work for someone, I do my homework. I have many friends in very well-placed positions. My sources are deep and impeccable. What I know about you is that you are the trustee for the American branch of the St. Clair Enterprises. I also know that the actual bulk of their fortune is almost limitless, but you personally are merely a middleman. So your, shall we say, need to bring this matter to a close probably involves something that will affect your position and perhaps your life. My guess is that you have made some unwise and unauthorized investments and have taken some big hits."

Duvigney stared at Randall and then slumped down in his chair. "What do you propose, Mr. Randall?"

Randall smiled, but the expression on his face was far from merry. "Ah, I seem to have struck the nail on the head. I'm going to lay out a plan and you just nod in agreement as I speak. First of all, you have lost a great deal of money that does not belong to you."

Duvigney nodded.

"Second, if these losses are discovered, you will lose your position which has afforded you a luxurious lifestyle and your masters might even consider you expendable."

Duvigney nodded.

"Third, the only way this malfeasance can be discovered is if Augusta St. Clair puts in a legitimate claim for the inheritance."

Duvigney nodded.

Randall stood up.

"Where are you going?"

"I am very close to locating Robert St. Clair's daughter. At that point, I will put a plan in motion that will bring all of the principals together so that we can deal with them in a judicious manner, so that the threat to you can be eliminated."

"You mean…"

Randall smiled again. "You needn't bother yourself with what I mean, Michel. All you need to do is get your checkbook ready. Now, please buzz the door so I can leave."

Randall turned to go. "And one more thing, Michel. Don't think about taking any action against me. I am your only hope."

The door clicked open and Randall was gone.

Chapter Eleven

The Connection

Bobby Halverson stood at the gate, watching the new black BMW pull up the lane to the Hershberger farm. He waved and the driver, who had started to pull in at the farmhouse, continued on up the hill and pulled in behind Bobby's old Ford truck. Bobby watched as the driver climbed out. He was exactly as Bull had described: clean-cut, well dressed, and very professional looking. The way his coat fit tightly around his shoulders told Bobby that the man was in good shape and, given what Bobby knew about him, would probably be a deadly opponent in a fight. He carried a leather briefcase. Bobby noticed there was no telltale bulge under his coat.

Carries himself like a pro and he considers us harmless enough to leave his gun in the car.

Bobby opened the gate and motioned the man inside. He walked up to Bobby and stopped. Bobby could tell he was getting the once-over, and for a moment, he regretted that the sessions at the gym had somehow gotten onto his drop-off list.

"Sheriff Halverson?"

Bobby chuckled. The only one who still called him that was Bull. "Ex-sheriff. I haven't been on active duty for almost ten years. Call me Bobby."

The two men shook hands and Bobby could feel strength in Gordon Randall's grip. Randall looked at Bobby in surprise at the return strength he felt from Bobby.

"Well...Bobby. Thanks for seeing me. Is Mrs. Hershberger joining us?"

"Yes, Mr. Randall, she's waiting inside."

The two men walked up the steps and into Bobby's bungalow. Jenny was sitting at the table. Bobby had arranged extra chairs, one beside Jenny and one across from her. He moved ahead of Randall and took the seat next to Jenny as he motioned Randall into the other chair. Randall got right down to business.

"I'm here on behalf of Augusta St. Clair."

"Concerning?" Bobby asked.

"The estate of Robert St. Clair."

"And what does that have to do with Mrs. Hershberger?"

Randall shifted in his seat and looked at Jenny. "You are the daughter of Robert St. Clair—?"

Bobby smiled. "Mr. Randall, you can direct your statements to me."

Randall frowned. "I'm not exactly sure how you got in the middle of this, Bobby, but—"

Bobby interrupted him. "Since her adoptive parents' deaths, I have been Mrs. Hershberger's guardian and advocate. She is here to listen to this conversation, but she is reluctant to make any comments at this time."

Jenny looked at Bobby. "It's all right, Bobby. I just want to say one thing. Mr. Randall, I will hear what you have to say, but I will make no comment on it, nor am I prepared to enter into dialogue with the St. Clair family or their representatives. Please give us the specifics of your request, and we will consider it after you have gone."

Randall frowned again. He obviously did not like to be told how he had to conduct his business. He nodded to Jenny. "Fine, Mrs. Hershberger."

He turned his gaze back to Bobby.

"Mrs. Hershberger is the daughter of Robert St. Clair and Rachel Borntraeger St. Clair. The American St. Clairs are a branch of the St. Clairs of Europe, one of the wealthiest families in the world, and Robert St. Clair was one of the main heirs to that fortune. When he died in a car wreck in 1949, he left Rachel St. Clair a widow and their small child, Jennifer Constance St. Clair—Mrs. Hershberger—without a father. In a normal course of probate, Robert's fortune should have passed to his wife. But the St. Clairs set up specific rules of inheritance several hundred years ago that ensure the bulk of the estate will remain in the family's control."

"And just what does that mean?"

"Rachel St. Clair could not have inherited the fortune, but her daughter could have, provided—"

"Provided what, Mr. Randall?"

"Provided she has the Key."

Bobby looked over at Jenny, who was staring at Randall with an expression on her face that Bobby had never seen before. "And just what is the Key?"

Randall reached down, picked up the briefcase, and put it on the table. The latches made a sharp click, click.

Bobby winced.

Like the bolt of my old M1903 being pulled back to load in a shell when I was waiting up on the ridge, just before the fight on Guadalcanal.

"Sheriff?"

Bobby shook his head and refocused. "Sorry. What were you saying about the Key?"

Randall pulled a document from the briefcase and laid it on the table. It was obviously old and it had been covered with a clear plastic shield. The border was a filigree of gold, surrounding the illustration of what appeared to be a knight. Only instead of an armored breastplate, the man was wearing a loose garment that was pulled back over his chest to reveal a red, key-shaped mark right above his left breast.

"This is a picture of Reynaud de Sinclair, Mrs. Hershberger's ancestor. It dates back to around AD 1200. That red mark is the Key. It's the St. Clair birthmark. Normally, it's found on the chest of the oldest son. Don't ask me how, but this has been true since the first St. Clair came to England with William the Conqueror in 1066. The Key has always determined the heir."

"But Jenny is a woman, so how can she be of interest to you?"

Randall smiled, but it was not a happy smile. "I'm getting to that. The daughter or granddaughter of a direct heir who dies can inherit, provided she meets two conditions: first, she must hold the Key and, yes, from time to time this birthmark has occurred in a female child. In fact, there are three known occasions when that has happened. If she does hold the Key, then the estate is put into trust until she meets the second condition."

"And what is that condition, Mr. Randall?" asked Jenny.

Bobby glanced over and started to speak, but saw the determined look on Jenny's face and held his peace.

Randall smiled again, but this time it was a bit more relaxed. "The second condition is that the female inheritor with the Key shall find a suitable male St. Clair and marry him after it is determined she is the true heir. Otherwise, she cannot inherit. This ensures that the fortune stays within the St. Clair family. In the case of discovering an adult heir such as Mrs. Hershberger, the woman has one year to fulfill the condition."

Randall looked at Jenny. Jenny stared back at him. "And if the heiress is married, Mr. Randall?"

"As I said, Mrs. Hershberger, the heiress must find a suitable male St. Clair and marry him within one year, if she wants to inherit."

Bobby broke in. "And if the heiress is a baby when it is found that she has the Key?"

Randall answered, still looking at Jenny. "In that case, the estate would be held in trust until the girl is eighteen, at which time the same condition concerning marriage goes into effect."

Jenny pushed her chair back and got up. "Well, Mr. Randall, it seems you've made a trip for nothing. I do not hold the Key and even if I did, I would not divorce Jonathan for all the money in the world. So you can tell your Augusta St. Clair that she can sleep easy tonight. I'll not be coming after her precious money. And why is all this coming up now?"

Randall twisted in his seat.

Bobby jumped in. "Well, Mr. Randall, can you answer that question please?"

"I'm not really at liberty to discuss Mrs. St. Clair's financial situation."

Bobby took a guess. "So, she's in some trouble, financially, and she's looking for a way to get out."

Randall didn't answer, but Bobby could see that his random shot had struck home.

"Well, if you won't answer that, how about this? Augusta is a St. Clair. Why can't she inherit the estate?"

"Very simple, Bobby. She is a St. Clair by marriage only."

"What about her children?"

"Augusta's husband died in the war. Her one son and his wife were killed in a ski accident in Switzerland over fifteen years ago. Her only living relative is her grandson, Gerald, and he does not hold the Key."

"So, as I guessed, Augusta is in a bind and is casting about for some way to get out. I assume that this Gerald would be a suitable St. Clair heir if a daughter or granddaughter with the Key could be found?"

Randall didn't answer that one either. Instead, he took a different tack.

"I understand that you have a daughter, Mrs. Hershberger."

Jenny's face turned pale.

"My daughter does not concern you, and she has no claim on the St. Clair fortune. As I said, you've made a trip for nothing. Bobby will show you out."

Randall stood and shook Jenny's hand. She turned and left by the kitchen door. The two men shook hands, and then Randall went out the front and headed to the car. When he got there, he stopped and looked around for a minute.

"Nice place you got here, Bobby."

"Yep. Thanks."

"If you have any other information, I'm sure Mrs. St. Clair would be more than happy to make it worth your while to share it."

Bobby nodded but did not answer. Randall got the message.

"Well, thank you for your time."

Randall climbed in the car, started it, drove around the circular drive in front of the house, and headed back down the hill. Bobby watched him go. Then he walked back into the house. To his surprise Jenny was standing in the kitchen. She had come back in after Randall left. She was shaking and pale.

"Jenny, what is it?"

"The Key, Bobby. I lied to Randall. Rachel holds the Key."

Bobby's chin dropped. "What?"

"Yes, Bobby. Rachel has the St. Clair birthmark right above her heart."

Bobby sat down at the table and motioned Jenny to sit. "Does Rachel know about this?"

"She knows she has a birthmark, but I never knew that there was any significance to it, so we have never talked about it."

Bobby tapped the tabletop with his fingers. "Are you going to say anything to her?"

Jenny looked down at the table. "Do you trust these people, Bobby?"

The question was almost a whisper.

"No, Jenny, I do not trust them. From what we know about Augusta St. Clair, she is a cold, scheming woman who won't hesitate to do what she thinks will best protect her interests. And this fellow, Randall, scares me. He's a thug of the worst kind because he's intelligent and highly trained. He's Augusta's tool and the extension of her wishes. I would not trust them with Rachel in any way."

Jenny sat down again and pulled her chair next to Bobby. Bobby put his arm around her.

"That's how I feel, too, Bobby. Rachel must never know."

Rachel trudged home from the King farm. The new colt was doing fine. The joy of working with Daniel's horses had lifted her spirits for a while, but now she had settled back into a gloomy mood. The sun was just going down over the western hills, and the soft scent of lilacs filled the air. Spring had burst upon Paradise with all the colors and sounds of the earth awakening after cold months in the grave of winter, but Rachel did not notice. For her, everything in her life was gray and flat. The offer from Cornell weighed heavy on her heart. She wanted to go so badly, but she knew that she would have to leave her faith do it.

I'm Amish and my papa will never say yes, and even if he did, the elders would never let me go in a million years. Oh, why was I born Amish? I can't stay here!

As she came to the lane leading home, she was surprised to see a black automobile come slowly down to the main road. The man behind the wheel saw Rachel and pulled to a stop. The electric window rolled down and Rachel looked into a pair of steel-gray eyes. For some reason, she shivered. The man smiled at her, but the smile made her feel creepy.

"Are you Rachel?"

Something about the man made Rachel's gut twist.

"Yes…"

The man smiled again. "Don't worry. I'm a friend of the other side of your family."

"The other side?"

"Yes, you did know that your mother was born a St. Clair, right?"

Without knowing why, Rachel was suddenly afraid. She stammered an answer. "I knew that Mama's birth mother was named Rachel, but that's all. She lost her mama when she was four, and then my *grossmutter*, Jerusha, found her in the storm and she went to live with *Grossdaadi* Reuben and *Grossmutter* Jerusha in Apple Creek. I was named after her."

Why am I telling him all this?

The man reached in his pocket and pulled out a card. "My name is Gordon Randall and I work for your great-aunt, Augusta St. Clair. She's trying to find out all she can about her relatives on both sides of her family. She lives in New York."

"Why is she so interested in her Amish relatives after all these years?"

Randall nodded, and though the air was warm, Rachel shivered again.

Randall's eyes were boring into Rachel. "I can tell you've got some of the St. Clair attitude. Augusta is getting old. She has alienated many of her relatives by her, shall we say, rough ways. Now she wants to set things right before she dies."

That's a lie!

Randall leaned out the window and handed Rachel the card. "I'm sure she'd like to meet you. If you're interested, give me a call and I'll arrange it."

Randall rolled up the window, nodded, and drove off. Rachel felt sick. She knew that she had been in the presence of evil. The words he spoke had twisted in the air like snakes. Rachel waited until the car disappeared around the bend and then quickly turned back up the lane. She wrapped her arms around herself to keep from running.

Chapter Twelve

The Secret Revealed

Jenny Hershberger went up the stairs and walked down the hall to her writing room. She opened the door and stood for a moment, looking in. Against the outside wall under the large picture window stood a beautiful birch-wood desk with an old-fashioned Underwood typewriter sitting on it. Jenny walked to the desk and ran her fingers lightly over the smooth surface.

Papa! How I wish I could feel your strong arms around me one more time.

Jenny stood with her hand on the back of the chair, touching the wood. Memories of her days in Apple Creek tried to push their way into her heart, tumbling over each other in a rush, so that for a moment, she was almost overwhelmed. She took a deep breath and turned away.

The walls of the room were lined with shelves, and the shelves were filled with folders, books, and stacks of paper and notebooks. But today they held no interest for her. She was looking for something else. In the corner, stood an old cedar chest. Jenny went over and knelt down in front of it. She closed her eyes and lifted the lid. The precious smell of cedar mixed with lavender rose softly from the box and caressed her senses—her mama's scent. For just a moment it seemed that

Jerusha was in the room with her. She knelt silently for a few moments and then opened her eyes and looked down into the trunk. On the top were several packages bound in brown paper and tied with string.

My books! Lord, will you ever let me publish these?

She lifted out the manuscripts, set them aside, and then dug down into the trunk. There were bits of material, scraps of batting, bolts of cloth, extra material for repairs and small samples of ideas for quilts that her mama had planned to make before she died. At the bottom was the bundle Jenny was looking for. It was large, wrapped in brown paper, and it, too, was tied with a string. Jenny took it out and opened it. There was a large, soft bundle inside, and she opened it and spread it out on the floor in front of her.

The Rose of Sharon, her mama's most beautiful quilt, lay before her. The deep red silk that comprised the magnificent rose centerpiece glowed softly in the afternoon light. The royal-blue silk behind it was set off perfectly by the cream-colored backing. Jenny held the quilt between her hands. She could feel the soft double batting that filled it, the batting that had kept her warm through long, freezing nights when her mama Jerusha was fighting to keep her alive in the heart of the worst storm in Ohio history. As she caressed the quilt softly, tears started in her eyes.

"Mama, oh Mama. I miss you so. I wish that you were here so I could talk to you. You were always so wise, you loved me so. Oh, Mama, I need you now."

Jenny pulled the quilt up around her as she knelt. She remembered the last time she had looked at the quilt. She had been with Jerusha in Apple Creek, after Jonathan had disappeared and they all thought he was dead. Jerusha brought out the quilt to comfort Jenny—to show her how the Lord had told the Springer family's story in the quilt's design. There was the rose that was for Jenna, her sister who had died; and the torn edge and the repaired batting that spoke of the places in Jenny's life that had been restored. Jenny remembered the conversation with her mama, as though Jerusha were there with her...

"The story of your life does not stop with Jonathan's death, my *dochter*," her mama had said. "It goes on until it is your time to go. You do not know which pieces you will discover tomorrow, but they are there, already determined by *die Vorkenntnisse des Gottes*. He has already planned them. Now let me show you one more thing as a reminder."

Jerusha moved the quilt until the rose was under her hand. "Look! Do you see it?"

Jenny looked, but couldn't see what her mama was pointing at. And then she remembered and looked closer. There it was! Sewn into the center of the rose—a small, key-shaped piece of red silk so finely stitched that it was almost invisible.

"*Ja*, Jenny, a key. The Lord had me add it to the quilt so that we would always remember—"

"That He is the key to our lives and without Him we cannot hope to comprehend what is happening to us and why?"

"Yes, Jenny, and if you put your life into His hands, He will guide your path and you will understand everything."

"I had forgotten all about the key."

Jenny looked more closely at it.

"It is the strangest thing Mama. Did you know that Rachel has a key-shaped birthmark right above her heart? She has had it since the day she was born, and it is almost the same color as the rose. That makes me think that I was wrong in what I wrote to Jonathan. Maybe *Gott* is still speaking to us through the quilt. Perhaps the journey is not over after all. In fact, we may be coming to a new beginning. That is a hopeful thought."

Jerusha had smiled at her then, and it warmed Jenny to know her mama was proud of her.

Now Jenny pulled the quilt closer, inhaling the fragrance of her mama. The Key—how had her mama known about the Key? But today the Key did not give her hope, only fear.

Augusta St. Clair sat quietly in the sunroom of her Connecticut mansion. She loved the view that overlooked the formal garden and carried down onto a lower lawn where there was a pool, a guesthouse, and tennis courts. Out beyond that was the sea, green and rolling, the waves like glass. Augusta could hear the cries of the gulls and the surf breaking on the shore. It reminded her of Martha's Vineyard—that summer with Jerod and...Robert...

Then the private phone rang quietly and Augusta was jolted out of her reverie. She looked around, but no one was there to answer it for her, so she got up and walked to the small table by the door where the phone sat.

"What?"

"Good morning, Augusta. I'm sure it's a nice day in Connecticut, no matter how you sound."

"Randall?"

"Yes, ma'am."

"Well?"

"I have good news and bad news. The good news; I located Jenny St. Clair. Her name is Hershberger now and she's married. She's Amish, like her mother."

"What's the bad news?"

"Jenny Hershberger does not, I repeat, does not hold the Key."

Augusta swore softly under her breath.

"Are there any other possibilities?"

"The Hershbergers have a daughter, but Jenny assured me that the daughter has no bearing on this situation. So it looks like Gerald will have to find a bride and produce an heir in order for you to get your hands on the money."

"I'll be dead by then, Randall."

"Well, as they say, Augusta, timing is everything."

The line went dead.

Ten minutes later, the phone in Michel Duvigney's office rang. Duvigney picked it up.

"Yes, what is it?"

"Michel, it's Randall. Just wanted to tell you that you're in luck. I found the daughter of Robert St. Clair and she does not hold the Key. Looks like you won't be subject to an audit for at least twenty-one years—that is if Gerald produces an heir tomorrow. If he doesn't, the audit will be sometime after that. In any case, you can rest easy tonight."

"Good job, Randall. Your check is in the mail."

"I hope you didn't forget to add the bonus we spoke about."

"You'll get your money, Randall. All of it."

"That's wonderful, Michel. We certainly wouldn't want to see the information I have about your inappropriate activities involving the principal of the St. Clair trust get into the hands of the wrong people, like, for instance, the board of trustees."

Duvigney gritted his teeth.

"No, Randall, we wouldn't. Like I said, you'll get your money."

The line went dead. Michel Duvigney got up slowly, walked over to the wine bar and got out the de Delamain Cognac. He poured himself a glass and then went back to the desk. He picked up the phone and pressed a number. When someone answered, he spoke.

"Order me another bottle of the Le Voyage de Delamain Cognac, please."

He set the phone back in its receiver and sat down behind the desk. Aside from Randall's outrageous demands, he felt much better. Lifting the glass in the air in a toast, Duvigney smiled. Things were looking up.

When Rachel came home, she stood in the hallway thinking about the man she had just met—and the woman he represented.

Who is Augusta St. Clair and why is she looking for us?

Rachel heard the soft sound of voices from the front room. It was her mama and papa, talking quietly. Rachel started to walk in when she heard something that made her stop and listen. Her mama was speaking.

"... and he's looking for someone who holds the Key."

Jonathan's low voice answered Jenny. "What is 'the Key,' Jenny?"

"It's the St. Clair birthmark. It's a key-shaped red stain right above the heart. It has been the main way that the trustees of the St. Clair estate have decided who inherits the fortune. My birth father, Robert St. Clair, was the heir to the St. Clair money. He had the St. Clair birthmark, the Key. When he died, all his money was put in trust until a new heir could be determined. Obviously, Augusta must be having trouble laying her hands on the money or she wouldn't be sending out agents. There's something going on and it does not bode well for us, husband."

"And this Key—is it the same one that Rachel has on her chest?"

"It seems so, Jonathan. The man, Randall, showed me a picture of one of the St. Clairs from around AD 1200. He had exactly the same birthmark above his heart."

"And the holder of the Key is the heir to all the St. Clair's money?"

Rachel's heart leaped. She couldn't believe what she was hearing. Her mama went on.

"Yes, Jonathan, but there is a catch."

"What's that, Jenny?"

"Rachel would have to marry a suitable St. Clair male in order to inherit. That would keep the money in the family."

"How does that affect Rachel?"

"Augusta St. Clair has a grandson, Gerald. From what Randall said—actually didn't say—Gerald would be a suitable male St. Clair."

"So, if Rachel married him, she would become wealthy?"

"Yes, Jonathan, very wealthy. And that is why we must not tell her."

As she stood outside, listening to her parents, Rachel felt a great knot forming in her chest. She could not believe that her parents were conspiring to deceive her. This was her life they were deciding. She was about to open her mouth and say something, but in that moment she felt the card in her hand. She turned and, being very quiet, walked back down the hallway and held it up in the light.

Gordon Randall
12 Plaza Way,
New York, NY 213-342-1200

Rachel felt something else rise up in her. It was a mixture of hope and fear. This was her way out! She was the heiress to a vast fortune. She could come forward and claim it, and then she could do anything she wanted with her life. No more Papa yelling at her, no more elders of the church telling her what she could or couldn't do. She could pay her own way through school and set up her veterinary practice wherever she wanted. It was like a miracle.

And yet, there had been something about the man's eyes that troubled Rachel. She sensed that he was very wicked. But still... As the prospects began to spin in her mind, as the reality of who she was and what she could have, merely by revealing herself, came into focus, something in Rachel's heart hardened.

In that moment, she made a fateful choice. She would leave here; she would leave this Amish life with all its rules and regulations, the hateful *Ordnung* that bound her with fetters of steel. She would escape from her papa's insanity, his moods and rages. This was her way out. As she stood there in the hallway, a great battle began to rage in Rachel's soul. She thought of her mama and her home, all the things that she loved...and... Daniel.

Daniel? He's just a friend. I could never marry Daniel.

And yet there was something, like a light trying to force its way into a very dark place.

Daniel! He loves me. He loves me with all his heart. Daniel...

For just another moment she hesitated. And then Rachel shut the door of her heart and walked down the hall to her room, clutching Gordon Randall's business card.

Chapter Thirteen

Who Am I?

Rachel sat on her bed for a long time staring at the wall, thinking. The light outside began to fade, and slowly the room darkened. But still, Rachel sat. She had just made a pivotal decision for her life, and yet, strangely, she felt drained and empty. She had expected to feel release and joy. Instead, her heart was heavy. She had turned a bend in the road of her life, and, right or wrong, she knew she must go on. She heard her mama calling her to dinner, but she did not answer. The gathering dusk shadowed the room and still she sat, thinking ...staring.

After a while, there was a soft knock on the door.

"Rachel, are you coming to dinner?"

"I...I'm not hungry, Mama. I don't feel well, and I think I will just go to bed."

"Are you sure, my darling?"

Rachel started to snap a sharp reply, but she bit her tongue. It wasn't her mama who made her crazy. After a moment, Jenny walked away from the door. Rachel slipped out of her clothes and climbed into her bed. She lay there for a while, feeling the softness of the sheets and the warmth of her quilt.

My bed... When I'm rich, I'll have a hundred beds to go in the big house I will buy.

And then a thought came across her mind.

The love of money is the root of all evil!

Rachel's eyes popped open.

I didn't think that. Who...?

And again, like a still small voice...

For the love of money is the root of all evil: which while some coveted after, they have erred from the faith, and pierced themselves through with many sorrows.

Rachel sat up. The room was dark and still. She waited, holding her breath. Someone lingered in the room—at least it seemed like it. She had heard a voice. She spoke into the darkness.

"Who's there?"

No servant can serve two masters: for either he will hate the one, and love the other; or else he will hold to the one, and despise the other. Ye cannot serve God and mammon.

A chill went down Rachel's back and she pulled the covers up over her head.

I don't want to listen. I've made up my mind. That's all there is to it, so don't try to convict me anymore. I don't need You.

The silence pressed down on her. Rachel's heart sank. She spoke into the darkness.

"Wait, I didn't mean that. I...I just want to live my own life. Can't You understand?"

But no answer came, only the mournful cooing of a dove in the oak tree outside her window.

When Rachel awoke, dawn's light was creeping through the window. A soft breeze swept in through the partly opened window, heralding another perfect morning in Paradise. The lace curtains fluttered softly. Rachel lay still for a long moment, enjoying the soft scent of lilacs blooming in the yard outside.

Then she remembered the previous night, and a little stab of fear touched her heart.

I need to talk to Mama.

Rachel got up and dressed. She washed her face and then brushed her hair and twisted it into a bun. She slipped on her *kappe* and then looked in the mirror.

Maybe I won't be wearing these plain clothes much longer.

The thought pressed against her mind like a headache. She went down the stairs and into the kitchen. Her mama was cleaning up some dishes from the table. Jenny brushed some errant curls from her forehead and smiled as Rachel came in the room.

"*Gut mariye, dochter.* Are you feeling better?"

"*Gut mariye.* Yes, Mama. I'm fine."

Rachel stood silently watching her mama, the weight of her presence demanding a response. Finally, Jenny put the rest of the dishes into the sink and turned to her daughter.

"What is it, Rachel?"

"Is Papa here?"

"No, he is already out in the fields. Why?"

"Mama, I need to ask you some questions, but I don't want Papa listening in. He would just interrupt."

"We have some time, Rachel. Sit down. Would you like some coffee?"

Rachel slipped into her chair.

"Yes, that would be nice."

Jenny poured two mugs and then sat down across from Rachel.

"So, what is it you need to know, Rachel?"

Rachel pulled her sleeve and looked down and then blurted out her question.

"Who am I, Mama?"

Rachel could see that she had ambushed her mother with the question.

Jenny paled. "What do you mean?"

"I want to know who I am, Mama. I heard you and Papa talking yesterday. I heard you say that you would never tell me what you were talking about. It made me angry, and then it made me sad that you would hide something from me."

Jenny looked at her daughter for a long time and then sighed.

"You are right, Rachel. It is not right for me to keep secrets from you. You are nearly grown. I am sorry."

"If you are sorry, you will tell me what you were talking about."

Jenny poured a little cream into her coffee and stirred it. Then she took a deep breath and began to speak. "We were talking about your grandfather."

"You mean *Grossdaadi* Reuben?"

"No, Rachel, my birth father, Robert St. Clair."

"You have never told me anything about that side of your family except that you named me after Mama Rachel Borntraeger and that she married an *Englischer.*"

"Yes. Rachel Borntraeger St. Clair. That was her married name. She was born here on this farm, just like you were. She grew up in Paradise and then when she was eighteen she met Robert St. Clair and fell in love. She became pregnant out of wedlock and her father, my *Grossdaadi* Borntraeger, who was a *Bisschop*, put her under the *meidung* because she would not give up Robert."

Rachel knew the answer to her next question, but she asked it anyway. She wanted to hear it from Jenny. "And who are the St. Clairs?"

"The St. Clairs are a very wealthy family, one of the wealthiest in America. They live in New York."

Rachel pushed harder. "And why have I never known anything about them?"

Jenny frowned and then stood up. "Come with me, Rachel, I want to show you something."

She led the way back upstairs and down the hall to her writing room. The two women went in and Jenny shut the door. Jenny went to the shelves and pulled down a manila envelope. Inside it was a small blue book. It was one of those books with empty pages that can be used for a diary or a journal. Rachel had never seen the book before. Jenny opened the book and showed it to Rachel. About half the pages were torn out.

"This was your *Grossmutter* Rachel's journal. It was given to me by Magdalena Bender, the mother of the man who was responsible for Mama Rachel's death."

On the inside cover, someone had written something at the top, but Rachel couldn't read it because it had been crossed out so thoroughly that it was illegible. Under that, written in neat cursive, was a name. The name was Rachel St. Clair. Rachel stared at the little blue book. The handwriting was strong and smooth, evenly spaced and written in cursive letters that slanted slightly to the right. The book was obviously a journal or a diary of some sort, because the entries were dated. Rachel read the first one.

April 23, 1950.

Today I arrived in New York with Jenny. I have a little bit of money and got a room in a hotel in Manhattan. The room is tiny and smells of cigarettes, but it will have to do. Jenny has been awfully fussy. I know she misses Robert very much. Tomorrow I will go to see Robert's parents. Robert told me where they live. It's in someplace called the Upper East Side, right on the East River. I hope they are as kind as Robert said. Surely they will love their granddaughter and want to help her. Robert, I miss you so much, too.

Rachel was puzzled. "What happened to Robert, Mama?"

"Robert was killed in an accident when I was three years old. That was why Mama Rachel went to New York. She wouldn't go back to her family because she was afraid they would reject her again. So she went to see if the St. Clairs would help."

Jenny pulled a stack of sheets out of the envelope. "These are pages that were torn out of the journal. When we were searching for my mother, we tracked her to the motel in Stroudsburg where she died. The police never identified the body so everything, including her suitcase was in storage in a cold file. We got the suitcase when we proved that the dead woman they found was Rachel St. Clair. There was a secret compartment in the suitcase and Jonathan found these pages where *Grossmutter* Rachel hid them to keep Augusta St. Clair from finding them."

"How did Rachel die, Mama?"

"She overdosed on heroin. The man who was with her, Joe Bender, took me and left for California. On the way, he crashed his car in Apple Creek and drowned when he fell through the ice on a frozen pond. Mama Jerusha found me in the wrecked car and saved me."

"Why would Mama Rachel want to hide the pages from Augusta St. Clair?"

Jenny took the top sheet from the pile of pages.

"Let me read some more."

April 24, 1950.

This morning I took the streetcar from the hotel up to Fifth Avenue to see Robert's parents. I found the address in his papers. It was difficult, but I finally got to the house. It's enormous! It sits right on a big park. The streetcar man said the name of the park is Central Park. My heart was pounding when I went up to the door. There was a big knocker so I knocked with that and after a while a young woman in a black and white uniform came and answered the door. I told her who I was and who Jenny was and that I wanted to see Robert's parents. She looked very surprised. She told me to wait and closed the door. After a while another young woman came to the door. She said her name was Augusta and she asked me what I wanted. I told her who I was and she smiled a strange smile at me. I asked if I could see Robert's parents, but she was very cold and suspicious. She told me that Robert's father had died shortly after he heard about Robert's accident, and his mother was in seclusion and would not see anyone. I told her about Jenny and she laughed at me. She said that I was just another fortune hunter who had heard about the family's tragedy and wanted to cash in. She told me to go away and then she closed the door in my face. I knocked again, but no one came. *After a while I went back to the hotel. Tomorrow I will take the proof and show her.*

Jenny read on.

April 25, 1950.

Today I took the papers and went back to the house with Jenny. Instead of a girl in a uniform, a big man in a black suit answered the door. He told me that Miss Augusta had warned him that I would be coming back and he told me to go away. I begged him to let me see Robert's mother, but he told me if I didn't go away he would call the police. Then he closed the door. I knocked and knocked. After a while a car pulled up in front of the house and two men got out. They didn't say anything to me. They just put me in the car and drove away from the house. Finally, one of them asked me where I lived. I told him the name of the hotel and they took me there. When I got out, they warned me that if I went back to the house I would be arrested and put in jail. Robert! Why did you leave me? I need you!

May 5, 1950.

For the last week I have been trying to call Robert's parents, but every time I get the house, whoever answers, hangs up on me. Finally, yesterday they told me that if I ever called again, they knew where I was staying, and they would send the police and take my little girl away and put me in jail. My money is almost all gone, and the man at the hotel told me I have one more day to pay him. God, why have you abandoned me in this horrible place? I feel so hopeless. I wish I had listened to my daed. I miss them all so much, but I can never go home. What can I do?

May 6, 1950.

Today something frightening happened. While I went to a restaurant with Jenny to get something to eat, someone came into my room. It was very odd because the door was not broken and the windows were locked. I knew someone came in because all of Robert's papers were gone. I have the most important ones hidden, though, and they didn't find them. I think that the woman, Augusta, sent someone to my room to make sure I couldn't prove anything. I had my diary

*in my purse so they didn't get it, but I'm going to take the
pages about Robert out and hide them, too. Maybe I can find
a way to see Robert's mother.*

Jenny stopped for a moment. Rachel looked up and saw with
surprise that her mama was crying. Jenny wiped her eyes with
her sleeve.

"There is one more entry. Let me read it."

May 10, 1950.

*I have been out on the streets since the two men came
with the hotel man and put me out. They said that Robert's
parents sent them and they would take Jenny away forever
if I didn't get out of New York. One of them slapped me very
hard and told me it was a warning. I've been sleeping under
the stairs behind an apartment building. Today I met a man
named Joe. He said he would let us stay in his apartment
and that he would help me, too.*

Jenny put down the stack of pages. "That's all there is.
Shortly after that, Mama Rachel was with Joe Bender when he
robbed a bank. The robbery went wrong but Joe and Rachel
escaped. I was with them. On their way west, Rachel died. I have
never told you this story because it is so terrible. I should have
but I didn't think you needed to know it."

Rachel still couldn't quite wrap her mind around what she
had heard. "So, this Augusta St. Clair…"

"Augusta St. Clair did everything she could to prevent
Rachel from meeting my grandmother, Robert's mother. She did
nothing to help Rachel. In fact, she sent the police to harass
Rachel, and finally had her put out on the street. After I read
this, it was many years before I could bring myself to find grace
for the things she did to my mother. That's why I never told you
about her."

Rachel reached in her pocket and pulled out the business
card. "I met this man when he was leaving here yesterday. Who
is he?"

Jenny took the card. "This man works for Augusta St. Clair. He is a very bad man. Bobby warned me about him. He is a professionally trained killer and he means us no good. Whatever you do, you must not contact him."

Rachel took a deep breath. "When were you going to tell me about the Key, Mama?"

Chapter Fourteen

Rachel's Choice

Rachel stared at her mama's face. The question lay between them like shards of broken glass. Jenny put her head down, sighed, and then looked back at Rachel. "You heard Papa and me talking, then?"

"Yes, Mama. You were talking about the Key. And there was something about the St. Clair fortune. What did it mean?"

"The Key is a birthmark that the legitimate heir to the St. Clair fortune must have. It is key-shaped and red."

Rachel reached to her blouse and unbuttoned it. She opened the top. There above her breast, over her heart, was a key-shaped red birthmark. "Does it look like this, Mama?"

Jenny put her face in her hands and slowly nodded. "I never wanted you to ever be involved with the St. Clairs, but I did not know what that birthmark meant until the man named Randall came to see me. I didn't know, Rachel, I swear it."

"But, what did he say about it?"

"Whoever has that birthmark is a legitimate heir to the St. Clair fortune. Your grandfather, my father, Robert, had it. He was in line to inherit his father's fortune, but he was killed before he did. My understanding is that the bulk of Robert's money was put into trust when he died. Randall didn't tell me, but I believe that Augusta St. Clair never told the estate about me. She just let them believe that Robert died without an heir. From my birth mother's journal, it seems clear that Augusta told my grandmother that Mama Rachel was a stranger who heard about Robert dying and was just after his money. Robert's father never accepted me as his granddaughter and he must not have told anyone about me. Augusta did her best to see that Robert's mother never saw me."

A whirlwind of thoughts rushed through Rachel's head—money and freedom and the power to live her own life. "Why is Augusta looking for you now?"

Jenny took another sip. Jenny's hands were shaking and the coffee in her cup did a tiny dance before she set it down. "I'm not sure, Rachel. Something must have happened with the money. If her grandson had the birthmark, he would have inherited. Augusta probably tried to lay her hands on the money and found out she couldn't get it. That's the only reason a woman like her would start looking for legitimate heirs after all these years. She probably needs me to get to the money."

"But if I have the Key that means the money belongs to me, right?"

"There are certain conditions, Rachel."

Rachel already knew the conditions. "That I have to marry a suitable male St. Clair, right?"

"Yes, that's the condition. And Augusta's grandson is the obvious choice."

"But then I'd have the money, and I could live my life any way I wanted."

The statement was thrown in Jenny's face like a challenge. Jenny cringed. "Yes, but…but, Rachel. Think of what that would mean. You would marry an *Englischer*. You would go under the *meidung*. You would lose everything you have, your life, your family, me, your papa…"

"What it would mean, Mama, is that I could do what I want to do. I could go to college, I could become a vet, I could live my own life without a lot of rules and regulations. And without…"

Jenny's face was white. "Without what, Rachel?"

"Without a crazy man yelling at me, ordering me around, making my life a living hell."

Jenny stood up. Her face blanched and her body shook. "Rachel Hershberger! Your papa is not crazy; he is ill. He…he…"

Rachel stood up, too. The two women stared at each other across the table. Rachel pointed her finger at Jenny. "He's not sick; he's a bully. He doesn't love me; he just wants to control me. Sometimes I wish…"

"What do you wish, Rachel?" Jenny's voice was icy cold.

Rachel took a breath and then the words came tumbling out, like water rushing through a sudden break in a dam. "I wish he would have drowned in the ocean. I wish he never came back. I wish…I wish he really were dead!"

Jenny's mouth moved but no words came out. Rachel turned and rushed out of the room. She ran down the hall into her room and slammed the door behind her.

It was late afternoon. Rachel stood at the bank of phones outside the general store. She looked at the card in her hand and started to lift the receiver, but something held her back. Her mama's words rang in her head like sledgehammers on an anvil.

"This man works for Augusta St. Clair. He is a very bad man. Bobby warned me about him. He is a professionally trained killer and he means us no good. Whatever you do, you must not contact him."

Rachel stared at the phone in her hand.

What can I do? Something tells me I should not call this man, but I need to know if what he said is true.

Then she had an idea. She dialed the zero. A voice came on the line.

"Operator, how may I help you?"

Rachel took a breath and then answered. "Yes, operator, I need to be connected to information in New York City."

There was a pause and a click, and then another voice came on the line.

"New York information, how may I help you today?"

"I need the phone number of someone in New York City."

"Do you have a name, please?"

Rachel paused. She thought she heard someone calling her name. She looked around but she was alone.

"I need a name, ma'am."

Rachel swallowed hard and then spoke. "Yes, I'm sorry. I need the number for Augusta St. Clair."

Augusta St. Clair sat at her desk, going over some papers. Randall's report had given her a severe case of indigestion. An open bottle of Tums and a glass of water sat on a tray in front of her. A quiet buzzer sounded on Augusta St. Clair's intercom. She pressed the answer button.

"What is it, Eva?"

"There's a call for you, ma'am."

Augusta waited and then sighed.

"Who is it? Surely you have a name?"

"Oh…yes, I do. It's a Rachel Hershberger."

"Rachel Hershberger? Who's that?"

"She says her grandmother was Rachel St. Clair."

Augusta's ears perked up.

"Rachel St. Clair?"

"Yes, ma'am, and she says she has the Key, whatever that means."

Augusta's heart skipped a beat.

"Well, let me speak to her."

There was a moment of silence, a click, and then Augusta heard the connection go live again. She spoke.

"Hello, who is this?"

A soft, youngish-sounding voice answered.

"Mrs. St Clair?"

"Yes, this is Augusta St. Clair. Who is this?"

There was a pause, and then the voice answered.

"This is Rachel Hershberger. My mother is Jenny Hershberger, but her birth name was Jennifer St. Clair. She is the daughter of Robert St. Clair and Rachel Borntraeger St. Clair."

Augusta could hardly contain herself, but she took a breath and answered back.

"And why are you calling me?"

"A man—he said his name was Randall—he came to our farm looking for the daughter or grandchild of Robert St. Clair. He talked about the St. Clair fortune and the birthmark that proves who the heir is. He called it the Key. I have that birthmark."

Augusta stood up from her chair. She kept her voice modulated to a low pitch as she began to walk back and forth behind the desk with the phone to her ear.

"Why didn't you just tell Mr. Randall when he was there?"

"I only met him for a few moments, and I didn't know why he had come to our house. Then when my mama told me who he was, I didn't want to call him. There was something...nasty about him. He made my skin crawl. I thought it might be better to just talk to you."

Augusta smiled to herself. Randall definitely could be creepy. She probed a little deeper.

"Well, Rachel, how do I know you are who you say you are? Maybe you're just a girl with a lucky blemish on your skin."

The voice on the other end flashed back at her. "That's how you treated my grandmother, isn't it? You just brushed her and my mama off and left them to die on the streets of New York. Well, my mama didn't die. I think you must be a very heartless woman. Maybe this isn't such a good idea, after all. I shouldn't have even called you. I'll just say goodbye now."

The girl has spunk, like her grandmother...

"Wait, Rachel, don't hang up. I didn't mean to offend. But there is a great deal of money involved here, after all, and I need to be very sure of whom I'm dealing with. You must understand. Now, let's just cool down and see how we can verify what you're saying. After all, if what you claim is true, you are my great-niece."

"As I said, Mrs. St. Clair—"

"Call me Augusta."

"As I said...Augusta, my *grossdaadi*, my grandfather, was Robert St. Clair. My mama showed me the marriage license and her birth certificate."

Augusta sat down in her chair.

"My men didn't find a marriage license. I mean..."

"That's right, your men didn't find it because it was hidden in the bottom of my *grossmutter's* suitcase. It's all in her journal: how you drove her away from Robert's parents, how you sent the police to harass her."

"Now listen, dear. I was only trying to protect my mother-in-law from further heartbreak. She had already lost two sons. There were several girls who showed up at our house trying to say they had relationships with Robert or Jerod. Why, one girl even had a red-haired baby she claimed was Robert's son. What was I to do?"

The voice on the other end was no longer shy. It was firm and direct. "What you should have done was to meet with Rachel privately and see what she had to say. Then, if she had legitimate proof, you could have introduced her to her mother-in-law. If you had any grace in you at all—"

Augusta laughed. "I'm sorry, Rachel. I'm not laughing at you. It's just that in the high-pressure world that I live in, there is not a lot of room for...for grace. And, personally, I am not a very gracious person, anyway."

"That is obvious from my *grossmutter's* journal."

"Point taken, my dear. Now, can we get beyond the unpleasantries and see what we can do about this situation?"

"What do you suggest?"

"I think the best idea would be to meet and have you show me the documents you referred to. Also, we would need to do a paternity test."

"Paternity test?"

"Yes, Rachel. I believe there are much more sophisticated ways to establish paternity than they used to have in the 1950s. I can have my personal physician—"

"I would prefer to have a neutral doctor do the test. I don't have a lot of faith in you...yet."

Augusta scowled, but her voice didn't show it. "That's fine, Rachel. However you want to do this. Can you get the documents?"

"Yes, I know where they are. I'll make copies to show you."

Augusta didn't like the initiative that Rachel was showing. "Well, I'd rather see the originals."

Rachel laughed on the other end of the line. "Right. I may be Amish, but I'm not stupid. I would bring the documents and your man, Randall, would take them from me, maybe even kill me, and then what proof would there be that I am related to Robert St. Clair? No, we will do this my way. You are not a nice person, no matter how pleasant you sound, and I do not trust you in the least. We will meet at a public place. I will show you the copies, and your bodyguard—or whatever he is—will not be there. You and I can go together, and I will give blood or whatever we need to take the test. I will show you the Key. And then you can decide what you want to do."

Augusta sat back down in her chair. She didn't like the way this was going. "You're pretty spunky for an Amish girl."

"I got it from Mama Rachel, the girl you treated so badly and my own mama. And remember, you need me. I don't need you. I'm sure there are others in the St. Clair family that I can contact."

Augusta frowned again. The last thing she wanted was for Rachel to bypass her and go to that pompous Duvigney.

"All right, Rachel. We'll do it your way. How can I contact you?"

"You can't. I'm Amish, remember? We don't have phones. I'll call you tomorrow at about this same time. I hope you will have all the arrangements made."

The line went dead. Augusta stared at the receiver in her hand and then plunged her finger down on the intercom button. Eva answered.

"Yes, Mrs. St. Clair?"

"Get that grandson of mine down here immediately. I need to talk to him right now!"

Rachel stood at the phone bank with the phone receiver still in her hand. She was shaking all over. The phone call had been the hardest she had ever made.

I'm glad she couldn't see me. She wouldn't have thought I was so tough.

Chapter Fifteen

The Meeting

Gerald St. Clair looked at his watch for the twentieth time. The two-hour trip from Manhattan had been boring—extremely boring. It was always tedious spending time with his grandmother, especially traveling. She didn't let him smoke cigarettes in the limo or listen to the radio. And now she was dragging him out to a farm to meet, of all things, an Amish girl. Augusta had briefed him carefully before they left, and now he was fidgeting in the back seat beside her. He could just imagine how this Rachel would look—cow-like features, big boots covered with mud and manure, and on top of it all, that stupid bonnet that the Amish girls wear. He needed a drink badly.

"Grandmother, do we really have to go through with this?"

Augusta looked up from her magazine. Her sharp face was set in "the look" and Gerald glanced away.

"Gerald, look at me!"

Gerald turned back and tried to meet her steely gaze.

"Do you want to be poor?"

"No, Grandmother."

"Do you want to live in some crummy apartment on the Lower East Side?"

"No, Grandmother."

"All the privileges and perks, the life of ease and comfort to which you are accustomed—do you want all that to just disappear?"

Gerald sighed. "No, Grandmother."

Augusta pulled a compact from her purse and checked her appearance. After another touch of lipstick, she snapped it shut and looked at Gerald. "Now I'm going to explain this one more time. This girl has the Key. That means she inherits everything except the tiny pittance left in my husband's trust fund and the house we lived in together. And she gets the New York house and the Connecticut estate. When I say she gets everything, I want you to know that means billions."

Gerald tried to counterattack. "When you say there's only a pittance left from Grandfather and my father, are you talking a few million, a few thousand, what?"

Augusta smiled the icy smile and reached into the Louis Vuitton bag that held her notebook. She opened it and leafed through until she found an official-looking document between two pages. She pulled a pair of reading glasses from the same bag, adjusted them on the end of her nose, and began to read. "The Trust of Jerod St. Clair—Current cash and bonds, value not including the properties in Manhattan, London and Connecticut: $15,985,000. Expenditures 1989: $4,000,000. Income and interest 1989: $500,000. Net debit 1989: $3,500,000."

Augusta removed her glasses and put the notebook away. Gerald looked out the window and frowned. It was worse than he thought. He shifted in his seat.

I really, really need a drink.

"So you see, darling Gerald, your profligate ways, your trips to Europe, the gambling in Monaco, the women, the drugs and alcohol, and whatever other vices you have picked up in your short but flamboyant life are grinding us right into the poor house. If you keep it up, we will be out of money in less than five years. And when it's gone, there isn't any more except for the property. If we have to sell all the property, we will be able to raise a few million, but that won't last. Why, you might even have to get a job."

Augusta chuckled but Gerald didn't think it was funny. He thought about mentioning his grandmother's penchant for Arabian horses, five thousand dollar bottles of wine, and trips to Paris for the latest fashions, but he thought better of it and tried a different tactic. "But, this Rachel...I mean, do I really have to marry her?"

"Rachel Hershberger cannot inherit the estate unless she marries a suitable male St. Clair within a certain time period after being verified as the genuine heir, or in her case, heiress. The St. Clairs put that stipulation in the inheritance protocols to ensure that the money would always remain in St. Clair hands. The only other option is for you to marry someone and produce a male heir who would inherit when he comes into his majority."

"Majority?"

"Yes, Gerald, when he turns twenty-one. So you see, given that it would take you a minimum of nine months to produce an heir if you started today, and assuming that it would be a male, you would still have to wait twenty-two years to get the money. That is, if you survived that long working at a Dairy Queen."

Augusta paused. "You know, Gerald, you really should have brought a book." She smiled again and returned to her magazine.

Rachel stood on the corner by the General Store in downtown Paradise. She had the manila envelope with copies of her grandmother's wedding license and her mama's birth certificate. The meeting was supposed to be at 10 A.M. but the St. Clairs were late. Rachel stood nervously shifting from one foot to the other. She was so intent on looking for the car that she didn't hear the footsteps coming up behind her.

"*Gut mariye*, Rachel."

Rachel's heart jumped. She turned to see Daniel King standing on the sidewalk.

"Daniel, why must you always come creeping up on me? You scared me."

His smile faded. A shadow crossed Daniel's face for just a moment, and then it passed. "A cat looking for a mouse creeps, Rachel. I just happened to be walking by. And judging by your face, I should keep on walking."

Daniel turned to go.

"Wait, Daniel. I'm sorry. I didn't mean to be rude. It's just...it's just..."

"Just what?"

"I have something very important to do, and I don't have time to..." She paused.

"To say hello to a friend?"

"Yes. I mean, no, I... Oh, Daniel, why do you always fluster me so?"

"Don't mean to, Rachel, really. But while we are here, can I ask when you will come to look at the mare and the foal again?"

Rachel felt a twinge of irritation.

Doesn't he know this is the most important day of my life? No, of course not.

"Really, I don't have time to think about that. I have a very important meeting."

At that moment, a long black limousine pulled into the parking spot in front of them. The back door opened and a young man got out. He was dressed in charcoal slacks and a white pullover sweater. He was very handsome with chiseled features and dark, wavy hair. He looked around, and then his eyes settled on Rachel. A smile crossed his face and he approached. Rachel noticed that his eyes were taking in all of her.

"Rachel Hershberger?"

Rachel blushed under his frank perusal and stammered an answer.

"Yes, I'm Rachel."

The man extended his hand and when she shook it, he held it a little too tightly.

"I'm Gerald St. Clair. It's very nice to meet you."

The intense blue eyes were focused on her face now. Suddenly, Rachel felt very uncomfortable. She pulled her hand away and glanced at Daniel. He was looking back and forth between Rachel and Gerald with a strange expression on his face.

"Gerald, this is my friend, Daniel King. Daniel, this is Gerald St. Clair, a…well, I suppose we are distant cousins."

Daniel extended his hand. "*Gut mariye*, Gerald."

"Excuse me?"

"It means good morning."

Gerald smiled. "Oh, oh sure. Good morning."

Ignoring Daniel's outstretched hand, he turned to Rachel and motioned toward the limo.

"Well, cuz, shall we go?"

Daniel looked at Rachel with a puzzled expression. Rachel found herself feeling very strange, almost like she was being torn in two. She patted Daniel on the shoulder awkwardly.

"I have to go, Daniel. I will talk to you later."

"But, Rachel, who—?"

Rachel interrupted. "I can't talk about it right now, but I'll tell you later. Now I must go."

Rachel turned and as she did, Gerald took her arm and steered her toward the car. As he did, he glanced back at Daniel.

"Nice to meet you, Dennis."

"Daniel. My name is Daniel."

"Right, Daniel. Come on, Rachel. We have an appointment and we're running a little late—all that traffic getting out of Manhattan really slowed us down."

Gerald opened the door, and Rachel started to get in. She paused and looked back at Daniel, then got into the car. The door closed and the limousine pulled away from the curb. Rachel looked out the back window. Daniel King stood alone on the grass by the edge of the road, staring after her. Suddenly, Rachel had a very sick feeling in the pit of her stomach.

Augusta St. Clair leaned forward in her chair as the man before her read from a thin binder.

"Although developed in the 1980s, polymerase chain reaction technique in DNA testing has only recently become the standard process for paternity testing."

Dr. Sanderson looked at Augusta over his glasses and then looked back down. The desk in front of him was empty of anything except the document he was perusing. The rest of the office was bare of furniture except for the three chairs that were now occupied by Gerald, Rachel, and Augusta. The doctor continued reading. "PCR is a technique through which samples of DNA fragments are copied and replicated many times until billions of copies are made. Because of the power of PCR, very small samples of DNA from any part of the body can be used in a DNA test. Additionally—"

Augusta broke in. "Yes, Doctor, I'm sure the science is very good. What I want to know is the probability factor for proving paternity, or in this case, grand-paternity."

The doctor gave Augusta a peevish look and went on. "As I was saying, because half of the child's DNA is inherited from the mother and the other half from the father, the child's DNA should match portions of both biological parents. It will also prove that even distant cousins, such as Rachel and Gerald, share the same common ancestor."

"To what degree, Doctor?"

The doctor looked down at the paperwork on his desk and traced a few lines with his finger. "99.999 percent accuracy, Mrs. St. Clair."

"Good. So, what do we have to do to complete this part of the procedure?"

"A buccal swab is all we need."

"A buccal swab, Doctor?"

"A buccal swab is a way to collect DNA from the cells on the inside of a person's cheek. Gerald and Rachel simply need to let me swab them—very simple and painless. The samples are analyzed to create the individual's DNA profile. The DNA profiles will then be compared to determine whether there is a genetic match."

"How long will it take?"

"We should have the results in about a week, Mrs. St. Clair."

"Good. And the birthmark?"

"After examining Rachel's birthmark, it is my opinion that it is a port-wine birthmark, which has been known to be hereditary in many cases. There is no evidence of tattooing or any artificial substances beneath the skin. I am not an expert in this field, but I can refer you to a man who is. However, as I said, I am quite sure that the birthmark is genuine."

Augusta glanced over at Rachel. The girl was leaning forward listening intently to the doctor. Augusta smiled to herself.

Come into my web, little fly...

Daniel King pulled his buggy up in front of his house and got out. His *maam* was out in the front beating carpets. Daniel unhitched the horse and began to lead him toward the barn.

"No greeting, son?"

Daniel looked up. "What? Oh, I'm sorry, Mama, I was thinking about something."

"Rachel?"

Daniel looked at his mother. He never could hide anything from her. "Yes, Mama. It is Rachel."

"I think you should try thinking about someone else, Daniel. That girl is never going to love you like you love her. Her mind and heart are out in the world out there. She will never be content to be an Amish wife."

Daniel felt the truth in her words, and they twisted in his heart like a knife. "You are right, Mama, but Rachel is in trouble."

"Daniel, Rachel is always in trouble. And it worries me to see you mooning over that half-*Englisch* girl."

His *maam* turned back to the rug and began to beat it. Daniel stared at his mother's back and then walked toward the barn. He led the horse into the stall and put some hay out for it. Then he walked out the back of the barn and took the path up the hill. He needed to go to his place. He needed to think.

As he walked up the hill, the afternoon sun warmed his back. The birds sang in the oak trees along the path, and the fresh air of Pennsylvania filled his senses. But Daniel's heart was heavy. He had seen something in Gerald's face as he had stared at Rachel. Lust and greed and wantonness—revealed in a way he had never seen so obviously before in a man. It sickened him. Daniel did not know who these St. Clairs were, but he did know in his heart that they were not good people. And he knew that Rachel would never find her dream with them.

Chapter Sixteen

The Breaking

Rachel sat at the restaurant table with Augusta and Gerald, looking down at the filet mignon in front of her. Augusta leaned toward her.

"Rachel, dear, you've hardly eaten a bite. Believe me, it's delicious."

Rachel pushed her plate away. "I'm sorry, Mrs. St. Clair."

"Augusta, dear. Call me Augusta."

"I'm sorry...Augusta. I just don't seem to have an appetite. I have so many things on my mind."

Augusta picked up her purse. "I'm going to powder my nose. Why don't you two get a little better acquainted?" She scooted her chair back, rose and walked away.

Gerald smiled as he took a sip of his wine. "I should think you would have many things on your mind, Rachel. After all, it's pretty much been confirmed that you are a St. Clair and—"

"And I am the heir to all the money? Well, when the DNA test comes back positive I will be."

Gerald let the remark pass. He gave Rachel another very appraising look and Rachel blushed. When he saw Rachel's response, Gerald put his glass down with a repentant expression on his face. "I'm sorry, Rachel. Did I embarrass you?"

Rachel paused, but then decided it was best to be honest with this man. "Yes, you did. I have never had anyone look at me the way you do, so openly, and it makes me feel…well, almost ashamed."

A strange look went across Gerald's face, and then he smiled at Rachel. "I'm sorry. I guess I'm not used to being with a girl who doesn't like to be looked at that way. I'm only staring at you because you're—well, you're very beautiful."

"And you weren't expecting that, were you?"

"Since we're being blunt, no, I wasn't."

Rachel smiled for the first time. "What were you expecting?"

"You won't be mad if I tell you?"

Rachel looked down at her meal. She wanted Gerald to keep talking. He was so handsome and no one had called her beautiful in a long time. Except Daniel, of course. "Go ahead. I think I have a pretty good idea."

Gerald took a sip of his wine and then smiled again. "When I heard you were an Amish girl, I had this picture in my mind of a large, shall we say, raw-boned girl, with calloused hands, laced-up boots covered with manure, and a hearty slap-on-the-back kind of attitude. You know, like what you would think a farmer is like—what my friends would call 'horsey.'"

Rachel laughed. "And I don't fit that picture?"

"You are as far away from that picture as the east is from the west."

Rachel looked at Gerald, and as she did, she realized that her heart was beating rapidly in her chest. He was well-mannered, friendly, obviously intelligent, and very handsome. He had a perspective on the world that was entirely foreign, yet somehow enticing.

Just then Augusta returned to the table. A waiter holding another bottle of wine followed behind her. Augusta leaned over to Rachel. "Won't you have a small glass of wine with us, Rachel? It's a naïve domestic, but it's surprisingly good."

"I…I don't know. My parents have never let me drink wine. Besides, I'm not twenty-one."

"Oh, just one won't hurt. After all, doesn't the Bible say, 'Thou dost cause the grass to grow for the cattle, and plants for man to cultivate, that he may bring forth food from the earth, and wine to gladden the heart of man, oil to make his face shine, and bread to strengthen man's heart?"

Rachel looked at Augusta with surprise. "You know the Bible?"

"Well, of course, dear. I've been an Episcopalian all my life. I find great comfort in the truths of the Bible."

Rachel was confused. After what she had read in her grandmother's journal, she had fully intended to despise these people. She blurted out a response. "If you think the Bible is so wonderful, why did you treat my grandmother the way you did when she came to New York?"

Augusta put down her fork and reached over and took Rachel's hand. "Let me be perfectly frank with you, Rachel. When your grandmother came to New York, she was the fourth or fifth girl who had shown up at my mother-in-law's house claiming to have a relationship with Robert St. Clair. It was terribly upsetting to Margaret, your grandfather's mother. So when Rachel showed up with a baby, how was I to know that she really was married to Robert? She showed me no proof. Max was dead, so he couldn't confirm that your grandmother really was a St. Clair. He was so disappointed with Robert that he never showed us any of the pictures Robert sent him. In fact, he hid them away and we never found them. As far as I could tell, I was protecting my mother-in-law from further heartbreak."

Rachel wanted to pull away, but she held her hand still. "But you were so mean to her. She got put out on the street and she died. You can't tell me that was just protecting my great-grandmother!"

Augusta glanced at Gerald who was looking down at his plate. "Yes, Rachel, you're right."

There was a pause. Augusta took a breath. "But here's the reality. This is a different world than your bucolic farm life. Those of us with lots of money are constantly attracting grifters and phonies, investment bankers and attorneys. They're like little parasites, everyone wanting to bite off a piece of what we have struggled to hold on to. They lie, cheat and steal to get what they want. It's a sad fact, but in order to keep them away, you have to become like them. And when you do, it is very easy to turn out to be hard and grasping. I don't like what I've become over the years, but I am a product of my environment. Knowing you, if I had to do it over again, I would probably treat your grandmother Rachel differently. But that was then and this is now. I'm very sorry about what happened to Robert's wife, and I want to make it up to you. How can I do that?"

Rachel sat very still for a long moment, looking back and forth between Augusta and Gerald. Augusta's request had taken her by surprise. Then the moment and the setting and the smiling faces of the two people across from her wore down her resistance. She took her hand away from Augusta and picked up the empty glass in front of her. "I think you might start with a glass of that wine, Augusta."

Jenny Hershberger sat in the silent house with Jonathan. The room was dark except for the low light from a fire that had burned down to coals in the hearth. Before it went out, Jonathan stirred himself to put a few more logs on. Then he stood by the fireplace, leaning against the large stones that framed the opening. The day had been overcast and chilly, strange weather for early summer in Paradise. But for Jenny, the chill was in her heart.

"Where could she be, Jonathan?"

Jonathan rubbed the side of his head where the scar ran along his hairline. It was an unconscious habit he brought with him when he had returned to the farm four years before.

"Daniel told us, Jenny. She's with them, and only trouble will come of it."

Jenny's heart was wrapped in a strange foreboding, tangible and oppressive. Around nine o'clock they heard a car coming up the driveway. The light from the headlamps cast strange shadows from the porch posts onto the walls of the room, like dark figures writhing in torment. Jenny heard a car door close and then the car drove around the circular driveway out front and retreated back down the lane. Soft footsteps came up the steps and across the porch. Jenny heard the screen door creak as it swung open. The latch clicked, and then Rachel was standing in the doorway. Jenny's eyes met Rachel's and her heart sank. There was defiance there, and by the set of her face, Jenny instinctively knew Rachel had made a decision.

"Rachel, where have you been? It's so late and we were worried."

"Mama, if Daniel came by, I think you know where I've been."

Rachel's words had a strange slur and her hands twisted nervously in front of her.

Jonathan stepped close to Rachel. He smelled something. "You've been drinking!"

"I had a glass of wine with my dinner, and a very good dinner it was. The St. Clairs took me to the nicest place I've ever been and...and I liked it."

Jenny got to her feet.

"The St. Clairs? Rachel, they are not good people. Augusta did terrible things to your *grossmutter*."

Rachel pulled off her shawl and turned to hang it on the peg by the door. "You know, Mama, there are always two sides to every story. Augusta told me all about what happened. She was very sorry for what she did. She told me she was only protecting her mother-in-law."

Jonathan took Rachel by the shoulder and spun her around. "She was only protecting her money, you little fool. Going off with those people and drinking! You are not twenty-one. While you live in my house, you will not go with *Englischers* or—"

Rachel jerked her shoulder out of Jonathan's grasp. "Your house? Again, Papa, it's your house? Well, I have lived here longer than you. This is more my house than yours. Or is it Richard Sandbridge's house? You don't even know and neither do I."

The sound of the slap was like a cracking whip. Jonathan's hand rose again, but Jenny leaped forward and grabbed her husband's arm. "Jonathan! No!"

Jonathan turned to Jenny. She felt the rigid arm relax and then it fell to his side. He looked at her helplessly.

Rachel stood holding her hand to her face. The red mark across her cheek flamed in the flickering light and tears coursed down her face. Her words came like rifle bullets. "In the years to come, Papa, you will remember that it was you who closed the door."

Then she went down the hall to her room. The sound of the door slamming broke the night.

The sun was trying to force its way into overcast sky when Jenny arose. She wrapped her shawl tightly around her shoulders against the unseasonable chill and looked down at her sleeping husband. The scar where he had been injured in the terrible explosion so many years ago was very visible along his hairline. Jenny reached down and softly stroked the hair into place.

Oh, Jonathan. You've changed so much. Somewhere along this road you lost the part of you that loves life. It is so hard for you, and it is not anything you did. I wish I could do something, but only du leiber Gott *can heal your wounded heart.*

Jenny sighed and left the room. She looked at the crack under Rachel's door to see if her daughter was up, but there was no light and no sound coming from the room. She went upstairs to her study.

Ever since she had come back to Paradise, this room had been her refuge. She went to the pale birch desk that sat under the long window, the desk her papa had made for her. Her hand caressed the smooth wood, sanded so beautifully that it felt soft to the touch. Jenny pulled out her chair and sat down. She pushed the piles of papers and notes aside and laid her head on the table.

"Oh, Papa! How I wish you were here. I would wrap myself in your arms and listen to your wonderful voice telling me that everything would be all right. I need you, Papa."

Jenny remembered another sunrise, long ago, when she had been despairing of ever living again. That dawn had come creeping into her room like a mischievous child, softly kissing her awake with the delicate touch of a rose-colored morning. Jenny remembered opening her eyes that long-ago morning and seeing the pale colors blushing in the fresh sky. She had risen and wrapped a shawl around her shoulders, just like she had this morning, and slipped outside.

The day was fresh and clean and warm, and the grass felt cool and damp against my bare feet. The plum trees were just sending forth their tiny, pink buds. A single wren twittered its call and stillness lay on the land.

Jenny rubbed the smooth surface of the desk. She could almost feel her papa's love emanating from the wood, the love that had sustained her and kept her all her life until the day...

Jenny didn't want to think about that other day, so she pushed her thoughts back to that morning, so long ago in Apple Creek. She remembered her papa coming out on the porch of their little house.

You were dressed for work and you were so handsome. The circle of your arms was like a fortress and a strong tower. I felt life coming back into me. It was as though I had been raised from the dead! Your words comforted me so.

Jenny put her head down on the desk and began to weep.

"Oh, Lord, where are You? I'm losing Rachel, and I've never really gotten Jonathan back. I am so alone. Why won't You help me?

And then a still, small voice that she had not heard for a long time spoke into her troubled spirit.

I never said there would not be hard times. I only said I would never leave you or forsake you.

Chapter Seventeen

Many Sorrows

Rachel looked up. Jenny stood in the doorway of her room looking at the half-packed suitcase on the bed. Rachel saw the look on her mama's face, but she steeled herself against it and continued packing.

"But where will you go, Rachel? How will you live?"

"Aren't you forgetting, Mama? I am about to become a billionaire. The St. Clairs have several apartments in New York, and I'll stay in one of them until Gerald and I are married. After that, we'll see what happens."

Rachel saw the pain on her mama's face.

"Please, Rachel, you must not do this thing. You do not even know this man. How can you even consider marriage? What about courtship? What about getting to know each other first?"

"Gerald is handsome, he is attentive, and I believe he has come to care for me. As of now, we have a business arrangement, but who knows? I may come to love him. That would be an added bonus."

"He only cares about the money, Rachel!"

"Gerald thinks I'm beautiful, and he told me that he feels more for me than just friendship, but that is beside the point, Mama. He is my ticket out of this place. I want to go to school to become a veterinarian. Gerald has no problem with that. The money I inherit will pay for the best schools in the world. I have already looked into the Royal Veterinary College. The St. Clairs have a house in London, and we could live there while I attend."

"But I thought you wanted to go to Cornell?"

"What does that matter to you, Mama? Papa wouldn't let me go to New York or help me financially, anyway. He could, you know. He made a lot of money when he was Richard Sandbridge."

Jenny looked away. "Rachel, your papa gave most of that money away when he came back to the church. He wanted to disconnect himself from everything that happened to him in those eight years he was gone."

Rachel turned back to her packing. "Another brilliant decision by Jonathan Hershberger, otherwise known as Richard Sandbridge."

"Rachel, why do you hate him so?"

Rachel felt her hands clenching as she stood with her back to her mama. Then the frustration of the last four years spilled out. "What do you expect, Mama? When he left us, it nearly killed me—"

"He did not leave us, Rachel. He couldn't help what happened."

"Mama, let me finish."

Jenny stopped and Rachel went on. "When he left us, everything changed. We went back to Ohio and you were so sad for so long. Everything was about you, your sorrow, your grief. What about my grief? You thought I was doing okay, but I was not. And you were so lost in your own pain that you had no time to really find out how I was feeling. At least I had *grossdaadi* and *grossmutter*, and they helped me for a while. Then they died and I was so afraid."

"Afraid?"

"Yes, Mama. I was afraid—afraid you would leave me, too. I used to wake up at night feeling like someone was standing on my chest. I just knew something was going to happen to you and then I would be completely alone. And then he came home and it did happen."

"What happened?"

"You left me, Mama."

"But how? I was right here all the time."

Rachel's voice rose. "No, Mama, you were not. Suddenly, we had a stranger in our house and everything was about him. Poor Jonathan, he's not well. Poor Jonathan, he shouldn't be disturbed. You never had time for me anymore and I hated that. It was like I was a stranger, standing out on the porch and looking into this house where all this love used to be, but I was out in the cold and you both were inside."

As she spoke, Rachel stepped closer to her mama until she was standing in front of Jenny, shaking like a leaf in a storm. "You left me, Mama! You may have been here physically, but you were gone. Gone taking care of a poor fool who couldn't even remember his name most of the time. He certainly didn't remember me. And all he could do was shove rules down my throat. The *Ordnung* says this, the *Ordnung* says that. I got to the point where I hated the word and I hated the rules."

Rachel took her mother by the arms and looked right into her eyes. "Don't you understand, Mama? I hate being Amish. And now God has opened a door for me to leave. And I'm going."

Rachel went to the closet and pulled down some more things.

"Rachel, I don't believe it is God who has opened this door."

"Who is it then, the devil?"

"If you consider the people you will be with, the man you are marrying—"

Rachel flung the clothes on the bed. "You don't know what you're talking about! You haven't even taken the time to meet them, to talk to them."

"But they are *Englisch*, Rachel."

Rachel pointed her finger at Jenny. "And so are you, Mama. So are you. You're a St. Clair, too, and if you will be honest, you will see that the St. Clair side of you has always fought against being Amish."

"No, Rachel, you are wrong. I have always loved being Amish."

"Right, Mama. That's why you write books, and get your column published in the paper and meet people from outside the church, while everyone looks the other way. Everyone says that an Amish girl can't become a vet. Well, what about an Amish girl who becomes a famous writer? The truth is that writing is the way you escape from everything Amish. Where do you go when you lock yourself in your room and write? You go away, Mama. You go away. For you to oppose me is so hypocritical. I expected better of you!"

Rachel turned back to her suitcase. She stared down at it for a moment and then slammed it shut. "I don't know why I'm packing anything. I certainly won't be wearing these clothes anymore!"

Just then, there was a knock. The bedroom door opened and Jonathan's face peeked around.

"Hey, what's happening? I heard yelling. Why can't we all just mellow out here?"

Rachel's stomach twisted. How she hated that voice! She didn't even look at Jonathan. Her words carried a nasty bite. "Good morning, Richard."

Jenny jerked as if she had been slapped.

Rachel re-opened the suitcase and put in a few more things. "Don't worry, Richard, everything's 'cool' in here. Jenny and I were just having a chat. I'm leaving, you know, and I'll be gone a long time."

Jonathan looked confused. "Where are you going?"

"I'm getting married, and I am moving to New York."

Jonathan's face brightened. "Oh, that's great. You can come by and visit me at my office. Who's the lucky guy?"

Jenny took Jonathan by the arm and began to lead him out of the room. Tears poured down her face. "Come, Jonathan. You need to lie down."

"But, uh…but Rachel's getting married. Aren't we invited?"

Jenny turned. The stricken look on her mama's face was almost too much for Rachel, but she pushed her regret aside.

"The wedding is a private affair, Richard, but when I'm settled, I'll get in touch."

Jonathan looked at Rachel. "Well, that's fine, just fine. The guy who's getting you is sure lucky. You're a beautiful girl."

Jenny began to pull Jonathan out of the room. "Come, Jonathan. You must rest."

Jonathan followed. Jenny closed the door behind them. Rachel heard Jonathan's feet shuffling down the hall. Then she heard his voice. It seemed far away, lost and lonely.

"Jenny?"

"Yes, Jonathan?"

"Jenny, where's Rachel? Where's my Rachel? I've looked and looked and I can't find her."

Rachel began to sob, quietly. She walked to the door and put her hand on the knob, but she couldn't turn it. She stood there, desperately wanting to fling the door open and run after her parents, but she didn't. Her hand slipped from the knob as tears streamed down her face. She spoke quietly into the empty space her parents had left behind them.

"I'm here, Papa, I'm here. Come and get me, Papa. I need you."

But there was no answer.

Jenny sat in the rocking chair at the foot of the bed. All the shades were pulled, and even though it was still light outside, the room was dark. Jonathan had been asleep for six hours, lying on his back like a dead man. Rachel's words careened around Jenny's thoughts like billiard balls.

"...what about an Amish girl who becomes a famous writer? The truth is that writing is the way you escape from everything Amish. Where do you go when you lock yourself in your room and write? You go away, Mama, you go away. For you to oppose me is so hypocritical. I expected better of you!"

"Lord, Rachel is right. I've used my writing to escape—from grief and sorrow, from hardship, from...from Jonathan, and yes, even from being Amish. I left her to fend for herself while I hid inside my thoughts in my room. And now it is too late. Rachel *fühlt sich verlassen*, she feels desolate, and so she is making a terrible decision. Oh, Lord, you must help me to make her see."

Jonathan groaned on the bed. His voice sounded weak in the darkness. "Jenny, who are you talking to?"

"I was praying, Jonathan."

"What about?"

"Rachel is leaving us."

Jenny could hear the bed creak as Jonathan twisted around. "Leaving? Where is she going?"

Jenny put her face in her hands and began to cry quietly. "She met with the St. Clairs. She has been certified as the true heir to the St. Clair fortune, and she is going to marry Gerald St. Clair."

"What! She can't do that! The *Ordnung* strictly prohibits Amish girls from marrying outside our faith..."

Something snapped inside Jenny's heart. She stood up from the chair and went to the side of the bed. She could see Jonathan's face in the dim light. It was twisted in anger and he was struggling to get up. Jenny pushed him down and stood over him. "*Ordnung! Ordnung!* You have crushed our girl beneath the weight of laws that none of us can keep. What has happened to you, Jonathan? You used to understand. The *Ordnung* cannot save us, only Jesus Christ can. You have taken refuge in the *Ordnung* and forgotten about grace. We are children of grace, Jonathan, not of the law."

"But, Jenny, the *Ordnung* is what defines us and makes us different. It's what keeps us from the things of the world."

"And what about love? Love for your family, for your only daughter. Love that would keep her warm and safe while she grew up and began to make real decisions for her own life. Times have changed, Jonathan. You could have helped Rachel. You have some of your royalty money left. You could have gone to the elders and helped them to see that an Amish veterinarian who understood our ways would be a great blessing to our community. You could have paid her way, guiding her and standing beside her. But instead, you beat her and broke her with the law."

Jonathan trembled. "I only wanted to protect her from the world. I—"

"But you never knew her. You never asked her what she wanted. And I have been your accomplice. Rachel was right in what she said to me. I left her. I put all my focus on you and my writing and I left her alone in the dark with her fear and her grief. She didn't need to be judged. She needed her papa and her mama. And we were gone, just as surely as if we had both been on that boat that blew up out on the ocean. And now she's gone…"

Jenny's heart broke and she sank to her knees. Great, gasping sobs tore from deep within her. Jonathan stared at his wife. He stretched a trembling hand toward her and touched her shoulder. Jenny twisted away.

"You have forgotten your first love, Jonathan. You have put your trust in the law but the law can't heal you. Only Jesus can heal your mind and your heart."

"But, Jenny, I need you."

"No, Jonathan, you need the Lord. You need to seek Him with all your heart. He is the God who will heal you. I can't do it anymore."

Jonathan stood up. "I'll stop her. I'll make her understand."

He went to the door and opened it. He started down the hall toward Rachel's room. Jenny lifted herself from the floor and screamed after him.

"You fool! Don't you understand? Rachel is gone and we have driven her away."

Jonathan stumbled down the hall toward Rachel's room.

"Rachel? Rachel, where are you?"

Jenny's scream cut through the air between them like a knife.

"She's gone! Don't you understand, you poor, sick fool! Our daughter is gone!"

And then Jonathan stood there helplessly while the sound of Jenny's sobs echoed through the dark and empty house.

Rachel stood beside Gerald, clad in a simple white dress. A touch of makeup highlighted her perfect features, and her auburn hair was swept into a cascade of curls—she was lovely, but her face was set like stone.

Gerald kept glancing over at her. Soft music from the organist filled the chapel. Candles and flowers decorated the altar in front of them, and Augusta stood beside them, dressed in a dark, expensive suit. The Episcopal Bishop continued reading from the wedding service, but Rachel didn't hear him. Her thoughts were far away, in a little blue house on a farm in Paradise, Pennsylvania.

Oh, Mama, Papa, what am I doing?

"Do you, Rachel, take this man, Gerald, to be your lawfully wedded husband, to have and to hold, for richer, for poorer, in sickness and in health, until death do you part?"

Augusta's soft voice interrupted Rachel's thoughts.

"Rachel?"

Rachel looked at Gerald and Augusta. She wanted to scream "no," and run. Run down the aisle, out of the church, and back to her home. But she didn't. She felt the words forming in her mind and then she heard herself speaking them as if from far away. She closed her eyes.

"I do."

Chapter Eighteen

A Two-Edged Sword

Daniel King hated days like this. The cold, blustery wind drove like nails through his coat. Icy rain slapped his face, and the gray clouds scudding overhead matched his mood. He pulled his coat tighter around him as his horse hauled the black buggy along the highway. An occasional car swept by, splashing water against the wheels and up on the floor. The red warning triangle was very visible on the back of Daniel's rig, but there were still some *Englischers* who took a perverse pleasure in coming as close as they could, especially on days like this.

The storm had swept in unexpectedly behind a thick layer of gray clouds. Daniel had not paid attention to the overcast sky before he set out, and now he was paying the price. He was miserable and wet. Finally, the sign for Old Leacock Road loomed up out of the rain, and Daniel turned off the highway. He reached up and touched his shirt pocket to make sure that the letter was still there and wondered why Rachel had sent it to him.

When Rachel left Paradise she had not even said goodbye. Then today, a letter had come in the mail. It was short and seemed chatty, but Daniel knew Rachel well enough to read between the lines. Underneath the bravado, Daniel could see that something was wrong. His thoughts churned and his heart ached as he drove into the teeth of the wind. Finally, the turnoff to the King farm appeared through the mist and rain, and he gratefully guided the horse into their lane. He drove straight down to the barn and turned inside. Water dripped off the brim of his hat as he climbed down and unhitched his horse. Grabbing a towel off a rack, he dried the animal off and then led him into a stall. He sat down on a bale of hay and pulled the letter out of his pocket. The envelope was damp from the rain. It was postmarked Greenwich, CT. He pulled the letter out of the envelope and read it again.

> *Dear Daniel,*
>
> *I hope this letter finds you well and happy. I just wanted to tell you that I am sorry I didn't say goodbye to you. Everything happened so quickly, but you are my best friend and I should have taken time to see you. Please forgive me.*
>
> *Right now, Gerald and I are staying at the St. Clair estate in Greenwich, Connecticut, with Augusta. It's a wonderful place, and the horses, oh Daniel! You would love the horses. They are mostly Arabians and thoroughbreds, and they are the finest money can buy. Augusta loves horses, so at least we have that in common.*
>
> *As for my inheritance, there seems to be a slight delay in receiving the money, so I have to wait to apply to vet school until the spring. Mr. Duvigney, who is the administrator of my grandfather's estate, tells me that there are quite a few financial technicalities involved in transferring such an enormous sum of money into our accounts. Of course, Augusta is not too happy about that.*
>
> *As for married life, it is not quite what I expected, but then Gerald and I basically have a business deal, so the romance part of it seems to be on hold for now. We do not see things the same way. That's because of our different backgrounds, I expect, but I am hoping that once we get to know each other better, we can resolve our differences amicably. The main thing that troubles me is that even though Augusta and Gerald go to the Episcopal Church, I don't see the fruit of real faith in their lives. In fact, I'm not sure Gerald even believes in God, and that troubles me. Not to say that I have been the most faithful adherent either, but*

I do know that Gott is real, even though He seems far away right now.

Well, enough about me. I am doing what I wanted to do and that's a good thing, I guess. When I get started at vet school I am sure I will feel a lot better about everything. In the meantime, I do get lonely for my folks and I miss our friendship. I hope this letter doesn't get you in trouble, since I know you are not supposed to communicate with those who have left the church. But I would love to hear from you sometime.

Anyway, look after my mama for me and Jonathan, too.

Rachel

Daniel sighed and shook his head. He spoke out loud.

"So, you don't see things the same way as a spoiled, rich *Englischer*? I wonder why!"

The horse snorted and jumped at his outburst, and Daniel looked around to see if anyone else had been listening. Rachel was right. When she married Gerald St. Clair, she was put under the *bann*, and the members of the Amish community of Paradise were forbidden to communicate with her. Daniel knew that his parents would be displeased if they saw the letter, so he looked around.

There was a loose board in the wall at the back of the stall, and he slipped the letter in behind it. Then he began to pace. After a moment, he made a decision. He left the barn and went into the house. He looked around to make sure nobody was downstairs, and then he went into the room his father used for an office and got an envelope, a piece of paper, and a pencil. He went back out to the barn and took his father's clipboard off the wall by the door. Then he went back in the stall and sat down again. Quickly he began to write.

Dear Rachel,

I got your letter and you are right. I am not supposed to communicate with you. But you are my friend, and I am responding because you sound very lonely. I know you well, Rachel, and I can read between the lines. It seems that in your haste to distance yourself from Jonathan, you have made a choice that is not turning out the way you expected.

But I don't care about all that. What I care about is you and your life. I am and always will be your friend, and if you need any help from me, or anything at all, please let me know.

Daniel

P.S. I do miss you.

He stared at the last words. What he wanted to say was how much he loved her, but she was married now, and he could not bring himself to write the words on paper. He lowered his head and was silent. A tear dropped from his eye and he quickly wiped it away. Instead of writing anymore, he prayed silently.

Lord, please be with Rachel in this time. Protect her and guard her. Set your mighty angels round about her and keep her safe. Danki. Amen.

Daniel put the letter in the envelope and sealed it, and then wrote Rachel's address on the front. He put it in the hiding place with Rachel's letter, and then went back into the house. He felt like someone had shoved a sharpened fence post through his heart. He could wipe away the tears from his eyes, but he could do nothing about the deep pain twisting him inside.

Two weeks later, Daniel was hanging around outside the post office. He had checked for a reply from Rachel as often as he could for the last week, but he had received nothing. Several Amish folk had come and gone this morning, and he was waiting until he could go in unobserved. Rachel had sent the first letter to Daniel in care of Mrs. Shoemaker, the postmistress, so Daniel wouldn't get in trouble. So he was expecting another letter to arrive in the same fashion.

Finally, the coast was clear and he went inside. Mrs. Shoemaker motioned for him to come to the counter. She looked around and then leaned forward and whispered in a conspiratorial way.

"Daniel, I have something for you from Connecticut. I hope it's from Rachel. It's too bad you kids can't just talk to each other instead of sneaking around. I never understood this shunning nonsense."

Mrs. Shoemaker saw the hurt in Daniel's eyes and stopped.

"I'm sorry, Daniel. I didn't mean to offend. I'm sure your customs serve their purpose, after all."

She reached under the counter, pulled out a small manila envelope, and handed it over the counter to Daniel. Daniel took it eagerly. The postmark was from the same town in Connecticut, but the return said Augusta St. Clair, not Rachel. The address was typed on the outside:

Mr. Daniel King
c/o Mrs. Shoemaker, US Post Office
1 Leacock Rd,
Paradise, PA 17562

Daniel tore open the envelope. Inside, he found a folded sheet of paper. He pulled it out and saw something else inside. It was the letter he had written to Rachel. The letter was unopened. Daniel looked at the letter, put it down on the counter, and unfolded the sheet. It was heavy linen stationery with the St. Clair family crest on the top above Augusta St. Clair's name and post office box in Greenwich, Connecticut. The message was short and to the point.

Dear Mr. King,

I am writing on behalf of my granddaughter-in-law, Rachel St. Clair. She wishes me to inform you that she wants nothing further to do with you or anything having to do with her old life. She requests that you cease annoying her by writing letters and that you refrain from attempting to communicate with her in any way. If you persist in your efforts, we will be forced to seek injunctive action.

Yours Truly,

Augusta St. Clair

Daniel's heart sank. He stared at the letter from Augusta and then at his unopened letter to Rachel. Something didn't feel right. He looked up. Mrs. Shoemaker was making strange pointing motions with her eyebrows. Then he felt a large hand rest on his shoulder.

"What's this?"

Startled, Daniel looked around. His father stood behind him, looking over his shoulder at the two letters in Daniel's hands. It seemed Mrs. Shoemaker suddenly remembered something she had to do in the back room, for she disappeared. Daniel faced his father.

"Can I see that?" his papa asked.

Reluctantly, Daniel handed over the letter from Augusta. His father read it and then sighed. He folded it and handed it back.

"And the other?"

Daniel pulled away. "It is personal, Papa."

"Also, *das ist persönlich?* And is it from Rachel?"

Daniel trembled under his father's stern gaze. "*Nein,* Papa. It is a letter I wrote to Rachel."

Mr. King looked at his son. And then he motioned Daniel to follow him and walked outside. He put his arm around Daniel's shoulders. "Walk with me, son."

They walked down the steps and turned left. The King's buggy was standing next to the yellow metal post next to the phone booth at the side of the building. Daniel's mother was waiting in the buggy, and she started to speak as they passed. But Daniel's papa motioned to her and kept walking. The fallen leaves crunched under Daniel's feet as he walked with his father, and the crunching sounded like bones breaking. The stark, bare limbs of the trees stood up like withered arms reaching out for a last bit of life from a cheerless sky. They walked a few blocks before Mr. King spoke. "You know that Rachel is under the *meidung,* the *bann?*"

"*Ja,* Papa."

"And you know that it is forbidden to communicate with her because she has chosen to live outside our faith and our *Ordnung?*"

"*Ja,* Papa."

Mr. King stopped and turned to his son. "Daniel, you are a good son. You are strong and faithful, yet you are also kind and gentle. You have never given me any reason to be other than very proud of you." He looked down at the letter in his hand. "The *Ordnung* may seem strict and without grace. It may seem to you that we are keeping rules by the letter of the law and not the spirit. And yet I know that the *Ordnung* are good if we understand that they have been written to protect our faith and our people and to keep us pure and undefiled from a world that is walking with the devil."

"I know that, Papa—"

Daniel's father went on. "I will not say anything about this to anyone. I trust you and know that except for your deep love for this girl, you would never have broken our rules."

Daniel dropped his eyes. The pain in his heart was almost more than he could bear.

"But I also know that if you continue on this path, it will only bring you great sorrow."

Daniel looked at his papa. "*Daed*, Rachel is in trouble. I just know it. She never would have said those things to me. Something's wrong. She sent me a letter a few weeks ago, and I could tell she was troubled."

"Of course she is troubled. *Sie wird gestört.* She disobeyed her father and mother; she married outside her faith; she is bound by enormous wealth. Son, you cannot serve *Gott* and mammon, too. Her sins have found her out and her conscience is tearing at her."

"But, *Daed!* She needs my help. I just know it."

Mr. King held up the letter from Augusta. "Daniel! You are so bound up by this girl that you cannot see the truth. You are so blinded that you don't see what this is. This is not a letter from" —he glanced down at the signature—"from Augusta St. Clair. It is a letter from *du lieber Gott.* He is telling you to stop, to give her up, to get on with your life. Don't you understand?"

There was a long silence while father and son stared at each other. Finally, Daniel spoke.

"*Ja*, Papa. I understand."

But he did not understand at all.

It was late in the day. Daniel sat on a stump among the trees on the top of the knoll behind his father's house. He was looking east. It had turned cold, and a flurry of snow had fallen before the family got home from the post office. But then the clouds had cleared and now the setting sun behind him cast long shadows toward the east. The remains of the brief storm scudded east on a brisk breeze from somewhere to the west and the trees above him rustled and shook. Daniel pulled his coat closer around him and then stood up and stamped his feet to get the circulation going.

That cold front is moving east. It will be snowing in Connecticut tonight.

He was stiff from the cold, but his thoughts were not on the temperature. Somewhere out there, Rachel was in trouble. Daniel could feel it in his whole being. Finally, he slipped to his knees, bowed his head and began seeking the Lord in prayer.

Lieber Gott im Himmel, I have to do something. Rachel needs me. Those people that she went with, they are bad. Helfen Sie mir, Herrn, show me how to help her.

And then, as clearly as if a voice had spoken, Daniel knew what he had to do.

Chapter Nineteen

Surrender

A month after their wedding, Gerald and Rachel flew to Italy for a honeymoon. Rachel wasn't sure she wanted to go on a long trip with a man she hardly knew and had resisted mightily, but Augusta finally prevailed by suggesting that they needed to keep up appearances for the sake of their position in society. She made light of their "business" relationship as she helped Rachel pack. "It will be relaxing and a lot of fun, my dear. You'll love the Amalfi Coast. Oh, it's my favorite place in Europe. Just wait until you see the Bay of Naples and Mt. Vesuvius."

Rachel had been pleasantly surprised at Gerald's treatment of her as they traveled. Her first impression of him was that he could be a bit pretentious and somewhat spoiled. But on the trip, she began to like him. He was most solicitous and charming. He wined and dined her, and, as a special surprise, took her on a five-day excursion to Capri.

When they boarded the huge yacht and sailed out onto the deep blue bay, Rachel was swept away by the beauty of her surroundings and by Gerald's attentive ways. She was drawn to him, infatuated with his good looks and intelligent conversation, and slowly she was pulled into the vortex of a new kind of life—

a life with no cares or worries, a life that held endless possibilities, fueled by an unlimited supply of money.

Capri was an experience beyond her wildest dreams. As their yacht sailed into the port, Rachel looked up toward the sky and the great spur of rock towering above the sea. Gerald pointed to an ancient villa perched like an eagle's nest at the top of the cliff, high above the sparkling waters. The stunning view stole Rachel's breath away, and she looked at Gerald in amazement.

"That's our hotel, Rachel, the Caesar Augustus. I've booked two suites, the best in the hotel, and they're incredible."

As they climbed down the gangplank to the small launch that was to take them into shore, Gerald took Rachel's arm to steady her. The touch of his hand was somehow intoxicating, and a strange thrill ran through her. She looked at him and he smiled and took her hand. Rachel blushed and turned her eyes away.

Is this what falling in love is? If it is I...I like it.

She pressed against him as the launch cut through water that spread like glass beneath the brilliant Mediterranean sun. His arm crept around her bare shoulders, and he pulled her close against him. She felt her face burning and hid against his shoulder. New and unknown feelings flashed through her, catching her by surprise.

This is just a business arrangement. I don't love him...or do I?

A chauffeur in full livery waited beside a limousine that was parked at the dock and they waited for a moment while the driver loaded their luggage. Then they drove up a cobbled, winding street to the top of the hill. When they pulled into the courtyard in front of the hotel, Gerald climbed out and held the door for Rachel.

"This is the only hotel on the Island that you don't have to walk up the hill to get to." He pointed west. A beautiful little town spread out before them. "You can walk a few hundred feet and be in Anacapri. We can go tomorrow. Then we can take a boat around to Grotta Azzurra. It's a cave under the cliff that you can cruise through—the bluest water in the world. Oh, and did you know that Roman emperors had villas on this island? There's a lot of history here."

Gerald's boyish enthusiasm amused Rachel. They stood outside for a moment, taking it all in, and then Gerald took her hand and they walked into the lobby. The concierge looked up and smiled. "Welcome back, Signor Gerald. And who is this lovely lady?"

Gerald took Rachel by the arm. "Hello, Adriano. It's good to be back. And this is my brand new wife, Rachel."

A big smile broke over Adriano's face. He came around his desk and extended his hand.

"*Buongiorno, signora St. Clair. Matrimoni e vescovati sono destinati dal cielo,*"

Rachel looked to Gerald for a translation. Gerald laughed. "He said that marriages are made in heaven. I hope that's true in our case."

Adriano looked puzzled but Gerald just smiled. "Just a little joke, Adriano. Now, what about our rooms?"

Adriano glanced down at the register and then back at Gerald. "You have reserved two suites, Signor Gerald?"

Gerald spoke to Adriano in Italian. "*La signora St. Clair proviene da un...un upbringing molto severo ed è molto timida. Vorrei dare a lei come molta...ah... privacy possibile fino a quando lei è più abituata a me.*"

Understanding crossed Adriano's face and he smiled and bowed. "*Sì*, Signor Gerald. I understand perfectly."

Rachel leaned close to Gerald. "What did you say to him?"

Gerald whispered back. "The truth. I told him you were very shy and I wanted to give you as much privacy as possible."

Adriano rang a small bell on his desk and a bellboy appeared magically. Adriano reached into his desk and brought out two sets of keys. He handed them to the young man. "*Si prega di prendere la signora St. Clair a Cesare Master Suite e il signor St. Clair a Capri.*"

The bellboy nodded and went looking for their luggage. Adriano smiled. "He will return in a moment and take you to your rooms. Again, *signora* St. Clair, welcome to Capri. *Congratulazioni e possono avete figli maschi!*"

Rachel glanced at Gerald. Gerald leaned over and whispered in her ear. "It's a traditional Italian wedding blessing. He says he hopes you have male children."

Rachel turned beet-red and looked at the floor while the two men laughed. Then the bellboy returned with their luggage and led them to their rooms. At the door of her suite, Rachel turned to Gerald. "Thank you for getting me my own room. I am very grateful. It is awkward, I know, but I appreciate it and hope you understand."

Gerald took her hand and bowed over it. Then he kissed it. "Think nothing of it, Rachel. I only want you to be comfortable and happy and to enjoy being together with me.

Gerald paused and then spoke softly. "My greatest hope is that when we sort through the...strangeness of this arrangement, you might come to have feelings for me as I am...as I am beginning to have for you."

Rachel felt something like an electric shock rush down her arms and the heat came into her face again. He looked into her eyes and held them for a long moment. Then he let go of her hand and nodded to the bellboy. "It's a beautiful suite, Rachel. I hope you like it. Say, I've got an idea. Why don't you meet me at the pool and we'll go for a swim before lunch. You won't believe the view."

The heat faded from Rachel's face and she gathered her emotions together.

"All right. That sounds fine. I'll see you there shortly, as soon as I unpack a few things."

Gerald turned and went off down the corridor. The young man turned the key, opened the door, and motioned for her to enter. Rachel stepped into the room and stopped, amazed. It was the most beautiful room she had ever seen. The walls were pristine white and beautiful matching drapes hung in all the arches that soared above the doorways, tied back with gray woven ropes. The parquet floors shone with a luminous glow and the accents in the room were gorgeous red and gray. The furniture was dark wood and there were lamps of gleaming brass set on the desks and on the tables by the couch. Rachel walked into the room. The young man came in behind her and set her luggage down. He turned to go. Rachel reached for her purse, but the young man smiled. "*No, la signora St. Clair. Il signor Gerald mi ha già dato un suggerimento.*"

He smiled at her puzzled look and tried again in English. "Mr. Gerald. He already tip."

Rachel nodded and smiled as the young man left. She turned back to the room. It was spectacular. Almost circular in shape, it had huge arches all around. The afternoon sun blazed off a glass door that opened out onto a terrace. White curtains framed the arches like clouds, and through them, Rachel could see the beautiful Bay of Naples. She stood entranced as the sun ricocheted off tiny, breeze-borne waves like a million bright candles.

She toured each room. The immaculate bathroom walls shone with white tile trimmed in blue, and the sinks were jade-green marble. As she looked in the bronze-framed mirror above the sinks, she could see the reflection of the sea through the enormous window behind her.

She went back into the living room. The master bedroom lay beyond an archway draped with diaphanous curtains. Rachel stepped through the archway. The material drifted against her skin like caressing fingers. She looked down at the huge bed. Strange feelings rushed through her, and for a moment she couldn't catch her breath. She sat down and felt the softness of the mattress, the touch of the magnificent coverlet. An image began to take shape in her mind. Gerald with her, in this room...

She stood up and returned to the living room. She picked up her suitcase and went back into the bedroom. There was a stand by the window, and she put her suitcase there and opened it. She sorted through the clothes that Augusta helped her buy until she found the swimsuit. It was a simple one-piece, modest but lovely. Augusta had tried to get her to buy a tiny bikini, but Rachel had balked.

Rachel undressed and put on the suit. She had seen some white terrycloth robes hanging in the bathroom closet, so she went in, found one that fit her, and put it on. Then she grabbed a towel from the cupboard and headed for the door. As she

Patrick E. Craig

passed the bedroom, she paused and then stepped back through the sheer curtains. As she stood looking down at the bed, the images came again. They were vivid and passionate; Gerald and her, alone in the room, as husband and wife. She tried to push them away, and then suddenly her heart was pounding and she could barely catch her breath.

What is happening to me? I've never had such thoughts.

She backed away from the bed, took a deep breath, and then turned and almost ran from the room.

The rest of the day was like a dream. They went swimming in the infinite horizon pool on the edge of the terrace. When Rachel was in the water, it seemed as though she were floating above the world. The sea stretched away to the north. On the horizon, an island rose out of the low-lying white clouds. It looked as though it was suspended magically above the water. Gerald swam up next to her. "That's Ischia. It's one of the Phlegrean Islands. It's beautiful, isn't it?"

Then she felt his arms slip around her. She had never felt the touch of a man's skin so intimately before. He turned her face to his and smiled. "But not as beautiful as you, Rachel."

And then his lips found hers, and she felt herself being drawn into his very being. They stayed there in the warm water, and it was as though she were looking down at another girl from high above. And then suddenly, it was so intense that she couldn't breathe and she broke away.

"What, Rachel? Didn't you like it?"

She reached out and took his hand. "Yes, Gerald, I like it. It's just that I never..."

He smiled again and put his finger to her lips. "It's all right, I understand. Come on, let's have lunch."

He turned and swam to the edge of the pool and pulled himself out. The muscles in his back and arms rippled as he did, and Rachel followed slowly, feeling suddenly alone without him.

Later that night, they sat on the terrace looking out over the bay as the full moon stood high above the Tyrrhenian Sea. The summer night was perfectly still, the surface of the water was smooth as glass, and the moonlight made a silver path on the sea. Gerald sipped his wine and then reached for Rachel's hand.

Rachel was stunning in a white, off-the-shoulder summer dress. Her long, dark auburn hair was pinned softly at the nape of her neck, and her violet eyes drank in Gerald's face. She was being swept away, and yet part of her was still saying no. Something inside her was clinging to the last bit of her old life, like someone in a flood holding desperately to a tiny bit of rock while the water rages all around them. Warning bells blared in her heart, but a heat was rising in her that slowly engulfed and silenced them.

Gerald stood and drew her to him. They walked to the edge of the terrace and lingered in the shadows. Gerald's lips found hers again and suddenly she was responding to him with her whole being. They stood in the embrace for what seemed forever, and then Gerald whispered in her ear.

"Shall we go back to your room, Mrs. St. Clair?"

She hesitated for just a moment. The strangest sensation washed over her—like a tornado tearing through her ordered little world, stripping away everything familiar and loved. Her head whirled and she didn't know where she was. She closed her eyes to steady herself, and suddenly she saw a man. But it wasn't Gerald. It was Daniel! He was standing on top of their knoll, under the tree where they had pledged their friendship and love so long ago. Daniel was looking east, and she could see that he was troubled. In that moment, she felt as though everything about her life was wrong. She wanted to cry out, to stop the folly sweeping her away in a white-hot flame. A thought came to her like a life preserver tossed to a drowning woman caught in a maelstrom.

Daniel, Daniel…come save me!

She wanted to scream it, but before she could say the words, burning lips pressed against hers. She opened her eyes but it wasn't Daniel that held her, it was Gerald—her husband.

For a moment she almost pulled away, but then the strange, unfamiliar heat began to course through her body again. Before she could stop herself, she was clinging to Gerald, pulling him close, and kissing him back with such passion that he was the one who pulled away in surprise.

He stared at her, and then he smiled in anticipation and his eyes asked the question again. Rachel nodded. The old world was swept away as though it had never been. Gerald took her hand. Rachel let go, opened her heart, and followed him into the darkness.

Part Two

The Prison

Too often, we make a prison of our dreams.

The Prison—From The Journals of Jenny Hershberger

Chapter Twenty

The Lie

Rachel sat propped up in her bed, looking out the ornate picture window in her private suite in the St. Clair mansion outside Greenwich, Connecticut. It was the first of November. The first winter storm had blown through during the night and dumped four inches of snow, and the grounds of the estate had been transformed into a wonderland. The snow had hidden the park surrounding the house, and the black wrought-iron benches that lined the path leading down to the ocean stood in stark relief against the soft, white blanket that covered the ground.

But Rachel could not see the beauty. Instead, she saw bare trees that rose like silent sentinels in a frozen world, naked branches raised in supplication as though imploring an unseen God for succor.

Like my heart.

A soft knock on the door roused her from her reverie.

"Mrs. St. Clair?"

Rachel turned at the sound of the voice. "Come in, Monique."

Rachel's French maid peeked her head around the corner, and then came in with a small tray. "Good morning, Mrs. St. Clair. I brought your coffee."

Rachel looked at the expensive silver pot and the cup made of white bone china. A picture came into her mind of her papa standing at the wood-burning stove in the kitchen in Paradise, pouring strong, black coffee out of the old aluminum coffee pot into big ceramic mugs and singing softly to himself. Her papa had a wonderful voice. Rachel remembered how he used to come into her room when she was a little girl, before the "gone" time. He would tuck her in and give her a good night kiss. Then she would take hold of the little finger of his strong hand and hold it tightly.

"Sing for me, Papa."

She recalled Jonathan's smile and his strength as he lifted her for a moment with his finger and then let her back down. Then his rich baritone filled the room as he sang. "*Loben wir ihn von ganzem Herzen! Denn er allein ist würdig.* Let us praise Him with all our hearts! For He alone is worthy…"

How she loved the *Lobleid*, the old praise song. Jonathan would sing it slowly and melodiously and she would feel herself beginning to slip into sleep. She would lift her tiny arms to him. "Now sing the other one, Papa. Mama's special song."

Jonathan would smile, wrap his arms around her and whisper in her ear. "All right, my darling girl, but just for you, because I love you almost as much as I love your mama."

And then he sang.

Tonight, I whisper in your ear, I always want you near, tonight
Tonight, I sing this song of love, You're the one I'm dreaming of
Tonight…

And Rachel would drift off to sleep, in the safest place that ever was—deep inside her papa's love.

"Mrs. St. Clair, your coffee?"

Rachel jolted back from her daydream. The girl was still standing next to her bed, holding the tray.

"Oh, I'm sorry, Monique. You can put it here by the bed, and please, call me Rachel."

"Yes, Miss Rachel."

Monique set the tray down and then turned to Rachel.

"Mr. Gerald wants to know if you are coming down for breakfast."

Rachel's heart twisted within her as she thought of Gerald. Gerald St. Clair, handsome, charming, beguiling, spoiled, petulant. Why had she rushed into marriage with this man before she really knew him?

The money, of course.

"Tell Mr. Gerald that I won't be coming to breakfast this morning. I'm not feeling well."

Monique nodded. "Shall I have the cook prepare you some soft-boiled eggs and toast?

"Yes, that would be nice."

Monique took the tray and left. Rachel roused herself from the bed and sat on the edge. She reached over and picked up her coffee, but before she could sip it, the strong smell twisted her stomach. She got up quickly and went into the bathroom. She stood by the toilet for a moment, and then she knelt down and threw up. She had been sick almost every morning for two weeks. At first, she thought she had the flu. But now she knew for sure what was happening. She sat on the edge of the huge tub and put her face in her hands.

Why wasn't I more careful?

And then the tears began to fall as she remembered Capri.

When Rachel had awakened after her night with Gerald, he was gone. In his place in the bed lay a single red rose and a note.

> *Rachel,*
>
> *Thank you for last night. It was truly delightful! If you're wondering why I'm not here, I've gone back to my room to change. The rose is the first of many. Please meet me for breakfast around ten and then we'll see the sights.*
>
> *Gerald*

She folded the note and leaned over to set it on the nightstand. Then she lay back on the pillow and stared at the ceiling. She wanted to feel like a new bride should feel after her wedding night—fulfilled and joyous. But instead, she felt only emptiness.

But it was all so wonderful last night. Why am I feeling like this?

She picked up the rose and smelled it, but it wasn't very fragrant. She closed her eyes and tried to bring back the memories of the night before, but strangely, the only image that came into her mind was the old chestnut tree on top of the knoll behind Daniel King's house. Her eyes opened in surprise and she stared at the ceiling again.

Why am I thinking of Daniel? I should be thinking of Gerald.

In the light of day, she didn't feel like she had the night before. The fire that had burned so fiercely in her body had dwindled down to ashes. As she lay there with her thoughts churning, she couldn't quite put her finger on what exactly she was feeling. And then in a moment of clarity she understood.

Regret! I regret what happened.

Remorse swept over Rachel like a huge, dark wall of floodwater. Something broke inside her heart, and she turned over and buried her face in the pillow. And then great sobs began to wrack her. She lay there for a long time, wrestling with the enormity of what had happened. She had given herself to a stranger. That precious gift she had saved all her life for the man God had for her had been tossed away in a moment of wine-induced desire. She felt violated and stupid and...

I feel like a prostitute. I sold myself for money!

Rachel finally stopped weeping and got up from the bed. She went into the bathroom and stared at herself in the mirror. Her eyes were red and swollen and there was no joy in her face. Her head hurt from the effects of all the wine and her body ached. She thought of Gerald waiting for her downstairs and a wave of revulsion swept over her.

She turned on the shower and stepped right in. The ice-cold water shocked her and cleared her head. She waited for a few minutes before she turned on the hot water. She stood under the water for a long time, but it did not make her feel clean.

Instead, shame swept over her, so intense that she had to lean against the wall to keep from falling. She roused herself and stepped out of the shower. A cool breeze from the sea floated in through the open window but it wasn't refreshing. It just chilled her, and she stood, shivering.

I'm so sorry, Lord. Please forgive me.

But there was no answer to her plea. She grabbed a towel, dried off and then went into the bedroom to dress. The rumpled bed, which had seemed so inviting last night, now gaped at her like an open mouth.

I have decked my bed with coverings of tapestry, with carved works, with fine linen of Egypt. I have perfumed my bed with myrrh, aloes, and cinnamon.

But my house is the way to hell, going down to the chambers of death.

She sat down on the bed and put her head in her hands. She wanted to pray, to throw herself on God's mercy—anything to take away the feelings she was having. But the words wouldn't come. Rachel hadn't talked to God in a long time.

After she got dressed, she made her way down toward the dining room. As she was walking through the lobby, she saw Adriano behind his desk. On a sudden impulse, she stopped and went over. The concierge was going over some paperwork that was spread out on his desk. He looked up and smiled at Rachel.

"*Buongiorno*, signora St. Clair. How are you this morning?"

Rachel got right to the point. "Adriano, you obviously know Mr. St. Clair very well. Has he been here often?"

The concierge looked uncomfortable. He hesitated for a moment and then answered. "*Sì, signora. Il signor Gerald è stato quello di farci visita diverse volte negli ultimi anni.*"

Rachel stared at him. Adriano shifted to English.

"Ah, excuse me. You do not speak our language. Yes, Mr. Gerald has been to visit us several times over the years."

"And did he bring women with him?"

Adriano spread his hands in a helpless gesture. Rachel stepped closer and spoke in low tones. "Adriano, I want you to know something. Mr. Gerald is not paying for this trip. I am, and I need you to answer some questions for me."

Adriano swallowed hard and nodded.

"Has Mr. Gerald brought women here before, and if so, how many?"

Adriano hesitated and then spoke. "Mr. Gerald comes twice a year. He started coming about five years ago when he was still in college."

"And the women?"

"Mr. Gerald always brings a woman—always beautiful, but always a different one."

Adriano hesitated and then went on. "You are the most beautiful of them all. When he introduced you as his wife, I was so happy to see that *si era sistemato e sposato*, ah, that he had finally *mettere la testa a posto*, how you say, was not so wild anymore, eh? Please don't say I have spoken to you, signora."

Rachel's heart pounded, but she tried to stay as calm as possible. "Thank you, Adriano. You have been most helpful. I will not betray you to Mr. St. Clair."

Rachel could see the appreciation in the man's eyes. She turned and walked toward the restaurant. When she went in, she could see Gerald sitting at a corner table. He was wearing white shorts, a blue shirt, and tennis shoes with a sweater draped around his shoulders. The dishes had been cleared from his table, and he was already sipping a glass of wine. Rachel walked up to the table. When he saw her, he stood up and smiled. "Good morning, Mrs. St. Clair.

He reached for her but she stepped back. "Gerald, I want to go home."

A blank look came over his face and he stared at her. Finally, he spoke. "Home?"

"Yes, I want to go home."

"You mean back to the hotel at Amalfi? But I thought you loved it here. And what about last night?"

Rachel raised her hand in a dismissive gesture. "Last night was a mistake that I...deeply regret. I realized this morning that I let you use wine and moonlight and this place to seduce me, and I am profoundly ashamed. And I don't mean that I want to go back the mainland. I want to go back to America—today!"

A strange look twisted Gerald's face, and then it was as if Rachel were seeing him for the first time. His mouth tightened.

"A mistake? No one ever called a night with Gerald St. Clair a mistake before."

His arrogance infuriated Rachel. "By 'no one,' I assume you mean the string of women you have brought here to conquer over the years. I must have been quite dull for you—a virgin who doesn't know the ropes in the bedroom."

Gerald's face clouded. "Well, you weren't exactly a professional—"

Before he could finish, Rachel reached over and slapped him hard across the face. Gerald's hand clenched into a fist, and he lifted it to strike her. Rachel could see the other patrons were staring at them. Gerald quickly put his hand behind his back. He spoke in a low voice.

"You are fortunate that there are people around, otherwise I would—"

"What? Beat me up and leave me here? I think I'm seeing you, really, for the first time. I don't know why I let you touch me."

Rachel saw rage grip him. Then his face became a stone mask.

"I'm Gerald St. Clair. Nobody slaps me."

Rachel put her finger on his chest and jabbed. Her voice was low and cold, and she felt strength in her that she had never known before. "The name Gerald St. Clair only means something now because I married you. Otherwise you would have squandered what meager inheritance you have left and then you would be Gerald Nobody. I may be a simple country girl, but I'm not stupid. Augusta would never have come looking for me if you people weren't in trouble financially."

Gerald's face paled under her onslaught.

Rachel bored in. "Let me explain this to you. The money belongs to me and I say how it is dispersed. If you want to continue living your degenerate lifestyle, that's up to you. But

I've got my own plans. I'm going to school in the spring. Now get your things. We are leaving."

Gerald looked at her helplessly. "But Grandmother always arranges everything…"

Rachel almost laughed. The man who had seemed to be so charming and poised was nothing but a lecherous little mama's boy. "All right, Gerald. I'll take care of it. You just run along and pack your bag."

Gerald gave her a look of pure hatred. "You'll regret this you…you…"

Rachel smiled sadly. "If you want to say 'whore,' go ahead. Because after last night, that's what I am."

Chapter Twenty-One

Deep Darkness

"What do you mean by 'financial technicalities,' Michel?"

Augusta St. Clair sat, fuming in her chair, listening to Michel Duvigney on her speakerphone.

"You must realize, Ms. St. Clair, that transferring the interest income from two hundred billion dollars in cash and various worldwide holdings into your accounts takes a great deal of effort and time. This whole business has taken us by surprise. After all, we never imagined that Robert had an heir, and you are directly responsible for that omission."

Augusta was not pleased at the answer. "Wait a minute, Michel. When I met Rachel's grandmother, I assumed that she was just another gold-digger after the money. How was I to know that the woman who showed up on my doorstep was really Robert's wife?"

Duvigney remained silent.

"And another thing. I thought that the money was held in trust."

Duvigney sighed and then responded. When he spoke her name it sounded like a snake hissing. "The money is held in trust, yes, that is correct, Ms. St. Clair."

Augusta glanced at Eva, her secretary. Eva scribbled something on a pad, stood up, and handed Augusta the note. Augusta squinted at it.

Don't get angry, Madam, your face is turning red. You know what the doctor said.

Augusta waved the fluttering woman away and asked another question. "If the money is in a trust, why don't you just make Rachel a trustee and let me, I mean us, control our own money."

Augusta could hear Duvigney sigh.

"The trust does not work that way, Ms. St. Clair. The principal of the St. Clair fortune is not transferrable. In other words, you cannot spend the inheritance; you can only receive the benefits from it. It was set up that way to keep the principal from being depleted in case the heir was profligate in his or her ways. And there are others who benefit from the principal that we must take into consideration. There are several lines in the St. Clair family, and all true St. Clairs benefit from the fortune.

"There are some cousins, and others, like yourself, who are widows of lesser heirs. And there are orphaned children of members of the St. Clair family who are receiving money from the smaller trusts that are drawn from the inheritance. Robert St. Clair's inheritance is only a portion of the total St. Clair fortune. Granted, it is the largest portion, but there is much more to this than just handing over a few bank accounts and some properties. Oh, no, Ms. St. Clair, we will not be making you a trustee. Besides, Rachel St. Clair is the heir, and she is the person with whom I should be having this conversation."

Augusta ignored the remark and pressed on. "And how does my grandson figure in all this?"

Another sigh from Duvigney. "If you wish an analogy that may help you understand, I will give you one. Rachel St. Clair is the heir. She fulfilled her obligations by marrying your grandson and taking the St. Clair name. Now all of her heirs will be St. Clairs and the fortune remains in the family. As for your grandson, Gerald St. Clair is like Prince Phillip of England. He is married to the Queen, but he is not the King. He is the Prince Consort. Oh, Phillip has an extraordinary income and high rank, as will Gerald, but Phillip does not have royal authority. That is held in Elizabeth's hands. And if she dies, the title will not pass to Phillip, but to Charles. At this point, that is Gerald's situation."

"What if Rachel should die?"

There was a pause.

"The estate passes to the eldest child, or to any one of her children with the Key."

"And if she dies and there are no children?"

"Then, and only then, Gerald St. Clair receives the income from the bulk of the St. Clair inheritance in his own name. However, if Rachel and Gerald do have children and if they ever divorce, then Rachel, having fulfilled her obligation under the terms of the inheritance, continues as the recipient of the income and passes it to her children, who would be considered legitimate St. Clairs. Gerald would receive an allowance, but he would basically be out of the picture."

Augusta stood up and began pacing. "Michel, it seems that the operative word here is recipient. That implies receiving, and to date, Rachel has received nothing. When is that going to change?"

"I have started that process and Rachel should be receiving the first check within a week. It will be drawn from the proceeds of some of the investments that I have transferred into Rachel's name."

And how much will that amount be?"

"Again, Ms. St. Clair, I should be having this conversation with Rachel."

"Rachel has given me power of attorney to act on her behalf, so you can talk to me, Michel."

There was a pause, and Augusta could tell that she had been put on hold. Then Duvigney's voice came back on the line. "If you will have your attorney send me those authorizations, I will then make a note in Rachel's file stating that you are a representative on her behalf."

"I sent them last week, Michel."

Augusta's face set like stone as she stared down at the phone. "Why do I get the feeling that you are stalling me?"

"I assure you, Mrs. St. Clair, that I am facilitating this process—"

Augusta interrupted him. "I may not be on your level, Michel, but I have many friends. I do not like to be trifled with. Rachel has authorized me to set up a joint account for her and Gerald, as well as an individual account for her. She wants part of the money placed in the joint account for the management of the estate and for Gerald's allowance. The rest will go into her private account. I would suggest that the first installments be put into those accounts as quickly as possible. I hope my friends don't have to intervene. Do I make myself clear?"

"Very clear, Augusta, but there is no need to pursue this matter. I have already sent a substantial check, and you should be receiving it within three days."

"And what do you consider to be substantial?"

"Around four million dollars."

"That's better. And I want an update next week as to the final resolution of the bulk of the estate. Good bye."

Augusta punched the speakerphone button. She turned to Eva. "Get Gerald down here, immediately. And then call Randall."

The calls had come in, just a few seconds apart. Randall sat in his apartment, watching the news and enjoying a very nice Zinfandel from California when his phone beeped quietly. His new caller ID showed Duvigney's phone number on the readout. He set the wine down, walked over to his desk, and picked up the receiver.

"Talk to me, Michel."

There was a short pause. Randall knew Duvigney was trying to figure out how he knew who the caller was. Then Duvigney began speaking.

"Randall, I've got a problem."

"I know. You wouldn't be calling if you didn't. Augusta is pressuring you to come up with the money. And, unfortunately, you don't have it available at this moment, due to your unwise investments and penchant for grand living. Am I right so far?"

There was another pause. Randall knew he was keeping Duvigney off-balance.

"The money is not gone, Randall. The principal of the estate is untouchable. It is held in several extremely stable, income-producing instruments. and the heirs enjoy the fruit of those investments. You are, however, correct in assuming that my firm made some unwise decisions and depleted the interest balance accounts for Robert St. Clair's portion of the inheritance. It will take some time for those funds to replenish themselves. In the meantime, I am keeping the St. Clair woman at bay by selling off some of my personal investments. But I think you understand that I cannot have her continue to pressure me. It would not be in the best interest of my firm if I had to open my records at this time. I was thinking that perhaps you might come up with a way to make the whole matter simply...disappear?"

"Well, well, Michel! I sense a bit of desperation here. You really are in a jam. I understand what you are proposing, and of course, it is not as simple as you think. The St. Clairs move in powerful circles. You will need to give me some time to come up with a solution."

Just then, a subtle click on the line let Randall know that another call was coming in.

"Hold on, Michel. I'll be right back."

Randall clicked over to the call that was waiting. "Gordon Randall Security."

"Mr. Randall, this is Eva Swanson, Augusta St. Clair's secretary. She wishes to speak with you."

"Tell Augusta that I will get right back to her. I'm on another call right now."

"Thank you, Mr. Randall."

The line clicked and Randall moved back to Duvigney's call. "Well, well. It seems that Augusta might be having some problems, too. Let me call her and then I'll get back to you.

Once I know what she's up to, I may have an answer to your dilemma."

"Very well, Randall, but don't keep me waiting."

"Not at all. Oh, and did I say that these kind of covert actions are very expensive?"

"How did I know that you were going to tell me that?"

"It's the nature of the beast. I'll call you soon."

Randall was amused. First Duvigney and then Augusta. Both of them needed his help quickly. That meant more money in his bank account. Duvigney's call was interesting, to say the least. The man was obviously worried. The old thief had probably been dipping into Robert St. Clair's estate for years.

And why not? There had been no known direct heirs when Robert St. Clair died. Only when Augusta had started pressing Duvigney for more money did the search for Rachel Borntraeger St. Clair and her daughter, Jenny begin.

Randall chuckled. Who could have guessed that a little Amish girl in a small Pennsylvania town would prove to be the heir to the great St. Clair fortune? Certainly not Duvigney!

Randall glanced down at the tape recorder on his desk to make sure the recording light was still on. Then he picked up the phone to call Augusta. This could prove interesting.

Gerald St. Clair sat stiffly in the chair across from his grandmother. Augusta could tell he was dying for a smoke, so she kept him waiting while she looked over some documents. Finally, Gerald spoke up. "Do we have some kind of a problem, Grandmother?"

Augusta looked up at her grandson. He was a true St. Clair. Devilishly handsome, a bottom-of-his-class graduate of the finest Ivy League prep school and college, accomplished tennis player, notorious womanizer, and altogether a totally non-productive, yes, even worthless, human being. Augusta sighed.

She wished that Gerald were more like Robert, Rachel's grandfather.

Robert St. Clair...The most beautiful man I ever met and the only one of the family with any gumption at all. What a team we would have made...

Yes, Robert had been the St. Clair worth catching, and she had made it very clear to him just how much she wanted to be with him. But he had spurned her. He fell in love with that Amish girl in Pennsylvania and married her. It was a bitter memory, for she had loved Robert passionately. And she could see Robert in Rachel. The same determination, the same passion...

"Grandmother?"

The apple doesn't fall far from the tree.

Then Augusta gathered her thoughts and smiled patronizingly at Gerald. Even with all his faults, she needed him. He was her only link to the St. Clair fortune. "Yes, dear, we do have a problem. I spoke with Duvigney today."

Gerald repositioned himself in the chair. "Well, what's the good news?"

"The good news is that he is sending us a check for four million dollars in the next three days."

Gerald scowled. "Only four million? We'll go through that in a few months. Where's my share of the big bucks? You promised me billions if I married Rachel."

Augusta got up and sat on the arm of her grandson's chair. She stroked his hair gently and gave him a kiss on the cheek. "There, there, darling. Your grandmother will come through for you. But there is a bit of a problem."

Gerald twisted away from Augusta's caresses. "And what might that be?"

Augusta got up and walked to the window. "It seems that even though you are married to Rachel, you don't really have any claim on the money as long as Rachel is alive. As Duvigney put it, she is the queen, but you are not the king."

Gerald reached toward his coat pocket for a smoke, but saw the warning in his grandmother's eyes and dropped his hand. "And if she dies?"

"Then you are the heir, but only if Rachel has no children."

Augusta paused and then came out with her question. "Have you fulfilled your...your husbandly duties yet?"

A strange look that Augusta could not read came over Gerald's face, and then he shrugged and smirked. "Grandmother, you're blushing. Of course I have. We are married, you know."

Augusta pointed at him. "You must stop those activities immediately. Rachel must not get pregnant. That would jeopardize our standing in the line of inheritance."

Gerald spread his hands. "You'll be happy to know that right now we're not sharing a bed. Rachel and I had a little tiff in Capri. She's a little distant right now, but I'm sure I can win her over."

Augusta sighed. "I don't think you will work it out, and the truth is, I don't want you to work it out."

"What do you mean, Grandmother?"

"Sometimes you can be very slow, Gerald. When Rachel came back from Capri, she told me that she will be submitting her application to veterinary school right away. With her money, I'm sure they will accept her. She will be moving to Ithaca in the spring. That means that you will be living on a simple allowance, which of course will not be enough to support us in the manner to which we are accustomed."

Gerald swore under his breath.

"It's probably for the best, Gerald. I don't want you to work it out. Go to your other women if you must fulfill your needs—but no more with Rachel. If you want to get your hands on the money, there must never be any children."

Augusta lowered her voice. "So you see, we have a problem to deal with that is not insurmountable. Rachel must never leave here. I have shared our little dilemma with Randall and he has assured me that he will find a solution."

Gerald's mouth dropped open and he stared at Augusta for a long moment. Then he shuddered. "Grandmother, you really are wicked, aren't you?"

Augusta turned to her grandson. "Yes, Gerald, I am very wicked. You can't even imagine how wicked I am. Always remember that."

Chapter Twenty-Two

The Guardian

Willy Oxendine sat looking out the front windows of the Old Greenwich Station in Greenwich, Connecticut. Most days his job as Station Master was fairly dull and so when the MTA afternoon train pulled in, he always played a little game as he watched the passengers get off. He tried to imagine where they were coming from, what they did for a living, and where they were headed. Of course, many of the passengers were from Greenwich and Old Greenwich, so he already knew their stories. That was why one passenger in particular caught his attention right away.

Hmmm. There's one that's not from around here...

Willy watched as the young man got off the train, turned up the collar of his dark pea coat, and looked around at the bustling crowd of commuters. The icy wind tugged at the coat, and Willy watched the young man button it even tighter around his neck. Then the stranger headed toward the red station building, his heavy canvas duffle bag leaving a trail of icy shards through the crusted snow as it dragged over the windblown hummocks. Willy kept an eye on the young man as he pushed through the lobby door and looked around. He stomped his feet and slapped himself with his arms to get the circulation going again.

Black watch cap, pea coat, duffle bag...maybe he's a sailor? Nope, doesn't have the swing in his walk.

The young man's cap was pulled down over his ears, and his face sported a two-day growth of blond beard. He walked straight over to the counter and looked Willy in the eye. "Excuse me, sir, but do you know of any folks who need an experienced stable hand?"

Willy gave him the once-over.

Ah-ha! Farm boy—lookit them hands. Seen a lot of hard work and that coat fits tight around them big shoulders. A hay-bucker if I ever seen one.

Willy looked up at the stranger's face. It registered in a good way—clean, honest, what ya see is what ya get kinda face, and Willy smiled. "Well, son, are you really good with horses? We got a lot of stables out here, lots of rich people that buy horses and don't know a dang thing about 'em."

"Yes, sir, I am very good with horses. Been around them all my life."

"You got any references? These folks are picky."

The young man hesitated and his face fell. "Well, sir, I didn't think to bring any when I left home. I...I had to leave in a hurry." Then he brightened. "But all I need is a chance to show somebody what I can do. I'm a hard worker and I'm dependable."

Willy stared hard at the honest face in front of him and right away he trusted it. "Okay, you don't look like a druggie or a thief. I'll take your word. Just so happens that Benny Peterson was in today and he's looking for another hand out at the St. Clair place.

A strange look crossed the young man's face. "St. Clair? I've heard of them. Very wealthy, aren't they?"

"That's right, son, very wealthy and very snooty. Young Gerald St. Clair just got married and his wife is a real looker. They're all staying up there right now. Gerald and his bride and that tarantula of a grandmother."

The old man looked around to see if anyone had overheard him. Then he picked up a pen and wrote something on a piece of paper. "Here's the address. 21445 Field Point Circle. Go around to the tradesman's entrance and tell them you want to see Benny. Tell him Willy at the station sent you. Oh, and what's your name?"

The young man hesitated. "Dan...David. It's David Kaufman."

The old man smiled and pointed across the street. "Okay, Dan David. Well, off you go. You'll have to find your own way out there. It's out at the end of Field Point Circle, right on the ocean—about a thirty-minute drive. Biggest place out there. There's a taxi stand right over there. I think it's only five bucks to get to St. Clair's. You got any money?"

The young man nodded. "Sure, I got some money..."

"But not a lot, right, kid?"

The young man grinned and shook his head.

The old man reached in his pocket and pulled out a twenty-dollar bill. "Here, this will get you out there and tide you over until you get paid."

"I can't take that, sir..."

"The name's Willy, and you can take it. I'm bettin' you'll get the job and then you can pay me back. I'm not going anywhere, so you know where I am."

The young man stuck out his hand and the two men shook. Willy pressed the money into the young man's hand.

"It's very kind of you, Willy. I'll pay you back soon."

Willy looked back down at his paperwork. "I know you will, son. Now get goin' or somebody else will get that job."

Forty minutes later, Daniel walked through the delivery gate at the St. Clair mansion. He asked a man shoveling snow by the gate where the stables were, and the man pointed silently toward the back of the property. In a few minutes, Daniel stood by the stable door, looking around at the magnificent estate. Off to the right, a huge stone house stood under sweeping elm trees. Meticulously tended grounds surrounded the house and everything seemed perfect and in order. Daniel looked in the wide front doors of the tall, white wooden barn. The long hallway inside ran the length of the building, and there must have been fifty stalls opening off the corridor. Daniel could hear horses nickering and the occasional whistle of a stallion.

Just then, a thin, wiry man with a ferret face walked briskly around the corner of the barn. He saw Daniel and stopped. "Wadda ya doin' here, buddy. Lost or somethin'?"

"I'm looking for Benny Peterson. Willy sent me. He said you were looking for some help."

The ferret-faced man looked at Daniel and then turned away. "Nah, we don't need any help. I don't know why Willy is always sending me charity cases."

Daniel stepped forward. "But he said you were looking for help. You are Benny, aren't you?"

Just then there was a loud crash from inside the stable. Someone shouted. Daniel and Benny ran inside. Down the long hallway they saw someone lying on the ground trying to hold onto the reins of a kicking, bucking horse. The animal had already knocked the door of his stall half off, and the man on the floor screamed for help. Benny pulled up short and grabbed Daniel. "Criminey, it's Diablo. I told Johnnie not to mess with him. That stallion is crazy."

Benny shouted at the man on the floor. "Johnnie! Don't try to hold him! Just get up out of there."

But the man on the floor stayed where he was. Then, before Benny could stop him, Daniel ran forward and grabbed the reins out of the fallen man's hands. He began to speak quietly to the excited animal as it reared up again. The man on the floor scooted away, leaving Daniel alone with the big stallion. Still speaking softly, Daniel inched closer to the horse. The animal began to calm, and soon he stood still. Then Daniel reached out slowly and put his hand on the stallion's face. The big horse snorted and then nickered. He stood still while Daniel began to rub his face and behind his ears, all the while talking in a quiet voice. In a moment, the huge animal was completely quiet.

Daniel looked at Benny. "Do you want him back in his stall?"

Benny's mouth hung open. He snapped it shut and pointed to an empty stall on the opposite side of the hallway. Daniel led the now quiet stallion inside and then closed the stall door and latched it. The big horse put his head out and Daniel stroked his face some more. Benny walked up. "Say, kid, where'd ya learn to do that?"

Daniel grinned. "I grew up on a farm. My dad raises the finest workhorses in Pennsylvania. Been around them all my life."

Benny put his hand to his chin. "What else do you know about horses?"

Daniel shrugged. "Like I said, I've been around them all my life. Anything that has to do with horses, I can do."

He turned to go. Benny quickly took him by the arm. "Hey, where ya goin', kid?"

"You said you didn't need anyone, so I better get back to town and see if anyone else is looking for help. I need a job."

Benny put his arm around Daniel's shoulder. "Now don't get all excited, buddy. How did I know you were some kinda horse whisperer? I actually could use another good hand, and if Willy liked you then I guess you're okay with me."

Daniel laughed. "He liked me well enough to loan me twenty dollars until I get paid."

Benny slapped Daniel on the back. "Okay, kid, you got the job. If Willy will part with a twenty, you must be all right. Get your gear and follow me. I'll show you where we bunk. Not real fancy, but the rooms are warm and the beds are comfortable...and we got our own kitchen. What did you say your name was?"

"I didn't, but it's David—David Kaufman."

"Okay, Davey-boy. We'll get you settled in and then you can get to work."

Daniel looked around. He breathed a silent prayer.

Danki, mein gnädiger Gott.

Daniel heard a soft voice answer back in his spirit.

You are welcome, Daniel.

Rachel sat at her desk, writing. She sighed and stopped. Then she crumpled up the paper and threw it in the wastebasket and started again. Then she sighed again and put her head down on her arms.

How can I tell Mama what has happened to me? I'm so ashamed. And besides, I'm shunned. They won't even open the letter.

The room suddenly seemed oppressive and close. Rachel's stomach churned. She got up and walked into her closet.

I need to get out and get some air...

She slipped on some jeans, a sweater, and a warm jacket. She wrapped a woolen scarf around her neck and pulled on a pair of warm, fur-lined boots. Then she went out through the French doors, onto the veranda outside her suite. The sun shone wanly through the clouds that hung in the gray sky. A few random flakes of snow were drifting down through the trees, carried in the arms of a brisk breeze, and the cold air slapped at her face like dead hands. Still, she felt better than she had in the overheated rooms of the mansion.

She walked along the path that led toward the tennis courts. A few leaves that had long passed beyond the flaming colors of fall were still clinging like dried pieces of skin to the branches of the trees. The snow had crusted, and the wind had sculpted the surface into haphazard hummocks. Away beyond the stables she could see someone working one of the horses in the exercise ring. For a moment she considered going over to the stables, but thought better of it. She wanted to be alone.

She had discovered a place earlier in the fall, an old caretaker's cottage that no one lived in out on the back part of the grounds. It had a wood stove and comfy old couches— much more to her taste than the overdone mansion. She headed toward the woods that surrounded the cottage. As she went past the trees that lined the entrance to the overgrown path, she saw a set of footprints in the snow. They were headed in the direction of the cottage.

I wonder who else knows about this place.

The last rays of the afternoon sun filtered through the trees, and the light in the woods grew dim. As she followed the footprints, she saw another trail of footprints come in from a side path to join the first set. She looked ahead through the trees and saw the cottage. Light shone in one of the windows.

A sudden caution gripped her and she stopped, wondering whether she should turn and go back to her rooms. But something pressed her on and she walked quietly up to the window and peeked in. At first she didn't see anything, but then movement caught her eye. Someone came out of the back bedroom. She ducked down and scooted behind one of the junipers that grew wild around the old cottage. She stayed that way for a moment and then she peeked up again. A man stood with his back to the window, looking toward the bedroom door. She couldn't see his face but she knew it was Gerald.

Rachel heard him say something to someone in the bedroom. Then she heard another voice—a woman's voice. She watched in dismay as the woman walked out of the bedroom, dressed only in her underwear. The woman stopped in front of Gerald and stood seductively for a moment before pulling a sweater on. It was Monique!

Then the maid walked up to Gerald and put her arms around his neck. His hands began to run over her body familiarly, and suddenly Rachel wanted to throw up. Gerald and Monique began kissing. They kissed for a long time and then Gerald pulled away, said something, and left Monique standing there as he headed for the door. She smiled after him and then bent down and picked up a pair of jeans from the floor by the bedroom door. The front door latch clicked and Rachel had just enough time to duck behind the bushes before Gerald came out.

From her hiding place she watched him as he glanced around and then headed off through the woods toward the mansion. Rachel watched him go and then peeked back in the window. Monique finished dressing. She had a satisfied smile on her face as she pulled on her coat and scarf.

Rachel couldn't stand it any longer. She turned and ran into the woods. She ran and ran. Branches whipped at her face and the trees loomed up like sentries, reaching for her as she ran and ran. Suddenly, her foot caught on an unseen root and she sprawled, face-first, in the snow. She lay there for a moment and then she threw up. Uncontrollable retching wracked her body. Finally, her stomach stopped churning and she got to her feet. The woods were dark and silent. The cold reached into her and she began to shake.

"Oh, God, oh, God, what have I done? Help me, please, help me. I need you so much!"

She felt weak and leaned against a tree. Then, softly and quietly, the words came.

I will never leave you nor forsake you.

Chapter Twenty-Three

Double Cross

The black BMW with the smoked windows drove up a hidden, tree-lined private driveway behind the St. Clair mansion. The snow creaked softly beneath the tires, the only sound to violate the perfectly still morning. The car eased to a stop and Gordon Randall stepped out. The sub-zero early November cold struck him like a fist, and he pulled the long, black cashmere coat tight around him to ward off the chill.

His professional gaze took in his immediate surroundings, and he instinctively looked for anyone hidden among the trees. Satisfied, he opened the back door, lifted his briefcase from the seat, and then walked briskly down a narrow paved path through the shrubbery to a small door set in an alcove in the side of the house. He glanced up and noted the small surveillance camera above the door. One of the wires attached to the back was hanging loose and Randall smiled to himself.

Amateurs!

Then he knocked twice. Augusta St. Clair opened the door. She smiled at him. The smile reminded Randall of a crocodile about to pull a wildebeest off the bank of an African river.

"Well, a personal greeting from the lady of the house. I must be moving up the food chain."

Augusta's smile disappeared. "I thought it would be best if you came in unobserved, since our business is so…personal. I gave most of the staff the day off. Please come in, Gordon."

Augusta motioned for Randall to enter and then led the way down a windowless hallway to a dark wood door. She opened it and ushered Randall in. She came in behind him. As the heavy door clicked shut, Randall felt a slight change in air pressure in his ears. Augusta motioned him into a chair and then went around the large oak desk and sat down. The room was paneled in dark wood with heavy beams crisscrossing the ceiling, and there was a small fire blazing in an iron-grated hearth in the wall. Books lined the shelves and there was a small, over-stuffed couch against the back wall with a side table and a reading lamp beside it.

"This is my private office. The window behind me is triple-pane glass and the door is hermetically sealed. The room is completely soundproof, so we can say whatever needs to be said in here."

Randall squeezed the handle of his briefcase and then set it on the floor next to his chair. He took a small notepad and a pen out of his pocket. "So, how may I be of service, Augusta?"

Augusta tapped her fingers on the desk for a moment. "This is a very delicate situation. I think you know most of the details since you were instrumental in helping us locate Robert St. Clair's heir. But to bring you up to speed, once we established that she had the Key and was the heiress, we were able to work out an arrangement with her."

"Yes, I followed the whole episode with interest. Rachel married your grandson and that allowed you to inherit the money."

Augusta nodded. "Yes, she did marry Gerald. The terms of the will dictated that any female heir who is not a St. Clair must marry an eligible St. Clair male to keep the money within the family. Gerald was that male. But you are wrong about the other assumption. Gerald does not have direct access to the money. His new wife is in control of where and how the money is dispersed. Of course, I have been able to act as her advisor on several matters but for the most part, she controls everything.

And since this was originally Robert's mansion, she is now the owner. If she ever divorces Gerald, we will be left with a pittance while she takes this house and the town house in New York City, not to mention several other properties of great value and the bulk of the income from the estate."

Randall nodded and made a note. "Well, Augusta, I'm beginning to see how difficult your situation is. I'm sure it's infuriating for you to have to go begging to a little country bumpkin every time you want to indulge your penchant for luxurious living. And isn't it true that if Rachel has children, Gerald is even further out of the picture?"

Augusta nodded again. "Yes, and despite our hopes when we met her, she has proven to be strong-willed, intelligent, and an independent thinker."

"In other words, you have discovered that she is not the simple little Amish girl you thought she was, and, contrary to your designs, you cannot manipulate her or control what she does with the money."

"You are as perceptive as ever, Randall. She and I have already had some clashes, and she is also discovering what kind of a person Gerald really is. I think she regrets her decision to marry him. I wouldn't be surprised if she decides to move out of here soon. So our dear, simple little Rachel has become a burdensome stone, as the Bible says.

"And you need to take that burdensome stone from around your neck, am I correct?"

"You are correct."

Randall made a note on his pad. "So, let me just put this as succinctly as I can. Instead of being your tool, Rachel has become an impediment to your plans to get your hands on the St. Clair fortune, and you wish me to devise a solution to your problem that will remove the impediment...permanently?"

"Yes, Randall, that is correct."

Randall closed the notepad and looked at Augusta. "Very simple problem, very simple solution—almost traditional in these cases. Arsenic poisoning. Small doses added to her food and in two to ten days she's gone."

Augusta scowled. "I'm not sure I like that idea, Randall. Won't people get suspicious?"

"When you contact me to solve problems, I cover all the bases."

Randall reached into his breast pocket and pulled out a piece of paper. He unfolded it on Augusta's desk. It was a newspaper clipping from *The New York Times*. He began to read:

U.S. Health Agency Declares Flu Epidemic

The Centers for Disease Control declared yesterday that a nationwide influenza epidemic exists and that it is the most widespread outbreak of the disease since 1984–85.

The flu, predominantly a strain called A-Shanghai, has been identified in every part of the country, and major outbreaks have been found in 35 states, epidemiologists at the centers say. Since reporting began, there have been 130 deaths attributed to the A-Shanghai flu nationwide.

"We're in an epidemic," said Dr. Walter Benson, a specialist in viral diseases in New York City.

"So you see, Augusta, it's simple. Rachel comes down with what looks like a flu bug, and five days later, she dies of A-Shanghai flu. You get your doctor to certify the cause of death and nobody is the wiser. You do own a doctor, don't you?"

"Yes, Randall, I 'own' a doctor. But usually he handles Gerald's miscalculations with married women. And what about her family? Won't they ask for an autopsy?"

"As I said, it's all very simple. Most Amish families will refuse or hesitate to solicit an autopsy of the deceased. Her parents will wish to have the body returned home as soon as possible so that family members can prepare it for burial. Then they perform the service and interment themselves. In three days she's buried and gone.

"As far as the means of death, arsenic has a somewhat sweet taste and a small amount can be added to food or drink without the victim noticing a thing. It's available commercially as rat poison, so you could keep it here on a large estate with horses and barns without suspicion. A very simple scenario: your granddaughter-in-law appears to catch the flu after a trip to the city, and five days later, your problem is solved."

Augusta looked hard at Randall. "And what part do you play in all this, Gordon?"

"What part do I play?"

"Yes. You see, I have no one here who has...shall we say, the professional expertise to handle this situation. I will need you to manage it for me."

Randall frowned. "I am available for this kind of operation, but the fee is extremely high. If you can meet my price, I'll come back in two days."

Randall wrote a number on a page in his notebook, tore off the page, and passed it across the desk.

Augusta's eyes widened. "One hundred thousand dollars!" She swallowed and then nodded.

Randall made another note in his book. "I will need a deposit today—say, half of the amount. The rest will be made available to me before I leave. You can tell your staff that you have had a few threatening calls, and you have brought in a security expert. Set me up in a nice suite somewhere out of the way. I'll be bringing a few of my special ops guys to put up a security shield around the operation. So I'll need a place for them also. I'm going to clamp a tight lid on this place, so order a week's worth of supplies out here. Anything else?"

"Gerald will help you."

"Gerald?"

"Yes. If my grandson is so eager to be a billionaire, he can get his hands dirty. He's a very bright boy and very willing to participate. I understand he's not too happy with his wife at the moment. All you need to do is 'train' him. I want his fingerprints all over this...operation. Do you understand?"

Randall stood and picked up his briefcase. He shook his head and laughed. "Forgive me for underestimating you, Augusta. You cover all the bases, don't you?"

"Yes, Randall, I cover all the bases. You and your men can use the old caretaker cottage at the back of the estate. Follow this driveway about a quarter of a mile when you return. You'll see an overgrown road on the right. Turn in there and the cottage is straight ahead. There is a bunkroom and it's heated. Bring your own supplies. I don't want anyone to know you are there. Oh, there's one more thing."

Augusta held out her hand. "Leave the notebook with me, Gordon. I'm sure a man of your skills has a perfect memory, and I don't want any incriminating evidence hanging around that might cause me embarrassment in the future."

Randall smiled. "If we're partners, shouldn't we trust each other?"

Augusta's face turned to flint. She reached in her desk and pulled out her checkbook. She wrote out a check, tore it off, and held it up. "It's not that I don't trust you, Gordon. It's just that I don't *really* trust you. I'll trade you this check for that notebook."

Randall shrugged, took the check, and handed over the small book. Augusta stood up and led him to the door.

"Down the hall to the right and out the door you came in. I'll see you in two days."

Randall nodded and left. As he walked down the hall, he squeezed the handle of his briefcase again. He felt the recording device inside vibrate and click off. Randall smiled to himself. He went out the door, climbed into his car, and drove away.

Rachel awoke the morning after she had seen Gerald with Monique. Her heart was filled with shame at what she had become. She lay in her bed for a long time, wondering what to do. Finally, a thought came to her.

I haven't prayed in a long time.

She slipped off her bed onto her knees. She felt strange and disconnected and awkward, but there was no one else to talk to. She bowed her head and tried to pray, but for some reason, the words would not come. She just did not know where to start. And then she remembered a scripture her mother kept on a little hand-stitched plaque on the kitchen wall in their home in Paradise.

If we confess our sins, He is faithful and just to forgive us our sins, and to cleanse us from all unrighteousness.

Another picture came into her mind. She was five years old and she was sitting on the grass under the old apple tree in their back yard. Her papa was sitting next to her and they were both munching the crispy last bites of a McIntosh apple from the tree over their heads. Her papa's arm was around her and they were enjoying the bright sun and warmth of an Indian summer day in Pennsylvania. All around them the trees were clothed in a riot of fall colors; orange, red, yellow, golden. White, fluffy clouds sailed the azure sky above. Rachel turned to her papa.

"Papa, what are the *Ordnung*? I hear the other kids talking about them and they sound scary."

Jonathan pulled his girl closer. "Ah, the *Ordnung*. Well, my darling girl, the *Ordnung* are something very special to the Amish people. Sometimes it is hard to understand why we are so different from everyone else, but here is why that is. We live differently than most of the other people in the world because we want to separate ourselves from the things of life that hurt us. So we have the *Ordnung* to guide us if we ever have questions about how we should behave when something happens and we need help to know what to do. I guess the best way to think of them is that the *Ordnung* are a way to arrange everything about the way we live so we have boundaries and guidelines to help us behave the way God wants us to."

Rachel remembered being puzzled. "What are bounaries, Papa?"

Jonathan pointed at the field where their sheep were grazing. "Boundaries, little one." He smiled. "Do you see the sheep in the field, Rachel?"

Rachel nodded.

"Well, the sheep need to stay in that field because they belong to us. If they got into someone else's field, they might eat their garden or wreck something. So what is it that keeps our sheep in our field?"

"The fence, Papa."

"That's right, Rachel, the fence. The fence is a boundary. It keeps the sheep where they belong. The Bible says that we are God's sheep. Now, God does not put us in a field and put a fence that we can see around us, but He does give us His Word and when we read the Bible, we learn how God wants us to behave and in that way, He sets a fence around our hearts. If we go outside that fence, we end up somewhere that God knows we do not belong."

"Is the Bible the *Ordnung*, Papa?

"No, little one. The *Ordnung* are not written down. Over the years, the men who lead our church have read the Bible and then they have decided on a way to behave that the church follows by learning it from those who go before, like *grossdaadis* and *grossmutters*."

Rachel pondered that for a moment. "Then, when we stay inside the boundaries, does that make God like us better?"

Jonathan laughed. "So many questions, my little curious one! No, Rachel, keeping the rules does not make God like us better. What makes God so very happy is when we let His Son, Jesus, come into our hearts. The boundaries, the *Ordnung*, are like a sign-post that tells us the right way to go. But they don't get us to where we are going. We need Jesus to do that for us. Let me explain…"

And so, for the first time in her life, Rachel heard the wonderful story of salvation from her beloved papa as they sat in the grass eating apples. And when Jonathan was finished, Rachel took his hand and looked up at him shyly.

"Papa, I want Jesus to live in my heart and help me to be good always."

And then her beloved *daed* held Rachel in his arms and helped her to pray the prayer of salvation.

And then came the "gone" years when her papa disappeared and they thought he was dead. Then he came home, but somehow he wasn't really her papa anymore. And he didn't talk about Jesus so much, but he mostly talked about the *Ordnung* and how Rachel was not keeping the *Ordnung* the right way. And something in Rachel broke, and she forgot about the boundaries and the Savior who had been in her heart since that day so long ago. And she began to live her life for herself.

And now she was kneeling beside a strange bed in a strange house, married to a man that hated God, and she was pregnant with his child. As she knelt beside the bed, she laid her head in her arms and began to weep. And she called on the name of her Savior, and for the first time in many years, she felt the sweet presence of the Lamb of God. As she opened her heart and told Him all of her troubles. The tears flowed from her eyes, and something inside her started to thaw.

Then, like the frozen streams of the Northland that feel the warmth of the spring sun, throw off the steel grip of winter and break free of the ice that holds them motionless and still, the river of life slowly began to make its way through her broken heart, and Rachel felt the love of her Lord and the soft touch of His nail-scarred hand.

Chapter Twenty-Four

The Plot

Rachel got up from beside her bed. She didn't know how long she had been kneeling there. Her legs were stiff and her back ached, but, for the first time in years, her mind was at peace. As for her problem with Gerald and Monique, she knew what she had to do. She went to her closet and found a plain skirt and a blue cotton blouse. In the bathroom, she washed her face but did not put on any makeup. When she was finished, she went back into the bedroom and dialed the kitchen. Collins, Augusta's butler, answered the phone.

"Yes, Ms. Rachel."

"Collins, I want you to send Monique to my room."

"She'll be right up, ma'am."

Rachel waited until the knock sounded on the door. "Come in, Monique."

The maid peeked around the door with a puzzled look on her face. "You are up early, madam. I usually don't come up until 7:00 o'clock Can I get you something?"

Rachel shook her head and pointed to a chair. "Sit down, Monique."

The girl sank into the chair across from Rachel. She started to say something, but Rachel put up her hand and the words died on Monique's lips.

"Monique, it's hard for me to say this. I am very angry with you."

Monique squirmed in her chair. "But why, madam?"

Rachel sighed and looked down at her hands.

What has happened to me? I used to live a peaceful life on a farm...

Then she looked back at her maid. "I know about you and Gerald. I was at the cottage last night and saw the two of you after you...well, after you were...together."

Monique's face turned pale. She started to say something, and again Rachel stopped her.

"There is nothing to say, Monique. I understand why you could be led astray by Mr. Gerald's persuasive ways, but the truth is, you didn't have to let him. You didn't have to..."

Rachel felt her face burning with embarrassment. "I want you to leave this house. Today!"

Tears welled up in Monique's eyes. "Leave this house? But madam, I have no place to go."

In spite of her anger and shame, Rachel's heart went out to the girl. She hated Gerald for what he had done. "Monique, this is for your own good. Gerald will only use you and then throw you away."

The girl couldn't meet Rachel's gaze.

"Monique, you need to leave immediately. Collins will drive you into town. I will ask Augusta to arrange for a hotel room in the city for you until you find work."

Monique wiped her eyes and then gave Rachel a haughty look. "But Mr. Gerald, he will be so angry. He will find me. He loves me."

Rachel's mouth dropped open in surprise. Monique stood up and pointed a finger at Rachel, and then acid-laced words spilled out of her.

"Maybe you are the one who should leave. Mr. Gerald is right. He says you are very mean to him and will not do what a wife should do. He will divorce you and marry me. I give Mr.

Gerald what he needs. He loves me, not you. I will be his wife and make him happy."

Monique stood there with a smug, self-satisfied look on her face.

Rachel put her face in her hands for a minute. Then she looked up. "Monique, you're a foolish, gullible girl. Gerald doesn't love you and he never will. You are just one in a long parade of women that he has used for his own satisfaction over the years. And there is something that Gerald obviously did not explain to you. He has no money. The money is all mine. This house belongs to me, the house in New York belongs to me— it's all mine, Monique. If Mr. Gerald divorces me and marries you, he will have nothing. You will live in poverty."

Monique drew herself up. "That is a lie! Gerald is rich, he told me—"

"Monique! Listen to me! Gerald has some money from his trust, but it's not very much and he will run out in a few years. He told you he was rich to get you into his bed. Don't you see? Gerald will never divorce me because I am his ticket to the lifestyle he loves."

Rachel stood up. She was trembling. "Monique, I want you out of this house in an hour. It may be true that I am not a good wife, but that does not give you an excuse to be Gerald's plaything behind my back. We'll find you a place to stay. Once you're gone, you might keep sneaking around and seeing Gerald, but you won't do it under this roof. Now go!"

The girl spun around and marched toward the door. Before she left she turned to Rachel. There was a challenge in her eyes and a smirk on her lips. "We will see what Mr. Gerald says when he hears you are sending me away."

Then Monique flounced out of the room. Rachel sank back down in her chair. She was shaking like a leaf and the room was spinning.

This can't be happening to me…

After a long time, Rachel pulled herself together and called Gerald's room. When he answered the phone, his patronizing voice grated on her like a carrot on a metal scraper.

"Well, good morning, Rachel. How's my darling wife?"

Rachel could almost see the smirk on his face. She got right to the point. "Gerald, I know all about you and Monique."

There was indifference in his answer. "So I heard. She came tearing in here like a nor'easter off the sound. It was most upsetting. I will probably have to take a valium to settle down."

"You don't sound too upset, Gerald."

There was a laugh from Gerald's end. "The truth is, I'm not. Actually, you did me a big favor in kicking her out. Monique was getting a little...clingy. Pressing me, and all that."

Rachel could hardly believe what she was hearing. "But, Gerald, you seduced her. You made promises to her..."

"Oh, those. Sometimes you have to stretch things a bit to get what you want."

"But that poor girl thinks you are in love with her. You used her, like you used me, just to satisfy your own lust. You're unbelievable!"

Rachel blinked back her tears. She felt trapped. Gerald's voice was hard, grinding into her like a dentist's drill.

"Don't play so high and mighty, Rachel. You didn't have to marry me, but you did. You didn't have to sleep with me, but you did. You could have stayed a good girl and passed on the whole deal. You could have lived out your life in your plain black dress, riding around in your rickety old buggy, but you wanted the money, so we made a bargain. You lusted after the money the same way I lusted after Monique. There's really no difference between you and me, now is there?"

Rachel took a deep breath. Rage rose inside her; rage at Gerald's indifference, rage at her own foolishness. Suddenly, she was screaming at him over the phone. "You are right. I'm no better than you, but I'm going to do something about it. Gerald, I'm divorcing you and I'm going home. I'm not going to raise my baby in this horrible place!"

There was a gasp of surprise from the other end of the line. "Your what?"

"My baby! I'm pregnant. I'm having your baby. It happened that night in Capri."

Rachel began sobbing. "I thought you loved me, but you just wanted sex. I was so foolish. I feel like a prostitute. My mama and papa were right. The world is a horrible place."

There was a long silence and then Gerald spoke. "Calm down, Rachel. Give me a minute..."

Rachel heard Gerald take a deep breath.

"This is a bit of a mind blow, and I'm not sure how I feel about it. You being pregnant changes things. I may be a jerk, but I do have some feelings. After all, it's my child, too, and it is a St. Clair. Can we talk about this when we calm down a bit? I don't really want you to divorce me. I...well, you might not believe this, but I do have feelings for you. Maybe I can change."

Rachel was caught off-guard. It was the first honest thing she had ever heard him say. She didn't trust Gerald, but he was right about the baby. She hesitated and then replied.

"All right, Gerald, we can talk, but don't expect much to change. I don't trust you at all."

Gerald's voice was soothing and contrite.

"I totally understand, Rachel. Give it a day or two and then let's talk this over like sensible people."

Augusta was in the barn, looking over her Arabian horses when Gerald caught up with her. He grabbed her arm and pulled her aside.

"Grandmother, I have to talk with you...privately!"

Augusta could tell her grandson was upset. She handed the reins of her stallion over to the young man who was helping her. She waved her hand imperiously.

"Take this horse back to his stall and make sure he's fed and watered."

The young, bearded man nodded in the affirmative. "Yes, Mrs. St. Clair, right away."

Augusta stopped the stable boy. "I haven't seen you around here before? What's your name?"

"I'm David, ma'am. David Kaufman. Benny hired me a few days ago."

Augusta scrutinized the bearded face. The young man looked familiar but she could not place him. "Well, if Benny hired you, you must be good with horses."

"Yes, ma'am, I am."

Gerald was standing there, obviously fuming. Augusta loved letting him know who was in charge. Finally, she let the young man leave and turned to Gerald. "Now, dear, what is it that seems to be troubling you?"

Gerald pulled her arm again. "Not here, Grandmother. Someone might hear us."

He pulled her into one of the empty stalls and then lowered his voice. "Grandmother, I have some disturbing news. Rachel says she is divorcing me."

Augusta scowled. "What precipitated this hasty action on her part, Gerald?"

Gerald twisted his hands awkwardly. "She...she caught me messing around with Monique. I guess my infidelity meant something to her. She's pretty upset."

Augusta raised her hand in a dismissive gesture.

"It's not something we need to worry about."

"Grandmother, that's not all."

"Not all? What is it then?"

"Rachel is pregnant!"

"What?"

Augusta stared at Gerald's face. Despite the cold, he was sweating.

"Rachel is pregnant."

Augusta looked at Gerald for a long moment and then slapped him, hard. The sound of her hand was like a whip crack. "You stupid fool! I told you to leave her alone."

Gerald rubbed his face and looked down. "When you told me that, it was already too late. She got pregnant in Capri. We only were together once..."

Augusta stared at Gerald as he cowered before her.

He really is a pitiful human being. If I could do this without him, I'd have Randall take care of him, too.

She sighed and took him by the arm. "Come with me, Gerald."

"Where are we going?"

Augusta put her arm around Gerald's shoulders. "I just want you to know that you are very fortunate to have someone watching over your interests."

"What do you mean, Grandmother?"

"I have already anticipated this situation and taken steps to remedy it."

Gerald stopped and pulled away. "Remedy? How can you remedy this? We're in big trouble here. She wants to divorce me."

Augusta opened the stall door and looked up and down the hallway. The barn was quiet, except for the occasional nicker of a horse and the cooing of the pigeons huddled above in the rafters. She turned back to Gerald.

"Our friend, Gordon Randall, and I have worked out a solution to all of our problems. He is coming for a brief stay. He will be here tonight. During that time you are going to be his assistant in facilitating the quick and unsuspicious demise of your obstinate wife."

"Assistant?"

Augusta stepped up close to Gerald. Her voice was like icy daggers ripping at him. "Yes, assistant, you helpless little pipsqueak. You keep pushing me to get the money. Well, there's only one way to get it, and you're going to be in it up to your eyeballs. You're going to poison your wife and we're going to make it look like she got a very virulent form of A-Shanghai flu. It should take about five days. Dr. Schumacher will certify the cause of death, and her Amish relatives will never ask for an autopsy. They don't believe in them. So Rachel will die, we'll ship her back to Pennsylvania, and you will be the heir."

"But, what about the baby?"

"Collateral damage. Can't be helped."

Gerald looked about the room as if trying to see a way to escape. "Look, Grandmother, I don't think I can go through with this."

"And why not?"

"Something's changed in my life. For the first time I've found a girl who is real, and pure, and honest. I've never known anyone like her. And now she's having my baby. I can't hurt her. I...I love Rachel.

Augusta's hand lashed out again and Gerald withered under the blow.

"Now you listen to me, you weak little boy. If I didn't need you I would have figured out a way to take care of you years ago, and you wouldn't be the first St. Clair I've dealt with."

Gerald went pale. "What do you mean, I wouldn't be the first one?"

"That, my dear grandson, is none of your business. As far as Rachel is concerned, I want you to understand something. Your life is worth nothing and you are standing on very shaky ground. I want that money and I want it now. That means Rachel has to go. If you mess this up, I will see you dead before you touch another dime of St. Clair money."

Gerald tried to take a stand. "You won't kill me, Grandmother, you need me. You can't get the money without me."

Augusta laughed out loud. "You're a fool, Gerald. The difference between you and me is that I see the whole picture, and I make preparations for the future. You're just a grasshopper, living from day to day. Do you really think that I don't have other options—that I have put all my eggs in the untrustworthy basket named Gerald St. Clair?"

She laughed again. "If you think that, you really are a fool. Now, if you want to live, you'll come with me and not say another word. And tomorrow morning you will begin the treatment that will resolve our dilemma. Do you understand me?"

Gerald's face was white. Augusta patted him on the face, but it was still a slap. "Gerald, my foolish, foolish boy. You need to understood how far your grandmother will go to achieve her purposes. Augusta could see the fear in his eyes.

He capitulated. "Yes, Grandmother."

Augusta smiled sweetly. She patted his face again. This time it was a caress. "That's better, dear. You just trust your devoted grandmother, and we'll see to it that you're well taken care of."

She took Gerald by the arm. Together they walked out of the stall, down the hallway and out through the big doors.

The barn was silent for a few minutes, and then the door of the tack room next to the empty stall, where Augusta and Gerald had been, creaked open. Daniel peeked out and then slipped out of the room and walked quickly through the barn and out the back door.

Chapter Twenty-Five

The Key

Jenny Hershberger stood at the window of the little blue farmhouse in Paradise, Pennsylvania. Outside, gray clouds scudded across the sky, signaling the coming of another storm. The chill wind had piled the snow from the last nor'easter high along the fences that marked the lane leading out to Old Leacock Road. Bare, brown trees painted with white frost lined the lane. A pine siskin sat on a branch of the dormant plum tree by the porch, waiting for someone to replenish the seeds in the bird feeder. Its chirping did not dispel the gray clouds, but it seemed oblivious to that and continued singing its plaintive song. Pennsylvania lay in winter's icy grip, but for Jenny, the winter was in her heart.

The sound of someone tramping onto the porch drew her away from her vigil, and she looked out the half-circle window that graced the one hundred-year-old, handmade door. Bobby Halverson was out on the porch stomping the snow off his boots. His old dog, Rufus, whined and fussed, anxious to get inside out of the cold. Jenny opened the door and motioned them both in, but not before an icy blast chilled the air in the entryway. Rufus trotted past Jenny and headed straight to the fireplace where he lay down as close to the burning logs as he could. Jenny looked up at her old friend. Bobby reached out, and then Jenny was inside the circle of his arms, weeping.

Bobby patted her awkwardly on the back until her sobs stopped. Jenny pulled a handkerchief from her pocket and wiped her eyes. She smiled at Bobby. "Sorry, Uncle Bobby. I'm still pretty *umkippen* over everything that's happened with Rachel. Come in and sit down. I'll get some coffee."

From the kitchen, Jenny saw Bobby sit down in a chair close to the fire. He held out his hands to the warmth. Rufus looked up and whined again. Bobby patted him on the head. "Yes, boy, it is cold. Our old bones can feel it today, can't they?"

Rufus inched closer to Bobby and put his head up for more rubbing. Jenny found Bobby sitting there, staring into the flames and absentmindedly stroking his dog when she returned with two mugs of steaming coffee.

"Sugar and cream, just like you like it, Bobby."

Bobby took the proffered mug and spoon and stirred the coffee a few times. Jenny sat down on the couch that was pulled up close to the fire, and the two sat there for a while, sipping the hot brew.

"Where's Jonathan today?"

Jenny sighed. "He's lying down. He got another migraine. They pretty much knock him flat." There were a few moments of silence, and then Jenny spoke again. "Bobby, what am I going to do?"

"Have you heard from our girl?"

Jenny sipped her coffee as she stared into the fire. "We heard from Rachel right after she got married. Gerald was taking her to Europe on a honeymoon. Her letter sounded cheerful enough, but I know my daughter. Underneath the excitement about going abroad, there was uncertainty. I think she was realizing what a mess she has made of her life. Jonathan was glad to get the letter, but the next day, he was in one of his moods and sent it back with a note reminding Rachel that she was under the *bann* and that we could not communicate with her. We haven't heard from her since."

Jenny got up and went to the window again. She looked out on the snow-covered yard. The past few months had taken their toll. She could see herself reflected in the glass, and there were new wrinkles in her once-smooth skin.

I'm aging every day. My hair is turning gray...

She turned back to the fire. "I feel old, Bobby. And I can't get anything done. I just stand here at the window, hoping I will see Rachel trudging down the lane carrying some sick animal she wants to take care of, or coming home from *schule* with an exciting discovery to share with me. It's a good thing it's winter and everything is on hold. If I'm like this in the spring, this farm will fall to pieces."

"What about Daniel King?"

"No one has heard from him. His *daed* came by after Daniel left. They had an argument over Rachel, and he thought Daniel might be staying here. I guess Rachel sent Daniel a letter and Daniel responded. He's such a good boy and he's loved Rachel since they were little, so he isn't about to let the *meidung* keep him from looking after her. Jonas tried to get Daniel to forget Rachel, but Daniel loves her too much. Daniel was very upset by the letter and worried about Rachel. He just packed up his clothes one morning and left. I think he followed her to New York."

Jenny set down her cup and put her face in her hands. After a moment she looked up at Bobby. "What has happened to my life? It used to be so peaceful here. The three of us were together on the land. We were always happy and Rachel loved her papa so much. I felt every day that *du leiber Gott* was walking with us, guiding us, and leading us. Then Jonathan disappeared and we went home to Ohio. And then Mama and Papa died. And when Jonathan came home, everything was different. It just seems that the Lord is so very far away. I don't know what to do..."

Jenny's voice trailed off and silence filled the room.

Bobby sat for a long time and then he spoke. "You don't sound like the Jenny Hershberger I know."

Jenny looked up in surprise.

Bobby went on. "The Jenny Hershberger I know has never ever quit, or whined, or complained. She takes the good with the bad and somehow finds a way to overcome all obstacles. And for an old agnostic like me, the one bright spot in my own search for meaning in life has been to watch my Jenny standing strong in her God. You've changed, Jenny. It seems like you stopped trusting God when Jonathan came home. You started trying to do everything on your own. I don't know much about how God works, but what little I do know about Him, I learned from your dad and mom and you and Jonathan. I know this is a long speech for me, but don't you think you should ask Him what to do instead of coming to a broken-down old Marine who can only shrug his shoulders when you ask?"

Jenny sat with her mouth open, staring at Bobby. He smiled and reached over to pat her arm. "Didn't expect that, did you? I'm just trying to say that it seems like you've given up on life. Why, I remember that when hard times came, the first place your mama, Jerusha, went was to her knees. I'm just making a suggestion that you might have gotten away from the source of your own strength."

Jenny sat for a long time and then she smiled back at Bobby. "Uncle Bobby, I didn't know you knew so much about our faith. You've always said that it was good for us, but you weren't interested."

Bobby ran a hand through his thinning hair and took a sip before he answered. "Look, Jenny. I never said I wasn't interested—I'm just kinda slow when it comes to these things. But I have learned this. You can't hang around Christians for the better part of your life without something rubbing off. I'm in my 80s now, and when you get to be my age, you start to understand that you are closer to the end than the beginning. I've seen enough to know that you can't wait to be a deathbed penitent, because you never know when you might come face-to-face with your own mortality. You would think I might have learned that in World War II, but somehow I forgot."

"Uncle Bobby, you sound like you have made some kind of decision…"

"Well, we will talk about that later. Right now, I want to know what you are going to do to get yourself out of this funk."

Jenny stood up. "You are right, Uncle Bobby. *Sie schlagen den Nagel auf dem Kopf.*"

Bobby smiled again. "So I hit the nail on the head, eh?"

"And you've picked up a little German along the way, also?"

"Some."

Jenny went and knelt by Bobby's chair and put her arms out. He reached out and put his arms around her. They stayed that way until she raised herself back up.

"You are right, Uncle Bobby. I've forgotten about prayer. I've been so focused on keeping everything organized that I forgot I'm not in charge. The Lord showed me that a long time ago when I was trapped in that cave waiting for my papa to come for me."

A voice behind them spoke. "I was there, too, Jenny."

Jenny looked around.

Jonathan was standing in the doorway. "I remember how it all happened. God kept showing Himself to me through miracle after miracle. The way I came to Apple Creek and met you, the way we rescued you from the gang that was chasing me, the way we found your birth mother; those were the things that opened my eyes to the truth that I needed Jesus in my life."

Jonathan walked into the room and came around the couch to face Jenny. "I haven't been a good husband or a good father for a long time, Jenny. I've been using my injury as an excuse to withdraw from you and Rachel. Now Rachel's gone because of me. Before I met Jesus, we used to laugh at Christians and tell them to stop beating us with their Bibles. Now I realize that is exactly what I've been doing to Rachel. The *Ordnung* does not save us. I used to know that, but somehow I forgot. I need your help, wife, to remember."

Jenny took Jonathan in her arms. Her heart went out to the gentle man who had suffered so much.

Then Jonathan stepped back and looked into Jenny's eyes. "I want to share something I believe the Lord showed me today when I was reading."

He went into the bedroom and came back with his Bible. He motioned Jenny to the couch and sat beside her. He opened the Bible and began to read: "Proverbs 12:25 says, 'Anxiety in the heart of man causes depression, but a good word makes it glad.'"

Then he turned to another section and read again: "Philippians 4:6-7 says, 'Be anxious for nothing, but in everything by prayer and supplication, with thanksgiving, let your requests be made known to God; and the peace of God, which surpasses all understanding, will guard your hearts and minds through Christ Jesus.'"

Jenny looked wonderingly at her husband as the Word sank into her heart.

Jonathan put the Bible down and took Jenny's hands. "I've been acting like some kind of a religious zealot. I've been strutting around, spouting the rules and there has been no place for grace in my heart. I have forgotten the way *Gott* has worked in our lives to restore our family. I have been depressed and I didn't know why. And then I read these verses and it became very clear to me. I'm anxious—anxious about everything. I'm afraid that I'm going to lose my mind or have a stroke or worse. And that has been making me depressed. And then I get *verrückt*, crazy and cranky and...oh, Jenny, I've been miserable to live with."

Tears welled in Jenny's eyes. She reached out and softly touched the cherished face.

"But then I read the last part: '...a good word makes the heart glad.' And then I remembered Philippians: 'Be anxious for nothing...' The Bible tells us, commands us, not to be anxious."

Jenny went on for him, quoting the beloved verse. "'...in everything by prayer and supplication, with thanksgiving, let your requests be made known to God; and the peace of God, which surpasses all understanding, will guard your hearts and minds through Christ Jesus.'"

Jonathan nodded. "Yes, Jenny, don't you see? We haven't been praying and it's my fault. I'm the head of this house. I need to lead you in prayer. And we need to make our needs known to God, with thanksgiving. And then we will have the peace that we need."

Jenny sat in amazement, looking from Bobby to Jonathan. And then, in a moment of understanding, she knew that God was working in her life once again. Another favorite scripture came to her mind. She spoke it softly. "'I will enter His gates with thanksgiving in my heart; I will come into His courts with praise.'"

Jonathan looked up. "Yes, Jenny, that's it. He's given us the key all along. He wants us to come into His presence and He has shown us the way. Prayer, thanksgiving, and praise will lead us right into His throne. Oh, Jenny, I'm so sorry."

Suddenly Bobby laughed out loud. "Hallelujah!"

Jenny and Jonathan stared at him.

"I feel like I'm in a revival meeting. It hasn't been like this in this house for a long time."

As Jenny sat there in the glow of what God was doing, a picture came to her mind. It was the second time she had remembered the Key, the one her mama had sewn almost prophetically into the Rose of Sharon quilt...

"...You do not know which pieces of your life you will discover tomorrow, but they are there, determined by *die Vorkenntnisse des Gottes*. He has already planned them. Now let me show you one more thing as a reminder."

Jerusha moved the quilt until the rose was under her hand.

"Look! Do you see it?"

Jenny looked, and there it was! Sewn into the center of the rose—the small, key-shaped piece of red silk so finely stitched that it was almost invisible. Jerusha smiled. "The Lord had me add it to the quilt so that we would always remember..."

"That He is the Key to our lives, Mama, and without Him we cannot hope to comprehend what is happening to us and why..."

And then Jenny remembered what she had said to Jerusha.

"Perhaps the journey is not over after all, Mama. In fact, we may be coming to a new beginning. That is a hopeful thought."

Jenny's heart leaped. The Key, she had forgotten the Key. And then Jenny knew that God was not finished with their family, and that in a moment of great love, He had once again touched their family with his great wisdom and power. And for the first time, she understood why *Gott* had put the Key into their lives. She slipped to her knees beside the couch.

"Lead us in prayer, husband."

Bobby started to get up. Jenny put her hand on Bobby's arm. "Please stay, Bobby. We need you to agree with us. You love Rachel as much as we do."

Bobby nodded and sank back down in the chair.

And so Jonathan began to pour forth their needs before a loving God, praying for his wife, praying for Rachel, praying for Daniel. And as their hearts softened and melted before Him, the gentle presence of the Holy Spirit filled the room and their hearts drifted out to that place where tears and laughter become one in the presence of the Master and giver of life. And hope began to rise within Jenny's heart; and a faith that somehow, someday, everything would be restored.

Chapter Twenty-Six

Pressure

"Michel, where is the money?"

The question was not posed in conciliatory tones, and the silence from the other end of the line was reflective of that. Finally, Duvigney spoke, the sibilance in his voice very pronounced, like the serpent in the garden offering fruit. "I am growing weary of your incessant badgering, Augusta."

"And I am growing weary of your incessant dodging and evasions, Michel. My granddaughter-in-law is the heir to the St. Clair fortune. As such, she should be receiving an immense income every month. So far we have received a pittance. Now, let me ask it once more, and I'll speak slowly so you can hear me. Where...is...the...money?"

"You should have received one million dollars on Monday."

Augusta laughed. "One million? That's a drop in the bucket. Rachel should have received ninety million just from the interest that has accrued since her grandfather died over forty years ago. And the ongoing income should be well over two million a month. Gerald and Rachel have been married since July. It's now the middle of November. That's ten million. So the way I see it, we should have received around one hundred million dollars. Where is it?"

"You must give me some more time. As I have said before, it is not so easy to move such a large amount of money—"

Augusta interrupted. "Michel, you're lying. There is something fishy going on here, and I intend to get to the bottom of it."

There was another pause. Then Duvigney began to protest. "Now, Augusta, I assure you..."

Augusta slammed her hand down on her desk. She wanted to reach through the phone line and grab Duvigney by his scrawny neck. But instead, she took a breath and then throttled her tone down from furious to threatening. The thought that had been scurrying around in the back of her mind like a rat in the attic came easily to her lips. "Do you know what I think, Michel? I think you've been spending the money. I think you and your friends thought that Robert St. Clair was the last of his line, that there would never be an heir with the Key and that his portion of the inheritance was sitting in a dead account. So you helped yourselves. Oh maybe not all of it, just a little here and a little there—enough to live a life of luxury. For all intents and purposes, Robert had died childless and no one was claiming the money, and what you took out would certainly build back up in the fifty years you had to play with before another heir was assigned. But you got greedy and spent too much—so much that an audit would be very embarrassing. But you didn't worry. After all, you're an old man. Six more years and then twenty-one years before anyone can claim the money. Why, you'd be long gone. And then out of nowhere, a little country bumpkin shows up with the proper DNA and, to make matters worse, she has the Key. And now you have to come up with money you don't have. That's what I think, Michel."

Augusta thought she heard a choking sound, and then Duvigney retorted. "Those are preposterous allegations. As I was about to say, before I was so rudely interrupted, I am making the final arrangements right now to resolve this whole matter."

"Michel, do you know Parker Salisbury?"

"The United States Attorney for New York? Why, yes, I know him."

"I'm glad you know him. You will get to know him even better because you will be hearing from him a lot in the near future."

"I have no reason to see Mr. Salisbury—"

"Oh, but you will, Michel, you will. You see, Parker is an old friend of mine. He would be happy to do me a favor."

Duvigney laughed but there was no humor in it. "You must have something on him."

"Nothing very important. Just some rather explicit photos of Parker with a much younger woman, that would be very embarrassing, to say the least. They would most likely put an end to his presidential aspirations. But the point is that if I ask him, which I will if we don't have ten million in Rachel's bank account tomorrow, he will be more than happy to launch an investigation into reported corruption and fund mismanagement by highly placed financiers. Do you get my point?"

"I understand, Augusta. You will have the money tomorrow."

"That's better. And the same investigation will begin if I don't have the bulk of the accrued interest from Robert's trust within thirty days."

Duvigney gasped. "I can't come up with ninety million dollars in thirty days."

"Michel, I would suggest you call in some favors. Otherwise, you will find that you are the focus of an anti-corruption campaign led by a very earnest United States Attorney who is dying to make a national name for himself and will leave no stone unturned to get to the bottom of things. Can't you just see the St. Clair name plastered all over the grocery store news racks as the crime-busting State Attorney digs up the mud? Parker would love that, but I know you and your friends would not. Therefore, if you don't want to trade your thousand-dollar suits for prison orange, I would start making some phone calls. Do you understand?"

A brief silence and then the click of the connection being broken was Augusta's answer.

"Randall, if you are going to help me out of this situation, you must do something now. The St. Clair woman is pressuring me, and I can't come up with the money she's demanding."

Gordon Randall reached for the pack of expensive French cigarettes lying on his desk. It was a habit left over from his tour of duty in Indochina and he indulged himself occasionally when he was working. Michel Duvigney's whining voice was music to his ears. He listened but his mind was already churning.

This is all working out as if it had been scripted...

He interrupted Duvigney. "Michel, I want you to relax. Things are moving along much more smoothly than you know."

"What do you mean?"

"I mean that I am going to be staying at the St. Clair mansion, and I will deal with all of the matters at the same time. The girl, Gerald, and Augusta will all be taken care of within the week."

"And how do you plan to do that?"

"I have certain professional methods that I will keep to myself, Michel. However, you can be assured that within seven days, your problems will be over...that is, if you meet my fee requirements."

"And just how much is this going to cost me?"

"One million dollars."

Randall heard Duvigney suck his breath through his teeth and then cough.

"That's absolute piracy, Randall. I'll need some time..."

Randall took off the gloves. "Michel, don't play games with me. Augusta St. Clair is putting the pressure on you for millions of dollars that you don't have. I can make that pressure go away, this week. Which way do you want to go? Try to find the millions, or write me a check for the pittance I'm asking. Or do you want me to bow out and let you find someone else, shall we say, less skilled than I am? Of course, that would take some time, and by then. the investigation would be under way."

"Investigation?"

"Why is it that people like you always think that people like me are stupid? Let me lay it out for you, so you understand that I'm already way ahead of you. You called me. You are agitated and want the St. Clair problem to go away today. It doesn't take an Einstein to figure this out. What this telephone call means is that Augusta has come at least as far along the trail of the missing money as I have. She knows you're stalling and she's guessed that you have misappropriated the funds. So she threatened you, probably with a criminal investigation since she has many friends in high places. Am I right so far?"

"Go on, Randall."

"You know what would happen if someone started poking around in Robert St. Clair's financial affairs. They would turn over a few rocks and there you would be, blinking in the light like an evil little salamander, with the evidence of your crimes sticking to your tiny webbed toes. Oh, no, Michel, you don't want Augusta to take one more step down that path. So just write the check, give it to one of your minions, and have him bring it to my favorite restaurant. You know where it is. I'll be having lunch there at…"—Randall glanced at his watch—"one o'clock p.m. That's in one hour. If your guy doesn't show up, I will assume you have decided to go elsewhere for help, and I will disappear from your life."

The sibilant voice was noticeably shaken. "Now, Randall, don't be hasty. My man will be there with the money."

"Very sensible, Michel. Once I have the check, you can be certain that your worries are over."

"Thank you, Randall. I won't forget this."

The line went dead. Randall chuckled and reached over to turn off the recorder. "I won't forget it either, Michel, not one word."

Daniel sat on the bed in his cubicle in the hired hands' quarters behind the barn. His heart was pounding. He had heard

Gerald and Augusta whispering together in the barn, but he had not been able to hear everything that was said. He did know two things. Rachel was pregnant and the St. Clairs were planning something that did not bode well for Rachel. Augusta had mentioned the name Randall, but Daniel did not know who he was. He slipped to his knees beside the bed.

"*Lieber Vater im Himmel*, I come to you for help today. Rachel is in trouble and I'm not sure what to do. Please show me what I must do to help her."

Daniel knelt there for a long time, and then, like fresh drops of rain on a green field, the words came into his heart.

Have not I commanded thee? Be strong and of a good courage; be not afraid, neither be thou dismayed: for the LORD thy God is with thee whithersoever thou goest.

And then again…

…the people that know their God shall be strong, and do exploits.

And one more…

Get up! Go out to the round pen!

The command was so resounding that Daniel literally jerked to his feet. He grabbed his coat and cap and went out the door. The sun had just set and the last few beams of light barely penetrated the gray overcast sky. Snow was piled up around the fences and along the houses. More snow had fallen during the day and the path to the barn was covered with a fresh layer. A chill wind blew steadily from the east, and there was a tang of sea air. Daniel started to walk faster.

Slowly, be cautious…

The command pulled Daniel up short. He looked around to find who was speaking, but there was no one. Carefully he made his way to the barn and then around it to the training pen. The enclosure was empty. All the horses were in their stalls and the ring was a foot deep in snow. The trees and shrubs pressed in close around the fence, and Daniel made his way carefully along the far side.

"What do You want me to do, Lord?"

Wait! Watch!

Daniel stood there in the growing dark, wondering just what he was doing. Then he heard the sound of a car coming down the private gravel road that ran around the back of the estate. He ducked down behind the fence and watched through the boards. An SUV drove out from behind the barn. It was headed out toward the back of the property, going slowly through the snow. The windows were smoked and Daniel could not see inside. It passed him and continued down the road. He rose and made his way through the bushes that lined the road. Ahead, he could see the lights of the vehicle as it drove through the snow. Then he saw it turning off the gravel road into the trees.

They're going to the old caretaker's cottage...

Quietly, he followed the tracks until he reached a point opposite the cottage that was concealed by trees and brush. He made his way through until he could see the cottage. The SUV was parked in front and four men were climbing out. One of the men gave the others some quiet directions, and they went to the back of the SUV, took out two large trunks, and carried them inside. As soon as the van was empty, one of the men drove it out of sight in back of the cottage and covered it with a camouflage tarp. Then he returned and went inside. As he passed the place where Daniel was hiding, his jacket flapped open in the wind and Daniel saw that the stranger was wearing a pistol in a shoulder holster.

Something terrible is happening, and Rachel is in the middle of it. I've got to get her out of here!

Chapter Twenty-Seven

Discoveries

The St. Clair mansion stood silent, a great dark hulk looming out of the surrounding blackness. The white drifts had piled up under the first floor windows, and the fitful wind blew an occasional gust of snow off the roof to fall in whispered whiteness down the walls like softly floating waterfalls. A slim crescent moon made a futile attempt to cast its light on the pale landscape below, but failed dismally as more ragged clouds began to blot out the night sky. A few light, icy flakes drifted down out of the indigo sky. The piled snow creaked softly under the feet of the man dressed in black clothing who was approaching the back door to the mansion. Gordon Randall was on a mission.

When Randall reached the entryway, he pulled out the key Augusta had given him and silently opened the door. He slipped off a pair of rubber shoe covers and left them outside on the step. Then he crept quietly down to Augusta's office. At the door he pulled a small black kit from his pocket, took out a stiff piece of wire, and worked it into the door lock. In another few seconds, he was inside the room. He went quietly to the window and pulled the curtains closed. Then he clicked on a small flashlight and looked around. The room was totally organized and neat; the desk, a model of efficiency with every pen in place, and the furniture was modern and spotless. Randall shook his head.

This will be easy. Augusta thinks she's on top of everything, but she's so easy to read. A person this neat is obsessive. They do everything the same way every time and never do the unexpected. So the safe…

Randall walked to the bookshelf that filled the wall behind the desk and began to run his fingers under the shelves until he felt the button, there was a click and the bookshelf slid sideways.

…is right here. And it's an old style walk-in Yale! Really, Augusta…

Randall reached into the kit of tools and pulled out a small stethoscope. Slipping it over his head, he placed the diaphragm on the front of the safe and began to turn the dial, first to the right, until he heard the tumbler fall, and then to the left and then back to the right. The safe lock clicked and Randall felt the door move slightly under his hand. Cautiously, he twirled the wheel, pulled the door open, and then stepped inside.

He tugged the safe almost closed and then looked for a light switch. He found it on the wall and switched it on. Randall's quick glance took in the small vault. There were drawers on the back wall and shelves with documents in folders to the sides. Randall pulled a few drawers out of the wall. They were filled with jewelry and gold coins. He pushed them back in and continued searching.

After a few minutes he found a large drawer that was locked.

A safe inside a safe. There must be something important in this one.

Randall looked through his toolkit until he found a strangely curved pick. He inserted it into the lock and manipulated it until he heard the click. He put the tool back in the kit and opened the drawer. Slowly, he leafed through the contents. There were several notebooks, what looked like a diary with a lock on it, a stack of pictures and several letters still in their envelopes. He took the pile out of the drawer and set it on a desk in the corner. He picked up the stack of pictures. There were about twenty. They were old Kodak prints that had been hand colorized.

The first one had three people at the beach, two men and a woman. He looked at the woman for a minute. She was young and beautiful, a real knockout in a one-piece bathing suit.

Suddenly, he realized that the beautiful young woman was Augusta. She was standing between the two men. One was well over six feet and had flaming red hair. The other was shorter and had dark brown hair. That physical disparity in size and coloring aside, the two men had remarkably similar features—strong prominent chins, broad foreheads, both very handsome. They were obviously related. The three of them were grouped together with Augusta in the middle and the men's arms around her. Augusta was staring up at the red-haired man. Her gaze betrayed the fact that she cared for him, but he was looking straight at the camera. The name, *Robert*, was written under his picture. The other man, who looked like a college boy, was staring at Augusta. Randall turned the picture over.

> *Robert and Jerod St. Clair, and me – August 1944 –
> Martha's Vineyard.*

Randall looked at the other pictures. All of them were of Augusta, and most had Jerod and Robert with her. There were many in nightclubs or at theaters or in a cozy-looking apartment. Randall scratched his head.

This girl knew how to play the game. She meets a rich kid, gets him hooked, and the next thing you know, she's making the high society rounds and renting a place in uptown Manhattan. I wonder where she got the money. I can just imagine how she played this poor sucker.

The last picture was dated February 15, 1945. There were only two people in the picture, Jerod and Augusta. Jerod was in an Army aviator's uniform and he had his arm around Augusta. They were at a train station. The trees were bare of leaves. Augusta was dressed in pants and a warm-looking coat and she was turned sideways to the camera. The coat did not hide the slight bump in her tummy. Randall knew what it was.

Jerod's baby…

He put down the pictures and picked up the letters. They were in a bundle held together with a rubber band. Randall slipped off the band and started scanning through them. One letter caught his attention. It was a letter addressed to Augusta but there were two letters inside. Randall pulled them out. The first one was from Augusta to Robert. It was dated December 15, 1944. Randall read it.

> *My Dearest Robert,*
>
> *It's been a month since you left to manage your father's factory in Lancaster, and I haven't heard a word from you. I am writing because there is something I must tell you, Robert. I am six weeks pregnant with your child and I am so happy. After our night together, I fell in love with you, deeply and truly. I know it is yours because, believe it or not, I have never been with Jerod. If you will only come home to me, we can be together. I want to be with you always. I know we can work it out with Jerod, he will understand that we are truly in love and won't stand in our way. He's a good kid. Please come home.*
>
> *Yours forever,*
>
> *Augusta*

Randall stared down at the letter.

Not Jerod's baby, Robert's baby! My, my, this is getting very interesting!

Randall unfolded the second letter in the envelope. He could see that at one time it had been crumpled and torn in two, then carefully smoothed out and taped back together. There were small, discolored spots on it. Randall was curious and then he realized what they were.

Tear stains!

The letter was dated December 23, 1944. It had been sent from Lancaster, Pennsylvania. Randall read on.

> *Augusta,*
>
> *I received your letter and I need to say a few things in response. The truth is, Augusta, our night together was a huge mistake on my part. I was drunk and if you are honest you will admit that you lured me up to your apartment and made yourself very available. I never would have done such a terrible thing to my brother if I had been in my right mind. He loves you with all his heart. I have done him a terrible wrong, and I am filled with remorse.*

*I don't want to seem cold, but I don't really believe your
claim that you have never been with Jerod. He is totally in
love with you and has hinted many times that the two of you
were involved in more than just a friendship. So it is difficult
for me to believe that I am the father of your child. If you
need anything, money, or help or support for the baby, I am
willing to do that, but I cannot marry you, because I do not
love you.*

I'm very sorry,

Robert

Randall stared down at the letters.

Not the Christmas present Augusta expected, I'll wager.

The story unfolding in the letters was almost too incredible
to believe. Jenny Hershberger and Francis St. Clair were siblings.
They had different mothers, but Robert St. Clair was their father.
That meant that Rachel and Gerald were half-first cousins. He
thought about the intricacies of their relationship and then
shook his head.

Randall put down the letters and picked up the diary.
Another twist with the lock pick and the book lay open before
him. The flyleaf had the name: Francine Bosnan at the top. And
then below that, another name: Augusta Moukhransky. Shoved
in between the flyleaf and the first page were several pictures.
Someone had drawn an X through all the faces, but Randall
could still see them. They were of Robert St. Clair and a
beautiful, dark-haired girl. A small baby was in Robert's arms.
Randall turned the top picture over. On the back was an
inscription.

*Dad, this is Rachel, my wife, and your granddaughter,
Jenny. Rachel is such a wonderful wife and mother and
Jenny is such a delightful little girl. I know you'd love them if
you would just meet them. Won't you relent and let us come
see you?*

Robert had signed the note. Randall shook his head.

So Augusta already knew who Rachel and Jenny were when they came to the house in 1950. She lied to me!

He leafed through more pages. The first part of the book was filled with girlish ramblings about finding a wealthy, handsome husband and leaving the Bronx and then, several pages in, there was an entry titled, "The Big Day". Francine was leaving the Bronx and her middle class status behind her forever, moving to New York and changing her name so she would be able to meet the right people. She had chosen the name Augusta Moukhransky.

Randall smiled.

Smart girl! Moukhransky is the name of a branch of the Russian imperial family. Her new background couldn't really be investigated because the Bolsheviks killed all the Romanovs. She did her homework and she arrived in New York with an exotic name, a mysterious but fabricated family background, and a beautiful face. She probably took the town by storm.

Indeed, she had, as the diary soon revealed. Within a month after arriving in the Big Apple, she met Jerod St. Clair at a USO dance in Manhattan in 1944 and began dating him. Randall read the entry.

July 15, 1944

USO Dance at the Stage Door Canteen. The Andrews Sisters were performing. I met a charming young man, Jerod St. Clair, and he was very attentive. My friend, Cecelia, told me that he comes from one of the richest families in America. I guess I don't have to look much further.

There were several entries after that detailing a whirlwind romance with Jerod St. Clair. Augusta was careful to point out that she was not in love with Jerod, but she certainly appreciated his money and the idea of marriage to the young man was certainly worth considering, despite the lack of feeling on her part.

And then Randall read an entry that was underlined in red.

August 15, 1944

Jerod has invited me to spend a week at his family's vacation compound at Martha's Vineyard!!!! This is the most exciting thing that has happened to me, ever! I'm sure Jerod is going to propose while we are there. We are leaving tomorrow and taking the train. I have so much to pack.

Followed by a very interesting entry two days later...

August 17, 1944

Yesterday, we took the train to Boston and then the Cape Flyer out to Woods Hole. From there we transferred to the ferry to Martha's Vineyard. And then the most amazing thing happened. When we arrived at Martha's Vineyard, Jerod's older brother, Robert, was waiting for us with a car. Robert is wonderful!!! He's taller than Jerod and has bright red hair and the handsomest face I have ever seen. As soon as I saw him, I actually started sweating and my heart pounded. I guess I fell in love with Robert at first sight. What am I going to do? Jerod is going to propose, I know he is, but Robert, oh, Robert! I have to be with him. I have to be careful with Jerod, though. He's madly in love with me. If I don't play my cards right, I could lose both of them and be back where I started. But I won't back down. I'll just put Jerod off until I know where I stand with Robert. One of the St. Clair boys is going to marry me. I'd prefer that it be Robert, but I'll take Jerod in a pinch.

The plan of seduction unfolded on page after page until Augusta found a way. Randall smiled as he read of Augusta's conquest.

October 22, 1944

Last night I was with Robert. We were all supposed to go out to dinner, but Jerod got sick, so he made Robert take me to the Stork Club anyway. It was a cold night and after dinner I invited Robert up to my apartment for a drink. After I plied him with some really good champagne, I turned on the charm and Robert couldn't resist me. It was wonderful! But it didn't work out exactly the way I planned.

There was much more to the entry, but Randall closed the book and pushed the knob on his wristwatch. The dim glow showed him the time.

My, how time flies when you're having fun! I'll get to this later but now I've got to finish up and get out of here!

Randall pulled a tiny camera out of his pocket, laid the diary down on the table, and quickly began taking pictures of all the pages. When he had photographed everything, he scanned through the notebooks. He photographed anything that looked interesting. At one point, he came across a list of negotiable securities that were being held at a local bank.

Nice! Over a million dollars' worth!

He snapped a picture of the list. When he was finished, he carefully put everything back in the order he had taken it out, closed the drawer, and locked it. Then, after looking around to see that everything was in order, he turned off the light, left the vault, and locked the safe. He checked everything to make sure it was back in place, opened the curtains in the office, and exited the room.

He slipped down the hallway, went out the door, put on his overshoes, and went back down the path. As he walked, he patted the camera in his pocket.

I've got you, Augusta. I've really got you now.

Chapter Twenty-Eight

The Diary

Back in his room, Randall opened the camera and removed the flash card. He put it into the memory card player, lifted up the small screen, and began to go through the material he had photographed in Augusta's office.

Digital cameras! Who would have believed it—you have to hand it to those Japanese. It makes you wonder who really lost World War II...

Randall opened the slides he had taken of the journal and flipped to the entry about Robert and Augusta. He began reading where he had left off and kept on reading. After a while, he whistled softly. The story read like a television soap opera.

Augusta, Augusta! So you had to fall back to plan B, after all. You are a very naughty girl...

October 22, 1944

Last night I was with Robert...but it didn't work out exactly the way I planned...

Augusta stirred. The bed was warm against the October chill of New York City. She pulled the covers up around her shoulders and snuggled down. From outside her window, the sound of brazen taxi horns and buses grinding their gears filtered up from the parade of traffic passing down 5th Avenue.

Augusta listened to the sounds of the city for a moment. Then, reaching out her arms, she turned to the place next to her in the bed, but there was no one there. The spot where Robert had slept was empty. Augusta raised herself up on her elbow and looked around her bedroom. The clock next to her on the bed stand said eleven. Bright sunlight streamed in the opened window blinds. Augusta stretched like a cat and lay back down. Memories and images from the night before flooded her mind with delight. Robert! Oh, Robert!

"Robert?"

There was no answer. Augusta called out a little louder.

"Robert?"

The silence in the apartment was deafening. Augusta got up, grabbed her silken robe off the chair next to the bed, and slipped it on. She remembered the look on Robert's face when she had taken it off the night before.

You've got the goods, girl! There's not a man in this city that could stay out of your bed if you really wanted him to be there!

The hardwood floor was cold against her feet as she padded to the closet and got her slippers. Then she went out into the living room. There was nobody there. She went to the front door of the apartment, opened it, and looked up and down the hallway. The morning *New York Times* was in front of her door. She picked it up. The headline blared at her.

MACARTHUR IN PHILIPPINES! HUGE YANK ARMY SWARMS ASHORE, CAPTURES CAPITAL OF LEYTE ISLE!

Augusta went back into the apartment. She dropped the paper on the coffee table and then looked around again. Where was Robert?

"Robert?"

She walked into the dining room and then into the small kitchenette. Robert St. Clair was gone! She glanced down and saw a note lying on the kitchen table. She grabbed it and read it.

Augusta,

I am very remorseful this morning about what happened last night. I have betrayed my brother and I feel like a lowdown heel. I am leaving for Pennsylvania tomorrow to take over my father's factory there. It will be a good thing. I want to be as far away from you as I can. You are a beautiful woman, and hard to resist, but I have made up my mind that last night will never happen again. Please don't try to contact me.

Robert

Augusta crumpled up the note and hurled it against the kitchen wall.

"That's what you think, Robert St. Clair! That's what you think!"

December 24, 1944

It was the day before Christmas, two months later. Outside her apartment window snow was falling lightly, filling the streets with a soft whiteness that matched the season. The sidewalks of uptown New York were filled with revelers, and Christmas music came from the department store across the street as people dashed in to do their last-minute shopping. Augusta sat at the kitchen table, her lovely face a stony mask. Tears ran from her eyes and fell upon the letter spread out in front of her. The news it contained was not good. Robert wasn't coming home. Robert didn't love her.

She sat for a long time in the dark room. Finally, her instinct for self-preservation took over. She folded the letter and put it back in the envelope. There was another letter with it. It was the one she had sent to Robert, telling him she was pregnant. He had sent it back to her along with his letter. Augusta rose slowly and went to the telephone sitting on the small desk in the living room. She dialed a number and waited. Finally, a voice answered. It was Jerod St. Clair. Augusta smiled faintly and then, working up a slight sob in her voice, began to speak.

"Jerod? Oh, hello, darling. Listen, I...I need to talk to you. Yes, I know we were going out tonight, but there is something I need to tell you and it can't wait. Can you come over early?"

She waited a moment until Jerod answered.

"All right, darling, I suppose I can wait until then. But come as early as you can. It's very important. Yes, dearest, I'll see you at five."

Augusta hung up the phone and smiled. Jerod was on his way. She went into the bedroom. She went to the closet and got the small box down from the top shelf. She opened it and put the letters on top of the diary inside. She closed the box and set it back on the shelf. Then she began to look through her clothes.

Hmmm, what shall I wear to bait the trap?

She looked through several dresses but passed over them.

Too hot, too naughty, too revealing... Wait, here's what I need.

She pulled the white dress from the closet and held it up in front of her as she looked in the mirror. It was modest, came below her knees and the neckline was high. Her long, blonde hair and her stunning figure would make her look like a Christmas angel in the dress.

Perfect! The innocent virgin, all in white, confesses her sin. If Jerod doesn't fall on his knees and beg me to marry him, then I am not the girl I think I am.

By five o'clock, Augusta was ready. She had put on just the tiniest bit of makeup because she wanted her face to look pale. Her long, blonde hair framed her lovely face and the white dress was exactly right. At five minutes after five, the doorbell rang.

We'll train the young man to be more prompt after we are married, won't we?

Augusta went to the door and opened it a crack. Jerod St. Clair stood in the hallway, an anxious look on his face. Augusta opened the door and the young man quickly came inside.

"I'm sorry I'm late, Augusta. Traffic was terrible."

Augusta managed a wan smile. "It's...it's all right, darling. I..."

And then she burst into tears.

Jerod stood for a moment and then took the sobbing girl into his arms. "Why, Augusta, what's wrong?"

"I'm so ashamed, Jerod. We should have been more careful..."

"More careful?"

Augusta pulled Jerod inside and closed the door. She leaned against the door, took a deep breath, and then turned to Jerod. Everything depended on what she said next. "Yes, more careful."

She paused and then put her face in her hands and began sobbing again. The words came out in a broken rush. "I'm...I'm...pregnant, Jerod."

Jerod's face was a study in bewilderment. "Pregnant? But when...how? We never..."

Augusta pulled away and looked at him, trembling. "You don't remember?"

Now Jerod really looked confused. "Remember?"

Augusta turned her back and began reciting the story she had gone over and over in her mind before he arrived. Her voice was pitched with just the right combination of sultriness and shame. "It was in October. We went to the theater and then to the Stork Club. We were both a little tipsy when you brought me home and you fell asleep on the couch and stayed until the next morning?"

Jerod smiled and looked embarrassed. "Yes, I remember. I made rather a fool of myself, didn't I?"

"Well, the truth is, Jerod, you didn't stay asleep the whole time."

"I didn't?"

Augusta changed her voice intonation to that of an innocent virgin. She turned back to Jerod and put her arms around his neck. "No, you did not. In the middle of the night you came into my bed. I was so sleepy that I didn't realize what was happening until you were kissing me."

She moved up close to him, very close. "You were so strong, so wonderful, I...I couldn't resist you. We made..."

Jerod looked into her wonderful eyes and Augusta knew she had won. Jerod's face flushed red and then white. "We did? And you got...well, in a family way?"

"Yes, dearest. And now I don't know what to do."

She flung herself down on the couch and began sobbing. Jerod stood helplessly, awkwardly, watching her. Finally her sobs slowed and she looked up at him.

"New York society is not very kind to girls who get in trouble. I expect…I mean, I'll have to leave here, find one of those homes for unwed mothers. When the baby is born, I'll have to give it up for adoption."

She choked back a sob.

Jerod pulled her up gently from the couch and held her tight against him. "Oh, no you won't!"

Augusta smiled with her face buried in his shoulder, but there was no smile in her voice, only fear. "I won't?"

Jerod took her shoulders and looked into her eyes. "Of course not! Don't you see, darling? I'm wild about you. I love you madly. I've loved you since the day we met. My only regret is that I truly don't remember that night, but if you will do as I ask, I'll make it up to you."

Jerod dropped to one knee. "I know this is not how it's supposed to be done, but, Augusta, will you marry me? You must marry me. I love you and I won't let our baby go without a name. Please, Augusta, say you will marry me."

Augusta looked down at the trembling young man. "Do you really mean it, Jerod? You want to marry me, even after…"

"Yes, my love, I'll marry you today if you want."

Augusta took Jerod by the hand and pulled him up. She pulled herself into his arms and clung to him. "Oh, yes, my love, yes, I will marry you. Oh, thank you. I was so afraid that you would hate me."

"Hate you? Augusta, you're the most incredible girl. You're beautiful and intelligent, and… Well, I just have to be with you always. I love you so."

Augusta sprang the final piece of the trap. She looked into his eyes, her lips parted, and her voice pitched slightly lower. "Jerod, darling, there's one more thing."

What, my love?"

"Ever since that night, I can't get you out of my mind. Your kisses, your strength, I'm obsessed with you and I don't know what to do."

Jerod looked at her again and she could almost feel the heat rise in his body. His face turned red and she could see passion in his eyes. "Do you mean...I mean, do you want me like I want you?"

"Yes, Jerod, I'm crazy about you, and I want to show you how much I love you."

"Oh, Augusta, I've dreamed of this."

Augusta dropped her eyes. "Please, Jerod, I need you, want you. Can we, I mean... Oh, I'm burning up. If we are going to be married, and I'm already... Well, won't it be all right? I love you so. I want to give you something, and this time you'll remember."

She pulled him after her as she turned toward her bedroom. Jerod followed her like a lamb to the slaughter. There was a slight smile on her face as she walked before him to her bed.

February 24, 1945

Augusta put the telegram from the war department down on the table. Outside the half-snow, half-rain turned to slush against her window. She felt the baby move inside her. She held up her hand, and the huge diamond ring sparkled in the light from the chandelier above her head. She smiled. This was perfect. She was a St. Clair, a bereaved war widow, another woman sacrificing her husband for the good of the country. Pity and compassion would solidify her position in New York society. And now she could make her plans to win Robert back. She looked down at the telegram. She would have to tell Max and Margaret, of course. They would be devastated, and then the baby would bond them all together so tightly. Perfect!

With my blonde hair, black should be most becoming.

She smiled. She couldn't have planned it better herself.

Randall read through more entries. Most of them detailed Augusta's attempts to see Robert or entice him to come back to New York. After the baby was born in June, Augusta tried mightily to use the boy as a lever to bring Robert home, but

Robert was steadfast in his refusal to see her or the boy, citing the pressing work of converting his father's wartime tank manufacturing plant into one that produced parts for automobiles. Augusta even tried to go to Lancaster to see him, but Robert arranged to be out of town. A year passed. And then Augusta received a surprising note from Robert asking her to meet him.

July 4, 1946

Augusta took one more look in the mirror. Yes, everything was perfect. Her long blonde hair framed her perfect face and the dress she was wearing was just the right mixture of modest and sultry. Her eyes, her strongest feature, were large, luminous pools of deep, almost-indigo blue. She smiled, and the effect was dramatic. Augusta St. Clair was a beautiful woman. She went to the phone and called a taxi. She mustn't be late, Robert was waiting.

When the taxi arrived at the Stork Club, Augusta went inside. The maître d' saw her right away. "Mrs. St. Clair, how nice to see you. Mr. Robert is waiting for you."

"How long has he been here, Angelo?"

"About twenty minutes. He seems a bit impatient to see you."

"That's fine, Angelo. A woman must always keep a gentleman a bit on edge, don't you think?"

Angelo smiled. "Yes, ma'am. Right this way."

Augusta followed Angelo through the tables to one of the small booths in the back. Her heart leaped. Robert was waiting for her, his red hair like a flash of fire even across the room. Robert saw Augusta coming and stood. He did not smile, but motioned her to a seat. Angelo nodded and left. Robert reached out his hand to greet her.

"What, no kiss or hug, Robert? After all, we are family."

Robert ignored her rather pointed remark. "Augusta, I need to talk to you about that. I chose this place because it is neutral ground, and I don't want a scene."

"Why, Robert, what could be so serious that it would cause me to be upset?"

"Augusta, I want to talk to you about Francis."

Augusta leaned closer. "You mean your son?"

"That is a debatable point. I spoke to my physician and paternity blood tests are unreliable when it comes to brothers. Jerod and I have the same blood type, O negative. So even a paternity test will not prove which one of us fathered the child."

Augusta stiffened in her chair. "And I'm telling you, Robert, that you are the father of my son. I never slept with Jerod before I got pregnant."

Robert sighed. "Look, Augusta, I'm going to be very blunt. I have come to know you as a manipulating, greedy woman who will do or say anything to get what you want. My brother wasn't three days in his grave before you were writing me, calling me, wanting to see me. You didn't even mourn him for a month. What kind of woman are you?"

Augusta's face flushed. "I'm that way because I love you, and I never loved Jerod. I only married him so I would have a name for my baby, and that's your fault. Obviously, it doesn't matter to you what happens to girls with no money who get into trouble. They are flushed down the drain like garbage. You weren't man enough to take responsibility and Jerod was. So I married him. Now I can take care of my child without having to take a waitress job or some other kind of work..."

"...not fitting to the style of life to which you have become accustomed? Augusta, I pity you. I believe that Jerod fathered your baby and I always will. You have his money now so you don't need me to support you. I think we should just go our own ways. You'll be fine."

Augusta lowered her voice and put a pleading tone in it. "But, Robert! I love you. I want to be with you. I don't even care if you don't marry me. I just want to see you, be with you."

Robert swallowed hard. He took a conciliatory tone. "Augusta, that will never happen. The truth is, I've met someone. She's carrying my baby and we're going to be married."

Augusta felt as though Robert had punched her right in the face. She gasped and struggled to catch her breath. "Who...who is she?"

Robert looked down. "She's an Amish girl I met in Lancaster. She's a wonderful, beautiful girl, honest and true."

"You mean unlike me, Robert?"

"Yes, Augusta, she's not like you at all. Her name is Rachel. I love her. I'll marry her as soon as she says yes. She moved in with me last week."

Augusta stared at Robert. She could tell he was not lying. A dead feeling began to creep into her heart, and at the same time a rage rose up and almost choked her. After a minute, she leaned close to Robert and her words were like icy daggers. "You will rue the day you ever set eyes on her. You and all the St. Clairs will learn that I am a woman who never forgets. You bastard! You get me pregnant and then you leave me for some country bumpkin? I don't think so. You think that you'll have a wonderful life with your Rachel. Well, I'm telling you that you and Rachel and your child will have nothing but sorrow for the rest of your miserable lives. I will personally see to it. You proud, arrogant St. Clairs! I will destroy you all."

She stood up, picked up her water glass, and threw the contents in Robert's face. Then she turned and marched out of the room, followed by the murmur of voices and curious stares.

Chapter Twenty-Nine

The Plan

Gerald St. Clair sat on the edge of his bed with his head in his hands. Fear gripped him. He knew that his grandmother had been deadly serious when she threatened his life. And what did she mean when she said she had taken care of other St. Clairs? He thought about Rachel and the plan to kill her. He hated his part in it, but he was deeply afraid of his grandmother.

Gerald stood up and went to the bathroom. The mirror told him he needed to clean himself up. He was about to begin shaving when there was a knock on his door. When he answered it, Gordon Randall was waiting.

"Good morning, Mr. St. Clair. May I come in?"

Gerald hesitated and then opened the door. There was something creepy about Randall that frightened Gerald. Randall walked in and shut the door behind him. Then he handed Gerald a small plastic vial filled with oval pills.

"These are for your wife, Mr. St. Clair. These are the pills Dr. Newberry prescribed for your wife's pregnancy. They are fifty-milligram vitamin B6 tablets. For our purposes however, they've been dipped in an arsenic solution. The arsenic is tasteless. These will help her morning sickness for a few days. But then she will start going downhill. It will look like she has a bad case of the flu. At that point, we will start giving her the poison in liquid form because she won't be able to keep these down. Give them to her with a glass of ginger ale about an hour after she gets up. Simple, tasteless, and painless... at first."

Gerald stared down at the bottle. Suddenly he knew that he couldn't go through with this. He looked at Randall. The man's face was expressionless.

"How long will this take, Mr. Randall?"

"About ten days."

"Will she suffer much?"

"In the last few days, she will be very sick, but she will sink into a coma and be unconscious most of the time. Does that bother you, Mr. St. Clair?"

"Not exactly. It's just that I have never done anything like this and I'm a little nervous, that's all."

"You're not backing out, are you?"

Gerald felt sick. He wanted to run away, go anywhere, get out from under his dominating grandmother and this dangerous man. His hand trembled and the pills made a slight rattle in the bottle. Randall noticed. He stepped close to Gerald.

"I want to tell you something, Mr. St. Clair. When I was in Vietnam, there was a village in Quang Ngai Province that we had reason to believe was supplying the Vietcong with food and weapons. I was a CIA dark ops advisor embedded with a small group of hand-picked mercenaries in a company of US soldiers. I had orders from Langley to make an example of the village, so we went in and massacred everyone—men, women, and children."

Gerald tried to move away but Randall blocked him. Gerald could feel his hands shaking.

"What's your point, Mr. Randall?"

"My point is that we massacred those people on my orders. The regular soldiers were uncertain about killing civilians, because they were mostly old people, women, and children— even babies. But I was not uncertain. I had my orders and I carried them out. Those soldiers knew that my men and I would kill the first soldier who balked. And this situation is no different. I have a job to do here and you are in this up to your ears. Don't balk at any of this or your life won't be worth a dime. Do I make myself clear?"

Gerald felt that Randall was telling the truth, but he had to make sure. "My grandmother is paying you. She wouldn't let you do anything to me. I'm her grandson, her own flesh and blood. I'm her lottery ticket."

Randall smiled. "You just don't understand, do you, son? If you don't play this the right way, you will become expendable. Your grandmother will do anything to accomplish what she wants. She's like a black, evil, monstrous old spider—spinning her web. She has planned this and she has covered all the bases. I'm here to see that her plans are carried out. And believe me when I say that, to me, there is no difference between the operation in Vietnam and this one."

Randall smiled, but there was no warmth, only cold steel. Then he turned and left. Gerald stared after him, the bottle of pills held in nerveless fingers. He shut the door and leaned against the wall, his heart pounding.

How am I going to get out of this?

Rachel knelt beside the toilet. The paroxysm of retching had passed, but she still felt weak and disoriented. Augusta's doctor had visited the day before, and after a cursory examination, he told her that some women respond to pregnancy more intensely than others, and she just needed to get some rest. He wrote a prescription for some medicine for the morning sickness and left. Rachel rolled off her knees and leaned against the wall. She really did feel terrible. There was a knock on her door. She dragged herself to her feet, wiped off her chin, and went out into her room. The knock came again.

"I'm coming!"

Rachel opened the door to find Gerald standing there with a tray.

"Can I come in?"

Rachel stepped aside and Gerald entered. He set the tray down and turned to Rachel. There were two white pills and a glass of golden-colored liquid on the tray. "I brought your pills. The glass has ginger ale in it. The bubbles will settle your stomach and the ginger will help, too."

Rachel stared at Gerald suspiciously. He seemed kind and solicitous, but she didn't know what he was up to. Her thoughts went back to Capri.

He just wants to keep me from divorcing him, so he's pouring on the charm. I've seen this before.

"Thank you, Gerald."

Gerald paused a moment and then he took her hand. There was a strange, troubled expression on his face. "Rachel, I'm sorry. I'm sorry that I have been so callous and hard. It's just that I never met anyone like you. I mean, a girl who was real and not just some tramp that was there to gratify me. You're real and honest and good, and I don't know how to deal with honesty and goodness. I...well, I'm sorry."

He turned to go, but Rachel took his arm.

"I'm sorry, too, Gerald."

"Sorry for what?"

"I'm sorry for the way I've used you to get what I wanted. I was so certain I wanted to get away from my papa, that when this chance came to do what I wanted with my life, I took it, no matter what the cost. Now I see that the cost has been terrible."

A tear ran down her face. "I'm supposed to be a Christian, but I threw all that away for the money. I forgot that nothing is worth more than a relationship with God. In the last few days, I've been praying again, and the Lord has really helped me to see what a fool I've been. Now I'm pregnant and I've hurt you and... Oh, Gerald, please forgive me."

Gerald stared at her with a troubled look on his face. He turned away. "Rachel, I don't know much about God. I know that when I was a kid I always liked church and the music and the stained glass windows. Somehow being there made me feel peaceful and safe, especially after my parents died. But I don't know what you mean when you say you can have a relationship with God. That just sounds so strange to me. And shouldn't you be the one forgiving me? After all, I seduced you under false pretenses and now…well, you are in real trouble."

"Trouble?"

A sense of nameless dread came over her, and she could feel her heart begin to pound.

Gerald turned back to her and took her arm in a powerful grip. "Yes, Rachel, trouble. I mean like dangerous trouble. You need to—"

Just then there was a knock on the door.

"Rachel, it's Augusta. Can I come in?"

Rachel stared up at Gerald. A terrified look had come over his face.

"I need to what, Gerald?"

Gerald looked at the door. "Ah…nothing, Rachel, never mind."

The knock came again, more insistent.

"Rachel?"

Gerald went to the door and let Augusta in. "Hello, Grandmother. I was just bringing Rachel her pills."

Augusta looked at Gerald curiously and then walked over and put her hands on Rachel's shoulders.

"How are you feeling this morning, my dear? Ever since Gerald told me the wonderful news I've been so excited for you and for us. Another generation of St. Clairs, and I get to see it. I really never thought I'd be a great-grandmother. How delightful!"

Then she scowled. "Gerald also told me that he's been a very naughty boy and that you're thinking of leaving us. Is that true?"

Behind Augusta she could see Gerald shaking his head. His face was pale. Rachel played along. "Well, I'm willing to at least talk about it."

Rachel could see the relief on Gerald's face.

Augusta smiled. "Excellent, Rachel, that's excellent. Now be a good girl and take your pills. You'll feel much better. The doctor told me you are a very healthy young woman."

She turned to go. "Come, Gerald, we must let Rachel get her rest. I'll have cook send up something that will be very soothing on your stomach, Rachel."

Augusta and Gerald went out. Before he closed the door, Gerald turned and gave Rachel another strange look. Rachel picked up the pills and took them with the ginger ale. In a moment, her churning stomach seemed to settle down. She went back to her bed to lie down.

I wonder what that was all about.

Gerald St. Clair followed his grandmother down the hallway toward the main part of the house. He felt hot and sweaty and flushed. She had almost caught him telling Rachel that they were poisoning her. He was about to go into the living room when he felt his grandmother's hand on his arm.

"I understand that Mr. Randall delivered my message, Gerald. I meant every word of it. You will not stand in the way of me getting what I want, so don't screw this up. You will be very, very sorry if you do."

"Just what do you want, Grandmother? And I don't believe that you would kill me. You need me alive if you want to get your hands on all that money."

Augusta smiled her icy smile and turned to go. "Sometimes money isn't everything, Gerald."

Daniel looked through the bushes at the house. He had not seen Rachel outside for days. He had to get inside to see her, but he knew he would have no excuse to be in the house. And those men, what were they doing here?

What can I do, Lord?

He turned and began walking back to the barn. As he came around the corner, he ran right into Gerald St. Clair. The two men collided and Daniel was knocked to the ground. Gerald reached down to help him up. "Wow, sorry, I didn't see you. I'm rather distracted at the moment. Are you all—"

As Gerald looked at Daniel's face, a light of recognition dawned in his eyes. "You look very familiar. Do I know you? I mean, I know you work here, but haven't I met you somewhere else?"

"No, I don't think so."

"What is your name?"

"David, my name is David."

Daniel's response caused Gerald to look at his face again. "No...it's not David. I know you, don't I?"

And then the penny dropped. "Wait...yes, I met you in Paradise. You're Rachel's friend. Dennis, right?"

Daniel shook his head. "I don't know what you mean."

Gerald held onto Daniel's arm. "Dennis...no, Daniel. You're Rachel's Amish friend, Daniel. You were with Rachel the first time I met her. But you were dressed in those funny clothes. And you didn't have a beard."

Gerald looked around quickly and then lowered his voice. "What are you doing here?"

Daniel looked for a way to escape, but Gerald held his arm with a grip of steel. Daniel capitulated. "All right, Mr. St. Clair, you're right. I'm Daniel."

"But what are you doing in Connecticut?"

Daniel looked Gerald straight in the eye. "I was worried about Rachel, so I came here to look out for her. I think you and your grandmother are not nice people and Rachel is my friend. So I got a job working in the stable. And now there is something going on here that is very strange. Two nights ago I saw three men arrive here. They had guns. Is Rachel in danger? What's going on? What are you up to?"

Gerald looked around quickly, and then pulled Daniel close. "Yes, Rachel is in danger. And if anyone hears me telling you that, I'm as good as dead."

"Dead? Are you serious? What is happening here?"

Daniel could see both fear and resolve in Gerald's face.

"My grandmother wants all of Rachel's money. But she can't get it because she's not an heir. And I can't get it if Rachel divorces me. The only way I can get the money is if Rachel dies without children. My grandmother has hired a man to kill Rachel. He's a professional and he's ruthless. They have started giving Rachel poison. I thought I could go along with the plan, but I can't. Rachel is good, she's beautiful and…and I've fallen in love with her. And there is a complication."

Daniel looked Gerald in the eye. "I know. Rachel is pregnant."

Gerald almost choked. "How…?"

"I heard you and your grandmother talking in the barn. I didn't hear everything, but I did hear that part. You were pretty upset."

Gerald put his face in his hands. "If they kill her, they'll kill my child, too. I can't let that happen. But I don't know what to do, and I need help getting Rachel away from here."

It was Daniel's turn to grip Gerald's arm. "I can't believe you have been poisoning my Rachel? How could you do such a thing?"

Gerald shook his head. "I thought the money was everything. But something Rachel said has been bothering me."

"What did she say?"

"She told me I could have a relationship with God. I thought I didn't believe in this Christian stuff, but ever since she said it, I can't get it out of my head. This morning I realized I'm basically a worthless human being, and now my grandmother wants to make me into a murderer. I just can't. It's…well, it's wrong. I have to get her out of here. Will you help me?"

Daniel nodded. "Yes, I will help. What can I do?"

"I can't talk any more now, but can you meet me here tonight?"

"What time?"

"I'll slip out around eleven. I have to be careful because my grandmother has men watching the house. She controls everything. They will stay until Rachel is dead. You must be very careful. These men are trained professionals and they won't hesitate to kill us if we get caught. My grandmother has something very evil planned for Rachel, and I think I'm on her list, too. I think it's much deeper than just getting the money, but I don't know all the details. We need to help Rachel."

Daniel could sense the urgency in Gerald's voice.

"I'll be here at eleven."

Chapter Thirty

Suspicion

Augusta picked up her private intercom and called out to the caretaker's cottage. A male voice answered.

"Yes?"

"I need to speak to Randall."

There was a moment's silence and then Randall came on the line. "Good morning, Augusta."

"Randall, something is going on with Gerald. I found him with Rachel this morning, and he looked very guilty when he saw me. I'm sure he is going to betray us."

"Well, he will at least try to wiggle out of his part in all this. I've seen his type before. He's weak and cowardly and has no stomach for this kind of operation."

"What should we do?"

"I'm already on it. My men are watching him to make sure he doesn't try to leave or mess up our plans. He is a liability, of course. I assume you will want to deal with him at some point."

"Yes, but not until he is vested with Rachel's inheritance. When he turned twenty-one, I had Gerald sign over all his powers of attorney and make me the sole beneficiary of his will. Of course, he didn't realize that he was signing those specific papers. He was too eager to start spending his trust fund to pay attention to the legal details. But be that as it may, if he dies before Rachel, there will be no money for me to inherit. And even then, I think we should wait awhile before we arrange something special for my darling Gerald—give everything time to cool down."

"That's right, but we might have to keep him on ice until then."

"Whatever needs to be done, that's up to you. There should be plenty of ways to keep him quiet, I imagine."

"Not a problem. As far as anyone is concerned, he will be a grieving husband who has locked himself in his room and is not receiving visitors. After a few weeks, the horrible and unexpected death of his lovely young bride will unhinge his mind until, being unable to face life any longer; he will drive out to a remote spot on his magnificent estate and shoot himself in the head. The authorities will inspect the scene but find no reason to suspect that any other people are involved, and they will put the whole matter down as a suicide. And life will go on as the billions of dollars are transferred to the grandmother's bank account."

Augusta listened to the scenario and smiled to herself. "Really, Randall, you are quite ahead of the game, aren't you?"

"I try to be."

Augusta was quiet for a moment.

"Augusta, you still there?"

"I'm just wondering, how difficult would it be to turn him into a vegetable without killing him. I mean, someone who is totally crippled, you know—in a vegetative state but totally aware of everything going on around him. As his conservator, I would be in charge of his money, so he could just sit there day after day while I did whatever I wanted. It would be very fulfilling to see him suffer as I have suffered."

"You, Augusta?"

"It's just a thought. Put it down to the musings of an old woman who has endured much at the hands of this cursed St. Clair family."

"I can arrange for any outcome you desire. A coma, a vegetable, or just dead. But it's like taking a choice from a menu.

As you add degrees of difficulty, you add more to the cost. So that's totally up to you. But the bottom line is that adding Gerald to my list is going to cost you, at a minimum, double my fee for Rachel. And I will need half up front, as usual."

There was a pause and then Augusta sighed. "No problem, Randall. I will have a check for you this afternoon."

The line went dead. Augusta stared at the phone in her hand. She put the phone down and walked over to a mirror that was hanging on her office wall. She admired herself and then pointed a finger at her own reflection.

"Be very careful, old girl. You're almost there. In a little while, all the St. Clairs will be dead."

Augusta laughed out loud.

Gordon Randall picked up a small bag and headed outside. He didn't want to make his next call on a line that Augusta might be monitoring. He walked into the woods and stopped under a large pine tree. He reached into the bag and made some adjustments to the equipment inside. Then he pulled a wireless handheld phone out and dialed a number. In a moment, the hissing voice of Michel Duvigney answered. "Well, Randall, how are we doing over there?"

"Everything is going as planned. Rachel will be out of the way in a few days and then we'll deal with Gerald and Augusta."

"I assume you have a plan for that?"

"Augusta is already counting the money she'll get when Rachel dies and her grieving grandson commits suicide. What she doesn't know is that you have lost or spent all her money, so there won't be any coming to Gerald and, consequently, none to her. If I were you, I would find some money to put into Rachel's account so that Augusta will take the pressure off you for at least a week. Then when Rachel is dead, I will send some very incriminating tapes to the police that reveal Gerald's part in murdering Rachel and how Augusta was his accomplice. When the police investigate, they will find the medicine bottle with the poison in it and Gerald's fingerprints all over it. Rachel's body will be exhumed and the coroner will find that death was caused by arsenic poisoning, not Asiatic flu. As a murderer, Gerald will be disqualified from inheriting the money and will spend the rest of his life in prison. Augusta will also go to prison, with no hope of ever inheriting anything, which will let you off the hook. Voilà! Michel Duvigney is never audited and the missing billions remain missing."

Duvigney actually laughed, although it sounded more like someone dying of tuberculosis. "Brilliant, Randall, absolutely brilliant. I'm delighted. If everything goes as planned, there will be quite a nice surprise in your stocking this Christmas."

"Thank you, Michel. I will keep you informed."

Randall turned off the phone, put it back into the bag with the tape recorder, and then walked back to the cottage.

After his conversation with Randall, Michel Duvigney sat quietly for a few minutes, thinking about what Randall had said. Then he picked up the phone and dialed a number. Duvigney heard the phone pick up.

"Rose, here."

"Rose, I have a feeling that Randall is double-crossing me. In a conversation today, he revealed that he has been making incriminating tape recordings of Augusta St. Clair. Knowing Randall, that means he has also been making recordings of my conversations with him. If those conversations ever leaked to the police or the press, it would be very disadvantageous for me. So I want you to be ready to eliminate him as soon as the project in Greenwich is completed. How many days until the girl is dead?"

"Three or four."

Duvigney nodded. "Good. Things are going as planned. As soon as you can verify that Rachel St. Clair is eliminated, I want you to take care of Randall. Does he have any idea that you're a double agent?"

"Colonel Randall trusts me implicitly. After all, we went through some very hot action in Nam together."

"Good. You'll be paid the usual fee and, Rose, be very careful. Randall has eyes in the back of his head."

"I can read the Colonel like a book. He trained me."

"Well, yes, that's true, but be careful anyway. I know I don't have to tell you this, but be sure you recover any tapes or information that will be incriminating to me. He will have them on his person or in his effects."

Duvigney disconnected from the call. He smiled and spoke to himself. "Money always trumps loyalty..."

Then he dialed another number. A woman came on the line.

"Charlene Esperanto here."

"Charlene, it's Michel Duvigney. Have you accomplished the task I requested of you?"

"Yes, Michel. We have tracked Randall as you requested and discovered both the attorney that he would use to deliver any incriminating evidence he might have collected against you and the safe deposit box where it is kept. When should we move on it?"

"Wait until I hear from Rose. He will be taking care of Randall, personally. As soon as Randall is dead, I will call you and you will get rid of the attorney. And what is the bank?"

"Manhattan Trust."

"Good, I will have my man there clean out the safe deposit box as soon as Randall and the attorney have been eliminated. You'll hear from me within five days."

Duvigney hung up the phone. Then he made one more phone call to the Manhattan Trust Bank. When he had passed on the information and instructions to his contact there, he got up and went to the Louis XIV Lion Head wine bar against the back wall. He got out the bottle of Le Voyage de Delamain Cognac and poured himself a drink. He held the snifter to his nose and reveled in the delicious bouquet. Then he raised it in a silent toast to himself. If all went as planned, he wasn't going to have to give up his expensive little habits after all.

A cold, bitter wind cut the night air like a scalpel. The moon was a slim crescent, high in the sky, but the pale light did little to illuminate the grounds of the St. Clair mansion. The clouds had blown through and the temperature had dropped again. A million stars set against the indigo backdrop twinkled in the high canopy of the heavens, but the effect was not delightful. Instead, it was almost ghastly. Daniel King walked quietly toward the huge horse barn. He made sure he stepped on already trodden paths to avoid the crunching of the icy crust under his feet. It was a few minutes after eleven. He slipped inside the open barn door and stepped into the shadows. He waited there silently for almost twenty minutes. Finally, he saw a shadow slipping down the path from the house. It was Gerald St. Clair. Gerald stepped inside the door. He whispered in the darkness. "Daniel?"

"Here, Gerald."

Daniel stepped out and pulled Gerald into the shadows. Gerald was trembling. "Sorry I'm late. I had to wait until Randall's men went for coffee. They were sitting at the end of my hallway. I think my grandmother is suspicious because she's had those men watching me more closely."

"I'm glad you were able to get out. How will you get back in?"

Gerald shrugged. "I'll just tell them I went for a walk, if it's any of their concern." Gerald started trembling again.

Daniel put his hand on Gerald's shoulder. "It is very brave of you to go against your grandmother and her evil plans. You have to gather your courage and trust God."

In the dim light, Daniel could see a puzzled look on Gerald's face.

"You talk like Rachel does, Daniel, but I don't understand what you mean. You both act like God is a real person."

"Oh, but He is a real person. And He's helping us right now."

"What do you mean?"

"Rachel is his daughter. He's concerned about her safety. He has moved on your heart to save her. Don't you see?"

"You mean these feelings that have been bothering me are from Him?"

"Have you been feeling guilty?"

"Very guilty."

"So think about it, Gerald. Here you are, a playboy who married someone you don't even love, just to get her money. She becomes pregnant and now you're feeling guilty, probably for the first time in your life. I would imagine you have gotten other girls pregnant and not given it a thought."

Gerald lowered his head and stood silently for a long moment. Then he looked up at Daniel.

"You're wrong about two things, Daniel. I have felt guilty before—not for a long time, but I have. I used to feel guilty when I was a boy and the priest talked about sin and doing the wrong thing. But after my parents died and I came to live with Grandmother, I learned to never feel guilty about anything I did."

"What is the other thing I'm wrong about?"

"You said I don't love Rachel, but I do. I don't know when it happened, but she's different from any girl I've ever met. She's strong, and sweet and pure. Well, she was...before..."

Daniel put his hand on Gerald's shoulder. "I understand, Gerald. I love her, too. So we must not be afraid to find a way to save her. Tell me where she is."

Gerald pulled Daniel to the door of the barn and pointed at a wing of the house. "She has her own suite in the east wing. It's on the ground floor and she has a set of French doors that open out into the gardens. She pretty much keeps to herself. But those men are watching everything very closely. It will be hard for you to get to her."

Daniel stood quiet for a moment. He tried to think of a way to sneak in to rescue Rachel. He thought of several, but discarded each one as impractical. Finally, he turned to Gerald. "First of all, you've got to stop giving her the poison. Then, I don't know how, you have to tell her I'm here and that I will come for her tomorrow night. Can you do it?"

Gerald looked at Daniel. "I'll slip her a note when I bring the pill in the morning. I'll tell her not to take it and that you're coming at midnight. I'll tell her to leave the patio door unlocked and that you will knock twice."

"Good, good, Gerald. Will she be able to walk?"

"I think so. We've only been giving her the poison for two days. She is very sick, though. Randall wants her to die in three more days so the dose has been strong. But the good thing is they can't give it to her all at once or it won't look like she died of the flu."

"All right. If she doesn't take it tomorrow, she might feel better. I'll figure out a way to get her off the estate between now and tomorrow night."

"Can you drive?"

"Yes. I learned during my *Rumspringa*."

"*Rumspringa?*"

"Yes, that's when we get to go out and see if the Amish way of life is really for us."

"Okay, then. My car is parked in the garage behind the house. It's a white Bentley. Here are the keys. If you go right down the path from Rachel's room you'll come to the garage. It should be open, but if not, this key opens the door. And this big one is the ignition key."

Gerald started away and then he turned. "Thank you for being here, Daniel. I don't know why you would do such a thing..."

"I prayed, Gerald, and this is what the Lord told me to do."

"Well, however it happened, you have to get her out of here. If you don't, my grandmother will have us all killed." He turned and slipped away into the darkness.

Chapter Thirty-One

The Fading

The next morning Gerald came to Rachel's room with her pills and the ginger ale. He was shocked when he saw her lying in her bed. Rachel looked very sick. Her face was pale and her hair was wet from perspiration and lay plastered against her skin. There was a rash on her neck and left cheek. He knelt beside her bed and took her hand. As he did, he pressed a piece of paper into it and folded her hand around it so it could not be seen. Rachel started to say something but Gerald gave a slight shake to his head. Then he spoke loudly. "How are you this morning, Rachel?"

"I don't feel well at all, Gerald. I've been throwing up and…"

Rachel blushed. "…I have to use the toilet a lot. I have a terrible headache and I feel very weak."

Gerald glanced around. The door had closed behind him. He leaned closer to Rachel as though he was going to kiss her cheek and as he did he whispered in her ear. "Read the note and don't take the pills."

Then Gerald leaned back from the kiss and spoke loudly again. Rachel was staring up at him, wide-eyed.

"The doctor says it's some sort of flu, Asian or something. You need to get a lot of rest and drink fluids. And don't forget to take your pill for the morning sickness."

Gerald stood up and walked toward the door. Before he left, he turned and smiled. "I hope you feel better soon, Rachel."

His lips mouthed the words "the note," and then he turned and left.

Rachel waited for a few minutes and then turned over to face the wall. She was trembling. She quietly opened the note and read the words.

> *Don't take the pills. They're poison! Try to eat something today. Daniel is coming to get you at midnight. Leave your patio door unlocked and be ready. He will knock twice.*

Rachel's heart leaped.

Daniel! Daniel is here. Oh, thank you, Lord!

She began to weep. As she did, she heard a noise and turned over. Two men were standing by her bed. One was dressed in black slacks and a black turtleneck. He was powerfully built and towered over her. There was another man standing beside him in black slacks, a pullover sweater, and a houndstooth jacket. He looked familiar. Then she remembered. Gordon Randall.

"Hello, Rachel."

Rachel's heart skipped a beat. "Hello, Mr. Randall. What are you doing here?"

Randall smiled, and the look in his eye sent a cold chill down Rachel's back.

He reached out and took hold of her arm. His grip was like a steel trap. The note fell out of her hand onto the bed.

"I see Gerald has given you a message."

"Let go of me! You're hurting me!"

Rachel began to struggle and scream. Randall reached in his pocket and then put his hand up and covered her mouth. There was a piece of cloth in the palm of his hand and Rachel noticed a faint chemical odor. Then the lights went out.

Randall picked up the note and scanned it. He turned to the second man. "Go get Augusta. I need her now!"

The man hurried out the door. In a few minutes, he returned with Augusta trailing behind.

"What's this all about, Randall? You interrupted my breakfast. Why, what's happened to Rachel?"

"Good morning, Augusta. Sorry about your breakfast, but we have a slight change in plans. You see, Gerald was planning to help Rachel leave, and I had to make an executive decision. What I need now is somewhere we can put her where we can lock her in."

"We have a safe room where we can go if anyone tries to break into the house."

Randall motioned to the second man, and he picked up Rachel like an empty sack. The two men went out the door and followed Augusta down the hall. She stopped in front of an undecorated section of the hallway wall and flipped open a large, ornamental light switch cover. Behind the cover was a keypad. Augusta punched in four numbers and a section of the wall slid back, revealing a door. She opened it and went through into the space behind. A light came on and she motioned the two men inside.

The room was small and sparsely but luxuriously furnished. There was a small kitchen area and a desk with a phone. A television set was mounted in one wall and two beds stood against the other. Two large leather chairs and a couch completed the furnishings.

Randall pointed to the first bed. "Put her there."

Randall's cohort carried Rachel to the bed and laid her down. She was still unconscious.

Augusta watched the procedure with alarm. "Now what do we do, Randall?"

"We keep going with our plan. Only instead of keeping her in her room, we keep her here until she's too sick to move. That way she can't leave and no one can interfere. When she's in the last stages, we put her back in her own bed where someone can find her after she's dead. We'll have to dose her intravenously because Gerald warned her about the pills. In the meantime, my men will watch the house but stay out of sight. According to Gerald's note, someone named Daniel is coming to Rachel's room at midnight to take her away. I assume that would be Daniel King, Rachel's Amish boyfriend. He'll find someone else there instead."

Augusta gave Randall a puzzled look. "How do you know about Daniel King?"

Randall slipped the note into his pocket. "Augusta, you pay me well to do my job. I have to know every detail about the subject of my investigations. Daniel King is a neighbor of the Hershbergers and has known Rachel since she was a small girl. That is the only Daniel that Rachel would know. When I was looking for the Hershbergers, the local postmistress in Paradise told me everything I needed to know about their family and friends. Now, is this room perfectly secure?"

Augusta nodded. "Yes. You have to know the code to open the sliding panel."

"What about that phone?"

"It's a direct line to the Old Greenwich police station."

Randall reached down and pulled the phone cord from the wall. "Not anymore."

Randall turned to the other man. "Headley, no one comes in or out of the grounds without my knowing about it. And nobody, I mean nobody, comes near this part of the house. And I want you to be ready in Rachel's room at midnight to intercept our would-be rescuer."

"Affirmative."

Headley turned and left the room.

Randall turned back to Augusta. "Does anyone else know about this room?"

"Only Gerald and my butler."

"Good. Tell your staff that Mrs. St. Clair is very ill and she is not to be disturbed. I don't want anyone going to her room. Is there a bathroom in here?"

Augusta pointed to a door at the back of the room. "Through there."

"Good, we have everything we need. No one comes in or out of this room except me."

"That's fine, Randall. But what about Gerald?"

"I'm afraid Gerald will have to stay under what we call 'house arrest'. My man will be stationed by his room, and he will remain incapacitated until all this is over."

"Fine, do what you have to do. I'm happy to stay out of this. The whole thing is very upsetting. I didn't know it would get so...so complicated."

"You're not getting cold feet are you, Augusta? We are in way too deep to back out now."

"No, no, Randall...I will be fine. I think I'll go to my room and have a drink. Just let me know when it's over."

"Fine, Augusta. A drink is probably a good idea—settle your nerves. I'll drop by later to collect my check."

Augusta left. Randall waited for a moment to make sure she was gone and then pulled a small walkie-talkie from his pocket. He thumbed the switch and spoke into the microphone.

"How's everything going with our little backup plan, Jamison? Both of the St. Clairs are getting antsy. Gerald has already betrayed us and I can see that Augusta is beginning to crack. The probability that she might turn on us is high."

The speaker crackled and a tinny voice answered. "Don't worry, our presents for the St. Clairs are being placed right now. This property has at least five propane tanks that I counted. If they explode, the house will go up like a torch. But I don't understand, Colonel. Why blow the place up?"

Randall chuckled. "Most likely we won't. But there is another party involved. My professional sense tells me he is preparing to double cross us. I have some very incriminating tapes linking this man to a desperate plot to eliminate the St. Clairs. When I send them to the police, along with a note describing the location of the bombs, some very uncomfortable light will be shed on our man's schemes—just a little payback to Michel Duvigney for thinking he could betray me."

"Good, very good."

Randall smiled and clicked off the device.

Rachel awoke with a pounding headache. She was lying on a bed in a room she did not recognize. Someone had left a light on in the bathroom and a dim light came into the room under the bottom of the door. Rachel sat up and swung her legs over the edge of the bed. The room began to spin and she nearly blacked out again. One of her legs suddenly cramped and the pain was so excruciating she almost cried out. She could feel her stomach begin to cramp. She looked around desperately and saw an open door that looked like it led into a bathroom. She lurched to her feet and stumbled toward the door. Before she could get there, she fell to her knees and vomited. Her stomach twisted and she retched until she was completely empty.

She crawled into the bathroom and found some toilet paper, which she used to wipe her mouth. Then she pulled herself erect at the sink and ran cold water into the basin. She dipped her hands into the water and splashed it on her face. She staggered back into the main room and collapsed on the bed.

As she lay there, she heard a click. She looked over to see Randall and the other man entering the room. Randall was smiling but it reminded Rachel of the pictures she had seen of great white sharks. The other man had something in his hand. It looked like a hypodermic needle. Randall stepped close and forced her down on the bed.

"Hello, again, Rachel. Sorry about the heavy-handedness in your room, but I have a job to do. You see, you have become a real problem for the St. Clairs."

Rachel looked into Randall's eyes. There was an evil there that chilled her heart. "Are you going to kill me now?"

He nodded to the other man who felt for a vein on Rachel's arm and then inserted the needle. "It will take a few more days, Rachel, but yes, I am going to kill you."

Daniel King crept up the steps to the French doors that led into Rachel's room. The bushes around Rachel's patio created good cover and Daniel was able to get close to the house without being observed. He tried to be absolutely quiet, but the hard crust on the snow crunched under his feet. The new moon was up and a low scud of clouds dimmed its already wan light. He looked around and then softly knocked twice on the glass door. There was no answer. He knocked again and then tried the handle. It was unlocked and the door swung open under Daniel's hand. He stepped inside into the dark room.

"Rachel, are you here?"

Daniel heard a noise and then something went over his head from behind and tightened around his throat. His hands went to his neck. There was a thin cord there that was being held so tightly he could not get his fingers under it. It cut deep into his skin, and whoever was holding it was incredibly strong. Daniel desperately tried to turn his body and get his shoulder against his assailant's chest. He managed to get a little leverage and threw himself against the attacker with all his might. The assailant lost his footing and stumbled out through the open door onto the patio. The noose around Daniel's neck loosened a tiny bit, and he could breathe again.

Daniel reached up and grabbed his opponent's wrists. He struggled to break the man's hold, but he felt himself weakening. Then he remembered something that he used when he had to lay a horse down. He pulled forward with all his might until he felt the man resisting. Suddenly, Daniel planted his feet and pushed his body sharply backwards. As he did, he reached under the man's knee and pulled it up.

His attacker slipped on the icy crust of snow and fell heavily against the wrought iron bannister that ran around Rachel's patio. Daniel felt the cord on his neck release and slide off and he turned quickly. His attacker was lying awkwardly against the pointed fence. The man's mouth opened, a groan came out, he jerked spasmodically, and then went limp. Daniel took some gasping breaths. Then he cautiously moved closer.

The man was very big and he was dressed in black clothing. He had slipped and fallen against one of the decorative wrought iron posts, and it had rammed upward into the back of his head. His body hung limply against the fence, and he did not move. Daniel grabbed the assailant's arm and felt for a pulse. There was none. The man was dead.

A shock went through Daniel's frame.

I have killed a man!

And then he remembered why he was there. He ran back to the open door and ducked inside. He waited until his eyes adjusted to the dark and then he looked around the room. The bed was empty. Rachel was gone! He stood there desperately trying to decide what to do. Suddenly, he heard a noise from somewhere in the house and panic gripped him. He ran out the door, and stumbled down the steps, staggering towards the barn like a drunken man. His heart was a sledgehammer in his chest and then the reality of what had just happened swept over him and he fell to his hands and knees and vomited. He crouched in the snow like an animal, shaking, and then he struggled to his feet and leaned against the house until the sickness passed. He turned for a moment, looking back at the mansion that was looming above him like a dark, evil castle in the pale moonlight. "I'll come back for you, Rachel. I'll get help. Hold on!" Then Daniel King turned and ran into the darkness.

Chapter Thirty-Two

Hopeless

Gordon Randall stared at the body hanging limply on the wrought iron bannister, the garrote still clutched in one hand. It was very clear what had happened. He could see the marks of the scuffle in the snow and the place where Headley's boot had slipped. He motioned to the two men standing with him, and together they lifted Headley off the fence. Randall motioned toward the door and they carried him into Rachel's room.

Randall pointed to the bathroom. "Grab a towel and wrap it around his head. And then we'll put him in one of these blankets and take him out to the cottage before it gets light."

Randall shook his head in disbelief while Jamison fetched the towel. Headley had been his best man since the days they fought side by side in the jungles of Vietnam. It was almost beyond comprehension that a highly trained, special-forces soldier had been taken out by an Amish farm boy. They bundled up Headley's body, and then Randall went back out on the patio and shined his flashlight around. It was still well below freezing, so the blood from the wound had coagulated quickly and there was only a small amount on the patio to be cleaned up. Randall looked at his watch. It was 1:30 a.m. The moon had gone down and it was cloudy, so there was little chance that anyone would see them. He went back inside and they picked up the body and carried it to the patio door.

"Walk along the edge of the patio under the roof where there's no snow. I don't want to disturb King's tracks."

The three men muscled the body along the edge of the patio until they reached the path. The bricks had been cleared of snow by the grounds crew the day before and the men did not leave any tracks as they carried Headley to the spot where the SUV was parked. They put the body in the back.

Randall turned to the third man. "Rose, I want you to go back and sanitize the room. Wipe down the fence and make sure there is no blood anywhere. Step in Headley's tracks and leave the mark of your boots, but don't obliterate the boy's tracks. We have to have evidence he was here. If the police come out, we'll tell them that you were the one who fought with King and kept him out of the room. Knowing the local boys, they won't get here until tomorrow and maybe not even then. After you're done, lock the room up tight. We've got to get some more men in here, so when you're finished with the room, call some men you can trust and have them drive up from the city as quickly as they can. I need at least two, three would be better."

"Got it."

Randall and Jamison climbed into the SUV and headed toward the cottage. Jamison shook his head. "It must have happened fast. Headley was good, real good."

Randall nodded. "It looks like the kid shoved him out the door backwards and then somehow Headley slipped on the ice and fell. This really messes things up. The kid is on the loose, Gerald is unconscious in his room, we have a dead body on our hands, and Augusta is getting nervous. It's not so simple anymore."

"What are we going to do, Colonel?"

"I'll call the local police and tell them there was an attempted kidnapping here, and they should be on the lookout for Daniel King. We have to neutralize him. I want a scenario that King can't turn over and the police will buy. Deranged ex-boyfriend shows up at mansion and tries to kidnap the girl but is driven off by security guards that had been alerted to a possible kidnap attempt. I want everything to look normal if the police show up. If they catch King, it will take him a while to get them to believe the truth. By then, the girl will be dead and we'll be long gone. Then Augusta can deal with the police."

"Okay, I'll handle it."

"Good, now let's get Headley into the cellar at the cottage and we'll pull this operation back together."

The phone rang at the Old Greenwich police station. Sergeant Oliver Cromwell Franklin jerked awake at his desk and looked up at the clock on the wall. It was 3 a.m. Sergeant Franklin scratched his belly and then picked up the phone. "Greenwich Police, Sergeant Franklin, how can I help you?"

"Sergeant Franklin, this is Gordon Randall. I'm head of security for Augusta St. Clair. We've had an attempted kidnapping here at the estate. The man escaped and I think he's headed your way. He's on foot."

Sergeant Franklin groaned. Why did this stuff always happen on his shift? And why at the St. Clairs'? Augusta was a tiger and made things miserable if his department didn't keep her happy. "Do you know who it was, Mr. Randall?"

"Yes. The intruder's name is Daniel King. He was an ex-boyfriend of Gerald St. Clair's new wife. He has been obsessing over her and had been sending her letters. When that didn't work, he followed her here from her hometown. He got a job in the St. Clair stables. He grew a beard and the St. Clairs didn't realize who he was until he snuck into Rachel St. Clair's room tonight through an unlocked patio door. She recognized him immediately, though, and called for help. He was ranting and raving about getting her away where she would be safe. When my man heard Mrs. St. Clair screaming and broke into the room, King fought with him and got away. The guy was acting crazy.

Mrs. St. Clair is very upset over the incident, and she's suffering from a bad bout of the flu, so we've moved her to a safe room in the house and we have our men on guard. It's pretty well buttoned up here, but you should put out an APB for King. He's tall, blond hair and beard, and dark clothes. And Sergeant, he is definitely dangerous."

"All right, Mr. Randall. Thanks for the call. Are you sure everything is okay up there?"

"Perfectly, Sergeant. I've called in more men and have them patrolling the estate. A squirrel couldn't get onto the grounds without us knowing it. We're good here. Oh, one more thing."

"What's that, Mr. Randall?"

"When you catch him, Augusta would appreciate it if you did everything you could to keep this incident quiet. She wants him locked up tight. We don't want King taking his crazy stories to the press, and we certainly don't want to put the kidnapping idea in anyone else's head. Rachel St. Clair is very ill with the flu and the St. Clairs don't want anything to upset her. Do you understand?"

"I sure do, Mr. Randall. You let Augusta know that we'll catch this guy and keep him locked up good and tight. I'll let my shift officers know what happened and tell them to be on the alert. As soon as we find King, we'll let you know. There's not too many places he could hide."

"Good, Sergeant, very good."

The line went dead. Sergeant Franklin picked up his dispatcher microphone. He clicked the button and turned the squelch knob so it wouldn't squeal. "Hey, Gary, you awake?"

A voice crackled in the speaker. "Very funny, Sarge. It's freezing out here. We're shaking so hard we're keeping each other awake. Just driving around keeping the car warm and waiting for this miserable shift to be over. What's up?"

"Just got a call from the St. Clair place. Seems as though they had an attempted kidnapping by a disgruntled ex-boyfriend of Gerald's new wife. He got away, and he's on foot. The security man said he was probably headed into town—tall, blond kid with a beard. And don't take any chances. He got in a fight with one of the guards out there and beat him up, so consider him dangerous."

"Right, Sarge. I just passed the St. Clair place and I'm coming in on Field Point Road now. We'll check along the road all the way into town."

Daniel King walked down the road toward Greenwich. He was still in shock from the events of an hour before. The snow had started again and it was bitter cold. The lights of a car approaching from the direction of the St. Clair estate reflected off the trees ahead of him. This part of Field Point Road was a little wilder with trees growing right down to the road. Daniel slipped into a clump of shrubs under the trees and waited for the car to go by. It was going slowly and someone was shining flashlights into the trees on both sides of the road. Suddenly, Daniel's insides twisted and his heart started pounding.

Maybe it's those men. They're looking for someone!

Daniel drew back into the heart of the shrubs. The car pulled up nearby and stopped with the motor running. It was a police car. Relief swept over Daniel. He was about to step out when he heard something in his spirit.

Stop!

He stopped dead in his tracks. Then he heard the radio crackle and a tinny voice came on.

"Gary, Augusta wants this Daniel King picked up and put on ice. If he puts up a fight, use whatever force is necessary to stop him. Do you understand me?"

"Sure, Sarge, I get you. A tough customer, eh?"

"Yes, and according to their man, Randall, very dangerous. So when I say whatever force is necessary, that's what I mean. Don't take any chances. If he struggles, defend yourself."

"Okay, Sarge."

Daniel moved quietly back into the bushes and then peeked through the branches. The police car was about fifteen feet away. He could see the officer take his gun out of his holster and chamber a round.

They're working for Augusta, too! They would kill me if they had to.

Daniel pushed further back into the brush and stood as still as he could. The two officers in the car swept their flashlights over the sides of the road and then drove slowly on toward town. Daniel watched them go and then crept out of his hiding place.

Augusta has this town under her thumb. Lord, I need help.

Suddenly Daniel remembered Willy, the stationmaster.

Willy liked me. And he didn't seem too fond of Augusta St. Clair. Maybe he can help me.

Daniel headed toward town. He stayed along the edges of the road in the shadows, carefully watching for more cars as he went.

Willy was nodding in his chair in front of a decrepit old television set in the office at the Old Greenwich station when he was awakened by a noise. At first he thought it was the wind rattling the windows, but then he heard it again.

Tap! Tap! Tap!

He swiveled around in his chair. There was someone at the side door. Willy got up slowly and shuffled over to the door. He looked through the glass. It was the young man that he had sent out to the St. Clair estate. Quickly, he opened the door. "Well, well! Dan-David. What are you doing here at this hour? Come in, before I lose all the heat in the room."

Willy pulled Daniel inside and slammed the door behind him. Then he turned to look at the young man. "You don't look so good. What's going on?"

Daniel sank down on a bench that was against the wall. "I'm in trouble, Willy. But worse than that, my friend Rachel is in great danger. They're going to kill her. I've got to help her."

"Whoa, hold on boy! Who's going to kill her?"

Daniel put his head in his hands. "Augusta and her professional killer, Gordon Randall."

Willy shook his head. "Now, son, you're a little upset…"

"But I'm not crazy, Willy. I'm an old friend of Rachel's. I've been kind of…well, watching over her. Gerald recognized me from when we met in Paradise. But he didn't turn me in. He was terrified of his grandmother and her killers. He told me everything. They tried to make him help them, but he couldn't go through with it. We were going to get her out of there tonight, but they caught on to us. There was a guy waiting in Rachel's room. He almost killed me, but I got away. I think he's dead."

Willy looked at Daniel closely and then went to the cupboard and got down a mug. He poured a cup of coffee from an old ceramic pot on a hotplate on the counter and handed it to Daniel. "Drink this, boy. Tell me your real name, and then start from the beginning."

Daniel took the coffee gratefully and then told Willy everything that had happened since he went to work for the St. Clairs. When he got to the part about being attacked in Rachel's bedroom and the death of his assailant, Willy's eyebrows went up and he whistled. Then Daniel told him about the conversation he had heard on the police radio.

"Right, Oliver Cromwell Franklin and his local thugs. Those boys are sold out to Augusta St. Clair—have been for years. They'll do anything Augusta asks."

Daniel put down his mug. "Willy, I have to call Sheriff Bobby Halverson. He lives at the Hershberger place in Paradise. That's Rachel's folks. He's an ex-cop and a decorated World War II vet. He'll know what to do."

Willy pointed to the wall by his desk. "Phone's right over there, Daniel." Just then, the lights of a car pulling up in front of the station flashed on the wall. Willy looked out the window. Quickly, he turned back and whispered to Daniel. "It's Gary Parkins, Franklin's right-hand man. You gotta get out of here. There's no place to hide. Go to my place on Railroad Street— number 432." Willy reached in his pocket. "Here's the key. Go out the back, cut down by the pizza place and keep walking. It's on the corner a block down. Do you have the number for this Sheriff Halverson?"

"I don't. You'll have to call information. He lives on Old Leacock Road in Paradise, Pennsylvania. His name is spelled H-a-l-v-e-r-s-o-n. You have to help, Willy."

Willy could see a flashlight approaching the front of the station. "I'll call him, Daniel. Now go, quick! Before these morons catch you." He shoved Daniel out the back door and went and sat down at his desk.

Just then the door opened and Gary Parkins called out. "Willy? Willy? You in here?"

"I'm in the back where it's warm, Officer Parkins." Willy glanced out the window. Daniel was gone.

Part Three

A Wind from the Sea

Mighty Angels of grace and hope
lift the heart of the sailor
and the fear that claimed his heart,
The tossing storm waves that carried him away,
Fade like the morning mist and are no more...
A sea change carries him back to shore,
Now from the crest of a wave he sees the haven
and his dear wife and child waiting by the fireside.

Home from the Sea—From The Journals of Jenny Hershberger

Chapter Thirty-Three

First Light

The single lamp on the desk shed a soft light in the room. Rachel St. Clair lay on the bed. Her head throbbed and her stomach churned. Her hair was plastered to her brow and her pajamas were soaked with sweat. She groaned and tried to sit up, but the room began to spin and she almost threw up. She collapsed back on the bed.

"Help me, Lord...please help me!"

Rachel!

Rachel's parched lips moved and she whispered an answer.

"Is that you, Lord?"

Fear thou not; for I am with thee: be not dismayed; for I am thy God: I will strengthen thee; yea, I will help thee; yea, I will uphold thee with the right hand of my righteousness.

Then the lamp seemed to flood the room with brilliance. Rachel reached her hand toward the light.

"Danki, lieber Gott!"

Then the light dimmed again and Rachel faded into darkness.

Willy looked up to see Officer Gary Parkins standing on the customer side of the counter. Willy nodded. "It's a little early to be buying a ticket isn't it, Gary?"

"I'm not here for a ticket, Willy, so you can keep your smart remarks to yourself. I'm looking for…" Parkins glanced down at a piece of paper in his hand and then back up. "I'm looking for a guy named Daniel King. He attempted to kidnap Rachel St. Clair out at the St. Clair mansion. He got in a brawl with the security guards and escaped, and we're trying to close up all the ways he could get out of town. Seen any strangers around tonight?"

"Nope. Haven't seen any strangers at all tonight."

"Well, when's the next train due?"

"Two hours from now. What's this stranger look like?"

"He's tall—blond hair and a short, blond beard. He was wearing jeans, a navy pea coat and a black watch cap. He's strong and desperate. We consider him very dangerous."

"Yeah, officer, he must be if he fought his way off the estate. I'll keep an eye out, and let you know if anything unusual happens."

"Okay, Willy. Say, you got a snort in that desk of yours for a policeman who needs to warm up a little?"

Willy shook his head. "Sorry, officer. I gave up drinking last week. Doctor's orders."

Officer Parkins mumbled something under his breath and then headed for the door. On his way out he stopped and looked at Willy. "Don't forget to call me if anything unusual happens." The door slammed shut.

Willy watched as the police car drove away. Then he reached into his drawer and pulled out a small bottle of Southern Comfort. He took a pull and put it back. A big smile creased his face. "Yeah, right, officer. I'll call you when I really quit drinking."

Willy waited until the lights of the police car disappeared. He looked at the clock on the wall. It was 5 a.m. Then he picked up the phone and dialed information. The operator came on.

"Information, what city, please?"

"Operator, I need the number for Bobby Halverson in Paradise, Pennsylvania."

"How do you spell that, please?"

"Halverson, H-a-l-v-e-r-s-o-n."

"Thank you, just a moment please."

Willy waited.

"That number is 717-687-2233."

"Thank you, operator."

"You're very welcome, sir. Have a nice day."

Willy dialed the number. It rang four times. "Come on, Sheriff! Pick up! Pick up!" The phone clicked over to an answering device. Willy's heart sank.

"Hi! This is Bobby Halverson. I'm not in right now, but leave me a message and I'll get right back—" In the middle of the message, there was a click and a voice came on the line. "Bobby Halverson, it's too early to be calling. What do you want?"

Willy almost cheered. "Sheriff Halverson, this is Willy Oxendine. I'm the stationmaster at the Old Greenwich train station and I'm a friend of Daniel King. He's in serious trouble here in Connecticut. Something about how the St. Clairs are trying to murder his friend Rachel. You have to come here immediately. Rachel is very sick and Daniel says she doesn't have much time. The police here are hirelings of the St. Clairs. They won't help Daniel and, in fact, are looking for him to throw him in jail. I have him hidden but they have the dragnet out for him..."

The bleary voice on the other end of the line interrupted. "Whoa, go a little slower, Willy. I just woke up. Now what's this about Daniel and Rachel?"

Willy took a breath. "Daniel King came into the station early this morning. He was on the run. He was working at the St. Clair place, kinda keeping an eye on Rachel, he said, and he found out about a plot to kill Rachel for her money. So he tried to rescue her but they were on to him. He barely got away. He's says they're poisoning Rachel and she's only got a few more hours left. I can't call the local police because they all work for Augusta. Can you get up here?"

"I hope this isn't a joke, Willy."

"Honest, Sheriff, it's all true. My phone number is 203-525-4415. I met Daniel a few weeks ago. I got him the job out there. He's a good kid and I know he's not telling me a lie. You've got to help him, Sheriff."

"Okay, I'm coming up there. Should take me about three hours. When I get there, I'll make some phone calls and see if I can get some help. In the meantime, where is Daniel?"

"I have him hidden at my house. Meet me at the station. It's right downtown. Then I'll take you to him."

"Okay, I'll see you soon."

The line went dead.

Jenny Hershberger sat on the sofa in front of the fire. A bitter cold had engulfed Pennsylvania, and the fire fought weakly against it. A great heaviness crushed down upon Jenny, and she did not know why. She had awakened at midnight with a deep need to pray for Rachel. She left the bedroom and came out to the front where she had been weeping and praying ever since. Finally, she went to the shelf and brought down her mama's old Bible. She opened it to the flyleaf.

Jerusha Hershberger 1937, From her grandmother, Hannah Hershberger

There was great comfort in holding the old Bible. Her mama and her *grossmutter* had both held this book. It was as though they were in the room to comfort her. Her fingers moved over the worn pages, and without looking for any verse in particular, she flipped open a page. It was Proverbs. Her eye caught the first verse on the page.

Trust in the LORD with all thine heart; and lean not unto thine own understanding.
In all thy ways acknowledge him, and he shall direct thy paths.

Jenny looked in wonder at the verse. It was as though *du leiber Gott* had spoken directly to her heart. She sighed and put the Bible down.

Suddenly, the door burst open. Bobby Halverson stood there. The look on his face was grim.

"Bobby, what is it?"

"Where's Jonathan?"

"He's lying down."

"Take me to him."

Jenny led Bobby down the hallway to her bedroom. She opened the door. Jonathan was lying on the bed reading his Bible. He looked up when Jenny and Bobby came in, and he laid the Bible down. A puzzled look came over his face. "Hello, Bobby, what's going on?"

"Jonathan, you've got to get up and get dressed. Rachel is in desperate trouble. I just got a call from Willy, a friend of Daniel King. Daniel is in trouble in Connecticut and he told Willy that Rachel is being poisoned by the St. Clairs. We've got to go get her, now!"

A pained look came over Jonathan's face. "I can't go, Bobby. Rachel is shunned. The *Ordnung* says…"

Jenny looked at Bobby. His jaw was working and his face seemed to set like stone. He walked over to the bed, grabbed Jonathan by his shirt and dragged him up to a standing position. Jenny cried out. "Bobby, what are you doing? Jonathan isn't well…"

"Stay out of this, Jenny." Bobby pulled Jonathan up close and almost shouted at him. "To hell with the *Ordnung*, Jonathan! This is your daughter who's dying. Now man up and get your clothes on. You are coming with me if I have to kick you down the hall!"

Jenny couldn't believe this was happening. She tried to pull Bobby's hands away from Jonathan, but Bobby's grip was like a steel trap. "Let him go, Bobby! Let him go! You'll hurt him!"

Then Jonathan took hold of Jenny's hands and pulled them away from Bobby's. He looked into her eyes and a sad smile came on his face. "No, Jenny, don't. Bobby is right. I've been hiding behind the *Ordnung* too long, and you've been helping me.

I know you mean well, but you can't protect me anymore. Rachel's in danger and I'm her father. I've got to go, no matter what."

Bobby let Jonathan go. "That's my boy. Now get moving. The truck's outside, ready to go."

"Give me five minutes."

"Okay." Bobby turned and walked out of the room.

Jenny's heart was pounding. Then a conversation she had with Rachel before all this happened came back to her. It was the day Rachel left. They had been standing in Rachel's room while she packed and Rachel's frustration and anger had poured out on Jenny...

"When he left us, Mama, everything changed. We went back to Ohio and you were so sad for so long. Everything was about you, your sorrow, your grief. What about my grief? You thought I was doing okay but I was not. And you were so lost in your own pain that you had no time to really find out how I was feeling. At least I had Grossdaadi and Grossmutter, and they helped me for a while. Then they died and I was so afraid."

"Afraid, Rachel?"

"Yes, Mama. I was afraid—afraid you would leave me too. I used to wake up at night feeling like someone was standing on my chest. I just knew something was going to happen to you and then I would be alone. And then he came home and it did happen."

"What happened, Rachel?"

"You left me, Mama."

"But how? I was right here all the time."

Rachel's voice rose. "No, Mama, you were not. Suddenly we had a stranger in our house and everything was about him. Poor Jonathan, he's not well. Poor Jonathan, he shouldn't be disturbed. You never had time for me anymore, and I hated that. It was like I was a stranger, standing out on the porch and looking into this house where all this love used to be, but I was out in the cold and you both were inside."*

As Jenny remembered Rachel's words, she felt as though she had been slapped. Rachel was right. She had protected Jonathan and tried to heal him in her own power. She had forgotten the lesson the Lord had taught her so long ago; to trust in Him alone and stop living life in her own strength. Jenny put her hands to her face and burst into tears. Jonathan turned as he was buttoning his coat. He came to Jenny and took her in his arms. Jenny sobbed. "I'm…I'm so…so sorry, Jonathan."

"Sorry for what, my darling?"

"Rachel…Rachel…was…right. I left her. I've been so focused on saving you that I…I…left her…alone."

Jenny felt strength flow back into Jonathan's arms as he held her tight.

"I know, Jenny. And I'm sorry, too. I've been so afraid of living that I've been like a dead man; to you and to Rachel. Now maybe *du lieber Gott* is giving me another chance; a chance to live again. Pray for us, my precious wife. We'll find her."

Jenny held him tight for one more minute.

Bobby's voice came down the hall. "You can do that when we bring Rachel home! Let's go!"

Jenny and Jonathan both laughed through their tears. Then Jonathan kissed Jenny quickly and walked out the door. Jenny was alone in the room. She looked down at the Bible lying on the bed. There was a bookmark in it. She picked up the Bible and opened it at the marker. Jonathan had been reading in Proverbs. The first verse leapt out at her.

Trust in the LORD with all thine heart; and lean not unto thine own understanding.

In all thy ways acknowledge him, and he shall direct thy paths.

Sergeant Oliver Cromwell Franklin was very grumpy. He had just hung up from a nasty phone call with Augusta St. Clair's man, Gordon Randall. Randall had been a little perturbed that the police department had not found Daniel King, and he told Franklin in no uncertain terms that his job was on the line if they did not find King soon. He also demanded extra police patrols around the St. Clair estate, which definitely put a strain on Franklin's manpower. In fact, it meant that Sergeant Franklin would have to get off his rear end and get out on the streets in a patrol car, a job that he thought he left behind when he got promoted. He flipped the switch on the dispatch microphone. "Parkins! Parkins, are you there?"

The unit squawked and then Parkins came on. "Yeah, Sarge, I'm here."

"Any sign of King?"

"Not yet, Sarge. I'm just about to go off shift."

"Yeah, well get your tail back in that car. Nobody goes off shift until we find Daniel King. Is that clear? I'm coming out there myself."

Parkins snickered. "Got a phone call from Augusta, eh, Sarge?"

Sergeant Oliver Cromwell Franklin snarled back at his officer. "It was from her security man, Gordon Randall. Now listen up, smart guy. You're in this as deep as I am. I suppose you forgot about the nice vacation to Aruba that Augusta popped for last summer. That wouldn't look very nice to the local yokels if some snoop dug up where the money came from, would it? Or any of the other little perks over the years."

"No, Sarge."

"Right! So I suggest you get in gear and find that kid. And keep your smart remarks to yourself."

"Okay, Sarge, okay. Sorry."

Oliver Cromwell Franklin lowered his voice. "Look, Parkins. There's something going on out at the St. Clairs', and if it blows up in our faces, we can kiss our jobs goodbye. So just find that kid and put him on ice. Do it now!" Franklin switched off the CB before Parkins could answer.

Chapter Thirty-Four

Deep Games

Gordon Randall looked at his watch. It was 8 a.m. and the police had not found Daniel King. He parked the SUV on the service road behind the house and turned to Rose and Jamison. "Things are spinning out of control here. First, Gerald betrays us, then Headley gets himself killed, and then Daniel King escapes. The local boys haven't seen any sign of him. That means he found a hiding place, he got out of town, or he's trying to get back to Rachel. We need to move up the schedule of events before King tries something."

Jamison scowled. "So what's plan B, Colonel?"

"The girl has to die today unless..."

Jamison glanced at Rose. "Unless what, Colonel?"

"I've got some business to take care of with Augusta before we finalize Rachel. I want the girl alive until it's all settled. If Augusta doesn't go for my proposal, we might have to use Rachel as our ticket out of here. What about Gerald? I don't want him interfering again."

Jamison grinned. "Gerald is pretty stoned. I've been giving him barbiturates, so he's out of it. As far as setting the guy up, I mixed arsenic into the ginger ale he's been giving her and I've got his fingerprints on the soda bottle, her glass, and the pill bottle."

"What about the hypodermic needles you've been injecting her with?"

"I used the very smallest needle you can get. Unless someone is specifically looking for an injection mark, they won't see it."

"Good. Has the girl gone into a coma yet?"

"No, but she's very weak. She couldn't walk three steps, much less get away. One more big dose and she's a goner."

"Okay, and what about Headley?"

"Everything seems normal with the staff this morning, which means that nobody knows about Headley's death. The basement of the cottage is like a meat locker. He'll keep until we leave."

"Good, Jamison. Are the other men here?"

Rose nodded. "Yeah they got here about fifteen minutes ago. They dumped their gear at the cottage, and they're waiting for orders."

"Okay, I want those guys out front, patrolling the gate and the service road. We have to keep everyone out of the St. Clair estate until tomorrow morning. I don't even want the cops in here. They can patrol outside but I don't want anyone on the grounds until we are gone. If everything goes right, we'll be out of here by ten, leaving Augusta and Gerald holding the bag for Rachel's death. If we pull this off, there will be a big bonus for you guys."

Jamison smiled. "How big, Colonel?"

"One hundred thousand each."

Jamison rubbed his hands together. "I like that, Colonel. I like that."

Rose's face was impassive.

Randall nodded. He picked up a briefcase from the seat next to him and tapped it. "I've got one more little card to play with Augusta and then we'll put this operation to bed." Randall got out of the SUV. "Okay, Jamison, I want you to watch Gerald and the girl."

Jamison nodded.

"Rose, you're a rover. Keep patrolling the grounds and stay visible so that the staff knows there is a security team here."

"Got it, Colonel."

"Oh, and one last thing. Is the nuclear option set?"

Jamison smiled and handed Randall a small paper bag. "All of the propane tanks are set with a small charge of Semtex and a wireless receiver. These are the detonators—a main and a backup."

Randall slipped the package into his pocket. Jamison walked off, headed for the east wing of the mansion, and Rose drove away on his rounds. Randall watched them go. His professional instincts were on high alert. Something was very wrong with this whole operation. It was time to play his trump card and get out before the police showed up. He thought about his options.

I'll keep the girl alive until Augusta signs over the securities. The last thing Augusta wants is the police talking to a live Rachel.

The wind picked up as Randall walked down the path from the service road to the main house. Snow was beginning to fall, hard, icy snow that stung his face. There was a big storm blowing in off the Atlantic and it would be arriving soon. In the distance, he could hear the sound of heavy surf pounding against the point. The Weather Channel had put out a winter storm warning and was broadcasting that the whole area would be shut down by that afternoon. Randall liked that. After his job was over and he had squeezed Augusta for the big bucks, he would send the incriminating material to the police. They would find Gerald stoned on downers in his room, the dead girl and the glass and bottles with Gerald's fingerprints in the secret room, and the taped conversations with Augusta. Randall and his men would be long gone under the cover of the storm.

Randall entered by the side door and walked down the hall to Augusta's office. He knocked twice and then went in without waiting for a response. Augusta was sitting at the desk with her head in her hands. When she heard Randall enter, she looked up. Her face was a question mark. "What's going on, Randall? Did you know Daniel King was here? How did he get away from your trained professionals? He's only a stupid, Amish farm boy."

"One question at a time, Augusta. Yes, we've had a little glitch in our plans. Daniel King was supposed to be eliminated by my man. Unfortunately, Headley underestimated the strength of the boy. He got himself killed because of his carelessness."

Augusta's eyes widened. "Killed? But…but how?"

"King got him out on the patio and Headley slipped on the ice. He fell backwards against a wrought iron post and it penetrated his brain. He was dead instantly."

Augusta stood up from her desk. There was panic in her eyes. "Gordon! You promised this would go off without a hitch. Now someone who can cause us a lot of problems is loose out there." She sank back into her chair and put her face in her hands. Then she looked back up at Randall. "I want that girl dead."

Randall nodded and then he reached in his pocket. "Yes, I wanted to talk to you about that, Augusta." He opened his briefcase and took out a bundle of photographs held together by a rubber band. "I think you should look at these first. You see, Augusta, one of the things that people in my profession always do is find out everything they can about their clients. I did a little exploring here a few nights ago and came up with some very interesting information about you. I printed up some copies. The original photos are in a very safe place."

Augusta took the photos from Randall and rolled off the rubber band. She began to leaf through them. After a moment, she looked up at Randall. He had never seen such a venomous look on a person's face. Augusta was trembling. "Why, Randall, you clever boy. You broke into my office."

"Yes, and I photographed everything—the diary, the letters, the photos, the papers. I finally figured out what you're really up to, Augusta."

"And what would that be, Gordon?"

"It's never really been about the St. Clair money for you, has it? It's always been about Robert St. Clair."

Augusta's face became set like flint. Her eyes seemed to focus somewhere beyond Randall. She whispered the name. "Robert St. Clair. Robert, my dear Robert." Then her eyes focused again and she looked up at Randall. "Yes, Gordon, it has always been about Robert St. Clair. Ever since the day I met him. He was so much different than that limp-wristed little pantywaist, Jerod. He was a real man, strong, beautiful, powerful. You know nothing about how I felt about Robert."

"You hated him, I know that."

"No, I loved him."

"You hated him with all your heart."

Augusta smiled and tipped her head to the side. The coquetry reminded Randall of a faded Bette Davis in *Whatever Happened to Baby Jane.* "Well, I suppose you could call it a love-hate relationship, Gordon. What's that to you?"

Randall pulled out some pictures from the pile. They were the ones with Robert, Rachel, and Jenny. "I'm assuming these are the pictures that Robert sent to his father in 1948, the ones you said you never found. You stole these from Max. You knew all along what Rachel Borntraeger St. Clair looked like. When she showed up in New York, you were ready for her. And you hated her. You had her put out of the hotel and you hired Joe Bender to degrade her, get her strung out on heroin. You didn't want her dead. You wanted her to suffer, like you had suffered."

Augusta sighed and then tittered. It was a strange, grating sound. "Well, Gordon, you're a very astute young man. You probed and you dug and you sneaked and you kept at it and you struck gold, didn't you? You've discovered my little secrets."

She got up and walked to the window. She stared out at the snow blowing wildly across the grounds of the estate. "Everyone has a purpose in life, Gordon. You are a professional killer. That's who you were made to be. You can't be anything else. I wondered what my purpose was for a long time. I knew I wasn't supposed to be some middle-class, dumpy housewife living out her life in the Bronx with a stupid husband and screaming brats. I was meant for much greater things.

"And then one day, it was the very day Robert St. Clair rejected me, everything became perfectly clear. We were sitting in the Stork Club and Robert was telling me that he was going to marry that Amish whore. While Robert was going on and on about the new love of his life, it was like I couldn't hear him anymore because there was another voice speaking to me. And I knew who it was. It was God himself, and in that instant, I knew that I had been called to serve God in a wonderful way. I had been chosen to be his hand of vengeance against the whole evil, corrupt St. Clair family. And I have performed my duty. Well, not quite all my duty."

She turned back to face him.

Randall stared at Augusta. Something had changed and Randall knew what it was. The mask had come off and Randall was looking at the real Augusta St. Clair—a conniving, climbing, murderess named Francine Bosnan—a woman capable of anything, a woman who was totally insane. The thought chilled him. He took a stab. "Max and Margaret, Robert's parents?"

Augusta nodded.

"Your own son, Francis, and his wife?"

Augusta shrugged. "He was Robert St. Clair's son, and I hated him as much as I hated Robert." Augusta sat back down and folded her hands together. She put on the glasses that hung on a chain around her neck. The change was startling. She looked like a prim, maidenly schoolteacher. She looked up at Gordon and spoke to him in a businesslike manner. "Well, Gordon, you didn't do all this sneaking and uncovering for fun. Obviously you want something from me. What do you want?"

"Money, of course."

"How much?"

"One million dollars."

Augusta stiffened. "That's a lot of money."

"Really, Augusta? I photographed the Swiss Bank Account Book under the name of Francine Bosnan. You've been siphoning money from Gerald's trust for years. Right now you've got eighty million in Zurich and two million in New York. I also saw the list of negotiable securities, which are held right here in the Greenwich bank. There are over a million dollars' worth within a fifteen-minute drive. I want you to call your banker and get him out here with enough securities to meet my price. You hand over the securities, I give you all my photos, Rachel dies, and my men and I disappear. You take it from there." He glanced at his watch. "It's eight-fifteen. You have one hour."

"And if I don't comply?"

"My men and I take the girl to the hospital and then we'll make all the other incriminating evidence available to the police and the FBI."

"Incriminating evidence?"

"The evidence that shows your complicity with Gerald in the plot to murder Rachel. Then when you are answering some very probing questions, your diary shows up in the mail at the D.A.'s office, and then the police will be looking into the murders of Robert St. Clair and the rest of his family. I cover all the bases. You should have learned that about me."

"Yes, Gordon. I have certainly been remiss."

"You have one hour, Augusta."

Willy was dozing at his desk when the creak of the front door opening woke him up. He looked up at the two men coming to the counter. One was of medium height. He was older but his hair was still sandy with a touch of gray at the temples. He carried himself like a military man. He wore a short green flight jacket with a sheepskin collar and a Stetson hat. Hanging at his side was a service revolver with the holster strap snapped over the handle of the pistol. The man with him was Amish, but the look in his eye was grim. He was tall, with long dark hair and a beard. A faint scar ran along the side of his forehead. The two men stood at the counter. Outside, the wind began to howl.

"You gotta be Sheriff Halverson."

"That's me, Willy. This is Jonathan Hershberger. He's Rachel's father."

"You made good time, considering the storm coming in."

"We got in just ahead of the front. I did kind of push it a little. Good thing the State Police were huddled somewhere along the road drinking coffee. It's really blowing up a mess out there." Bobby looked around to see if anyone else was in the waiting room and then spoke quietly. "Where's Daniel?"

"He's at my place. It's only a block away."

"How do we get out to the St. Clair place?"

"It's out on Field Point Road. Daniel knows where it is. But they're not going to let you in there. In fact, Sergeant Franklin and Augusta's security boys have buttoned that place up tight. As soon as they see Daniel, they'll arrest him."

"How do we get in there, then?"

"There's only one way. You've got to go out on Long Island Sound and go around the back of the point, by boat. I've got it all worked out. My cousin, Frank, has a Boston Whaler and he'll take you. I've already talked to him. It'll be tough because the wind is really starting to blow. But you can make your way along the shore and stay out of most of it."

Bobby glanced over. Jonathan was staring at Willy and there was anguish written on his face. Jonathan took a deep breath. "Out on the ocean? Long Island Sound?"

"Yes, sir, Mr. Hershberger. It's not far and it's fairly protected. The St. Clairs have a big dock with a covered boathouse, and once you land, it's only a short walk to the house... Why, what's wrong, Mr. Hershberger?"

Jonathan's eyes had a strange look. He passed his fingers over the scar. They were trembling. He sat down on a bench and put his face in his hands. "I can't go out there, I just can't."

Willy looked over at Bobby.

Bobby stepped over to Jonathan and put his hand on his shoulder. "Jonathan, we've been friends for a long time. So I feel like I can speak straight to you. I once had a discussion like this with Jenny's father, Reuben. He didn't think he could go into battle because of his conflicting fears. But in the end, he went, and he saved my life. Now is the time for you to put everything aside, all your fear, all of the past, all of the terrible things that happened to you out on that ocean, and think only of your duty to Rachel. If we don't go now, she will die. That's the bottom line."

Jonathan took a deep breath, almost a sob. Then he slowly lifted his head. As Willy watched him, a change passed over his face and a fire kindled in his eyes. He stood up. "You are right, Bobby. We'll say no more about it. Let's go."

Bobby slapped Jonathan on the shoulder and smiled. He looked out at the storm blowing wildly through the square in front of the station. He turned to Willy. "Can I use your phone?"

Willy pointed to the desk.

Bobby pulled out a notebook and looked up a number. He dialed. When a man answered, Bobby quickly filled him in on the situation. Then he shook his head. "Over an hour, Jerry? That's too long for us to wait. Rachel may be dead by then. Tell you what. We're going after Rachel. You get out to St. Clairs' as fast as you can. We'll hold the fort until then."

Bobby hung up the phone and looked at Jonathan and Willy. "That was my friend, Jerry Cowell, head of the Connecticut State Police. The closest large force he has is at Milford, but it's going to take an hour to get here because of the storm. So we have to go get Rachel on our own."

Bobby looked out the window at the gathering fury of the storm. "It doesn't look good out there, Jonathan, but suppose we put our trust in this God of yours and see what happens."

Jonathan smiled and turned to Willy. "Take us to Daniel, Willy."

Chapter Thirty-Five

The Greatest Trial

Daniel King, Jonathan, Bobby, and Willy stood on the dock looking at the old Boston Whaler as it rode in its moorings. Willy's cousin, Frank, was cranking up the engine and getting the boat ready to go. He motioned to the men to come aboard. They clambered over the side onto the deck. Waves from off the sound were starting to move into the harbor and boats up and down the quay were pitching and rolling in their slips.

Frank slapped the side of the boat. "She's old, but she's the most sea-worthy craft on the sound. It's just a short run down to St. Clair's place, biggest boathouse on the North Shore. We'll slip this baby right inside, and nobody will be the wiser."

Jonathan walked to the bow of the boat and looked out over the water. Grey-green, choppy swells rolled toward him from off the Atlantic. A mist rose from the water. The waves were endless, moving toward him out of the mist and disappearing away toward the unseen horizon. It was dark, so dark, and the strange smell of the salt water was overpowering and somehow terrifying. A stiff breeze drove the icy spray off the tops of the waves into Jonathan's eyes. He raised his hand to wipe his face, but the mist and spray were continuous, blinding him. The chill of winter not yet dead...the gulls circling behind the boat...the plaintive cries whirling away on the wind. The sea ominous and lifeless...

And then he was in the darkness and the cold and the spray and the waves, the endless waves, rolling, rolling, rolling by and where were they going? Suddenly, a great longing to see Jenny and Rachel swept over him like one of the swells rolling ceaselessly and vanishing away, beyond his sight. He was lost, gone, alone on the bridge of a ghost ship that cut through the waves like a sword... He was frozen, dead, lost on the sea. He looked in through the porthole and watched the ship's wheel spinning crazily and no hand was on it—there was no one to pilot the boat. Where was the captain? Then he felt a hand touch him...

"Jonathan, are you all right?"

Jonathan jerked around. The hand on his shoulder did not belong to his father. His father was dead. He had died out on that lonely sea a long time ago. The hand on his shoulder belonged to his old friend, Bobby Halverson, who was staring at him with eyes filled with concern. And then Jonathan knew he wasn't lost on the sea. He was here with his friends, and they were going together to save Rachel. Jonathan shook his head and passed his hand over his eyes. "Bobby! I...I kind of got lost there for a minute..."

Suddenly, the wind blew straight in on them and the boat leapt up in its moorings and twisted to the left. They heard a cry, then a thud and a groan behind them. Bobby and Jonathan looked around. Frank was lying on the deck, holding his arm. Daniel was bending down. He looked up at Jonathan and Bobby. "The boat twisted and Frank slipped on the ice and fell." He turned back to Frank. "Are you okay?"

Frank groaned. "I think I broke my arm. I've been on this boat for thirty years and I've never fallen. Ooooh!"

Bobby and Daniel crouched over Frank, checking out his arm. Bobby nodded at Daniel and then looked up at Willy. "Willy, Frank did break his arm. You're going to have to get him to the hospital."

Frank grimaced in pain. "But what about the girl, Sheriff? She's going to die if you don't get her and this is the only way."

From behind them came a voice, soft but unafraid. "I'll take them, Frank."

Bobby looked up at Jonathan. "Are you sure, Jonathan?"

Jonathan nodded. "Look, Bobby. I grew up on Long Island. I've cruised these waters in a six-foot sailboat. I've been up and down every inch of the north shore in a boat just like this. We've got to get Rachel, and I'm the only one who can take us. You and Daniel are landlubbers. You couldn't sail your way out of a paper bag."

Bobby laughed. "You're right about that, pal."

Jonathan looked back out at the sea. "Besides, I can't let this ocean beat me again."

Bobby slapped Jonathan on the back. "Okay, Jonathan, let's do it then."

Willy clambered back onto the dock and they lifted Frank over the side. He stood morosely on the dock, holding his arm.

"Sorry, fellas. I let you down."

Jonathan waved back. "Frank, we're good. Daniel knows the St. Clair place and he can show me the boathouse. We'll be back with Rachel before you know it."

He turned to his crew. "Bobby, you and Daniel cast off those two hawsers...those ropes."

Jonathan stood at the wheel, his dark hair flying in the wind as he eased the boat out into the wild waters of Long Island Sound.

Gordon Randall watched the storm through the window of the cottage. The wind had picked up in intensity. Through the blowing snow he saw a figure approaching. It was Jamison. He came inside banging his arms across his chest to get warm.

"Temperature's dropping, Colonel, and the wind is picking up. Pretty soon it's going to be locked down tight out here."

Randall looked at his watch. It was 9:45. Augusta was half an hour late.

Jamison got right to the point. "Colonel, when I was patrolling the house, Augusta pulled me aside and tried to buy me off. She said if I would kill you she would give me the securities. She has them, but she hasn't called you yet. I played along and said I'd do it. She cackled like a chicken. That old lady is crazy. She's coming unglued. She'll do anything to stop you."

Randall's senses were on high alert. "Jamison, this whole operation is coming unglued. Augusta is extremely dangerous and the King kid is out there somewhere. He has to have contacted someone by now. We've got to get the men and get out of here, before the whole thing blows up in our face."

"It's not Augusta you have to worry about, Colonel."

The two men turned. Rose was standing in the entryway. He had slipped in unnoticed and was holding a small but deadly looking pistol equipped with a silencer. Randall saw the look in Rose's eye, the connection between brain and trigger forming, and knew he was about to be shot. It was a skill he had developed over the years and it had saved him many times.

He pushed Jamison to one side and at the same time leapt the other way. Rose hesitated for a split-second deciding which man to shoot and then shot at Jamison. That gave Randall time to drop his arm. The concealed throwing dagger slipped into his hand, and with a flip of his wrist, the knife flew through the air and caught Rose in the neck. Rose looked at Randall in surprise and then collapsed. Randall stepped over and kicked the gun away. Rose's eyes were glazing over.

"Who paid you, Rose? You might as well tell me, because that knife has killed you."

Rose grimaced and then gasped. "Duvigney."

Then his eyes closed and he was gone.

Randall went to Jamison. Jamison was clutching his arm.

"Are you okay, Jamison?

Jamison grimaced. "The bullet caught me in the fleshy part of my arm. It went clear through but I think it broke the bone. Thanks for pushing me out of the way. He had me for sure."

Randall shook his head. "For some reason, Rose forgot that I trained him."

Randall pulled off Jamison's coat and rolled up his shirtsleeve. Blood poured from the wound and Randall could see that the arm was indeed broken. Randall went in the kitchen and grabbed some kitchen towels and a wooden spoon. He broke the end of the spoon off and, using it as a splint, set Jamison's arm and tied a compress over the wound. "That should keep it from bleeding." Jamison put his coat on over the bandage. Then Randall used the other towel as a sling. "You okay?"

Jamison winced, but nodded. "It doesn't hurt too bad, but I'll need to get it in a cast soon. Say, Colonel, if Rose was working for Duvigney, that means the guys he brought in are working for Duvigney, too."

Randall nodded. "That's right. So we have three guys working for Duvigney and the cops working for Augusta. I think we need to redefine the mission."

Randall grabbed his briefcase and opened it. He took out some small cassettes and put them in Rose's pocket. Then he took the bag with the two detonators out of his pocket and put one in Rose's hand and wrapped the hand and the thumb around it. Jamison looked puzzled. Randall pointed at the detonator. "We take the girl with us and use her as a shield. On the way out, if they don't let us through with the girl, we can use our detonator to blow the propane tanks, and in the confusion, we slip by the cops at the front. When the cops get back here, they'll find Rose with the cassettes and the detonator. They'll think Rose blew the tanks before he died. The tapes will implicate Duvigney in the plot against the St. Clairs. That will take care of that treachery. Then we'll send the D.A. the info on Augusta. It will take them a while to sort everything out but Duvigney and Augusta will both be in deep water. We'll just have to cut our losses and disappear."

Jamison shook his head. "It's a good plan, Colonel, but there's only the two of us and my arm is broken. There's three of Rose's men and all of Augusta's cops. We'll never carry that girl out to the car and be able to cover ourselves at the same time."

Randall scowled. "You're right, Jamison, we're in a real bind here."

Randall took a pair of binoculars out of his case, walked to the window, and scanned the grounds. He could not see the front of the house, but he knew the men were there. He swung the glasses toward the back of the estate. And then stopped in amazement. Out on the storm-tossed waters of Long Island Sound was a small boat. It was heading in toward the St. Clair dock. Randall looked closer. There were three men on the boat. "Halverson."

Jamison walked over to the window as Randall pointed. "What did you say, Colonel?"

"Out there, on the sound, there's a boat coming in and Sheriff Bobby Halverson is on board with two men. I think we may have just gotten our help."

Bobby Halverson watched as Jonathan eased the boat out into the sound from the protective confines of Greenwich Harbor. The wind began to blow straight in at them. The six-to-eight-foot waves were running before the wind in a chop that was like riding a bucking bronco. Jonathan looked at Bobby. He shouted over the wind. "There's only one way to get through this! I've got to power the boat up and jump the tops. It's going to get rough so hold on tight."

Bobby held on to a stanchion and nodded to Daniel to do the same. "Whatever you have to do, Jonathan. You okay?"

Jonathan smiled and in that smile, for the first time in years, Bobby saw his friend. He glanced at Daniel and saw that he was holding on tight and then turned back to Jonathan and nodded. "Cut'er loose, cowboy."

Jonathan pulled back on the throttle and the boat picked up speed, heading straight into the waves. As the speed increased, the boat lifted up out of the troughs and began to skip along the tops of the waves. Soon they were flying along, lifting off from the top of one wave and crashing down onto the next. Bobby looked at Jonathan. He was staring up into the sky and shouting something, but the wind snatched the words away, and Bobby didn't catch them. Jonathan's hair was flying in the wind, and he stood strong and powerful against the storm.

After about twenty minutes, Daniel yelled and pointed toward the shore. Through the spume and the spray, they could see a large, brick boathouse nestled on the shore in a protected cove. Daniel shouted over the wind. "That's the St. Clair place. Take her right inside and we'll be out of the wind."

As they entered the cove, the waves dropped down and Jonathan was able to navigate safely into the large boathouse. He pulled the boat up to the dock and Daniel and Bobby jumped over the side and made the boat fast to the pilings. Jonathan stood staring out at the ocean. Then he clambered over the side onto the dock. The boathouse was cavernous and there were several other boats in the water or drawn up on hoists.

Bobby pulled his hat off and knocked the water off against his leg. "Boy, quite a place the St. Clairs have here." He turned to Jonathan. "Say, what were you yelling out there when you were in the middle of that storm? Who were you yelling at?"

Jonathan grinned. "I was yelling at God. I told him that if He wanted to kill me in the ocean, after all, there wouldn't be a better time to do it. And if it was not yet my time, would He mind helping me get this tub around the point and into safe harbor. Looks like it was not my time."

Bobby looked at Jonathan's face. Years of pain and sorrow, fear and confusion, had been washed away by the fierce blast of the storm. The man who stood before him was the Jonathan Hershberger he knew and loved. Bobby put his hat back on. "Well, let's go find Rachel. And keep an eye out for Randall and his men."

"You won't have to go far to find me, Sheriff."

The three men turned. Two men walked out of the shadows behind one of the boats. One had his arm in a sling but his good hand held a large pistol. The other man was Gordon Randall. Bobby's heart sank. Then Randall nodded to the other man who holstered his pistol. As Bobby, Daniel, and Jonathan looked on in surprise, Randall lit a cigarette.

"Sheriff, I know we've been playing on two different teams here, but Jamison and I find ourselves in a tight squeeze. So we came out to make a deal with you. Rachel is not in her room. She's hidden in a safe room and I am the only one that can get you in. She's very sick."

Daniel lunged at Randall, but Bobby held him back. "Yes, she's sick because you've been poisoning her!"

"That's true, son, but we were only doing what Augusta paid us to do. It was nothing personal, believe me. Now the game has changed and we find ourselves in need of some help. And then you show up. It seems that timing is everything."

Bobby nodded. "Go on."

"Here's the deal. We give you the girl and you take us out of here. We have an SUV and if the sheriff here is driving, he can get us past Augusta's cops out front. She's probably given them orders to shoot us. We have another car in town. I've got the information the doctors need to save the girl. As soon as we're at the hospital, Jamison and I walk away and you never see us again. We let bygones be bygones. But you have to decide now so you can get the girl out of here. Once you're there, you give the doctor this." He showed Bobby a note and a small glassine bag with pills in it. "This will tell him exactly how to treat the girl. She will probably live if we go now. What do you say?"

Bobby looked at Jonathan and Daniel. Jonathan concurred. "Rachel's life is more important than anything, Bobby. We have to do what he says."

Bobby nodded. "Lead the way, Randall."

Chapter Thirty-Six

The Truth Will Set You Free

The five men left the boathouse and made their way through the storm to the east wing of the house. Randall led them in the side door. He signaled for them to be quiet, and they all moved silently down the hall. They came to the panel that hid the secret room, and Randall keyed in the combination. The door slid silently back and Randall ducked inside. Before the others could enter, he came back out.

"Rachel isn't in there. Augusta must have taken her."

Daniel grabbed Randall by the arm. "How could she carry Rachel by herself?"

Jamison spoke up. "I didn't give Gerald his drugs this morning. There was too much going on, so he could have been alert enough to help. She must have forced him to carry her."

Randall walked a little way up the hall. He saw something on the floor. "Someone vomited here."

The rest of the men gathered around. Randall looked in the direction that the stain indicated. "Augusta's taking Rachel back to her room. She wants the perfect scenario. Rachel dies in her bed, her grieving husband commits suicide by the bedside, Augusta leaves the country and lives off the eighty million she stole from Gerald. She may be insane, but she's not totally crazy, yet."

Together, the group of men made their way up the stairs and then down the hall toward Rachel's suite. Randall motioned for them to move to either side of the door. Then he slowly opened it. Rachel was lying in the bed. The covers had been pulled up over her and she looked like she was sleeping. Randall could tell she was slipping into a coma. Her face was pale and her hair was matted against her head. Gerald was standing next to her holding her hand and Augusta was holding a gun on him. When Augusta saw Randall, she shoved Gerald aside and jammed the barrel of the gun next to Rachel's head.

"Well, well, Gordon Randall. I thought Mr. Jamison was going to take care of you. Your friend, Mr. Jamison, is a very naughty boy."

Randall moved into the room. "Some of us retain a sense of loyalty, Augusta."

Augusta saw a movement outside the door. She pressed the gun tighter against Rachel's head. "Everybody inside or the girl dies. Move!"

Daniel came into the room, followed by Bobby and Jonathan.

"Daniel King! Join the party! Uh, uh, don't come any closer. At this point it no longer matters to me how Rachel dies. I will shoot her if you take one more step."

The men halted. Augusta looked at Jonathan. "And this must be Rachel's papa." Augusta snickered. "You certainly don't look non-violent."

Jonathan stiffened. "Where my daughter's life is concerned, you might be surprised what I am capable of."

Augusta motioned for the men to stand against the wall. Then she began a weird sing-song chant over Rachel. "Dearly beloved, we are gathered here today to celebrate cleansing the earth from the stain of the St. Clair family. Rachel and Gerald will be crossing over today and soon all the St. Clairs will be gone." She snickered again. "Except me, of course, but then I'm not really a St. Clair, am I?"

She looked at the grim faces of the men. "It seems like we've got a standoff here. I guess I'll just have to be happy with killing these two and then see how the rest plays out."

Randall looked at Gerald. He was staring at his grandmother in disbelief. Randall took a shot—anything to keep the crazed woman talking. "Gerald, why don't you ask your grandmother what she did to your family? I'm sure she would be happy to tell you. It was all done so brilliantly, and I'm sure she wouldn't want her secrets to follow her to the grave, would you, Augusta?"

Augusta looked at Randall. The gun was still pressed against Rachel's head. "It was brilliant, wasn't it, Gordon?" She turned to Gerald. "Yes, my darling grandson. You should hear how smart your grandmother has been. All these years, you thought I loved you, that I was just a doddering old grandmother with a few peculiarities." She laughed at her own joke. The effect was chilling. "Shall I start with your grandfather Robert?"

Gerald's mouth dropped open. "What?"

"Yes, Gerald, your grandfather, Robert St. Clair. Jerod St. Clair wasn't your grandfather. He was a weak, little mollycoddle. Robert St. Clair fathered my child. But he rejected me and married that Amish tramp. And then I knew that I would have my revenge, and that I would be God's instrument in wiping the St. Clair family from the face of the earth. Oh, how I hated Robert. Men don't understand that a woman's love can turn to deep hate if she's wronged. What is that old saying, 'Hell hath no fury like a woman scorned'?"

Her eyes narrowed. "How could he do that to me? How could he marry her instead of me? She gave him a daughter. I was the one who loved him. I gave him a son. I gave him everything—and he spurned me for her, that Rachel Borntraeger."

Randall moved an inch to his left, trying to get into a position to get the jump on Augusta. Jamison saw it and moved slightly to his right. "Tell Gerald what you did to Rachel, Robert's wife."

Augusta smiled as if reliving the memory. "I should have killed her like I killed Robert. But I wanted her to suffer horribly. When she came to the house in New York, I knew her right away. I had Robert's pictures. I got them from Max. Joe Bender worked for me. It was easy for him to get Rachel addicted to heroin. She was already in so much pain. The heroin was her escape. And I loved that. I wanted her to stay alive, a slave to drugs, knowing that Robert was dead, gone, and that she would never have him."

Gerald's hands were shaking. "You killed Robert St. Clair?"

"Ah, yes, Robert. Of course I killed him and I'm happy to say he died horribly. Did he really think he could spurn me and walk away? Did he really think he could leave me for that little slut? Bender said it was easy. He stole a truck, waited for Robert to go to work and then, when he was driving through an intersection, Bender ran him off the road into a tree. Robert's car exploded and he burned to death. He roasted in hell before he died. That was the best part."

Bobby Halverson spoke up. "Joe Bender worked for you? He was your hit man? You had Robert St. Clair killed and Joe Bender did the deed?"

"Yes, Sheriff, you are correct. Didn't dig that one up when you were looking for Jenny's parents, did you?"

Bobby shook his head. Augusta looked at the men. Her face was like flint but she smiled seductively at them. The effect was repulsive.

There was a pause and then Augusta shrugged. "Bender would do anything for me. He loved me. I could get any man to love me...except Robert. I...persuaded Bender to kill Robert. Of course, Robert had it coming. Everyone thought Robert was such a nice man, but he didn't hesitate to climb into my bed or seduce Rachel Borntraeger. But it's not just Robert I swore revenge on. I have taken care of all the St. Clairs."

Randall nodded at Gerald. "Gerald, she had your grandfather Robert's parents killed, your great grandfather and great grandmother."

Gerald stared at Augusta. She shook her head.

"Well, actually, Gerald, I killed Max and Margaret myself. Nobody ever noticed the little mark where I injected the air bubble into his neck. They all thought it was a stroke. And Margaret. That was a lot of fun. The old lady was half crazy already, and I would show her the pictures of her granddaughter and tell her that the little girl had been run over by a car. It didn't take long until she had a heart attack and died."

"And who else, Augusta? What about Francis and his wife?"

"Oh, Francis! That was so easy. They had been drinking. My agent lured them off the trail when they were skiing in Switzerland, suffocated them and buried them in the snow. Everyone thought it was an avalanche."

Gerald moved closer. "You killed my father and my mother?"

"Well, of course, Gerald. He was Robert's son, the devil's spawn. I couldn't let him live, now could I?"

Randall pressed the attack. "Why didn't you just confess that Gerald is Robert's grandson? Wouldn't the DNA prove it?"

Augusta gave Randall a condescending look. "Without Robert, the DNA could only prove that Gerald is a St. Clair. But there was nothing left of Robert to make the final connection, and Gerald didn't have the Key so it would have been my word. But it was never really about the money..."

Augusta tittered.

Randall nodded toward the bed. "And now you're going to kill Rachel."

"Oh, that's not all, Gordon. You forget about the little red-haired brat in Paradise. She thought she could escape me. But she'll find out."

She gave Gerald a venomous look. "And then, of course, I have to do something about little Gerald, don't I?"

Randall looked at Bobby and Jonathan. They were staring at Augusta with shock and disgust on their faces. Randall kept going. "Jenny Hershberger, too? Augusta, you are insane."

"No, Gordon—bitter, thwarted, frustrated, hateful maybe, but not insane. Otherwise I wouldn't have worked so hard to get my hands on the money. You see, when I'm finished with this branch of the St. Clair family, all the money will be in my bank account, and all of Robert St. Clair's heirs will be dead."

Jonathan stepped forward. "If you hurt Jenny..."

Augusta waved the gun at him and then quickly put it back to Rachel's head.

"Oh, didn't I tell you, Mr. Hershberger? I've already dispatched my messenger."

Jonathan looked desperately at Bobby. "Bobby..."

Bobby shook his head and motioned Jonathan back.

Randall looked at Augusta. "I hate to burst your bubble, Augusta, but there's something you are not aware of. Even if you could get your hands on it now, there is no money in Robert St. Clair's trust. Duvigney spent it all."

Augusta's face twisted in disbelief.

Randall nodded. "Yes, Augusta, the money's gone. Your plan backfired. When you killed Robert, Duvigney didn't know about Rachel Borntraeger St. Clair and her daughter, Jenny St. Clair, because you kept that a secret and they had disappeared. Duvigney thought Robert's trust was a dead end, no heirs, no disbursement. So he spent it. It's actually kind of funny. Something else you don't know is that I've been working for Duvigney all along to set you and Gerald up for the murder of Rachel. Then when Gerald went to prison, he couldn't inherit and so your demands for the St. Clair fortune that wasn't there would cease and Duvigney was off the hook from an investigation of the trust. Not to mention your part in the whole plan, which I conveniently recorded. You would have ended up on death row next to Gerald. But then Duvigney tried to have me killed, which means that I'll just have to make sure that his part in all this comes to light. I'm sure the board of trustees for the St. Clair estate won't be too happy about the missing money. If they don't have him killed, he will end up in prison with you."

Augusta hissed. "Why, that sneaky rat. I suspected he had been raiding the till, but I never thought he spent all of it. That's why he was stonewalling me on the money."

As Randall had been speaking, Gerald slowly moved closer to Augusta. When Randall mentioned Duvigney, her attention was diverted for a split second and Gerald reacted. He leaped at

Augusta and grabbed her arm. He jerked it away from Rachel's head and held it against his own body. They wrestled for the gun.

Gerald began shouting at Augusta. "You're insane, Grandmother! You're out of your mind! I've known it for years, but I was always too afraid of you to say anything. It was you all the time. You killed my parents. You killed my real grandfather. But you are not going to kill Rachel."

They struggled violently for the gun. Augusta was like a crazed animal, and Gerald had all he could do to control her. Suddenly, the gun went off. Gerald's body jerked and then with one violent shove, he threw Augusta against the wall. Her head smacked against the corner of a mirror with a sickening sound. She went limp and slid down the wall. The gun dropped on the floor. The men rushed forward. Gerald sank down on the bed next to Rachel, holding his chest.

Daniel grabbed him. "Gerald, Gerald!"

Gerald looked down. The front of his shirt was soaked in blood. Blood was pouring from a terrible wound. He looked at Daniel. "Take care of her, Daniel."

He smiled and started to fall over. Daniel knelt on the bed next to him and held him up. "Wait, Gerald! You saved Rachel. Let me help you."

Gerald tried to lift his head. "Grandmother's killed me, Daniel. I'm going."

Daniel pulled Gerald closer. "Then you need to give your life to God before you go. You saved Rachel, now let God save you. Just ask him to forgive you, tell him you believe he died for you, quickly Gerald, while you still can."

Gerald gasped. "Yes, Daniel. Ever since we talked, I've known that you were right. I asked Him to forgive me, and I...believe..."

He choked, and a bloody froth colored his lips. "Tell Rachel that for the first time in my life I loved someone, truly and deeply. I...I...loved her..."

And then, as the men watched, it seemed as though a beautiful, ethereal light illuminated Gerald's face, and he smiled at Daniel. He reached out and placed his hand on Daniel's arm. "Take care of her, Daniel."

Gerald's eyes closed and he slumped against Daniel. He was gone. The men all stared down at him.

Daniel laid him down next to Rachel. He turned to Bobby. "Gerald's gone. There's nothing we can do for him. We've got to get Rachel to a hospital, now!"

The spell was broken and the men leaped into action. Randall pointed at Rachel. "I'll go get the car and bring it around to the back. You men carry her down. Hurry."

Daniel and Jonathan wrapped the blanket around Rachel and Daniel picked her up. Bobby stood in the doorway and looked at Randall.

"Which way?"

Randall nodded toward the hallway. "Down the stairs, turn left, go down the hallway until you see the first outside door. I'll be waiting there. Hurry!"

Chapter Thirty-Seven

Rescued

Rachel opened her eyes. The lights were dim and she was confused, but she could tell she was being carried down some stairs. Everything was spinning and she had to fight the urge to vomit. Her vision was blurred, but slowly her eyes focused on the face of the one who was carrying her. It was a beloved face, the face of a friend. Slowly, she reached her hand up and touched the face. The unfamiliar beard was soft under her fingers. It was Daniel. His strong arms held her tight, and she felt safe. When he felt her hand, Daniel looked down at her. Rachel could see the love in his eyes.

"Daniel, are you married? You have a beard."

Daniel smiled and pulled Rachel closer. "What a question to ask me, little one!"

She could see that he had almost laughed. Then he spoke softly. "No, Rachel, I'm not married."

"How did you find me? Why are you carrying me?"

"We're taking you to the hospital. You are very sick. Your papa is here."

Rachel turned her head. It made her dizzy. Her papa's face swam into view, but it was a different face. It was strong and powerful. It was the face she remembered—a face she had not seen for a long, long time. She could not see Richard Sandbridge, just her precious papa.

"Papa, I'm so sorry. I..."

Jonathan took Rachel's hand as they walked down the stairs. "It's not your fault, *dochter*, it is mine. And when you are well, we will talk. *Du leiber Gott* will bring restoration. Right now, all I want is for you to get well. Daniel and I and your Uncle Bobby will see to that. Just hold on and stay with us."

Rachel could see the love in her papa's eyes. It was the last thing she saw before the world around her faded into darkness.

At the bottom of the stairs, Bobby watched as Jamison turned left and then directed the men to follow him down the hall to the door. They pushed through. The wind and snow tore at them like a flock of furious white birds. They stood in the blast for a moment and then Randall pulled up in the SUV and climbed out. He nodded and Bobby slid in behind the wheel. Jonathan opened the back hatch and Daniel laid Rachel down on the floor. Together, they wrapped the blankets around her and then Daniel crawled in next to her. Randall and Jamison got in behind the driver's seat and Jonathan joined Bobby in the front. Bobby put the car in gear and they headed for the front gate.

The wind whistled around the SUV and they could see only about twenty feet ahead through the driven snow. As Bobby drove slowly, looking for the gate, a picture came into his mind. He was sitting in the cab of an old tractor. His friend, Reuben Springer, was sitting next to him. They were slowly plowing through enormous drifts of snow toward an old, deserted cabin in the woods. The wind was howling and the snow was blowing sideways through the dark and twisted trees...

"Bobby, you okay?"

Bobby turned. The Amish man sitting next to him was Jonathan, not Reuben. Bobby pushed his hat back on his forehead. "Yeah, Jonathan, I'm good. Just thinking about another time I was on a rescue mission in a blizzard."

"When you and Reuben saved Jerusha?"

"Yep. That was a long time ago."

Jonathan pointed ahead. They were coming to the gate and there was a police car with flashing lights on top, blocking the way. They rolled to a stop. A short, stout man in a police uniform climbed out of the car. He waved at someone out of sight out on the road, and in a few seconds, another police car pulled up. The policeman started toward the SUV.

Sergeant Oliver Cromwell Franklin had been out in the storm for three hours and for the last two he had been parked in front of Augusta St. Clair's house trying to keep a kidnapper from getting back on the grounds and keep from freezing at the same time. He was very cold and very cross. As he watched the service road, he saw an SUV coming toward the front gate. He looked closer. There were several men in the car. The SUV pulled up to the gate and stopped by the cruiser. Franklin pulled his coat collar up around his pudgy neck and climbed out of the car. He waved at Gary Parkins who was parked down the road and motioned him to come closer. He waited until Parkins arrived and they started toward the SUV.

Franklin crunched through the snow to the driver's side of the SUV and waited while the man behind the wheel rolled the window down. There were two men in the front, two in the middle and a man in the back next to someone rolled up in blankets. As Franklin scrutinized the passengers he realized the man in the back matched the description of Daniel King. His hand went to his pistol.

"Say, what's going on here?"

The man behind the wheel looked up at him. He was an older, sandy-haired man wearing a Stetson hat. Franklin suddenly realized that the driver looked like someone he did not want to mess with. The man seated next to him was Amish, but the look in his eye was not a peaceful one. The sandy-haired man opened his jacket. Pinned to his vest was a silver sheriff's badge. Next to it was a combat medal. Franklin looked closer. It was the Silver Star. Then he noticed that there was also a police-issue revolver strapped to his waist. The sandy-haired man smiled.

"I brought these because I thought I might have to do a little convincing. My name is Bobby Halverson. Sheriff Bobby Halverson. The reason you can still call me Sheriff is because the citizens of Wayne County, Ohio saw fit to bestow the title on me permanently in light of my long service to them. We have a very sick girl in the back. Her husband and his grandmother have poisoned her. Daniel King tried to rescue Rachel but was prevented. He escaped from the house and then called me for help, knowing that he could not trust you or the local police. When we arrived at the estate, we had to sneak in by way of Long Island Sound. These men are Augusta St. Clair's security chief and his assistant. By the time we arrived, they had discovered the plot to kill Rachel and offered to help us rescue her. You should know that the three private security men who are helping you guard the house are also in on the plot and should be arrested immediately. Now, if you will kindly move your car, we need to get this girl to the hospital fast!"

Franklin looked in the window again. He pointed to Daniel and fumbled at the snap on his holster. "You fellas don't seem to realize the bind I'm in here. One of our most prominent citizens has filed a very serious complaint against that man back there, the one you say is Daniel King. She—"

Before he could continue, the sandy-haired man interrupted.

"She has instructed you to arrest Daniel King and keep him under wraps, and you're buying into it because she owns you."

Franklin felt heat infuse his face. "Say, you can't talk to me like that! I'm the police around here."

Sheriff Bobby Halverson opened the door of the car and got out. He moved in front of Franklin and put his finger in Franklin's face. "Let me explain something to you, officer. The grandfather of the girl in the back of the car was a Congressional Medal of Honor winner who single-handedly turned the tide of the battle for Henderson Field on Guadalcanal. This man next me is Rachel St. Clair's father. I have many friends in the National Sheriff's Organization. The current police commissioner of New York City and I served as officers together on the board of the Fraternal Order of Police. Colonel Jerry Cowell of the Connecticut State Police is on his way here from Middleton with twenty of his troopers to take over this investigation. And we have a sick girl who will die if you don't get your fat behind out of the way. You would be better off going up to the house and arresting Augusta for the murder of her grandson, Gerald, and the attempted murder of Rachel St. Clair. You had also better round up the three men who are on the estate as guards."

Franklin felt his secure little world start to crack around the edges. Sheriff Halverson continued. "If you want to buck me on this, I will make some phone calls and the law enforcement bigwigs who show up here will make Augusta St. Clair look like a pussycat. If Rachel dies while I'm doing that, I will personally beat you to a pulp. When you recover, you will find that your next position will be as a weather balloon operator in Goose Bay, Labrador, if you're not in jail with Augusta. Am I clear?"

Oliver Cromwell Franklin looked at Sheriff Bobby Halverson. There was a fire in Halverson's eyes that guaranteed the truth of what he was saying. The fight went out of Franklin, and his shoulders dropped. He was about to start back to his car when he heard a voice.

"Just stay where you are officer. We have some business with Colonel Randall."

Franklin turned. Three men armed with nasty-looking automatic weapons were standing behind Parkins. The leader motioned for everyone to raise their hands. "Get out of the car, Colonel."

Randall looked at Jamison and slowly started to open the door. Just then the blast of a bullhorn cut through the wind.

"You men there! This is Colonel Jerry Cowell of the Connecticut State Police. You are surrounded. Lay down your weapons, put your hands behind your heads, and kneel down. Now!"

Oliver Cromwell Franklin looked toward the sound of the voice. As he watched, several tough-looking State Troopers materialized out of the storm. They were armed with shotguns and rifles. They had come upon the confrontation and surrounded the group unnoticed. The three men dropped their weapons and did as Colonel Cowell told them. Then a tall man with a bullhorn walked out of the whirling snow up to Sheriff Halverson.

"Bobby, what's going on here?"

"Jerry! It's pretty complicated, but first of all I have a very sick girl here, who will die if I don't get her to the hospital." Bobby nodded at Sergeant Franklin. "The sergeant and his men have been obstructing us on the orders of Augusta St. Clair, who just shot her grandson, Gerald. She is still in the house. Gerald is dead. Those three men are in on the plot. These two men are helping us. They discovered the plot to kill Rachel, and I need to take them to the hospital with me so they can talk to the doctors. I know that's a lot to digest and there's a lot more, but I can sort it out with you later. Right now we have to go!"

Colonel Cowell nodded and turned to one of his men. "Take your cruiser and get these people to the hospital as quickly as you can."

The trooper nodded and started for his car.

Colonel Cowell pointed to the three men on their knees and motioned to some of his troopers. "Take these men into custody!"

Colonel Cowell turned to Franklin. "You! Get your car out of the way but give me your pistol first, and then I want you and your men to accompany me to the house."

Franklin stood in bewilderment, watching his world come crashing down. Then he handed over his gun and got in the police car. When he had moved his cruiser, Colonel Cowell motioned to Bobby.

"Get the girl to the hospital and then call me when she's in good hands. I'll need you to debrief me on everything that's happened here."

Bobby shook the Colonel's hand and then jumped in the SUV and followed the trooper down the road toward town.

Oliver Cromwell Franklin shook his head and wondered how cold Goose Bay, Labrador got in the winter.

Chapter Thirty-Eight

The Road Home

Bobby drove like a madman following the State Patrol cruiser's flashing lights through the blinding snow. As he watched the car in front of him guide him to the hospital, he remembered a day over forty years earlier when he had taken another precious girl on a race for life. For the first time in a long time, Bobby prayed.

"Lord, I know I don't know you very well, but I have the feeling you know me. I have a girl here who is very sick, just like my little Jenna so long ago. Please let this time be different. Please let Rachel live."

Jonathan glanced over at Bobby and smiled. He said a quiet, "Amen."

After about twenty minutes, they pulled up in front of Greenwich Hospital. The wind had died and the storm clouds were beginning to open above them. Bobby and Jonathan leaped out of the car and ran to the back. They opened the door and Daniel climbed out with Rachel in his arms. Daniel and Jonathan headed for the emergency entrance. Gordon Randall grabbed Bobby's arm. He handed Bobby the folded piece of paper and the glassine envelope.

"And now it's time for Jamison and me to take our leave. This note will tell the doctor exactly what Rachel is suffering from and there are some of the pills in this bag. Follow the directions and there is a good chance Rachel will live."

Bobby grabbed Randall by the coat collar and stared at him. "I'm only letting you go because we made a deal. As for your part in this, if Rachel dies, I will spend the rest of my life hunting you down. If I were you, I would take up another line of work or retire. Because if I ever see you again, there will be real trouble."

Randall smiled. "I think I'll take your advice, Sheriff. Things have definitely gotten a little warm for me around here. Now you should get in there and help the girl."

Bobby turned and ran into the hospital.

Randall stood in the snow watching Bobby go. He turned to Jamison and noticed the sour look on his face.

"This operation sure blew up in our faces, Colonel. All that work and nothing to show for it."

Randall reached into his coat pocket and pulled out an envelope. "Not exactly, Sergeant. Before I got the car, I broke into Augusta's office and grabbed these off the desk. They're the securities. They're worth over a million dollars and Augusta signed them over. So maybe it is time for us to think of another profession, like beach bums in Costa Rica. We've been fighting this war too long."

Jamison smiled. "I'm with you, Colonel Randall."

"Is the back-up SUV still parked downtown?"

Jamison pointed down the street. "It's in a parking garage out of the snow, about a ten minute walk from here, down that way. We have plenty of supplies and a medical kit. You can put a cast on this arm when we stop."

Randall nodded. The two men turned and disappeared into the falling snow.

Bobby ran through the door. Jonathan and Daniel were remonstrating with a nurse who was trying to explain hospital protocol. Bobby ran up to her and showed her his badge.

"Get me a doctor, quick!" he shouted at her. "This girl is dying."

The nurse dropped her paperwork and pencil, ran into the office and got on the intercom. In a few minutes, a white-haired man with a puzzled expression on his face came down the hall.

"I'm Dr. Wilson," he said. "What seems to be the trouble?"

Bobby handed the note and the glassine envelope to the doctor. "This girl is suffering from acute arsenic poisoning. She needs treatment immediately. The exact poison is in this envelope and instructions for treatment are in this note."

The doctor pulled back the blanket and looked at Rachel. He opened the note. He held the pills as he scanned the instructions. Then he turned to the nurse. "Get a gurney in here, stat! Move this girl into the ER and start her on fluid and electrolyte replacement immediately. I want her stomach pumped as quickly as possible, and I want her chelated with dimercaprol."

The nurse nodded and motioned for another nurse to help. They grabbed a gurney that was standing in the entranceway. Daniel laid Rachel down on the gurney. The doctor did a quick exam and then nodded, and the two nurses pushed the gurney through the emergency room doors into intensive care.

The doctor shook his head. "She's in bad shape. I'll do the best I can."

Daniel took hold of the doctor's arm. "There's something else, Doctor. She's pregnant."

The doctor frowned. "That's not good, not good at all. I may be able to save the girl, but the chances that the baby will live... Well, that would take a miracle."

The doctor pointed to an area off to the left. "The waiting room is right over there. I'll let you know their status as soon as I can." He turned and followed the nurses through the swinging doors.

Jonathan took Bobby aside. "Bobby, what about Jenny? Augusta St. Clair said she had sent someone to hurt her."

Bobby remembered. "Jonathan, that's right. I'll call the local boys in Paradise and get them out to the house to guard Jenny. In the meantime, we'll leave Daniel here with Rachel and drive home as quickly as we can. Maybe the troopers can run interference for us. It's going to be crazy out on the road."

Bobby went over to the desk, showed them his badge, and asked for a phone. In a few minutes he returned. "The police in Paradise will send some men out to the house to guard Jenny. I talked to Jerry Cowell. He's dispatching three cruisers to get us through to the Pennsylvania state line. He's making some calls and should have some Pennsylvania boys there to take us in to Paradise. So let's tell the officer what's happening and get going. We'll meet them when we pick up my truck at Willy's place."

Bobby shook Daniel's hand and patted his shoulder. "Daniel, I want to thank you for watching out for Rachel. Jonathan and I have to see about Jenny. Will you stay here with Rachel and take care of her?"

Daniel nodded and looked at Jonathan. "That's all I've ever wanted to do."

Jonathan smiled. "*Das ist gut*, Daniel. We'll call as soon as we know what's happening."

Bobby took Jonathan's arm. "Come on, pal. We got a long drive ahead of us."

Then he and Jonathan headed out the door.

Colonel Jerry Cowell and his men entered the St. Clair estate with guns drawn. As they came in through the kitchen, they found the frightened staff huddled together. When they saw the state police, a tall, dignified man approached the Colonel.

"I'm the butler. We heard a gunshot and screaming upstairs. We don't know what's going on, but we want to leave."

Colonel Cowell motioned to one of his men. "Let them get their coats and then take them out and put them in the cruisers. I want them taken into town to the police station along with Sergeant Franklin and his men and held until I get there. Are there any other buildings where people might be hiding?"

The butler pointed out the back window. "There's a caretaker's cottage just through those trees. The security men have been using it."

Colonel Cowell signaled to two of his men. "Go out to the cottage and check it out. We'll go upstairs and see what's happening with the St. Clairs."

He pointed to the butler. "I need you to show me where you heard the shot. Then you can go."

The two men left by the back door with the rest of the staff while Cowell and his men followed the butler down the hall to the stairs. The man stopped and pointed. "Go up the stairs and turn left down the hall. You'll pass another set of stairs and then you're in the east wing where the living quarters are. Ms. Rachel's room is two doors down."

The state police crept silently up the stairs following the butler's directions. They passed the stairs and came to a room with the door partly open. From inside they heard a weird, crooning sound. Slowly, they pushed the door open. An old woman was sitting on a bed by a man who was obviously dead. She was caressing the man's forehead and singing. "Rock-a-bye Gerald, in the tree top, down came the cradle, Gerald and all..." And then the old woman giggled.

Colonel Cowell spoke. "Mrs. St. Clair?"

The old woman turned. Her coiffed hair had fallen apart and she had a vacant stare. "Mrs. St. Clair? Oh, no, not Mrs. St. Clair. I'm Francine, Francine Bosnan. I'm not a St. Clair. They're all dead and I'm alive. Gerald's dead, and Rachel will soon be dead, and then Jenny and then they will all be dead. No more St. Clairs...all gone...all dead."

Colonel Cowell moved up beside the old woman. "Mrs. Augusta St. Clair, I am arresting you for the murder of Gerald St. Clair. Please stand up and put your hands behind your back."

Out in the cottage, the two state policemen opened the door and proceeded cautiously into the room, guns drawn. The body of a man was lying by the front door. He had a throwing dagger in his throat and a surprised look on his face. One of the troopers stooped down and took a small box with a flashing light on it from the dead man's hand. There was a button below the light.

"I wonder what this is."

His partner started to speak. "Don't press—"

The first policeman pressed the button. There was a short series of beeps and then a roar as the propane tanks around the house exploded.

Colonel Cowell and his men were thrown to the ground by the force of the explosion. One of the men crawled to the window. "The house is on fire, Colonel, looks like the propane tank exploded."

"Get everyone out of the house now."

Colonel Cowell turned to assist Augusta. She was gone.

Augusta ran down the stairs to her office. Behind her, she heard the pounding steps of a state policeman in hot pursuit. She pulled open the door, ran in, and slammed it in the trooper's face. "Can't get in, can't get in, I made a special door."

The trooper pounded on the door. "Mrs. St. Clair, come out. The house is on fire."

Augusta ignored him. Her safe door stood open. She ran inside and opened her lockbox. Inside, she found the diary and the pictures. She laid them on the desk and spread out the photos of Robert and her. Outside, the flames roared and the policemen shouted but she took no notice. She reached in her desk and pulled out a brush and some lipstick. She walked to the mirror and began to brush her hair. Then she smeared lipstick on her mouth. "Here I am, Robert. Aren't I beautiful? More beautiful than her. Why did you choose her, Robert? I loved you; I gave you a son…"

Augusta could hear the troopers trying to break down the door but it was solid steel and she knew they would never get in. She heard someone shouting that the mansion was going up like a torch—that the whole east wing was on fire. She smiled when she heard Colonel Cowell order his men out. Above her, she could hear the house groaning and cracking, but she ignored it. The reflection in the mirror held her spellbound. She was young and beautiful again. She began to sway seductively in front of the mirror, the picture of Robert St. Clair in her hand. "You're all dead, all the St. Clairs. You should have chosen me, Robert. You never should have left me."

Above her head, a circle of fire began to eat its way through the ceiling. The chandelier crashed down as the support was eaten away by the flames. Augusta looked up as the ceiling began to fall. She held up the picture and screamed. "Robert St. Clair, I'll see you in hell."

As the whole east wing collapsed in a roar of fire right on top of her, the last thing Augusta saw was the face of Robert St. Clair smiling at her.

Bobby and Jonathan drove through the snow, guided by the state police cruisers. The storm had started to blow itself out, and the further east they got, the clearer the weather became. They met an escort of police at the Pennsylvania border and drove on toward Paradise. The snowplows had been out in force and the road was fairly clean, but it still took them four hours to get there. They drove up the Lincoln Highway to Leacock Road and headed toward the farm, followed by the police cruisers. Bobby and Jonathan pulled into the lane. A local police car was parked in front of the house, but they didn't see anyone on guard. Bobby signaled to Jonathan and they ran up the road. They looked around, and then Bobby saw someone lying off to the side of the house. It was a local policeman and he was groaning and holding his head. Bobby grabbed him. "Where's Jenny?

The policeman pointed. "She's in there. Someone came up behind me and knocked me out. I think they must be in there with Mrs. Hershberger."

Bobby and Jonathan ran into the house. Outside, the wail of sirens proclaimed the arrival of the state police.

Jonathan shouted. "Jenny? Jenny, where are you?"

There was a faint sound from the back bedroom. The two men ran down the hall and burst through the door. There was a man in the room. He was holding Jenny from behind and had a gun at her head. He pointed the gun toward them. "Don't come any closer or she's dead."

Bobby stepped forward. "Do you really want to do that? There are a dozen state policemen outside. You wouldn't get two feet out the door. And besides, Augusta St. Clair won't be paying you, she's been arrested."

The man smiled. "I already got my money, mac, so that's not an issue. Now I'm taking the woman and I'm getting out of here. I want everyone to step aside and let me go. As soon as I'm clear, I'll turn the lady loose."

Bobby could see the lie in the man's eyes. As he looked at Jenny, he saw her move her head and then she suddenly grabbed the man's arm. Bobby and Jonathan jumped him as Jenny pulled the gun down. There was a roar as the gun went off, and Bobby felt a blow to his side, like someone jabbing hot icepicks into his hip. He crumpled in a heap.

He saw Jonathan's dark hair fall over his face as he fought ferociously with the killer. As Bobby watched, the scene changed. He was in a trench on top of a hill on Guadalcanal. He couldn't move. Above him, a tall, dark-haired Marine was fighting hand-to-hand with a crush of Japanese soldiers. Bobby called out. "Reuben, Reuben…" And then everything went black.

Rachel opened her eyes. She was in a dark room lying on a narrow bed. Everything was blurry and it was hard to see. There were tubes attached to her arms and going up her nose. Next to her on a stand were several pieces of equipment that were either softly beeping or showing jagged green lines on small screens. She had a terrible headache and her stomach felt sore. She turned her head a little. There was someone seated in a chair next to her bed. It was Daniel! She tried to speak, but the tubes were in her way.

Daniel saw Rachel move and took her hand. "Don't try to speak, Rachel. Just rest. The doctor says we got you here in time, but we have a hard road in front of us. You must save your strength. Close your eyes now and sleep."

Rachel squeezed Daniel's hand but when he tried to take it away, she would not let go. She closed her eyes. She knew everything would be well. Daniel was with her, and the Lord was with Daniel.

In another hospital room in Lancaster, an old Marine lay in a bed. Beside him sat Jonathan and Jenny Hershberger. Jenny was crying. The old Marine slowly opened his eyes and smiled. He reached over and patted Jenny's hand. "Don't worry about me, kid. This old gyrene is too tough to kill."

Jenny took Bobby's hand. "Oh, Bobby, we were so worried."

"What happened after I passed out?"

Jenny glanced lovingly at Jonathan. "Jonathan grabbed the man and knocked him out. I guess he wasn't expecting an Amish prize fighter."

Jonathan reached in his pocket. "Here's something the doctor gave me for you, Bobby. He dug it out of your hip when he got the bullet out."

He leaned over and handed Bobby a twisted shard of metal. "This is the shrapnel that's been in your hip since 1942. He figured you might want it as a souvenir."

Bobby reached out and took the chunk of metal. "Well, I guess this story has come full circle. I've got a special place for this, Jenny, right next to a picture of your father. Now I just need to know how Rachel is doing."

Jenny patted Bobby's arm. "She's alive and slowly getting better. The doctor told Daniel that she and the baby have a fighting chance. Daniel's with her and that's the best care she could have right now. We are going down there tomorrow. We are confident that the Lord will keep her."

"Me, too," Bobby said. "Me, too."

Chapter Thirty-Nine

Home from the Sea

On a cold morning in early January, an ambulance drove slowly up the gravel drive from Leacock Lane and stopped in front of the blue farmhouse. Jonathan and Jenny were standing on the porch along with two other Amish men. Bobby Halverson sat on a bench against the wall of the house, a pair of crutches and his dog, Rufus, lying next to him. The driver and an attendant got out and opened the back of the ambulance. Daniel King climbed down and helped the two men pull a gurney out and extend the legs. The girl on the gurney stirred and a wan smile crossed her pale face. Daniel walked beside the gurney as the attendants rolled it up the path and lifted it onto the porch. The girl lifted her hands and Jenny reached down and took them, pulling her girl into a warm embrace. Rachel was home.

After the attendants wheeled Rachel inside, Jonathan and Daniel conversed in low tones with the two elders of their community, *Bischopp* Hochstetler and Daniel's father, Jonas King. The *Bischopp* put his hand on Jonathan's shoulder "*Und so*, your *dochter* has come home? And what of her *Englischer* husband?"

"Her husband is dead, *Bischopp*. It was a terrible tragedy."

"But Rachel is still pregnant with the man's child?"

Jonathan nodded. "It is a miracle that the baby is still alive, but it is. The doctors don't know how the poisoning affected the child, but Rachel is a very strong girl. She was in intensive care and then in an intermediate care unit at the hospital in Greenwich for a month. Then we brought her to a managed care facility in Lancaster for another three weeks. She is healing from the effects of the arsenic much quicker than the doctors expected, and we hold great hope that the baby will be born undamaged."

"And has Rachel repented of leaving the church?"

"We have not yet had that conversation with her. We only want to see her get well."

The *Bischopp* stroked his beard. He turned to Daniel. "*Und Sie, junger Mann?* You violated the *Meidung* when you left against the wishes of your papa to follow Rachel after the church shunned her. That put you under the *Bann* also. What do you have to say for yourself?"

Daniel looked at his papa and then took a deep breath. "I do not regret following Rachel. I believe the Lord spoke to my heart that she was in great danger, and she needed someone to look after her. I am very sorry that I violated the *Ordnung,* but if I had to do it again, I would. I have always loved the Amish life and never want to live any other way, but *Gott bringt Rachel in meinem Weg.* He gave her to me to love, and there is nothing I can do about that. If she stays under the shunning, then so be it, I will be shunned also, because I am going to look after her."

Jonas King put his arm around his son's shoulder. "I was *sehr böse,* very angry, when Daniel ignored my counsel and left to follow Rachel. But because of Daniel, Rachel is alive. If he had not listened to the Lord, she would be dead. I am very proud of my son and will support him in whatever he does."

The *Bischopp* looked back at Jonathan. "And you, Jonathan? Rachel is still under the *Bann* until she repents and returns to the church. If she stays here you are violating the *Meidung* also. Would you and your wife risk being excommunicated from the church for that?"

Jonathan nodded. "*Bischopp* Hochstetler, I know this is difficult for you, but, although I love the ways of the Amish and

I trust that the *Ordnung* protect us from the evil out in the world, in this case, I believe that grace will trump all. In the last few days, I have found myself again. I have been touched by *du leiber Gott* and the old wounds and fears have fallen away. I am Jonathan Hershberger again. Not the foolish hippie, or the *Englischer*, Richard Sandbridge, but the Jonathan Hershberger who came to love Jenny Springer and the Amish way with all my heart. And out of that love came my girl, Rachel. Her well-being is the most important thing now, and I will risk all to make sure she lives and is restored, no matter what her decision about the church. To that end, in spite of the fact that she is under the *Bann*, she will stay here with those who love her until she is well enough to decide about her life. If we are excommunicated for that, well, so be it."

There was a cough from behind them. They all turned to see Bobby Halverson leaning on a crutch and smiling. He hesitated a moment and then spoke. "Gentlemen, I am not Amish and I don't mean to intrude in matters of your church, but I have something to say here. I live on this farm because I have no other family except the Hershbergers and they have opened their home to me. I have been a friend of this family for over forty years. During that time I have always called myself an agnostic because I was never really sure if there was a God. I should have known better, because as I look back over my relationship with this family, with Reuben and Jerusha, with Jenny and Jonathan and now Rachel and Daniel, I realize that I have seen the hand of God at work through them many times in my life."

Bobby put his hand on Daniel's shoulder. "I have seen God working in this young man's life to save a girl who is more than precious to me."

Bobby looked at Jonathan. "When we were out on the ocean and Jonathan became the captain of the ship, I saw God reach out of heaven and heal a man that has been lost for many years."

Bobby looked straight at the *Bischopp* and Jonas King. "So, while you are considering what to do, you might factor in that a man who has never really believed has, through this incredible journey, come to realize that I was a fool. At last, in the lives of these two men, I have come to know that God is real and that

He indeed sent His son for me, too. And I'm a better man for it."

Jonathan smiled and then walked over and embraced his old friend. He whispered in Bobby's ear. "Welcome, you old prodigal. Tonight we kill the fatted calf."

Bischopp Hochstetler looked around and smiled as he shook his head. "*Ja, das ist ein Rätsel.* It seems I have a small rebellion on my hands. And yet I, too, see the hand of *Gott* in all these things." He pulled Jonas King aside and spoke to him for a moment. Jonas nodded in agreement and then the *Bischopp* turned back to the men. "We will put any decision on hold. While not setting aside our *Ordnung*, I believe, as Jonathan says, we must allow for the grace of God to work its healing now. Rachel may stay at home until she is well enough to decide what she will do with her life. Daniel, you are on probation, under your father's watchful eye. You may come and care for Rachel, as you are needed, for who are we to deny a calling that God has made so plain in your life. We will talk of these matters more when Rachel is well."

The *Bischopp* turned and walked out to his buggy. He climbed in, waved to the group on the porch, and then drove away. Above them, the ragged clouds opened, and for the first time in days, the sun shone through to warm the land and the hearts bound to it.

And so the days passed. January was a cold, snowless month, and Rachel was still so weak that she was most often confined to her room. She would sit in her rocking chair with her mama's shawl wrapped around her. Outside her window, the bleak fields were locked in the grip of winter's death, and as she watched the unchanging landscape, her mind lay in a strange dormancy, with only the promise of the baby growing within her, bringing a small sense of life to the cheerless days.

Daniel would come as often as he could to sit with her and talk, mostly of his work on the farm and the new foals born to his father's mares. Rachel would sit quietly and listen, but for the most part, she did not enter into the conversation. A deep darkness lay on her soul, as though she was floating far down under the sea where only a few rays of some wandering sun could penetrate to the depths.

One day she looked up at Daniel and spoke quietly. "I am ruined, Daniel. Because of my stubbornness and unforgiveness, I have destroyed my life. I am not worth your love and the care you give me. You should go home and stay away. Leave me to my fate."

Daniel patted Rachel's hand and smiled. "I am your truest friend, Rachel. I will never leave you or forsake you, no matter what you have done or what you say."

Rachel looked at Daniel's face. It was a strong and handsome face—the face of a true and noble man, and Rachel could see that he was telling her the truth. And in that moment, she had a glimpse that perhaps…perhaps something might be made of the disaster she had brought upon herself.

Early in April, on a still, dark night, Rachel awoke. Something was happening in her body, and she knew what it was. She called out in the darkness. "Mama! Mama!"

She heard the sound of her mama's feet coming down the hall and then the door opened and Jenny came in holding a lamp. "What is it, *dochter*?"

"It's my time, Mama. I feel the contractions and my water broke."

Jenny went to the door and called to Jonathan. "Get up, Papa, you are about to have a grandchild."

Jonathan came into the room. He was buttoning his shirt. "I need to get the nurse from the birth center. I will go now. It shouldn't take long. I'll ask Bobby to drive me."

Jonathan left and Jenny turned to Rachel. Rachel turned her face toward the wall. Jenny came and sat by her daughter's side. "What is it, Rachel?"

Rachel sobbed. "I am so ashamed, Mama. I am having the baby of a man that I did not love. I gave myself away for money. I feel cheap and degraded, and I feel so sorry for this baby because I will have to leave here and my baby will not have a father."

"Why will you have to leave, my darling?"

Rachel turned back to Jenny. "I am not worthy to stay with you. I have disgraced myself, and you, and I am not worthy to be loved by anyone. So I will go and live alone with the bitter fruit of my own making."

Before Jenny could answer, Rachel gasped. Jenny held her hand. "A contraction?"

"Yes, Mama."

"Well, let's get ready for this baby. It's coming soon."

Daniel stood with Jonathan and Bobby on the porch. The sun was just coming up over the eastern hills, and the sweet fragrance of apple blossoms from the orchard filled the air. Out in the fields of the Hershberger farm a light mist clung to the trees and rose from the ground like gentle fingers reaching toward the awakening sun. Above their heads in the plum trees by the porch, tiny pink flowers were alive with brilliant color as they painted the day with God's palette. A single wren twittered its call and stillness lay on the land. From within the house, they heard Rachel give a great cry. Then the silence of the dawn was broken by the lusty cry of a newborn baby. Daniel looked at Jonathan in apprehension.

Then the screen door flew open and Jenny stood there, breathless. "It is a boy, Jonathan, strong and big. He is fine and handsome and the nurse says he will live and not die."

Daniel looked at Jenny. She smiled. "Rachel is very tired, but she is well."

Daniel took his hat off and held it in his hands, nervously shifting from one foot to the other. "May we, I mean, can I..."

"Yes, Daniel, you may go in and see Rachel."

"May I see her alone for a few minutes?"

Jenny looked at Jonathan and then nodded her assent.

Rachel lay still and quiet, her eyes half-closed and her dark hair spread out against the white sheets. The nurse stood holding a bundle in her arms. Rachel could see the tiny arms waving and her heart filled with a love she had never known before. She reached up. The nurse put the baby down beside her and Rachel took the newborn into her arms. She could see Gerald in the small face and she thought back to all that had happened to her in the last year. Then the door opened quietly and Daniel stood there, his face aglow. The nurse nodded to him. "I'll let you speak with her for a moment while I go clean up. Do not excite her. She is very tired. It was a hard labor."

The nurse left and Daniel came and looked down at Rachel. Without thinking, he reached out and stroked her brow.

Rachel looked up at him. "The baby is well, Daniel."

Daniel nodded.

"You have been so good to me, Daniel. Why have I been so blind?"

Daniel touched her lips and silenced her. Then he knelt down beside the bed. He took her hand in his. "Now, Rachel, you will listen to me for once in your life."

Rachel stared at him.

Daniel went on. "I have loved you since we were children. God has put you in my way, and there is nothing I can do about it. You are going to marry me and this baby will be my son. His name will be Levon King and he will be Amish and his children will be Amish."

Rachel started to protest. "But, Daniel, I am not good enough for you to love me. I am ruined. I cannot be a good wife to you. I can't give you what I should, my purity…"

Daniel looked at Rachel. "I, too, am ruined, Rachel."

"What do you mean, Daniel?"

Rachel could see Daniel struggling with himself. Then he spoke, so quietly she almost could not hear.

"I killed a man."

Rachel's eyes opened wide. "Daniel…when?"

"When I came to rescue you there was a man waiting in your room. We fought and I killed him. I violated the deepest tenant of our faith. So, we are both broken. But don't you see? That is where *du leiber Gott* wants us to be—having nothing in ourselves and putting our lives in His hands. Rachel, He has given you to me and me to you. We are broken and hopeless, both of us faithless. But it is His plan for us to be together for the rest of our lives, depending on Him and helping each other to walk each day in faith and love. Now, say that you will marry me, and let me be a father to this boy."

Daniel reached over and tenderly touched Rachel's face. Then quietly and gently he leaned down and kissed her. Rachel felt a stirring in her heart that she had never felt before and her arm went around Daniel's strong shoulders and then she was kissing him back with all the strength and passion and love that was in her.

And like the golden sun that awakens the day after a long dark night, the truth and strength of Daniel's love for her poured into Rachel's heart and the emptiness and despair were swept away by the power of God reaching through Daniel to her. And like a flash of lightning on a hot summer night, the truth came to her. She loved Daniel. She had always loved Daniel and now their love would somehow make everything right again. And she would be Amish, and her son would be Amish, and she would live her life with this man, and the mighty angel that had turned her away from the gate of the garden would lower his flaming sword, and she would return with joy to live again in Paradise.

The End

Epilogue

The Rest of the Story

The tall writer put down the last page of the manuscript and looked up at the clock. It was four-thirty in the morning. He had been reading since six o'clock the night before. He took a handkerchief out of his pocket and wiped his brow. Then he turned to the phone, picked it up, and dialed a number. The phone rang a few times, and then a voice came on the other end.

"Who's calling me at four-thirty?"

"I finished the manuscript. It's an amazing story. It's so far outside anything she ever wrote before. I couldn't put it down. It's really a thriller."

The writer could hear the interest in the other man's voice. "That good, huh?"

"That good. She's a brilliant writer. The literary world lost an icon when she handed these manuscripts over to me."

"How long will it take to re-write it?"

"Not long. There's not a lot to do. It will be very hard not to just copy it word for word."

"No, don't do that. We need the man's point of view in this story. We need the adventure angle and the words and observations that only a man would see."

"Yeah, I know. I'll get to work on it right away."

"What else does she have?"

The writer shuffled through the stack of manuscripts. They were hand typed on a manual typewriter and then tied with a red ribbon.

"There's a story here about Jonathan's great-great-great grandmother. She was an Indian princess who converted to the Amish faith. And there's another one about a Polish princess who became the matriarch of the Hershberger family. Pretty heady stuff."

"Good. I'll call our publisher—at a decent hour—and tell him you're ready to go on to the next book."

The line clicked and went dead.

The writer picked up the manuscript he had been reading and started to tie the ribbon back around it. A handwritten note that he had not seen before slid out from between the pages. He picked it up. It was written in Jenny's smooth cursive and was addressed to him.

> *Dear Friend,*
>
> *I just wanted to fill in a few of the details in the rest of Daniel and Rachel's story. They married and went to live on the King farm with Daniel's family. Jonathan, Bobby, and Jonas helped them build a fine house on the knoll by their tree. Daniel adopted the baby and he and Rachel named their boy Levon St. Clair King, in honor of Gerald. Interestingly enough, Levon was born with the Key, the birthmark above his heart—the same one that caused Rachel so much trouble. Someday there may be another story there for you to write.*
>
> *A year after they were married, Jonathan received an unexpected royalty check from a reprint of one of Richard Sandbridge's old albums. With the agreement of the elders of our church, Jonathan used the money to pay Rachel's way through a local veterinary school. Now our community has a real Amish vet.*
>
> *Rachel returned to the church and as Jonathan so lovingly put it, "Grace trumped all."*
>
> *I see that the first three books did very well. I read them and I appreciate your honesty and clarity in telling the story of my family. May the Lord bless your further endeavors.*
>
> *Jenny Hershberger*

The writer remembered the day several years before that he sat with Jenny on the front porch of the old farmhouse. Cups of tea stood on the small table in front of them and a warm summer breeze had heralded the coming of another beautiful evening in Paradise, Pennsylvania. He had come all the way from California to meet her, and she had unfolded the story of her family as she had unfolded the marvelous quilt that held the secrets of the Hershberger saga. After she told the story of her sister, Jenna, and of her husband, Jonathan, he had asked her a question.

"What about your daughter, Rachel?"

Jenny smiled. Her *kappe* was slightly askew and the rebellious curls, now turning white, fought to escape at the urging of the evening breeze. And then the breeze picked up and the golden light of the setting sun touched the leaves of the trees and they began to dance, and then they flamed into fire.

"It was hard for Rachel when her papa came home. She was fourteen, she was becoming a woman, and Jonathan had missed such a big part of her formative years. They were at odds for a long time. I think she felt like he came between her and me. Eventually, they found what they once had when Rachel was little, but it took circumstances far outside the boundaries of our quiet Amish life to heal Jonathan. And Rachel…well, Rachel went through her own trials before she came home. But then, that's another story."

The writer smiled as he remembered. He picked up the manuscript and looked at the title.

Yes indeed, Jenny Hershberger. That was another story…

24952629R00205

Made in the USA
San Bernardino, CA
12 October 2015